Diane Armstrong  Australia with her gaining a Bachelor Sydney, she became articles have been published in Australia and around the world, winning national and international awards, including the *Pluma de Plata* from the Mexican government and the George Munster Award for Independent Journalism in Australia.

In 1998, Diane's internationally acclaimed memoir, *Mosaic: A Chronicle of Five Generations*, was published and was shortlisted for the National Biography Award and the Victorian Premier's Literary Award. Her second bestselling book, *The Voyage of Their Life: the Story of the SS* Derna *and its Passengers*, was published in 2001 and was shortlisted for the New South Wales Premier's Literary Award. It was followed in 2005 by her first novel, *Winter Journey*, which was shortlisted for the Commonwealth Writers' Prize for Best First Book, South East Asia and South Pacific region. *Winter Journey* has been translated into Polish and is currently translated into Hebrew.

Nocturne is her second novel.

Diane lives in Sydney with her husband, Michael. They have a daughter and son, and three grand-daughters.

Also by Diane Armstrong

Mosaic: A Chronicle of Five Generations

The Voyage of Their Life: The Story of the SS Derna and its Passengers

Winter Journey

Nocturne

a novel

DIANE ARMSTRONG

HARPER **PERENNIAL**

Harper Perennial
An imprint of HarperCollins*Publishers*

First published in 2008
This edition published in 2009
by HarperCollins*Publishers* Pty Limited
ABN 36 009 913 517
harpercollins.com.au

HarperCollins*Publishers*
Level 13, 201 Elizabeth Street, Sydney NSW 2000, Australia
Unit D1, 63 Apollo Drive, Rosedale, Auckland 0632, New Zealand
A 53, Sector 57, Noida, UP, India
1 London Bridge Street, London, SE1 9GF, United Kingdom
2 Bloor Street East, 20th floor, Toronto, Ontario M4W 1A8, Canada
195 Broadway, New York NY 10007, USA

National Library of Australia Cataloguing-in-Publication data:

Armstrong, Diane–
   Nocturne / author, Diane Armstrong.
   Pymble, NSW: HarperCollins, 2009.
   ISBN 978 0 7322 8431 2 (pbk.)
A823.4

Cover design by Matt Stanton
Cover images by Getty Images and Shutterstock
Author photo by Keith Arnold, Red Rocket Design
Typeset in Hoefler Text by Kirby Jones
Printed and bound in Australia by McPhersons Printing Group
The papers used by HarperCollins in the manufacture of this book are a natural,
recyclable product made from wood grown in sustainable plantation forests.
The fibre source and manufacturing processes meet recognised international
environmental standards, and carry certification.

To my darling grand-daughters,
Sarah, Maya and Allie

Author's Note

POLISH PRONUNCIATION

Ę/ę elongates the 'e' so it sounds like 'eh'

Ł/ł sounds like the English 'w' (so 'Miła' is pronounced 'Mi-*wa*')

Ń/ń sounds like 'gn'

Ó/ó sounds like 'oo'

Ś/ś sounds like 'sh'

W/w sounds like the English 'v'

Ż/ż sounds like 'Zh' in 'Zhivago' (so 'Elżunia' is pronounced 'El-*zh*un-ia)

Prelude

August 1939

That year, summer was more beautiful than ever, as though God was bestowing one final gift before turning his back on them forever. That's how it seemed to Elżunia Orłowska whenever she heard her parents discussing the impending war. But despite the gloomy predictions, life went on as usual, and as she strolled arm in arm with her girlfriends in Warsaw's Łazienki Park after Mass one sultry afternoon in August, she dreaded the thought that their lives would soon change.

Heads together, gossiping about the other girls in their class, Elżunia and her friends pulled the petals off the daisies and chanted, 'He loves me, he loves me not.' Elżunia tossed the stalks away. Hers always ended 'he loves me not'.

Love was on their mind because of the new American novel everyone was talking about. Like Elżunia, all the girls fancied themselves as Scarlett and longed for a masterful Rhett Butler to burst into their lives. They read and reread the scene where Rhett carried Scarlett upstairs to the bedroom, hoping to find some clue that might reveal the mysteries of sex.

Elżunia thought it was the most romantic story she had ever read. But, as usual, Elżunia's parents had a different interpretation. Her father said that *Gone with the Wind* was about a society destroyed by war and the end of a way of life, while her mother argued it was about illusion and self-deception.

Although the prospect of war unsettled Elżunia, in some ways she was secretly excited by it. War gave people the opportunity to be noble and brave, and freed them from their meaningless existence. And perhaps it would give her the chance to fulfil her dream.

Ever since she had been given Florence Nightingale's biography for her thirteenth birthday almost a year before, she had been fired up with longing to become a nurse. She couldn't wait to use the first-aid box the Red Cross had recently issued to all the girl scouts, and, as she rearranged the bandages, scissors and elastoplast, she imagined herself tending selflessly to wounded soldiers on bloody battlefields, and being rescued by a dashing officer as bullets whizzed past and buildings blazed.

Before going their separate ways, the girls stopped at the ice-cream barrow under the lime tree. The vendor was a cheeky fellow who winked at them as he scraped the vanilla ice-cream against the metal tin, placed a scoop of the heavenly stuff onto one wafer, and squashed it flat with another.

'Definitely not Rhett Butler material,' Elżunia whispered and her friends laughed as they licked the ice-cream oozing from the sides.

'Not even Ashley,' Lydia giggled, but turned around to sneak another look at him, just the same. 'I can't believe there's going to be a war.' She waved her arm to encompass the park. 'Does this look like a war's about to start?'

Elżunia and Gosia exchanged glances. Lydia could be

incredibly childish. 'You're absolutely right,' Elżunia said. 'Hitler will take one look at Warsaw, see us enjoying ice-cream in Łazienki Park, and give up his plan to conquer the world.'

But Lydia wasn't listening. She was ogling the boys who swaggered past and whistled under their breath as they gave the girls the once-over. Their eyes were glued to Lydia's bust and Gosia's Veronica Lake hair. Elżunia noted that they never looked at her. Why would they? Her hair was the colour of dried mud, and her chest was as flat as their maid's ironing board.

When the girls reached the lake, the boys hung around, pretending to look at the swans. Lydia suddenly stopped as though to shake a pebble from her shoe, and Gosia tugged at Elżunia's arm. 'Come on, Elżunia,' she said. 'Let's have some fun.'

Elżunia shook her head, irritated with her companions for sounding so frivolous. She felt much older than Gosia and Lydia, but, where boys were concerned, she sensed she was younger than they were. She had an hour to fill in before meeting her parents at the café in the park, so, leaving the girls to flirt with their pathetic Romeos, she headed for the rose garden for the Sunday-afternoon concert.

At three on the dot, a portly woman in a black taffeta skirt swishing against her thick ankles stepped onto the platform, acknowledged the audience with a curt bow, and sat down at the piano. Almost immediately she struck up Chopin's Military Polonaise with such fervour that the hair piled on top of her head wobbled and the pins flew off, loosening strands of hair around her jowly cheeks. Elżunia thought she looked comical but everyone else was listening with such reverent attention that she buried her face in a handkerchief to stifle her giggles.

It was music that she knew well. On these long summer evenings, when the sky was still blue at nine o'clock, and a light breeze billowed the lace curtains in their salon, her mother often sat at the piano and played Chopin. Whenever she played the nocturnes, their haunting cadences made Elżunia feel sad, as though someone close to her had died. Her mother's fingers flew over the keyboard, and with each movement the light glanced off the amber brooch that she always wore on the lapel of her jacket.

As a child, Elżunia was fascinated by the honey-coloured light that shone through the amber, and loved touching its smooth surface, but as she grew older she felt sorry for the helpless insect embalmed in the resin. She sometimes wondered whether it had sensed the approaching danger and attempted to escape from the engulfing mass that had trapped it for all eternity.

As the stirring notes of the Military Polonaise hung in the warm air, in her mind's eye Elżunia could see her father galloping into battle, sabre raised. Like his ancestors, Edward Orłowski had fought for Poland's independence and could trace his lineage back to medieval times when the Lithuanian prince Jagiello married the Polish princess Wanda to merge their two countries to form one nation. From time immemorial, knights, counts and crusaders of the Orłowski family had been ready to lay down their lives for their country. Poland's history was defined by battles and invasions, and Elżunia often wondered what was the point of all that sacrifice and suffering, because no sooner had they helped to repel one lot of invaders than others appeared. But for the past twenty years, ever since the end of the First World War, Poland had been independent, and the white eagle on Poland's scarlet flag fluttered proudly from all the public buildings in Warsaw. Her father always said that courage was the noblest human quality and Elżunia longed to live up to his ideals.

The pianist was playing a ballade and the dreamy cadences formed a peaceful background for Elżunia's reverie about her father. Even though she was almost fourteen, she still rushed up and hurled herself into his arms the moment she heard his key turn in the door in the evening.

'You're getting too old for that! Father's had a busy day at the law courts; let him sit down!' her mother would scold, but her father would just laugh and twirl Elżunia around the room while her mother shook her head.

From her mother's quick, sharp glances and critical comments, Elżunia knew she wasn't the daughter of her dreams. She was active and boisterous, and preferred climbing the cherry trees on their country estate to spending hours at the dressmaker's studying pattern books and having pins jabbed into her during endless fittings.

Unlike her daughter, Lusia Orłowska spent hours perfecting her hairstyle and translucent complexion. Which was only to be expected of a woman who owned the most exclusive beauty salon in Warsaw, where the wives of diplomats, politicians and businessmen had their faces pummelled with creams and their egos soothed with compliments. Lusia's only competition was Madame Françoise's Salon. Madame Françoise, who pretended to be French, was so envious of her rival that she spread lies and rumours in an attempt to try and lure her clients away, but she never succeeded.

The concert was over and Elżunia walked along the avenue of beech trees to meet her parents. As they walked towards her arm in arm, she saw that people turned to look at the towering man with the thick moustache smiling down at the slender woman with her upswept blonde hair and a face like a Florentine cameo. She resembled the mannequins in the *Warsaw Illustrated* magazine that was her bible. Lagging behind her glamorous parents in her long socks and comfortable sandals, strands of fine hair flopping over her face, Elżunia felt like a pale moon trailing in the shadow of a brilliant sun. The outdoor café was filling up and they made their way to a vacant table, past flustered waitresses carrying trays of walnut tortes, sugar-encrusted doughnuts and cream-cheese pancakes.

As she bit into her vanilla slice and sent a puff of icing sugar over the table, Elżunia studied her mother delicately sipping black tea with lemon and no sugar. No food ever entered Lusia's mouth before she considered its potential effect on her waistline. Elżunia considered her spoilt and vain. Although she was ashamed to admit it, even to herself, she knew she was jealous of her mother because of her father's admiring glances and compliments. Gosia and Lydia, whose parents often fought, envied Elżunia's happy home life, but she thought it was more painful for a child to grow up in a family where the parents were so besotted with each other.

None of this bothered her brother. Four years older and a revolting know-all, Stefan inhabited a different world, especially now that girls were running after him all the time. What they saw in him she couldn't imagine, but when one of them told him he looked like Cary Grant, he started smearing brilliantine in his hair, parting it on the side, and talking through his teeth in what he imagined was English.

At the next table, two men raised their voices as they argued about Germany's plans. One of them said Hitler was bluffing, while the other banged his fist so hard on the table that his glass crashed to the ground.

'Are you going to tell me he was bluffing when he invaded Sudetenland, Austria and Czechoslovakia?' he shouted. 'Wake up, for God's sake. We're next on the list!'

Images of German soldiers marching through towns, arresting, torturing and shooting ordinary people, tightened Elżunia's stomach with dread.

'But how come Hitler can do those things?' she asked as she sat between her parents in the back of the horse-drawn *doroszka* on the way home.

Her father leaned over and squeezed her hand. 'Don't worry, Dzidzia,' he said, using the pet name he'd given her when she was a child. 'Worrying about tomorrow sucks all the pleasure from today.'

She nodded. After all, he would always be there to protect her and whisk her away from danger, like the knights in the stories he used to tell her.

The *doroszka* driver flicked the mare's rump with his whip and the horse turned into Okopowa Street and trotted along Nalewki. This was the Jewish part of Warsaw and it seemed to Elżunia that, compared to the rest of the city, this was a bubbling cauldron. No one walked or talked slowly here; everything was speeded up. Merchants ran to and from their storerooms, haggling, arguing and gesticulating. Wherever she looked, carters were loading or unloading trucks, hauling oranges, sacks of flour or bales of cloth onto waiting barrows that they wheeled at a run into open doorways. Every wall was pasted with notices and hung with advertisements, and tiny workshops in passageways resounded with hammering and whirring. Some of the men had long beards and the women strolling along the street had dark eyes and long skirts. Craning her head out of the carriage, Elżunia asked the driver to slow down so that she could have a better look at these exotic people, but her mother made an impatient gesture and told him to drive on.

Suddenly everything stopped moving. The street became as still and silent as a tableau. It reminded her of the time at the movie theatre when the projector had jammed and she had sat staring at a frozen image of soldiers with bayonets poised, ready to strike. Elżunia couldn't hear the horse's hooves

7

clattering on the cobblestones, the sound of doors banging or people calling out. In the ghostly stillness that descended over the street, she had a vision of an enclosure that surrounded these houses, sucked out the air and entombed all the people. She was holding her breath when her mother's exasperated voice brought her back to the present.

'Elżunia, did you hear what I said?'

She blinked several times and everything returned to normal but she was silent all the way home because her mouth was as dry as sand. The late-afternoon sun lit up her mother's amber brooch and Elżunia's gaze rested on the insect trapped inside, engulfed by a pitiless force that it had been powerless to resist.

Part I

One

The ballroom of the Europejski Hotel opened out onto a large semi-circular terrace and, as Adam Czartoryski propelled his companion towards the French windows, the band leader climbed onto the podium, raised his baton in his plump hand, and the orchestra struck up 'Perfidia'. Weaving between the dancing couples, Adam smiled to himself. The sensuous movements of the tango seemed a musical version of foreplay.

On the way to the terrace, Adam had to navigate around the buffet table where people were piling caviar, mushroom pancakes, smoked salmon, pike in aspic and chicken kiev onto their gold-rimmed plates. August was coming to an end, and all around him people were discussing the coming war, but the only campaign on Adam's mind at that moment was his conquest of the enchanting brunette he'd finally managed to lure outside.

Elena's bare shoulders and black hair gleamed in the moonlight, and Adam could already visualise her stretched out on his settee like *The Naked Maja*, her hair cascading over her soft white body. Leaning against the wrought-iron balustrade, he breathed in Elena's perfume and found it spicy, secretive and full of promise.

He caressed her bare back and felt her quiver as she leaned her head on his shoulder. Things were looking good. His colleagues, who tended to categorise women by their nationality, often said that English girls had cool eyes but hot bodies, while Spanish girls set you on fire with their glances but never delivered. But Elena's back felt warm and pliant under his hand, and he was convinced that by the end of the evening he'd prove them all wrong.

It had been the best summer Adam could remember. Being a trainee diplomat had opened doors to exclusive soirees, receptions and balls like this one, hosted by the Spanish ambassador, whose daughter he was presently courting. Like a keen angler, he assessed each season by the catch, and this one had been quite remarkable. In fact, in order not to disappoint all the eager mesdemoiselles, fraüleins and señoritas who flitted in and out of his life, some evenings he'd had to bid a hasty farewell to one so that he could keep his rendezvous with another.

He swung Elena around to face him and squeezed her waist. 'Let's get away from here,' he whispered. 'I know a nightclub where they serve shashlik and play wild music all night. We'll dance the *czardas* and you'll feel like a gypsy princess.'

She shook her head. 'This is my father's party. I can't leave.'

Adam dropped his arms and turned away without saying a word. He never pleaded.

'Perhaps I could slip away a little later,' she said after an awkward pause.

'Perhaps you could,' he murmured, pressing his lips passionately into her palm as a shadow fell across the terrace. He looked up to meet the compelling gaze of a tall blonde in the doorway and cursed his bad luck. Coming across past conquests had become an occupational hazard in these circles, but to make matters worse, this was a woman he had dropped rather abruptly.

He breathed out again when he noticed a faint smile on her lips and a flute of champagne in her hand. As she raised it in his direction in a silent toast, Adam bowed. He was still bowing when she took three rapid steps towards him and tossed the contents of the glass in his face.

Elena leaped back as though attacked by a tiger. '*Santa Maria!* My dress!' she shrieked. Glaring at Adam, she uttered a torrent of Spanish invective, and rushed across the dance floor, holding out her dripping skirt.

Alone on the terrace, Adam mopped his face and scanned the ballroom. The architect of his misfortune had vanished inside and Elena was surrounded by a group of babbling women examining the wet stain on her dress, offering suggestions, and pointing to the washroom. The band leader tapped the lectern, raised his baton, and the orchestra struck up a Strauss waltz. The ballroom swirled with chiffon, silk and organza, and the French chandeliers sparkled with the refracted flashes of diamonds, sequins and pearls.

As the couples waltzed past the terrace, they whispered and cast disapproving glances in his direction. He wasn't surprised. The men envied him his reputation as a Lothario, while their wives, some of whom knew him far more intimately than their husbands suspected, felt a vicarious satisfaction in seeing him humiliated in public.

'See, that's what you get for burning your candle at both ends.' His friend Piotr had come out on to the terrace and was shaking his head with mock disapproval. Adam sensed a touch of *Schadenfreude* in his friend's playful remark. Piotr was timid with women and couldn't understand Adam's success. 'I don't get it,' he would often complain. 'You're certainly no Adonis, but the women are always falling over themselves to get into your bed.'

Adam had no illusions about his appearance. His jaw was long and bony and his cheeks were pitted with pock marks, but he knew that success with women had nothing to do with looks. Women desired you because you liberated them from their inhibitions, not because you had regular features.

'Well, it looks as though my candle has gutted tonight,' Adam said as he looked across the ballroom where Elena was standing provocatively close to the French consul and pealing with laughter at everything he said. She caught Adam's eye and jerked her head away as she led the consul on to the dance floor.

There was no point prolonging the embarrassment. Adam was heading for the door when a tall man with a neatly clipped moustache came towards him, hand outstretched.

'How do you do? I'm Charles Watson-Smythe,' he said in halting Polish.

Adam couldn't disguise his astonishment. Polish was a language very few diplomats bothered to learn, especially the British ones.

'I'm really an honorary Pole,' the Englishman was saying. 'I've lived in your beautiful city for several years. In fact, I'm engaged to a lovely *Warszawianka* — that's what you call the girls from Warsaw, don't you?'

'We can speak English if you like,' Adam said. 'I spent three years in London doing postgraduate work in political science.'

'That's very tempting, but I do feel I should practise my Polish whenever I get the chance.'

Watson-Smythe had come to his rescue at an awkward moment. A real gentleman. There was no equivalent of this word in Polish, with its connotation of discretion, breeding and courtesy. According to some of the Polish diplomats, the English said one thing to your face and another behind your back. They had a reputation for being evasive, non-committal and sometimes downright duplicitous, but their manners were always impeccable. 'They smile and say, "So sorry" while they're stabbing you in the back,' his foreign-office colleagues used to say.

'I must say, I don't know how you Poles manage to drink that vodka of yours by the glass. I went to the shindig your people gave at The Bristol last week. It was some air-force do. Those airmen can drink anyone under the table, and they certainly know how to charm the ladies!'

Adam laughed. 'That's why I've joined the air force!'

His infatuation with flying had begun fifteen years before, when he had read about the airman who had made the first solo flight from Warsaw to Tokyo. Adam was ten years old at the time and he cut out every article he could find about the flight. He spent so much time studying the aviator's head-hugging leather helmet and huge goggles that his mother said he'd wear out the newsprint.

He'd almost jumped out of his skin with excitement when his uncle took him to an air show. The moment he set eyes on the Potez two-seaters with their huge silver wings, he saw himself in the cockpit. His throat closed up when the planes lifted off like gigantic metal birds. One moment they soared into the sky and the next they were hurtling towards the ground. *Jesus Maria!* The spectators clutched their throats and covered their mouths with trembling hands, hardly daring to look. But at the last moment, as they all gaped in disbelief, the planes suddenly rose again in a series of somersaults, loops and arabesques.

After they touched down, the prettiest girls Adam had ever seen rushed towards the pilots and walked away with them, arm in arm. It was then Adam thought that being a pilot and having girls vying for your attention must be the closest thing to heaven on earth.

At first, his father had regarded his fascination with flying with indulgence. After all, most boys wanted to be train drivers or firemen but they outgrew their childhood fantasies. Later, he approved of Adam's decision to enter the diplomatic service, but he was shocked when earlier that year Adam had announced his intention of joining the Polish Air Force.

'War's coming and I'm not going to sit back. I want to fight for Poland,' Adam had said.

'Polish Air Force? You mean Polish air circus!' his father thundered. 'These machines are made for entertainment, not war. Airmen are undisciplined louts, only interested in womanising and carousing. I don't want to hear any more of this nonsense. Our family has always fought in the cavalry and that's what you'll do.'

Adam had choked back his anger. Nothing had changed since he was a little boy. His father still dismissed his ideas and persisted in laying down the law. The Russian campaign of 1920 in which he had distinguished himself was long over, but in his own mind he was still the colonel demanding unconditional obedience, even though his son was now twenty-five.

'Father, with all due respect, the cavalry is a relic of the past,' Adam said, ignoring his mother's desperate gestures in the background signalling him to not upset his father.

'You call the cavalry a relic? How dare you insult Poland's heroes! You're not fit to polish their boots. All you've ever done is chase girls and drool over photographs of aeroplanes.'

Adam clenched his fists. The morning light slanting from the window caught the glass on the photograph that stood on the walnut sideboard. It depicted his father in his cavalry uniform. The peculiar elongated tasselled cap on his head, and the sabre at his waist reminded Adam of a chocolate soldier in a Viennese operetta, an image that gave him the courage to press his point.

'Flying isn't a novelty any more, Father. Even Marshal Piłsudski's daughter is learning to fly. As a matter of fact, she's joined my aeronautical club.'

But his father refused to be mollified by this reference to the Polish hero with whom he had fought several campaigns.

'Your ancestors fought the Teutonic Knights, the Swedes and the Turks. I fought the Russians to gain this nation's independence ...'

Adam suppressed a yawn. 'Well, I'm not going to fight for it on the back of a horse, tilting my lance at tanks like a Polish Don Quixote. The cavalry is an anachronism. It will make Poland a laughing stock —'

His father swung his arm back and struck Adam's face with such force that he reeled back against the sideboard and sent the photograph crashing to the floor. Adam strode out of the house without another word and, for the first time in his life, didn't kiss his father's hand before leaving.

Lost in his painful reverie, Adam had to ask Charles Watson-Smythe to repeat his question.

'So, have you broken many hearts since you joined the air force?' the Englishman asked in a genial voice.

Adam suppressed a smile. 'I do my best.'

'I *bet* you do.'

The Englishman was no longer smiling and his comment had a jarring tone. Adam supposed it was due to his poor command of Polish.

'That reminds me,' Watson-Smythe said. 'Would you be good enough to wait a moment? There's someone I'd like to introduce to you.'

Adam was leaning on the balustrade with his back to the ballroom when he heard footsteps on the tiled terrace behind him.

'I'd like you to meet my fiancée,' the Englishman said.

Adam turned and the smile died on his lips. It was his former lover, the woman who had thrown champagne in his face half an hour before.

As Adam raised her hand to his lips and murmured the usual pleasantries, the Englishman's expression remained affable. His fiancée gave Adam a mocking smile and returned to the ballroom, but Charles Watson-Smythe continued to make small talk, clearly enjoying Adam's discomfiture. It was Adam who lost the contest and made an excuse to leave. As they shook hands, the Englishman said amiably, 'We allies must stick together in these troubled times, you know.'

Cursing under his breath, Adam collected his hat and coat from the pert cloakroom attendant and, without paying her his usual compliments, hurried out into the night.

Two

As soon as Elżunia heard the drone of aeroplanes high above the city, she rushed to the window and started counting.

'Look at them all!' she shouted and ran for her father's field-glasses. Before she had time to use them, Stefan had grabbed them from her hand.

'It must be the air force on an anti-aircraft training exercise,' he said.

'Gosia's cousin reckons our pilots are the best in the world,' Elżunia said. 'He says they'll knock the Germans out of the sky in no time.'

'I'd like to know how they're going to do that with their antiquated planes,' Stefan scoffed. 'They don't even have a retractable undercarriage. Junkers are the best planes ever built.'

Elżunia pulled a face. She didn't know what a retractable undercarriage was and she certainly wasn't going to ask. Stefan was an insufferable know-all. Just because he was four years older and understood mechanical things, he always made her feel ignorant.

'You don't know everything,' she said.

Her mother gave her a sharp glance. 'Don't be rude to your brother,' she said.

Elżunia glared. It wasn't fair. Their mother always made excuses for Stefan. She always sided with him — never with her.

'Well, I know more than a snotty thirteen-year-old who goes around with a toy Red Cross box and thinks war's a game,' he sneered.

Elżunia turned to her mother. 'How come he's allowed to be nasty to me?' she complained, but Lusia didn't seem to hear.

With an irritated gesture, their father put down his newspaper. 'Leave your sister alone, and stop the quibbling,' he snapped at Stefan. 'You should have more sense at a time like this. It's about time you pulled yourself together and acted your age.'

Stefan turned back to the window, red-faced at the rebuke, while Elżunia shot him a triumphant look. At least her father stood up for her.

Stefan peered through the field-glasses. 'They don't look like ours,' he said slowly.

A moment later a shrieking sound turned Elżunia's skin to gooseflesh. An explosion followed that sounded as though a thousand cannons had gone off at once.

'Quick, Elżunia, get your mask and run!' her father shouted, and they all rushed down the stairs three at a time, hardly taking a breath. A nearby nightclub was the closest shelter and they reached it just before the next bomb hit. Crouching in the basement, Elżunia clamped her hands over her ears and shook each time she heard the explosions. Every bone in her body vibrated with the shaking of the cellar walls. Did this mean they were being attacked? How long would the bombing last? All around her, the adults discussed the situation, their faces tense. Some of the women were white-faced and their eyes were full of fear, while others murmured prayers. The men said that Hitler must have finally carried out his threat to invade Poland, but the Polish army and air force would soon repel them and show them what Poles were made of. With each explosion, Elżunia's breathing became so rapid that she felt dizzy. So was this how war began? What if their building was hit? What would happen to all their things? Where would they go? Would they be buried under the rubble?

A fine heroine you are, she told herself. She had broken out in a cold sweat and her moist hands could hardly hold her first-aid box. She prayed she wouldn't need to use it.

Her father put his arm around her trembling shoulders. 'It'll be over soon, Dzidzia,' he said.

Her brother leaned forward. 'Is poor little Dzidzia scared?'

She turned away from his mocking glance. If only the bombing would stop.

As soon as they emerged from the shelter, she knew the world had changed. It wasn't just the fire engines racing through the streets, the pall of dust that dulled the brightness of the September sunshine, or the sparks from all the fires that rose into the sky. It was the smell. At first she thought it was the smell of smoke and burning buildings but it was more pervasive, more frightening. It was the smell of fear.

Over the next few days, Elżunia's hair rose on her arms each time the sirens shrilled to warn them of imminent bombardment. 'Why hasn't our air force shot down those Stukas?' she kept asking.

Every morning they huddled around their large wireless to hear the latest news, pressing their faces against its walnut case to ensure they didn't miss a single word. The air alerts were interspersed with mysterious announcements that made no sense at all but made Elżunia feel uneasy with their stuttering urgency. *Attention attention, arriving arriving between eight and twelve*. Her father explained that these messages were in code for the army. But what if the soldiers weren't listening and missed them?

Three long days had passed since the Germans had attacked, but if this was war, it wasn't what she had expected. She had envisaged gallant warriors performing heroic rescues and fighting courageous battles. She had not anticipated huddling in dark shelters, teeth chattering, as they waited for the next bomb to fall.

It was all so confusing. From her history lessons, she knew that battles were either lost or won, but right now no one seemed to know what was happening. Someone said that the Polish Air Force had repelled the Luftwaffe, the army had taken over Gdańsk, the English and French had attacked Berlin and General Bortnowski was on his way to save Warsaw. When she heard that, she jumped up and cheered, but then someone else said the exact opposite and painted such a bleak picture of what was happening that her stomach folded in on itself and she picked the skin around her thumbnail. She didn't know what to believe and the worst thing was that her parents didn't either. And all the time the air alerts kept coming, buildings kept falling and fire kept raining down from the heavens until the sky glowed scarlet, and she closed her eyes, pressed her hands together and whispered urgent prayers to the Blessed Virgin to protect them and their house.

In the days that followed every hope was crushed. It turned out that General Bortnowski's army had been cut to pieces and the Germans with their panzer tanks had cut across Poland like scythes mowing down fields of wheat. They were rushing towards the capital. Hardly anyone could believe the news that the Polish army had been decimated and everyone was asking, 'How could this happen to our army? Where's the cavalry? When will our allies come to our aid? Why hasn't our air force protected us from German dive bombers?' To Elżunia, these questions were more unsettling than the rumours because no one had any answers.

She was still trembling after another air raid when her mother placed her finger against her lips. 'Ssh. Szpilman's playing Chopin,' she said. In between the air alerts, coded messages and news bulletins, Warsaw Radio broadcast the city's popular pianist playing the Military Polonaise.

Elżunia glanced at her mother. Lusia's eyes were closed and an ecstatic expression smoothed out the anxious lines on her face. The stirring notes rekindled a fierce patriotism. There was still hope in a world where such music existed. It reminded them who they were, and reaffirmed their pride in their nation and boosted their spirits. But Elżunia didn't feel comforted. This time in Chopin's rousing music, she could hear the tread of soldiers' boots and the rumble of approaching tanks.

The polonaise ended, and the notes were still lingering in the air when a fanfare introduced an important announcement. They blanched when they heard Colonel Umiastowski announcing that German panzers were racing towards Warsaw. He ordered men of military age to leave the city to avoid being captured, and eventually to regroup.

Panic gripped Elżunia's chest as she heard her parents discussing the situation.

'We've all been misled,' her father said bitterly. 'Our military and political leaders have miscalculated the disparity of weapons between us and the Germans. Or else they deliberately deceived us. And now they're telling the men to abandon the capital.'

Elżunia's hands shook at the thought of being separated from her father. She looked at him anxiously. Thank God he was too old to be mobilised.

'Miss Elżunia, are you ready?' Their maid, Tereska, was standing in the doorway holding a string bag. Tereska could barely read and write but she was very shrewd. 'Put this ribbon around your hair,' she said while Elżunia protested that she wasn't going out looking like a child. 'Go on,' Tereska cajoled. 'The younger you look, the better chance we'll have of getting food.'

Elżunia muttered as the ribbon was tied on top of her head and hoped she wouldn't meet anyone she knew.

As they turned the corner a few blocks further on, all thoughts about her appearance vanished. Several buildings had toppled onto the pavement, leaving jagged towers of masonry pointing at the sky. Bits of doors and windows were strewn over the pavement and a balcony hung precariously from a wall. 'You, miss, out of the way, quick,' a man shouted.

People were wandering around like sleepwalkers, poking among the rubble, shouting the names of loved ones. Some lay on the ground moaning while others bent over them, trying to make them comfortable. One of them, a stout woman with a double chin, was propping a man's head on her lap and was about to place a glass of water to his lips when Elżunia rushed forward.

'Stop!' she shouted. 'Don't give him anything to eat or drink. He might need surgery.'

The woman put down the glass. From her narrowed eyes, it was clear that she didn't take kindly to being corrected by a mere girl.

'Well now,' she said. 'Since you know so much, don't just stand there. Come and help.'

Elżunia inched forward. Sickened by the blood, she couldn't remember what she had learnt at first-aid classes. First you had to make sure they were breathing, but what were you supposed to check next: bleeding or broken bones?

She wanted to back away but the woman fixed her with an insistent stare.

Tereska was pulling her arm. 'Come on, Miss Elżunia,' she drawled in her slow country accent. 'This is no place for you. The ambulance will be here soon; they'll know what to do. We have to hurry and get some bread before they sell out.'

Elżunia walked on, reproaching Tereska for dragging her away but secretly grateful to have an excuse to leave the frightening scene.

Back home, she sat on her bed daydreaming. In a scene like the one she had just witnessed, the handsomest boy she'd ever seen was lying injured on the road while bombs were falling all around him. Risking death, she ran over to him and, as she splinted his broken arm and wound a bandage around his head, he gazed at her with admiration and said —

'Elżunia, I want to talk to you!' Her father's voice cut through her fantasy. With a sigh, she went into the lounge room.

'It's too dangerous for you and your mother to stay in Warsaw,' he said. 'I want both of you to go to our country house until things settle down. Stefan and I will stay here.'

No amount of arguing could dissuade him. He was too old to fight but too proud to abandon his city. To him, leaving smacked of cowardice, and he refused to join the exodus. From Stefan's expression, Elżunia could see that he was thrilled to be asked to stay with his father and have the opportunity of gaining his approval. She longed to stay too but her father was adamant. 'This is no place for women and children,' he said. 'The air raids are getting worse and this morning the bastards even bombed firemen trying to put out the fires.'

For once, he didn't apologise for swearing in front of the children.

That night, Elżunia tossed in her bed, too agitated to sleep. For the first time in her life, the family was about to be split up. She quailed at the prospect of staying with her mother and dreaded what lay ahead, especially as she wouldn't have her father to protect her. 'Let it be over quickly,' she muttered over and over before falling into a dreamless sleep.

Three

Everyone was scrambling to get out of Warsaw. That's how it seemed to Elżunia as their black Skoda inched along a road clogged with cars, bicycles, trucks and horse carts. Petrol fumes, combined with the smell of the leather upholstery, made her breakfast rise up into her throat.

'Mama, I'm going to be sick.'

'Can't you hold on just a bit longer? If we stop now, we'll never get back into this traffic. If you could only —' She didn't get any further because Elżunia was gagging. 'Pull over, quick,' she ordered their chauffeur.

A moment later, Elżunia was bending over a ditch, holding her stomach and retching while people streamed past like pebbles pushed along by a powerful current. When she straightened up, she saw cars with bedding, boxes, bundles and valises tied onto the roof, stretching as far back as she could see.

She had never seen so many people all at once. In between the cars, old women with scarves on their heads and men in battered hats and threadbare jackets sat on top of wooden carts pulled by scrawny horses, while their children sat on the edge, their legs swinging over the side as they tried to hold on to the bird cages, baskets and pots and pans heaped beside them.

Some pushed overloaded barrows, stopping frequently to wipe their sweating brows with the back of their hands; others carried their belongings in rucksacks on their backs or changed suitcases from one blistered hand to the other as they shuffled along the endless road. Mothers shifted fretting babies from one hip to another while crying toddlers pulled at their skirts as they dragged their tired little feet in the dust.

Occasionally a woman had held up a child and pleaded with Lusia and Elżunia's chauffeur, Pan Maciej, to let them ride for a while but Lusia had given him strict instructions not to stop for anyone. 'You don't know what kind of people they are. Once they get in, there'll be no getting rid of them. Besides, we're squashed as it is.' Elżunia had argued that someone could sit beside their chauffeur but her mother was adamant.

While Elżunia was wiping her face, Lusia moved into the shade of a tall poplar, undid a couple of the tiny covered buttons on her cream silk blouse and fanned herself with a bough she pulled off the tree. Although it was mid-September, the sultry weather showed no signs of making way for autumn. In the distance, peasant women in kerchiefs and big aprons were bending over corn stalks that glistened in the sun. It was the kind of idyllic rural scene that city artists loved to paint but none of the travellers on this road were interested in their surroundings. Their minds were focused on the journey's end and where they would sleep that night.

'Come on, Elżunia, we have to get going,' her mother said, glancing at her watch for the hundredth time, as if afraid of missing an urgent appointment.

Elżunia climbed back into the Skoda but the road was so jammed with traffic that no one would let them in, and, when the chauffeur pressed the horn, he only succeeded in enraging the refugees.

'Look at them. Just because they've got a car, they think everyone has to make way for them,' shouted a woman pushing a wheelbarrow. Sweat ran down her face and the tendons on her neck stood out. 'You wait; everything's going to change from now on. Your lot won't be so high and mighty any more!'

Lusia sighed. She couldn't come to terms with the chaos or with the ineptitude and dishonesty of their leaders who had misled them about everything. Only a few days before, everyone had been jubilant because Churchill had announced that England was now at war with Germany. Crowds had rushed to the British Embassy, whistling, blaring car horns and tossing flowers to the English ambassador who came out on to the balcony waving to the crowd like a Roman emperor after a victorious campaign. But, apart from issuing declarations, Britain and France had done nothing to help. And the night before leaving Warsaw, Lusia had heard the shocking news on London radio that the head of the Polish army, Marshal Smigły-Rydz, had left the capital, along with the entire government of Poland. She still shook with anger at the fact that their leaders had deserted them — left them to face their invaders alone.

Now, surveying this endless throng of refugees, she saw it as purposeless and panic-stricken as a swarm of bees after the death of its queen, and cursed the cowardly marshal and the ministers.

A group of young soldiers, some of whom looked no older than Stefan, trudged past, heads down. Their boots were covered in dust and their shirts hung out of their stained trousers. Some hobbled along, leaning on their companions; others had slings around their arms and blood-stained bandages around their heads. The able-bodied ones walked with the slow, dragging gait of the defeated, their heads full of images they would never describe. No wonder they were dejected, Lusia thought. Losing a battle so fast was demoralising enough without being deserted by your commander.

When a big Humber halted to let them into the traffic, their car shuddered and stalled. Cursing under his breath, Pan Maciej turned the key in the ignition again but the engine was dead.

He got out and raised the bonnet and poked about while Lusia drummed her fingers on the leather seat. For this to happen now, of all days. She leaned out the window. 'Is this going to take long?'

'*Proszę pani*, I don't know how long it will take. It might take a minute or it might take an hour. That's if I can fix it at all.'

She groaned. 'We should have taken the train.'

'Madame, the Germans have bombed the railway lines.' He spoke slowly with exaggerated patience, as if speaking to a dim-witted child. 'The trains are held up for most of the day while they repair the lines, and, when they finally get going, they're jammed with soldiers. Thousands of civilians are stranded on the railway stations. I've even heard of people being trampled and falling under the trains in their rush to get on.'

Elżunia had listened in sullen silence to the conversation. She felt aggrieved that while she had been retching by the roadside, her mother had shown no sympathy for her at all. Now, as she contemplated the image of people being squashed beneath trains, she quivered on the edge of another bout of nausea.

'Mother, it's no use going on about it,' she said. 'Stop nagging Pan Maciej, so he can fix the engine.'

Lusia fluttered her hand in a helpless gesture. She thought of Edward and Stefan sitting comfortably back at home in their apartment, drinking tea while she was stuck on this highway going nowhere. It had been a mistake to listen to Edward and leave Warsaw.

Pan Maciej was tapping on her window, wiping his blackened fingers with a cloth. 'I can't get the engine started. We need an automobile mechanic.'

'So what's supposed to happen now?' Lusia demanded. 'Where are we to find a mechanic? And how do we get out of here?'

She was still railing at him when a covered truck drew level with them. The driver, a cheerful fellow with a snub nose and pink cheeks, leaned out. He looked as though he'd just walked off the farm except for the air-force cap perched at a jaunty angle on his head. As his eyes fell on Lusia's delicate face and desperate expression, he pulled up and turned to his companion.

'We can give them a lift to the next town, can't we?'

But the other airman was staring moodily out of the window and merely shrugged.

Lusia glanced at the khaki tarpaulin that covered the truck and an expression of distaste flitted across her face. But before she could refuse, Elżunia said, 'Thank goodness you came along or we'd be here all day.'

When the driver untied the thick rope that secured the canvas cover, they saw that the back of the truck was filled with airmen. After they'd hoisted Lusia and the chauffeur onto the truck, the driver said to Elżunia, 'You're so tiny, you can sit up front with me.'

As he turned the key in the ignition, he said, 'That was bad luck your car breaking down back there.'

'But it was good luck coming across you.' Elżunia smiled.

'An optimist, eh? That's what I like!'

As they crept along the highway leading south, Elżunia and the driver chatted while his companion stared gloomily out of the window, not saying a word. Out of the corner of her eye, she could see that under his air-force cap, his angular face was pitted. There was something interesting about his melancholy air and the bitter curve of his mouth but, no matter how hard she tried, she couldn't engage him in conversation.

'We're on our way to Lublin to regroup, so we can go on fighting from there,' the driver was saying.

'Don't tell me you believe that?' As the other man said this, his heavy-lidded eyes rested on Elżunia.

The driver turned to her. 'Don't let him upset you. Ever since our defeat, he's been in this grouchy mood and he can't snap out of it.'

As the truck lurched to a stop once more, Elżunia looked around. In a wayside shrine, Christ hung on the cross. Blood poured from his wounds and a garland of cornflowers and daisies rested on his head. To their right, past a clump of spindly sunflowers, two girls with kerchiefs on their braided hair were walking through the field, laughing. Occasionally they straightened up and shielded their eyes against the sun as flocks of black jays flew overhead.

Elżunia was about to say that these country girls didn't even seem to realise that their country was at war when suddenly they heard a whistling, shrieking sound far above.

'Bloody Stukas with their Jericho trumpets,' the driver cursed. 'Probably heading for Warsaw.'

The other guy gritted his teeth until the hinge of his jaw jumped under the skin. The Stukas were coming closer now, and the shrill sound puckered the skin on the back of Elżunia's neck. They weren't flying past, they were diving, darting, swooping low over the highway, so close that she could see a pilot's face clearly in his brown leather helmet. From his expression, he might have been on his way to a party.

Firm hands grabbed her by the waist and, before she had time to protest, the taciturn airman had pulled her off the truck and thrown her, like a sack of potatoes, into a ditch. She wanted to shout at him but her face was in the dirt and all the breath had been squeezed from her lungs as he flung himself on top of her.

She was still struggling to push him off when she heard the explosion. The ground trembled violently and for the next few moments her head was spinning. She could hear nothing at all. As soon as she felt his weight lift off, she tried to scramble to her feet but her legs buckled and she sank to the ground. Far away, someone was screaming. Around her, everything was ominously silent. Two horse carts lay on their sides, their contents spilled across the highway and there were bodies on the road. There was a deep crater in front of the truck. Then she heard a woman screaming, and in the background the murmur of prayers. 'Holy Mary, full of grace ...' A horse whinnied and a woman yelled, 'May they roast in hell for eternity, the filthy murderers!'

Elżunia looked over and saw a patch of scarlet on the cornfield. There was no trace of the two girls but one brown boot lay on the ground. She looked again at the red stains and froze. That grinning Stuka pilot must have fired at those girls as if they were targets in a shooting gallery.

She clasped her arms tightly around her body. Her mind was blank and the sound of the explosion still reverberated in her ears.

'Thank God you're not hurt.' Her mother was kneeling beside her and her voice was breaking with emotion. Dead leaves and clumps of soil clung to Lusia's silk stockings and her coiled hair had come loose. 'You were in the front and, when they started firing ... thank God you had the sense to jump into the ditch.'

In a hoarse whisper Elżunia said, 'It was that airman.'

She remembered his strong arms lifting her out of the cabin, and the pressure of his lean, hard body lying over hers. She sprang up. 'I have to find him.' She looked around, hoping to spot him in the crowd but her mother swayed and tottered backwards. Elżunia caught her in time and sat beside her on the ground, her arm around her mother's trembling shoulders.

'Warsaw can't be worse than this,' Lusia said. 'We're going back.'

Four

As the truck inched its way towards Lublin, even the garrulous driver fell silent and Adam noticed that his face was white and his hands were trembling. He, too, was shaken after the air raid that had left so many dead and wounded on the teeming highway, and, grateful for his companion's silence, he tried to comprehend the swiftness of the catastrophe that had befallen Poland in the first week of the war.

When the order to take to the skies had finally been given, he had felt a sense of relief. The incident at the Europejski Hotel and the argument with his father had left him feeling flat. In the last days of August, when the air force was put on alert and the planes were sent to a secret airfield outside Warsaw, he had paced up and down, impatient to fight the Germans and prove himself in aerial combat. He couldn't wait to see his father's face when it was over and he could tell him that the air force had destroyed the Luftwaffe.

While the airmen had waited, they'd speculated about the relative strength of Polish and German air power.

'We're better pilots but they've got more bombers and fighters than we have horse carts,' his friend Stasiek had said. 'And, let's face it, our planes can't match their Junkers and Messerschmitts. It'll be like putting snails in a race against cheetahs.'

'It's training, skill and stamina that count,' Adam had argued. 'That's why we'll beat them.'

As soon as their squadron had received the order, they'd hurled themselves against the enemy planes that blackened the sky over Warsaw, but the German bombers and fighters just kept coming, wave after wave, like swarms of locusts. No matter how fiercely they fought, how many sorties they flew, or how many enemy planes they shot down, within one week the Germans had control of Polish skies, and Warsaw lay defenceless beneath them.

Adam was flying in formation beside Stasiek during one of the sorties over Warsaw when he spotted the Junker above them. He cursed his Potez P-11 for not being able to fly high enough to reach it. Just then a Messerschmitt swooped down and riddled Stasiek's plane with bullets. He must have hit the petrol tank because a moment later the cockpit burst into flames. Adam watched, gripping the column with white knuckles until he saw that Stasiek had managed to bail out and a few moments later his parachute opened up like a mushroom floating in space. Thank God. In a few moments he'd touch the ground. Then he heard the staccato of machine-gun fire and Stasiek crumpled and plummeted to earth like a stone. Adam's mouth was dry and his hands shook so much he needed all his strength to control the plane. 'The bastard,' he kept repeating. 'The fucking Nazi bastard.'

Ignoring everything he'd been taught, he pushed the Potez beyond its limits, wheeled around and headed straight for the Messerschmitt. He smiled when he saw it plunging to the ground, trailing black smoke.

But one week later it was all over. As he travelled towards Lublin with the remains of his squadron, Adam had a hollow feeling in his stomach and the bitter taste of defeat in his mouth. Watching the endless column of refugees who trudged along the road, he couldn't stop thinking of the crushing defeat and had felt too depressed to make conversation with that chatterbox they'd picked up. He didn't know what had prompted him to fling himself on top of her during the raid, and he didn't want to be thanked. If only the Polish planes had matched the pilots. All those aerial combats, all those brave young airmen lost, all for nothing.

He had told the guy driving the truck to Lublin that he didn't believe their squadron would regroup there, and as it turned out, he'd been right. There didn't seem to be anyone in charge, there weren't any planes, and the lack of organisation maddened him. All around them, artillery battles were raging, bombs were dropping and the airmen had to hang around, waiting for someone to give an order or make a decision. This wasn't war. This was chaos. So several days later when they got the order to cross the border to Romania and wait there for new fighter planes from Britain and France, his spirits lifted. The bombing raid on the road to Lublin, his rescue of the girl, and the disappointment of being unable to regroup all receded. Soon he'd be in the air again, fighting for Poland.

But no sooner had his squadron crossed the border, expecting a friendly welcome, than armed guards appeared, grabbed hold of them and took them to filthy barracks inside a compound surrounded by barbed wire. Inside the hut, other Polish airmen were lounging on narrow bunks, smoking, playing cards or staring at the ceiling. Adam looked around, astonished to see colleagues from other Warsaw squadrons.

'Welcome to Romania,' one of them said. As he ran his hand through his thick hair, he reminded Adam of a Hollywood movie star whose name he couldn't recall. He tamped out his cigarette on the floor and stretched out his hand. 'I'm Romek.'

'What's going on?' Adam asked. 'Are we supposed to wait in this dump until the planes arrive?'

Romek laughed mirthlessly and the other occupants of the hut joined in. 'There aren't any bloody planes and there won't be any, either,' he said. 'And, in case you're wondering, this isn't a holiday camp for displaced Polish airmen. It's an internment camp.'

'There must be some mistake,' Adam said. 'Romania promised to help us; that's why we're here ...'

'Our Romanian friends have changed their fucking minds. They've suddenly realised that alienating the Germans might be risky, so they've become neutral. Oh, and they won't be taking delivery of any Allied planes, either. Instead, they're going to keep us here to make sure we can't fight again.'

Adam sat heavily on the hard bunk, his head in his hands. It couldn't end like this. A rat scuttled across skeins of dust on the floor and ran under his bunk. He leapt off. 'Bloody hell!' he shouted. 'This place is a stinking cesspit. Are we just going to vegetate here?'

Romek lit another cigarette and walked over to him, a cautionary finger across his lips. 'Calm down, pal. Things aren't as bad as they look,' he whispered. 'We've been waiting for instructions and we got them today, together with false papers they've smuggled in for us. They want us to escape as soon as possible and make our way to Bucharest. From there, our people will get us to France so we can fly again.'

So there was a plan, after all. They sat up planning their escape in hushed voices long past midnight. According to

Romek, who seemed to know everything, the guards at the internment camp were lazy and their surveillance was sloppy. It wouldn't be difficult to distract or bribe them, cut through the wire and get away.

When Adam finally fell asleep, he tossed from side to side on his narrow bunk. He dreamed he was crawling under barbed wire, running across fields, and being pursued by French border guards. But when he woke, his head was clear. He wasn't going to join the others in France. He'd had enough of schemes that came to nothing and he refused to hang around in another foreign country in the hope of being given a plane. He would return to Poland and find some way of fighting the enemy on his home ground.

Weary and dejected after weeks of wandering from place to place and sleeping in barns and stables along the way, to avoid being captured by the Germans, Adam got back to Warsaw. But the city he knew had been buried beneath a pile of rubble. It now belonged to helmeted soldiers in grey-green uniforms, and officers with death's-head insignia on their peaked caps who strolled around the streets with the self-satisfied expressions of those who dispense death with impunity. As the tram swung across what remained of the city, he noticed that on some walls residents had scrawled 'Poland lives on!' but, from what he could see, the graffiti said more about the defiance of the writer than about reality.

On the corner of Marszałkowska Street and Aleje Jerozolimskie, a group of people had gathered around a pile of flowers heaped on the pavement. Some held lighted candles while others knelt in silent prayer.

'We keep vigil here every day from dawn till curfew,' the elderly woman beside him murmured as she wiped her eyes. 'They shot thirty people on this spot last week. Someone in that restaurant over there fired at a German soldier, so they rounded up everyone inside, stood them against that building and shot them. You can still see their blood on the wall.'

As the tram rattled towards the Old Town, he stared at the burnt-out ruins and piles of broken masonry. To think it had only taken three weeks for so much of the capital to be demolished. When he saw what was left of the old market square, he tightened his grip on the back of the seat until his hands cramped up. Those ancient buildings whose baroque façades had depicted scenes of eighteenth-century life had become tragic heaps of rubble.

Gone were the lively pavement cafés, the artists with their easels, and the horse-drawn *doroszki* that used to clatter over the cobblestones of the alleyways beneath the city's medieval walls.

Gone was the Royal Castle with the gilded apartments that had left him awestruck as a boy. Gone was the ornate opera house where Milicja Korjus's thrilling voice had made him forget to breathe. Gone, too, were his favourite haunts, like the Hungarian nightclub where he'd invited Elena that disastrous night at the Europejski Hotel, and the Polonia Restaurant whose dim lights and romantic music had always put his girlfriends in the mood for making love. He had left a city that bustled with life and returned to find a violated corpse. He slumped in his seat, feeling helpless and ashamed because he'd failed to defend his city.

The people in the streets moved with an air of wary alertness, as though ready to flatten themselves against a doorway or to dart into an alleyway at a moment's notice. Food queues stretched for blocks and exhausted people shifted from foot to foot, terrified that by the time their turn came the bread would have sold out. A crowd had gathered around a kiosk where Germans were dispensing soup to demonstrate their beneficence. Adam bristled. How could people accept soup from their oppressors? It was a wonder it didn't choke them.

His fellow passengers spoke in hushed tones, looking around from time to time, as if to check that no one was listening, even though the Germans rode in compartments designated exclusively for them. As the tram squealed to a halt, he heard a shout from across the road. Two SS men had grabbed hold of an old man with a white beard, struck him across the face so hard that he staggered backwards, and proceeded to kick him with boots buffed to a high polish. One of them took his pistol from his holster and a shot rang out in the golden light of that autumn afternoon.

Adam felt the blood drain from his face. All conversation on the tram ceased. After a pause, his neighbour commented, 'At least they'll get rid of the Jews for us.'

'And then they'll get rid of us,' Adam retorted.

'I never believed we'd have to capitulate,' a man across the aisle was saying to his neighbour. 'I don't know what happened to our army. And, as for our air force ...'

Adam clenched his fists. Didn't these people understand anything? He thought of his colleagues and all the sorties they'd flown back to back while they were reeling with exhaustion after not having slept for thirty-six hours. He wanted to tell his fellow passenger about all the Messerschmitts and Junkers they'd knocked out of the sky so that they couldn't drop their obscene bombs on people like him who didn't care about the pilots' lives that had been lost and the sacrifices that had been made.

He could feel the heat coming out of his eyes and longed to grab this ignoramus by the scruff of his neck and not let go until he'd told him what had happened and why it had happened, but he was too angry and too confused, and knew he wouldn't make any sense. The whole thing didn't make sense, anyway.

As he got off the tram and walked towards his parents' house, he braced himself against his father's derision of the air force. He couldn't blame his father for gloating: the cavalry he'd maligned had put up a valiant fight against the deadliest tanks and artillery the world had ever seen.

He pressed the bell, and waited for an effusive welcome from his mother. But, when she opened the door, there was something remote, almost frozen, in her expression. She led him into the lounge room without a word and twisted a handkerchief around her fingers before bursting into loud sobs. 'Thank God you're all right!' Her trembling fingers stroked his hand. 'The Blessed Virgin has answered my prayers. Every day I prayed that you'd come back safe.' Tears splashed down her thin cheeks and the corner of her mouth twitched.

He held her away from him and looked into her face. Her cheeks were furrowed and her lips, which had been pressed together after a lifetime of keeping her feelings inside, had become a thin line.

He looked around. Everything in the apartment was as he remembered. The heavy Gdańsk sideboard, the crocheted doilies on the table, the Persian rugs on the polished floor, and his father's large armchair by the window.

'Where is Father?' he asked

She shook her head, unable to speak.

'Is he ill?'

She pulled at the cross around her neck, and fiddled with the handkerchief again.

'What happened?'

She swallowed and wiped her eyes. 'He joined the army.'

He stared at her. 'At his age? But that's insane.'

Her answer came in gulps. 'He said he wasn't going to wait around until the Gestapo came for him. *Poland needs me and, as long as I have a drop of blood left in my body, I'll defend my country*. That's what he said. You know your father. You can't argue with him.' She blinked to push back the tears. 'I know he was sent east, but I haven't heard a word from him, and, now that the Russians have occupied Poland east of the Bug River, it's impossible to find out what's going on.'

'What company was he with? Where were they fighting?'

She wrung her hands. 'I can't find out anything. I've heard rumours that the Russians took our soldiers prisoner but everyone says something different. I just don't know what to do.'

She placed the kettle on the tiled stove and brought two glasses in silver holders to the table. 'There's no sugar in the shops but I've still got a bit of that raspberry jam you like.'

Adam waved the jam away. 'There must be some way of finding out where he is.'

Her hands shook as she poured black tea into the glasses. 'You say that because you don't know them. My neighbour has a cousin in Lwów and she says the Bolsheviks arrest people and send them to Siberia for the slightest thing. They don't answer to anyone.' She looked at him anxiously. 'Anyway, what are you going to do now?'

Adam shrugged. He was too depressed to gather his thoughts.

That night, in his old room, he paced up and down. He'd been consumed by the prospect of coming back to Poland but, now that he was here, he felt like an insect that had flown into the web of a waiting spider.

Five

Many of the city's parks had become graveyards, but roses as vivid as tropical sunsets still bloomed in one secluded corner of the Saski Gardens, and pale green buds were appearing on the chestnut trees. Sitting on his usual bench in the park, Adam shivered. April had brought the usual sudden downpours but none of the warmth that should herald the beginning of spring. He took out his packet of Klubs and, as he lit up, he wondered idly whether the blood of those buried in the park had nourished these rose bushes.

Apart from a harassed young mother wheeling a baby carriage, and a stooped old woman with a string bag, the park was empty. You didn't venture outside these days unless it was necessary, but it was four months since he had returned to Warsaw and he needed to get away from his mother's misery.

As he did each day, he unrolled the *Nowy Kurier Warszawski* and skimmed its contents. Ever since the Nazis had banned Polish newspapers and arrested their publishers and editors, the only paper sold openly was this German-sponsored rag, which spread rumours, lies and misinformation. Today's issue, marked April 1940, announced that publishing and selling the work of Polish authors and playing the music of Chopin were all strictly forbidden. Adam gave a sardonic laugh under his breath. So novels and nocturnes were now considered subversive. The paper also reported Hitler's threat that his next conquest would be Britain. From what Adam remembered of the English from his postgraduate student days, he knew that the more they were pushed, the more they'd dig their heels in, but anything was possible in a world where Poland had been carved up between Germany and the Soviet Union like a Christmas goose and had virtually ceased to exist, and where German boots were stomping across Europe.

Adam didn't know how long he'd been sitting there brooding when an elderly man, with a little hunting hat perched at an angle on his unruly white hair, came hobbling along the path, muttering to himself like an absent-minded professor. There was something familiar about the man but Adam couldn't place him. For the briefest moment, as he walked past, the man gave him a sideways glance. It could have been significant or totally meaningless; you couldn't trust anyone these days. Every day people were dragged to Szuch Avenue, and, after the Gestapo had finished its interrogation, not even their mothers could recognise them.

That night, as usual, Adam couldn't sleep. The floorboards in the adjoining room creaked and he heard the clicking of rosary beads and his mother's low murmuring voice. He marvelled that she didn't run out of prayers for divine intervention. Suddenly he sat up. Of course! The old man in the park was Pawel's father, Dr Wieniawski. He and Pawel had been sparring partners at the university fencing club and he had stayed at their place in Żoliborz. Over coffee and the delicious cheesecakes and walnut tortes that Pawel's mother baked for them, they'd spent hours discussing philosophy and politics. How extraordinary that he hadn't recognised him straightaway. The turmoil of the past few months had affected him so profoundly that events before the war seemed to have taken place in another lifetime.

Puffing thoughtfully on his pipe, Dr Wieniawski had always listened to his ideas and hadn't made him feel stupid, as his own father did. After all these years, he could still hear the quietly authoritative voice saying, 'We must go on believing that everything is possible,' whenever Adam argued that Poland's conservative ruling class would never surrender its power to make the government more democratic. Strange how some phrases stuck in your mind.

Next morning, Adam hurried to the same spot in the Saski Gardens but Dr Wieniawski didn't appear. When he called the Żoliborz number listed in the telephone directory, there was no response. A few days later, when he'd almost given up hope, the white-haired doctor came hobbling along the path, a briefcase under his arm and his hat askew, as though he'd rammed it on his head while running for the bus.

'Dr Wieniawski, I'm so glad to see you,' Adam began. 'Ever since I returned to Warsaw —'

Ignoring his greeting, the old doctor tapped the ground with his cane, drawing Adam's attention to a half-smoked cigarette in front of his right foot. 'All you young people are the same; you think that just because there's a war on you can make a mess everywhere.' He poked Adam's arm with the walking stick. 'Pick that up, young man, and don't litter the park in future!'

Startled, Adam bent down to pick up the cigarette and Dr Wieniawski whispered, 'Come at four,' and hobbled away. The cigarette butt on the ground was a clumsily hand-rolled brand made with cheap tobacco and there was some writing on the tissue paper. It was an address.

Dr Wieniawski no longer lived in a mansion but in a damaged apartment block in the riverside suburb of Powiśle where every morning the mist rose from the river and swathed the damaged buildings of the surrounding streets. The façade was crumbling and pocked with bullet holes and the bell swung from the end of a rickety doorpost.

Inside the small room on the fourth floor, a pink geranium wilted in a little pot on the window sill. In this part of town, the Vistula flowed sluggishly, and in the intense light of the late-afternoon sun it glinted like a wide band of steel.

'As you can see, I'm living like a bachelor here,' Dr Wieniawski said. 'My dear wife passed away before the war and Pawel ...' His voice faltered and he bowed his head. When he looked up again, his eyes were blazing. 'The bastards shot him three months ago. So now I have nothing to lose.'

Adam was shocked and started to offer his condolences but Dr Wieniawski rose and left the table so hurriedly that his chair scraped the floor. While he bustled about making tea, Adam sensed that something was being left unsaid but stifled his curiosity, not wanting to appear insensitive. As he looked around at the chipped tiled stove, rough pine table and the sofa against the wall, which probably opened up into a bed, a hundred questions crowded into his head.

'I remember you used to live in Żoliborz,' he said, recalling the elegant villa in one of Warsaw's garden suburbs.

'Ah yes, that was then.' Dr Wieniawski was clattering around with the cups.

He obviously didn't entertain very often because he forgot the saucers and spoons, and the biscuits he placed on the cracked plate were stale and broken. Adam sipped the tea, declined the biscuits, and they continued to engage in awkward small-talk.

After an awkward half-hour, Adam started shifting impatiently in his chair.

'I'm sorry to be blunt, Dr Wieniawski, but I have no idea why you bothered with that fake cigarette butt or why you wanted me to come. Anyway, thanks for the tea.'

As he rose to leave, his host chuckled. 'Sit down, young man, sit down. I'd forgotten what a hothead you are. Do you always expect a declaration of love on the first date?'

Adam bristled. 'No, but I did think there might be some point in us getting together.'

Placing his finger on his lips, Dr Wieniawski switched on the wireless and turned up the volume. 'One can't be too careful.'

Unable to control his anger, Adam burst out, 'How long are we going to continue living like this? What's going to become of us if we keep knuckling under, while those bastards grind us into the dirt? I wanted to fight for my country, not sit back and watch it being crushed. I can't find out whether my father is alive, dead, or rotting in some Nazi jail. I just can't live like this any more.'

Dr Wieniawski was holding a cup and seemed to be weighing it in his hand. He looked at Adam intently then said in a quiet voice, 'You know, not all of us feel as powerless as you do.'

Adam looked up. 'What do you mean?'

'Some of us have become quite active. There's no freedom when you live in fear.'

Adam's heart was racing. Although he didn't fully understand what the doctor was saying, he sensed something that offered hope.

'What kind of action? Are you talking about an organised group? Can anyone join?'

'Not so fast, Adam. I'm talking about resistance. To be

more exact, I'm talking about an Underground army that's under strict military discipline.'

Trying to steady his voice, Adam said, 'How do I join?'

'You should think it over very carefully before you decide. It's dangerous.'

Adam shrugged. 'Living in Poland is dangerous. Just tell me what to do.'

Several days later, he was standing in front of a typical Warsaw apartment block, three storeys high with a grey cement façade and small balconies that were ornamental rather than functional. Adam climbed the dusty staircase to the top floor, and gave three rapid knocks followed by two slow ones on the door marked *Import Enterprises*, as he'd been instructed. A few moments later, a tall thin woman with grey hair pulled back into a wispy bun opened the door and looked at him suspiciously.

'*Pan Direktor* is out at the moment. Would you like to leave a message?'

'I've come about Dutch clogs,' Adam replied, feeling foolish as he recited the code he'd been given.

She nodded and ushered him into a small bare office where a middle-aged man with a luxuriant moustache sat typing at a table. Adam cleared his throat several times but the man continued his work without acknowledging Adam's presence.

He walked towards the small window and looked down on the trams clanging below, drummed his fingers on the sill and turned to the man at the desk.

'If you're too busy to see me, perhaps I should come back some other time.'

Without looking up from his typewriter, the man said, 'I see patience isn't one of your virtues.'

'And courtesy isn't one of yours,' Adam retorted.

The man stopped typing and looked up. 'Have you brought something for me?'

Adam handed him the scrap of newspaper that Dr Wieniawski had torn from the first page of *Nowy Kurier Warszawski*. The man opened a drawer and took out the corresponding piece. When he was satisfied that the two pieces dovetailed, he motioned for Adam to sit down.

'Our mutual friend warned me that you were impetuous,' he said. 'This work requires a calm, detached mind. Impatience and arrogance can lead to serious trouble and cause disaster for us and our work. You must control yourself.'

Adam felt like a schoolboy being rebuked in the headmaster's office. He was about to say that he'd made a mistake and was obviously the wrong person for the job when the man stood up and pumped his hand.

'He also told me you were bright, enthusiastic and patriotic. I'm delighted that you're joining us. I know you'll be a great asset. I'll be known to you as Zenon.'

Speaking so rapidly that Adam had trouble keeping up, Zenon explained that all the members used code names so that if they were captured and tortured real names wouldn't be betrayed. One of their rules was 'no contact upwards', which meant that he would only know his immediate superior but would be unable to contact him unless summoned. He'd be issued with false identity documents and a capsule of potassium cyanide, in case he was caught.

'How do you want to be known?' Zenon asked.

Without hesitating, Adam said, 'Eagle.'

Secret signals, passwords, torn bits of paper, code names, fake documents, poison capsules. He couldn't suppress the thought that he was being inducted into a game instead of a dangerous Underground body vital to the survival of the nation.

As though he had read Adam's mind, Zenon said, 'Make no mistake about it, *Armia Krajowa*, as we call the home army, is a military organisation. It's strong, disciplined and well organised.'

He explained that the AK was answerable to the exiled Polish government, which was now based in France. 'You need to understand that the AK is more than an organ of resistance and reaction against oppression. We want to ensure the continuity of the Polish state in secret until our nation is independent again. We will fight the occupier any way we can — by sabotage, subversion or propaganda, and ultimately by armed insurrection. We don't recognise the occupation and don't collaborate with the occupiers in any way. Collaborators and traitors will be shot.'

Adam was pensive. 'Do you really think it's possible to create a secret state under the very noses of the Germans?'

'We have to believe we can,' Zenon replied. 'As our mutual friend says, we can never know what is possible until we try it.'

'Poland seems to be like Sisyphus, doomed to fight for its existence over and over again,' Adam remarked.

Zenon nodded 'That's been our curse, but it's also been our blessing.'

Adam frowned. 'I don't follow you.'

'This eternal struggle for sovereignty has given us our strong national identity and the determination to survive invasions, partitions and occupations.' Looking at Adam's downcast face, he chuckled. 'If you want a quiet life, go and live on the moon. Anywhere other than in Poland!'

A hush fell over the room as Zenon took the crucifix from the wall and handed it to Adam who cleared his throat and raised his other hand before taking the oath of all those inducted into the Underground. 'I swear before God to serve my country for honour and freedom, and for that honour and freedom I am ready to sacrifice everything I have.'

Adam felt elated and at the same time filled with solemn reverence. This was how he used to feel whenever he stepped away from the altar after taking holy communion, head bowed, the wafer dissolving on his tongue like a blessing from God. But this time, what he had received was not absolution for past sins but the promise of a future with honour.

Later, as he walked along the street, his step was faster and lighter than before. He noticed that a high wall had been erected on Okopowa and Pawia Streets but he was too preoccupied with his thoughts to pay it much attention. For the first time since the air force had been disbanded, he had a purpose in life. He'd found another way of fighting for his country.

Six

On the pavements of Marszałkowska Street, peasant women wrapped in dark shawls and headscarves held out bunches of lilac and lily-of-the-valley to passersby, a reminder that May had come. This year, however, the sun shone with a pallid light and the sky was watery. The German occupation had already lasted for seven months and the heroic promises and defiant pronouncements the Allies had made to protect Poland at the beginning of the war had evaporated into the heavy air, leaving a trail of dejected footprints that led to food queues and funeral corteges.

Now that their maid Tereska had returned to her village, Elżunia joined the silent queue that stretched for several blocks each morning to buy bread. Behind her, two women were whispering in distressed voices and she caught the word 'Holland'. So her father had been right. The Nazis had marched into Holland. Elżunia shivered. Who would stop them?

A car door slammed and everyone fell silent as two SS men jumped out of the black Opel, the wheels of which reflected off their shiny boots. They strolled along the queue, examining faces and documents. *'Schnell! Schnell!'* they screamed in voices that made her stomach churn.

Pedestrians scattered and melted into side streets while the measured tread of the SS men's boots resounded beside the queue. Their hands, encased in fine leather gloves, held riding crops, and their eyes, harder than the paving stones, scanned identity papers for any irregularity that could put those whips to use. Elżunia tried to shrink inside her coat to make herself invisible. She started counting. It was a game she had played ever since she was a child, a bargain with God or a challenge to fate. If she got to ten, it meant they'd walk past her. Their steps were louder now; they were coming closer. Eight, nine, ten. She held her breath, letting it out only when she saw the back of the black uniforms. A moment later the footsteps stopped beside a boy in front of her. They pointed to his trousers. 'Drop them! Now we'll see if you're a Jew or not!' He shook his head too vehemently and the look in his eyes gave him away. They pointed to his trousers. Silence fell over the crowd as his fingers fumbled with the buttons.

Elżunia had read the notices stuck on walls and lampposts all over town that ordered Jews to move into an area that had been labelled *Seuchensperrgebiet* and cordoned off from the rest of the city. That didn't make any sense because why would they force anyone to live in an area that they said was contaminated with typhus, when they were so terrified of disease? But so many things didn't make sense these days that she didn't bother questioning it.

'*Verfluchte Jude!*' the younger SS officer swore at the boy. 'I'll teach you what happens when you don't wear your armband!' He raised his whip, the boy ducked and, holding the waistband of his unbuttoned trousers in both hands, made a run for it. A shot ripped through the air. He stood quite still, as though frozen mid-flight. Elżunia's heart bounced against her throat as he tottered and fell, his eyes wide open.

Elżunia screamed, a long, piercing scream. The older SS officer swivelled around, hands on his solid hips, his face so close to hers that she could smell the eau de cologne he'd dabbed on his smooth cheeks.

'You should be grateful that we are ridding you of these subhuman *Untermenschen*.'

She glanced at the small body sprawled on the road and felt too sad to cry. Only a minute earlier he had felt the sun on his face, but now he felt nothing and never would again. Because of an accident of birth, he had been cheated of the rest of his life. She had always thought of her life as stretching ahead like an endless golden thread rolling towards infinity, and perhaps he'd thought the same. The dead boy would never see his parents again. Thank God she had hers. Mingled with pity, she felt a shameful sense of relief. It was terrible to be a Pole in Warsaw these days but it was even worse to be a Jew.

She struggled with herself to stay in the queue instead of running home to her father to be folded in his arms and comforted. She couldn't go home empty-handed.

She was still trembling when she reached the head of the queue and her teeth were chattering so much that she could hardly speak.

'Hurry up! People are waiting!' the baker snapped, wiping his big hands on his floury apron.

In her haste, she dropped the ration card and groped for it under the counter, red-faced. The baker's gruff manner softened and, putting a warning forefinger over his lips, he placed an extra loaf in her basket.

As she hurried home, the thrill of surprising her parents with the miracle of the two loaves pushed thoughts of the dead boy from her mind. She burst into the lounge room, holding up the bread, and then sensed the heavy stillness in the room. Her mother's face was white and strained and her father didn't jump up to hug her. They were both staring at two men in grey coats, whose dark fedoras tilted over their hard faces.

One of the men pointed to Elżunia. Addressing Lusia in a disrespectfully familiar way, as if she were a child, he said, *'Das ist deine Tochter, nicht wahr?'*

Elżunia glanced at her father, who looked as though someone had tied all the muscles of his face together and yanked the rope tight.

The Gestapo agent turned to him. 'You, come with us.'

'But what is this about?' Her mother's face had a yellowish hue. 'There must be some mistake.'

'No mistake,' the Gestapo agent snapped. 'You will come by yourself or we will take you.' He put his hand into his pocket and Elżunia froze as he pulled out a pistol.

Edward turned to his agitated wife. 'Don't worry, Lusia. It's just routine. I'll be home soon.'

But his expression didn't match his words. Even Elżunia knew that there was no such thing as routine questioning at Szuch Avenue.

As Elżunia moved towards her father, the Gestapo agent shouted, *'Komm mit! Los!'*

She clung to her father but he pushed her away gently. Placing his hands on her shoulders, he looked into her eyes and said, 'Never forget who you are. Smile at adversity, laugh at death and always keep a straight back.'

Without saying another word, he embraced his wife, placed his hat firmly on his head and walked out of the apartment.

Elżunia ran to the window and looked down at his retreating figure. Instead of her powerful father, she saw an ordinary, middle-aged man. That frightened her more than anything that Hitler had done. She watched as the Gestapo pushed him into the back seat of the waiting car. A moment later they sped away.

Elżunia turned away from the window. Her mother was sitting at the table, her head in her hands. She spoke in a low, hoarse voice. 'What are they going to do with him?' She looked wildly around the room. 'Where is Stefan when we need him? He should be here with us. I only hope he's safe. What in heaven's name are we going to do?'

Elżunia was shaken. Her mother was supposed to know the answers. The light faded and darkness filled the room but Lusia continued to sit without moving or drawing the curtains. Finally, with a deep sigh, she rose and walked slowly to the telephone. 'We know a lot of people. Surely someone can help.'

Elżunia could see her mother's fingers were shaking so much she could hardly dial the numbers. She tried one friend after another but although they spoke consoling words, their tone belied their optimistic phrases. In some cases she detected a hesitation that shocked her and she realised they were unwilling to make inquiries on behalf of anyone arrested by the Gestapo. Lusia slumped in the chair while Elżunia chewed her nails. Surely someone would help. But what if they didn't and her father never came home again?

As she turned towards the window, her eyes fell on a small flat object lying on the table beside her father's armchair and caught her breath. Father's silver cigarette case. Knowing that he had left it behind made her aware of the gravity of the situation and she felt she had fallen into a deep, dark well. As a child she had always loved tracing the acanthus leaves around the initials embossed on the case with her fingertips, proud that the initials, EO, were the same as hers. Comforted by the smooth patina of the cigarette case, she turned it over and over in her hands, then put it in her pocket.

'Why did they take him away?' Elżunia asked. 'He hasn't done anything.'

Lusia shrugged. 'Maybe because he was an officer in the Polish army.'

'But that was over twenty years ago!'

Lusia looked thoughtful. 'He's been going out a lot lately and he's been very secretive about it. Maybe it's to do with that.' She didn't tell Elżunia that it had crossed her mind that he might be seeing another woman. She had often noticed women giving him coquettish glances, and he seemed to enjoy their attention. But when she accused him of encouraging them, he denied it, insisting that she was the only one for him.

They sat in silence for a while and to Elżunia it seemed that the room was closing in on them. She looked at the piano. Music always soothed her mother's nerves. 'Play something, Mama.'

Lusia shook her head but a few minutes later she placed a sheet of music on the carved stand between the candlesticks.

As the haunting notes of a Chopin nocturne rippled from her long slim fingers, they filled the room with all the sadness, suffering and beauty in the world, and tears sprang to Elżunia's eyes. Lusia closed the lid but continued to sit at the piano, her head bent over the keys.

It was past midnight and they were in bed when they heard footsteps thumping up the stairs. Lusia and Elżunia both sat up with a start. Someone was banging on their door, shouting 'Open up!' Lusia pulled on her silk dressing-gown and tried to fasten it with shaking fingers.

'Who is it?' she asked in a tremulous voice.

'Open up or we'll break the door down!'

Standing behind her mother in her flannelette pyjamas, Elżunia clutched Lusia's arm as she slid back the bolt. Two

SS men, pistols in hand, pushed them out of the way and barged inside.

'You're too late; they've already taken him away,' Lusia said angrily.

The younger man had a long face and a sour expression. Scanning the sheet of paper in his hand, he barked, 'Lusia Orłowska? And is this your daughter?'

Lusia nodded.

'And your son? Where is he?'

She shrugged. Stefan often stayed out all hours with his friends, despite the curfew. She had often argued with him about his reckless behaviour, but now, although she longed to have him with her at home, she was relieved he'd stayed out.

The men strode around the apartment, knocking over chairs, pulling out drawers and throwing things out of cupboards and wardrobes as they searched every room. Elżunia and Lusia looked at each other white-faced. The men were obviously not searching for valuables. What could they possibly be looking for?

Search over, the officers returned to the lounge room. 'Come with us. Now!' the sour one said.

'But why? What have we done?' Lusia asked.

'You're Jews pretending to be Aryans.'

Elżunia couldn't contain herself. 'That's a rotten lie. We're Catholic. Ask Father Skowronski; he'll tell you.'

She ran into her room and came back with a photograph of herself in a white dress with frills and flounces and a veil attached to the garland of flowers on her head. 'That was my first communion, see?' She thrust the picture into the face of the younger man. 'We go to Mass every Sunday. You've mixed us up with someone else.'

The other officer was expressionless as he removed a letter from the inside pocket of his long coat and jabbed his finger at it.

'It says here you were born a Jew, Leah Bronsztajn, and in 1921 you converted to Catholicism at St Aleksander's Church in the Square of the Three Crosses,' he told Lusia.

Elżunia stared at her mother whose face was ghostly white.

'Quick, tell them it's a pack of lies,' she shouted, but her mother's legs had buckled under her and she had sunk into a chair, unable to speak. She watched while the younger officer tamped his cigarette on a gilt-edged Dresden plate.

'Enough talking!' he shouted. 'You have thirty minutes to pack.'

'But where are you taking us?' Elżunia cried out.

'All Jews must live in the *Seuchensperrgebiet*, the special area we've set aside for them so they don't spread typhus.'

Elżunia clamped her hands over her ears. 'Stop!' she shouted. 'This has nothing to do with me. I'm Catholic. You can't make me go and live in an area meant for Jews.'

He gave a cruel laugh. 'The children of Jews *are* Jews, *Fraülein*.'

She coughed as he blew cigarette smoke into her face.

'And I warn you to be polite.' He blew another ring of smoke in her direction and, with a pointed glance at his watch, flopped into her father's armchair.

Elżunia's mind lurched from one crazy thought to another. None of this made any sense. Her mother a Jew? It was an outrageous idea, concocted by a sick mind. Jews didn't even believe in Christ or the Blessed Virgin. If only her father was here, he'd explain that they'd made a terrible mistake. Then she realised the futility of that idea: her father had been unable to prevent his own arrest. Her scalp prickled. No one could help them. They would have to struggle alone.

'Please listen to us!' she burst out. 'You're making a big mistake, and when your superior finds out that you've taken away innocent people, you'll be in big trouble.'

'*Ach so?*' The sour one stepped closer and struck her face with the flat of his powerful hand. Her hand sprang to her stinging cheek and suddenly the room was swaying, the Dresden ballerinas were spinning on their pedestals and the walls were closing in.

Lusia hissed, 'Don't ever argue with them!' and the other Gestapo agent bellowed '*Schnell!*'

A key turned in the lock and four pairs of eyes swivelled towards the door. Stefan's hair was dishevelled, his collar was loose and his tie was twisted but the sight of the peaked caps with the death's-head insignia sobered him up immediately.

With a cry, Lusia rushed over to embrace her son but one of the SS men pushed her away.

'Stefan Orłowski? Hands up! Now!'

He raised his arms and looked at his mother questioningly. The SS officer pulled a blunt-nosed pistol from his coat and waved it at him.

'You. Get ready. Now! You have twenty minutes.'

Stefan was staring at his mother. 'What's going on?'

Lusia looked at him with such love and sorrow in her face that Elżunia felt a stab of resentment. Her mother was distraught that her beloved Stefan would have to share their fate. She doubted whether her mother was equally distressed on her account.

'I'll tell you later,' Lusia whispered.

Elżunia saw her mother's eyes sweep helplessly around the room. Paralysed with anxiety for her children and herself, Lusia was stuck between panic and indecision as she tried to decide what to take and, even harder, what to leave behind from a household filled with objects acquired over an indulgent lifetime.

'Elżunia, quick, get your things together and come and help me,' she said, still not moving. What would they need and what could they carry? With a huge effort, she began making an inventory in her head. Valuables that could be offered as bribes or sold for cash. Clothes, but which ones? Something warm.

What if she failed to pack something essential? Bedding was essential but it was bulky and they could only take what they could carry.

She ran from room to room, pulling clothes from their hangers, then discarding them in favour of others. She grabbed silver candlesticks and ornaments from the sideboard and threw them on her eiderdown, ready to roll up, then changed her mind and replaced them with other ornaments. When she was ready to bundle it all up, the ends of the eiderdown didn't meet, so she had to tip everything out onto a sheet. For the hundredth time, she checked her watch. Not much time left and there was still so much to sort through. Photographs. How could she leave without photographs of her wedding, of the children, and of their holidays in the country?

Panic-stricken, she wanted to sink into the centre of the eiderdown and surrender to despair. Throughout her life, the need for security and comfort had guided all the decisions she had made, and now she felt like the French aristocrats who invoked God and government to come to their aid as they mounted the guillotine. She was being flung from her safe, cocooned existence into a frightening world of persecuted outcasts. If only she had gone to their country house and stayed there.

Through Stefan's open door, she could see her son emptying drawers, and throwing shirts, trousers, shoes and books on the floor, swearing loudly as he did so.

Heart pounding, she glanced at her Tissot wristwatch again and her legs seemed to dissolve, unable to hold her up. Only ten minutes left. The piles of belongings had grown, but how was she to sort them and how could they carry it all? Her mind raced in all directions. She tried not to contemplate what awaited her and her children.

In her room, Elżunia rubbed her aching jaw as she looked at the floral curtains and the white dressing table with the heart-shaped mirror and the row of dolls on the top shelf as if seeing them for the first time. Her room had never looked so cosy, and her bed had never felt so soft. As she stuffed clothes, the Red Cross box and her favourite books into her rucksack, her mind was roiling. Why had someone written such vicious lies about her mother? How long would it take to prove it was false? What if no one believed them? And what if Gosia and Lydia heard that she was in the Ghetto with all the Jews? She could see their disgusted expressions and hoped they'd never find out. None of this could be real; surely it was a nightmare from which she would soon wake. But the two Germans pacing impatiently in the lounge room and littering her mother's precious ornaments with their cigarette butts were all too real. When her rucksack was bulging so much that she could hardly fasten the buckles, she ran back to the bookshelf and squeezed *Gone With the Wind* into the side pocket beside a pair of her father's trousers that she had grabbed on impulse from her parents' room. She closed her hand over her father's cigarette case in her pocket and, taking one last look at her room, walked back into the lounge room.

In her parents' bedroom, she found her mother sitting on the floor, staring into space. Her fragility made the ground tremble beneath Elżunia's feet. She helped her mother up and they tied the ends of the sheet together. As they fastened the unwieldy bundle, Elżunia looked closely at her mother.

'What's this rubbish about you being Jewish?'

Without looking up, Lusia gave the ends one more tug and started throwing suede pouches into her leather handbag. 'We have to hurry,' she said dully. 'This isn't the time to discuss it.'

'Mama, I have to know,' Elżunia insisted.

Lusia swung the hold-all over her shoulder and dragged the bundle along the floor. 'Just get your coat,' she said.

As the three of them walked out of the apartment prodded by the SS men, Stefan supported his mother while Elżunia followed. She felt alone. Suddenly an image of the dead boy leapt into her mind. His open eyes were fixed on her and his reproachful look seemed to be saying, *You were glad it was me and not you.* It was true. She had been relieved that she wasn't a Jew. God has punished me, she thought.

Seven

The wall cut the courtyard in two, leaving half inside the Ghetto and the other half outside it. It was about three metres high and topped with barbed wire and broken glass. When Elżunia looked out of the window, she saw that the boy in the house opposite was watching her as usual. She pulled a face at him and he wagged a reproving finger, laughed, then disappeared inside. He looked about seventeen and she hated him. Hated the way his yellow hair stuck out all over his head as though he'd jumped out of a haystack, hated the carefree freckles across his nose, but most of all she hated the fact that he was free to live in his own home on the other side of the wall while she had been forced to live in this loathsome place for the past two months. If only they would release her father so that he could get them out. He was never far from her thoughts and the longing to run into his arms always filled her eyes with tears.

The wall divided more than just courtyards and streets. It split the world in two. On the boy's side of the wall, people didn't have to struggle to find a corner to sleep in, but on hers the streets were so crowded that you couldn't walk without being pushed or jostled. The summer of 1940 was coming to an end, but the heat seemed to rise from the pavements and walking on them was like trying to fight your way through treacle. The Ghetto was already bursting at the seams but refugees kept pouring in from the towns, *sztetls* and villages that the Germans were clearing of Jews. Streams of newcomers trudged in every day, lugging as much as they could carry on their backs, or pushing barrows heaped with bedding, clothes, pots and pans and anything else they could carry. Elżunia knew what they were thinking as they looked around with pale, worried faces. Would they be able to find a place to live, and would they manage to survive in a place where they knew no one and had no way of earning a living? With haunted expressions they told of entire *sztetls* being rounded up and their residents clubbed, shot, set on fire or deported God only knew where. They camped wherever they could, in the corner of a hall, on stairways or in corridors with their silent children. Elżunia's heart twisted when she saw their despairing faces as they begged passersby for a piece of bread or a glass of water.

The restless activity in the street reminded Elżunia of the ants' nest she had observed while sitting beside a stream at their country estate the summer before the war. An endless line of insects, lugging blades of grass like an army of soldiers bearing jade-green pennants struggled to and from their nest in an activity imposed on them by forces beyond their control.

Standing at the window beside her daughter, Lusia shook her head. 'How many more people are they going to push in here? What's to become of us all?' she asked for the hundredth time. She looked forlornly at the cramped, shabby room on the first floor that they'd occupied for the past two months.

The three of them slept and ate in that room, tripping over each other as they moved around. She and Elżunia shared the only bed while Stefan slept on a battered sofa with broken springs. They hadn't been able to bring any furniture with them and had to make do with what was already there.

'To think I had to leave my beautiful apartment for this slum,' Lusia lamented yet again, looking at the broken plaster on the wall. The former Christian tenants, who had been evicted by the Germans and ordered to live in the Aryan part of the city, had torn out the sink and taken it with them.

Elżunia looked at her mother resentfully. 'At least we've got somewhere to live,' she pointed out, irritated by her mother's constant complaints. She missed her father's cheerful nature and equanimity more and more. If only they had some news of him.

Each time Elżunia had broached the subject of the letter that had been sent to the Gestapo, her mother had refused to discuss it. She was always too exhausted, too busy or too distraught to talk about it. She even became angry with Stefan when he raised the subject. Concerned about their mother's fragility, they had desisted, but this time Elżunia decided she wasn't going to be fobbed off any longer.

'Mama, I have a right to know the truth.'

Her mother looked down. She couldn't meet her daughter's unflinching gaze.

Elżunia took a deep breath. 'I'm sick of your excuses. This is my business too. You have to tell me,' she insisted, amazed at her own daring.

There was a tense pause. Finally Lusia whispered, 'It's true. I was born a Jew.'

A dark pit opened in Elżunia's stomach. Her mother a Jew! The priest had called Jews Christ-killers, and the nuns had said they were devils, destined to fry in hell.

She tried to speak but her tongue didn't move.

67

Finally she gasped, 'It can't be true! How come you never told me? How could you hide something like that?'

Lusia seemed to be speaking through broken glass. 'There was no need to tell you. I didn't see the point.'

'I don't understand,' Elżunia was trying not to shout. Did Father know? When did you convert?'

Lusia opened her mouth then closed it. There was no way of explaining why she had turned her back on her heritage. Past emotions were impossible to recapture, let alone to convey. How could Elżunia possibly understand how embarrassed and insecure she had felt belonging to a despised group? All her life she had felt that hatred like a miasma that hung over every aspect of her existence. The school friends who whispered that Jews drank the blood of Catholic babies, the college students who moved away from her as though she had the plague, the hooligans who threw rocks through her father's tailoring workshop or scrawled insulting slogans on the walls. Jews weren't considered to be true Poles, and she had yearned to belong, to be the same as everyone else. She gravitated towards Catholic friends and came to look at her fellow Jews with the critical eyes of their detractors.

Her favourite escape had been skating. Gliding around the skating rink, she felt carefree. Dressed in the long fur-trimmed coat and arctic-fox hat that her father had stitched for her, and her hands snuggled into her white fur muff, she skated around the rink to Strauss waltzes or Mozart's *Rondo alla Turca* and felt no different from anyone else. In between brackets, the skaters gathered at the buffet table at the side of the rink, where she tasted food that would never have passed her parents' lips. Smoked ham canapés, crumbed pork, and smoky country sausage spiced with garlic.

She was relishing these forbidden delicacies when a tall cavalry officer with a moustache that almost brushed his ears stood before her and bowed with a flourish. As his gaze slid from her blonde hair and delicately moulded features to her fur-trimmed coat, he kissed her hand and said, 'You must be a Romanov princess who escaped from the Tsar's palace and galloped over the steppes in your troika.'

She laughed and, as the band struck up the Gold and Silver Waltz, he stretched out his hand. 'Would you like to take a turn around the rink with me?'

As they glided arm in arm, Edward Orłowski told her that he'd recently been fighting the Bolsheviks in the east of Poland. Lusia was certain she was the envy of all the women at the ice rink because her striking partner looked like a hero straight out of a Sienkiewicz novel. Soon she was meeting him secretly in Łazienki Park, hoping that her parents wouldn't find out.

Six weeks later, when he proposed, she was so besotted that she didn't hesitate to accept, even though she knew her parents would never consent to her marrying out. Although she didn't want to admit it to herself, his proposal offered an entry into a world that had always been closed to her. His parents belonged to the *szlachta*, Poland's aristocracy, and although he avoided discussing their reaction to his marrying a Jewish girl, she sensed their disapproval. All he said was that they insisted on a church wedding.

When she told her parents that she had decided to marry Edward and convert, her mother wept while her father's face turned white with anger. 'I never thought my own daughter would turn her back on us,' he said.

Tears welled in her eyes. '*Tateh*, I didn't mean to hurt you, but I have a right to be happy. You know religion has never mattered to me.'

'Religion!' he exclaimed. 'It's not a matter of religion. It's a matter of heritage, of identity. Just because a bird nests in a stable, it doesn't become a horse. To them, you'll always be a Jew.'

'I love Edward and I can't live without him,' she insisted.

Her mother gave her a penetrating look. 'And how much does this Edward love you? He'll only marry you if you change your religion. Your great love affair sounds very one-sided to me.'

At that moment, Lusia hated her mother so much that she was too choked up to reply coherently.

'You don't know him,' she shouted through her sobs. 'He's the most noble, unselfish person.'

Unable to change her mother's mind about Edward's character, Lusia burst out, 'Anyway, I'm entitled to live my own life.'

'So go live your life,' her father said, 'but for us you are dead.' And with that he walked out of the room and slammed the door behind him.

Her parents observed the traditional mourning ritual. For seven days they covered the mirrors in their home, ripped their clothes, donned slippers and sat in low chairs. At night they said the Kaddish prayer, as if she had died. She never saw them again and the ache in her heart never went away.

Nearly twenty years had passed and now Lusia recalled her father's words and shivered. It was as though she had been cursed. And she still hadn't been able to find out what had happened to Edward. With every passing day, she grew more anxious about his safety. If he had been released, she knew he would move heaven and earth to get her and his children out of there. If only she knew where he was.

Elżunia watched her mother and waited. She longed for an honest answer that would not only explain why they were in this predicament but would also indicate that at last her mother considered her as an adult and not a child whose questions could be dismissed with a flippant wave of the hand.

But Lusia only said, 'I fell in love with your father and we couldn't get married unless I converted.'

At least she hadn't brushed the question aside. Elżunia decided to push a little further. 'Who do you think wrote that letter?'

Lusia sighed. 'I'm sure it was that Madame Françoise.'

Elżunia was frowning. 'But why would she do that?'

'Envy sometimes eats people up,' Lusia replied. 'She finally found a way to pay me back for my success.'

After musing over this for a while, Elżunia asked, 'But how come she knew you'd converted?'

'Once she came up to me in the street and told me her cousin was the parish clerk at St Aleksander's Church. She said it in such an insidious tone that I knew immediately what she meant. I was terrified, and wondered whether she was going to blackmail me. I suppose when the Germans occupied Warsaw she saw her chance to get even with me.'

The expression on her mother's face aroused Elżunia's suspicion. 'There's more to it than that, isn't there? It wasn't just professional jealousy, was it?'

Lusia nodded. 'A friend told me that Madame Françoise had been in love with your father before he and I met. So I was her rival personally as well as professionally.'

Anger stuck in Elżunia's throat like a fishbone. If only she could get her hands on the vicious woman who had caused all their misfortune. 'It's incredible that someone would do such a horrible thing.'

'You can never tell what people are capable of, for good or evil,' her mother said.

'I hope one day she'll pay for what she did to us,' Elżunia said.

The front door opened and Stefan swaggered in, looking very pleased with himself. The drastic change in their circumstances seemed less painful for her brother, who didn't appear to miss his friends as she did. He had found new pals in the Ghetto and spent most of his time with them. Elżunia and her mother rarely saw him during the day.

Elżunia eyed him curiously. 'What's that you're wearing?' she asked, and couldn't resist adding, 'Is there a fancy-dress party on somewhere?'

He smoothed down his belted jacket and adjusted his cap, which was too big and slipped down his forehead. 'You're looking at the latest recruit in the Jewish police force!'

Lusia gave him a wan smile. 'You look very smart in that uniform. How come you joined up?'

'So he can throw his weight around,' Elżunia muttered.

'In case you haven't noticed, Miss Smartypants, we can't survive on the pathetic ration of three hundred calories a day that the Germans dole out. Now I've joined up, I'll get better rations and I might share them with you if you stop needling me,' he said. 'Even if we start selling off Mother's jewellery, how long will that last when a loaf of bread already costs one zloty on the black market? That's if we're able to get to the market at all. Once they close the Ghetto, we won't be able to get out.'

'They said they wouldn't do that,' Lusia said in a tremulous voice.

Stefan shrugged. 'You can't believe anything they say. But that's what they reckon at the Judenrat and they should know.' He brushed an imaginary speck from his boots and pushed the cap back from his forehead. 'Anyway, now I'll be able to protect you.'

Elżunia eyed her brother's uniform, from the top of his

navy cap with its six-sided oblong metal emblem to the yellow band on his right arm with the word *Judenrat* on it.

Lusia knew that the Germans had set up a Jewish Council they called *Judenrat*, to liaise between them and the Jewish inhabitants. She also knew that many people in the Ghetto were alarmed when the Judenrat appointed Jews to police their own people, but, seeing how pleased her son was with his new job, she kept her doubts to herself.

'I thought you had to be twenty or twenty-one to join up,' Elżunia said.

He gave a smug smile. 'I told a fib about my age and they believed me.'

'Anyway, what are you going to protect us with?' she asked. 'Where's your pistol?'

'We didn't get pistols. We got truncheons.'

She looked contemptuously at his wooden baton. 'The Polish police got pistols. How come you lot didn't?'

'You're such a nosy brat!' he shouted. 'Why don't you just shut up and mind your own business?' He stalked off, fuming. His sister always misconstrued his good intentions.

'Oh my God! What if he's right and they do close the Ghetto? What'll we do?' Lusia lamented. 'And what's happened to Father? If only we could find out whether they've released him.'

Whenever her father was mentioned, a tight knot twisted in Elżunia's stomach. With every passing day, her optimism waned. It became increasingly difficult to maintain the conviction that he would soon be released and come to their rescue, but the thought that something terrible had happened to him, that she might never see him again, was unbearable. But if he was safe, surely he would have contacted them. The uncertainty was agonising. But she didn't voice her suspicions for fear of distressing her already fragile mother. In the past six months, the lines on her doll-like face had deepened and the dark hollows under her eyes gave them a tragic expression.

'Perhaps it isn't true about them closing the Ghetto,' she said to comfort her mother. 'Anyway, as soon as they let Father out, he'll get us out of here.'

She spent so much of her time trying to raise her mother's spirits that she sometimes believed her own optimistic predictions. Despite her anxiety about Lusia's fragile state of mind, it gave Elżunia a sense of satisfaction to know that for the first time in her life her mother was listening to her.

Lusia nodded. 'You're right. After all, he knows so many influential people.'

Elżunia knew that these days the influential people themselves were being arrested, deported and killed, but there was no point adding to her mother's anxiety over her father. Lusia had managed to contact one of their friends and asked him to make some discreet inquiries about Edward but so far he hadn't been able to find out anything. Elżunia tried to brush aside the sinister thoughts that crept into her mind. Life inside the Ghetto was terrifying enough without anticipating tragedy.

There was a tap on the door and their neighbour Pani Szpindlerowa was hovering apologetically on the doorstep. She had always lived in the Jewish part of Warsaw with her cobbler husband, she wore a wig and she spoke Polish with a Yiddish accent.

'I have nothing in common with people like that,' Lusia had often complained to Elżunia. She regarded the orthodox men with their beards and long black coats and the women with their wigs and dowdy ankle-length skirts as clannish and backward. It was the bitter irony of her life that she was now lumped in with them and abandoned by those whose society she had always sought. With an obvious lack of enthusiasm, she invited her neighbour inside.

Pani Szpindlerowa's husband, Chaim, had been deported to some camp or other, and hadn't been heard of since. The woman never tired of regaling her with stories about Chaim's wisdom and goodness. With each story, he sounded more saintly than before. Lusia had no patience for these monologues, which usually ended with her neighbour begging the Almighty to intercede on her husband's behalf.

'I just saw your Stefan in his uniform, *kenaine horeh*,' she said, invoking the universe to keep the evil eye away from him. Then she launched into a stream of Yiddish.

Lusia's face twisted in distaste. 'I'm sorry, Pani Szpindlerowa, but, as I've told you, I don't speak Yiddish.' In fact, she understood every word but pretended she didn't.

'I keep forgetting,' the woman said. 'Didn't your parents speak Yiddish?' she asked with a touch of commiseration.

Lusia didn't reply.

'Thank God we now have our own police force, *Boruch Hashem*.' Her neighbour peppered her conversation with pious thanks to the Almighty. It was a habit Lusia usually found irritating but on this occasion she was mollified by the woman's admiration of Stefan.

Pani Szpindlerowa turned to Elżunia. 'You must be proud of your big brother.'

Elżunia made a non-committal reply and busied herself in another part of the room. Her stomach was growling. She tried not to think of the crusty kaiser rolls that Tereska used to place on the table every morning, and her mouth watered at the memory of their yeasty smell and crispness. She rummaged through the jars and scoured the cupboard in the hope of coming across a forgotten slice of bread but all she could find on the shelf was a small packet of buckwheat *kasza*.

After their neighbour had shuffled back to her own place, Elżunia cooked the buckwheat into a gluggy porridge and stirred some burnt grain into boiled water, and tried to believe it was coffee. As she sipped the bitter liquid, she made a mental inventory of their belongings to figure out what she could sell at the market the next day to buy bread. But when she broached the subject with her mother, the little equilibrium Lusia had gained from contemplating Stefan's new status immediately evaporated.

'To think I've become reduced to selling my own things, Elżunia, like those common women in the markets. Never in my life did I imagine that something like this could happen to me.' Her eyes brimmed with tears. 'What would Edward say?'

It seemed to Lusia that she was inhabiting someone else's skin, living someone else's life. She could hardly grasp the sequence of events that had smashed her beautifully ordered, comfortable existence in such a short time. One moment she was running Warsaw's most exclusive beauty salon and entertaining high society, and the next she was an outcast, selling her belongings to buy food. And what had happened to poor Edward?

Lusia watched as her daughter spooned the porridge as slowly as she could into her mouth to make it last and then scraped the last grains from the edges of the plate. She felt guilty that she had allowed Elżunia to take over the running of their meagre household, but over the past two months the girl had become more capable and energetic while she herself had become increasingly weak. She pushed her own bowl towards Elżunia. 'I'm not hungry,' she said. 'Have mine.'

Elżunia looked away from her mother's bowl and shook her head. 'After class tomorrow, I'll sell something at

Kiercelak Market and buy some bread and maybe a pat of cottage cheese.'

Her mother unpinned her brooch. 'Sell this,' she said with a sigh.

Elżunia was dismayed. 'Not your amber brooch!' Of all her mother's jewellery, this modest piece was the one she loved most, with the insect stuck in the honey-coloured resin. 'Amber isn't very valuable,' she said. 'It won't fetch much.'

Lusia nodded. 'You're right. I'll find something else for you to sell.'

Lying down on her bed in the corner of the room they shared, Elżunia tried to distract herself from the gnawing emptiness in her stomach and memories of mushroom pancakes, *bigos* stew with sausage and sauerkraut, and chicken kiev. She let her mind wander, as it often did, to the taciturn airman who had saved her life on the highway leading from Warsaw. Recalling the weight of his body lying on hers almost a year before, she felt a guilty rush, as if blood was simmering in her veins.

Although she didn't know him at all, not even his name, he had risked his life for her, just like the heroes in the books she read, but she had been too dazed to realise it at the time and hadn't even thanked him. She replayed the scene on the road once again but this time it ended with him carrying her up a wide staircase like Rhett Butler, and saying in a low voice hoarse with passion, 'Tonight you won't lock me out of the bedroom again ...'

The following morning, Elżunia stood in line at one of the gates, waiting for the young German guard on duty to check her permit. Stefan never tired of pointing out that, thanks to his job as a policeman, he had managed to obtain a Red Cross pass for her. Because of that pass, she was able to leave the Ghetto for a short time each morning to train as a nurse at a medical clinic on Marszałkowska Street. The guard studied the words on each pass slowly and deliberately, as though learning them by heart, and occasionally stared at the person before him with such malevolence that Elżunia's blood froze. With his hard, colourless eyes, he reminded her of a wolf stalking its prey, but she noticed that when he was chatting with the other guards the predatory expression was gone and he looked like any ordinary young man enjoying himself.

While waiting her turn, she wondered about his family. His mother was probably proud of him and had no idea how cruel he really was. She wondered whether this happened when you took someone out of their familiar surroundings and gave them a uniform and the power to hurt people. Her thoughts turned to people she knew. How would they behave in similar circumstances? She wondered uncomfortably about herself. Some years ago, she had been playing with the girls next door when their mother had gone out, leaving the baby in his cot. When he'd stretched out his arms to be lifted up, his sisters had rocked the cot violently from side to side and giggled while he screamed in terror. Elżunia had looked on but said nothing. He was their little brother and it wasn't her business. After a time, she had stepped in to stop their game. She knew she should have done it sooner but, in some deep dark place she was ashamed of, she had been stirred up by seeing the child at their mercy.

Wolfman was taking longer than usual at the gate and the pretty young woman whose pass he was studying made an impatient sound. His eyes glittered dangerously as he set aside the pass, said something to the other guard, and they both looked at the woman and sniggered in a way that made Elżunia feel sick. They grabbed the girl by the arms, pushed her onto the ground and, while she tried to fight them off, pulled off her panties and made her crawl across the yard on her hands and knees, laughing heartily as they fired shots above her head to make her go faster. Their sport over, they returned to their post.

Elżunia looked at her watch and hoped she wouldn't miss her class. It took so long to get around the Ghetto these days because the walls blocked off so many exits. Instead of walking around the corner, as she once had been able to do, these days she had to make a huge detour around Nowolipki, Zamenhof and Gęsia Streets, which added forty minutes to her journey. In an effort to calm herself down, she thought about her father and his parting words. *Never forget who you are. Smile at adversity, laugh at death, and always keep a straight back.* But Father had overestimated her courage, just as he'd overestimated his own power to influence events. She felt the guard's wolflike eyes on her. He snatched the pass from her hand, read it, and waved her through.

Outside the Ghetto gate, she looked around to make sure no one was watching and slipped off the humiliating white armband with the blue Star of David. She looked enviously at the other people on the street. They could go wherever they pleased without armbands and permits, just as she had done only three months earlier, not realising how brief that freedom would be. Instead of the turgid air in the Ghetto's sweltering, overcrowded streets, out here there were open spaces, trees and bright flower beds.

Casting a quick look around, Elżunia flew up the stairs to an unmarked apartment. Although most schools had been closed down, clandestine classes called *komplety* had mushroomed all over the city and that's where she went early every morning before the clinic. Although attending these classes was very risky, she was determined not to allow the Germans to deprive her of her education.

The nine students who gathered in Professor Kowalski's tiny flat each morning entered one at a time so they wouldn't arouse suspicion, and tip-toed inside so as not to alert the neighbours. The professor, a tall thin man with liver spots on his bald head and wrinkled hands, addressed them with exaggerated courtesy, which amused them.

'Miss Elżunia, would you be kind enough to remind us what we learned yesterday about our national hero Kościuszko?' he asked, and nodded as she gave an enthusiastic account of the general who led the 1794 uprising against the Russians.

'Ladies and gentlemen,' he said in his tremulous voice when she had finished, 'it's very important for you to learn about the achievements of Polish heroes, especially our scientists and musicians who have left such a rich legacy.

'You are the custodians of our culture for the future, now that the Germans have forbidden us to play the music of Chopin and to read the poems of Mickiewicz and the epics of Sienkiewicz. And today I have some interesting news for you. Our great astronomer Copernicus, whose observations revolutionised mankind's perception of the universe, has just received a posthumous honour.' He paused for dramatic effect. 'The Nazis have turned him into a German.'

Elżunia was still bristling with indignation at the way the Germans were trying to stamp out Polish culture when Professor Kowalski placed a glass bowl on the table, took out some stones from his briefcase, and filled it to the top. 'Is the bowl full?' he asked.

The students nodded. Without commenting, he tipped in some pebbles that filled the spaces between the stones. 'Is it full now?' he asked.

This time they were certain it was. Again he said

nothing and they craned forward as he emptied some sand into the bowl.

Finally he poured in a glass of water, which was absorbed by the sand. Turning to them, he said, 'The bowl is your life. The stones are the values for which you must make room before everything else. The pebbles are your important relationships for which you must always make time. The sand stands for the things you enjoy doing that vanish almost as soon as you've experienced them. And the water is your brain, which is capable of absorbing far more than you realise.'

After their lessons had ended, he said, 'Tomorrow we will discuss the work of Marie Curie-Skłodowska who discovered radium. May the Lord watch over you.'

The students left the class as they had arrived, stealthily, one by one. Elżunia tip-toed down the stairs, and looked both ways before stepping into the street. As she neared the corner, a boy suddenly appeared in a doorway and stuck his leg out. She fell and dropped her briefcase with her exercise books and notes.

'You moron, why don't you watch where you're going?' she shouted as she scrambled to her feet, rubbing her grazed knee. As she reached out to retrieve her briefcase, the boy was already stuffing it into his rucksack and, before she could grab it, he darted away.

She was about to chase him when a German voice behind her yelled 'Halt!' Her blood froze and she turned around. A plainclothes man in a trenchcoat, like the ones who had burst into their apartment that fateful night months before, was shouting at one of her fellow students who had just emerged from the building. Elżunia crept into an alleyway and flattened herself against the wall, hardly daring to breathe. She dug her nails into the palm of her hand as she heard the Gestapo agent order the girl to open

81

her bag. Any minute he would see the Polish books and find out about their secret classes. There would be no lesson about Marie Curie-Skłodowska tomorrow and no Professor Kowalski. As Elżunia walked away, her legs shaking, she realised that if it hadn't been for that thief, she would have been caught as well.

That evening there was a soft knock on the door of their room in the Ghetto. It was the boy who had tripped her in the street and, from the look on his face, it was clear he was enjoying her astonishment. 'I've brought your briefcase back,' he said.

Eight

He was just a kid with a cheeky smile, a cloth cap over his springy brown hair, and eyes the colour of strong cocoa. Shaking her hand with a man's grip, he said, 'I'm Edek. Sorry about tripping you up this morning but that Gestapo guy was hanging around. Had to grab your satchel before he did.'

'You could have been caught with my books,' Elżunia pointed out. 'Weren't you scared?'

'I'm nearly twelve,' he said proudly. 'I don't scare easily.' Then he shrugged. 'I suppose it's different for girls.'

'That's rubbish,' she retorted. 'Girls are just as brave as boys.' But she wasn't brave at all. Even though she was nearly fifteen, she was scared all the time, with a fear that crept up from her toes and made her scalp prickle.

'Prove it then,' he said and pointed to the apartment block on the next corner. 'Come over this evening and meet the gang. There's four of us and we get together every day and plan stuff.'

She was intrigued. 'Like what?'

'Like rescuing schoolgirls from being caught with forbidden books,' he said with a grin.

The noise in the tiny flat made her head swim. Two toddlers were running around while Edek's weary mother pleaded for quiet in a voice that didn't expect to be heeded. She was nursing a listless baby who had the face of an old man. 'He's nearly a year old but he's never smiled,' she told Elżunia, and added, 'not that there's anything to smile about in here, especially since they shot my poor husband.'

The room had a bare floor, one rickety table in the centre, and three sagging mattresses stacked up against the wall. Edek led her to a corner where three boys in patched trousers and threadbare shirts sat cross-legged on the floor, shouting across each other. Elżunia was shocked to see how young they were. One of them looked about nine. Why had she bothered coming? They were just little kids playing at being grown-ups.

As though he'd read her mind, Edek said in a defiant tone, 'I suppose you think we're just kids because we're younger than you but we know what's going on, and we're going to fight them.'

It sounded like bravado but he had a determined manner that made him seem much older than his years. The others were watching her with doubtful expressions and she felt she had been assessed and was found wanting.

Two of the boys were Edek's brothers Izio and Mosze. The only outsider was a boy with a pointed chin, who turned out to be their neighbour Dolek.

Surveying her with obvious distaste, he muttered, 'Told you not to get mixed up with girls. They're more trouble than they're worth.'

Ignoring him, Elżunia turned to Edek. 'How on earth did you know who I was or where I lived?'

He laughed and gave a sharp salute. 'We scouts always have to be prepared, right?' In a serious tone, he added, 'I keep my eyes open, that's all. When I saw that Gestapo guy nosing around, I thought I'd better think of something fast. I reckon a sore knee's better than a trip to Szuch Avenue!'

Then he asked, 'Are you any good at sewing?'

Recalling the handicraft lessons at school that always ended with a pricked thumb and clumsy stitches that soon unravelled, she shook her head. 'Why?'

His brother Izio cut in, speaking so rapidly that saliva sprayed through the gap in his front teeth. 'We sneak out with the work groups in the mornings, see, to get some food on the other side, and then we sneak back later, but it's hard to smuggle anything in, and it's going to get much harder if they close the Ghetto.'

'Aren't you scared you'll get caught?' she asked

'I told you it was no good starting with girls.' Dolek was scowling at Elżunia. 'They're scared of everything.'

Edek interjected. 'What he's trying to say is if we had big pockets on the inside of our trousers, we could bring more food in and the guards wouldn't see it.'

Suddenly Elżunia's eyes lit up. 'I'm hopeless at sewing but I know someone who might help.'

Her mother stared at Elżunia with the expression of a Michelangelo being asked to paint a chicken coop. 'False pockets?' she repeated incredulously. 'You expect me to become a seamstress?'

'Well you've got nothing else to do. It's not as if anyone in here needs your beauty treatments, but Edek has five little brothers and their mother is so poor that she had to sell some of their shoes yesterday to buy them something to eat. If those boys don't smuggle some food in, they'll all starve.'

'I thought the Judenrat organised soup kitchens for people like that,' Lusia said vaguely.

Stefan walked into the room, fastening the belt of his police jacket. He pushed his loose cap more firmly on his head but it dropped over his forehead. 'You haven't got a clue what's going on out there,' he told his mother. 'You should see the thousands lining up for soup every day, and there are more people being forced into the Ghetto all the time. There's no way the Judenrat can keep up. The Germans are cutting down the rations and most of the vegetables are rotten. And I reckon it's going to get worse.'

Seeing her mother hesitate, Elżunia said quickly, 'You could make pockets from that old sheet you used to tie up our things when we moved here.'

A week later, Elżunia knocked on Edek's door holding a neat pile of pockets ready to be pinned to the inside of their trousers. While the other boys were examining them to see how they'd fit, she took Edek aside.

'I've figured out a way we could get through the wall without going past the guards,' she said.

After dark, the five of them crept towards the part of the wall that was farthest from the gates and so less closely monitored by the guards. After Elżunia had counted the number of bricks they needed to loosen, she marked the bricks with a piece of chalk she had found.

'We'll have to get something sharp to gouge out the cement and then we'll put the bricks back so they won't suspect anything,' she said.

'Not a bad idea for a girl,' Dolek said grudgingly, and Elżunia felt a glow of pride at having earned his approval.

Among his dead father's tools, Edek found a small hammer and chisel. While four of them scratched and scraped out the cement and drove in the chisel with a hammer to loosen the bricks, the fifth stood guard, ready to warn them to run if any policemen appeared.

After they'd gouged out the bricks, they tested the opening by squeezing through in turn. Elżunia was the only one who had trouble getting through, and emerged red-faced, pulling her blouse down. She hadn't realised how much her breasts had grown in the past few months. They stood back, slapping each other on the back as they admired their work. The bricks slid in and out easily and, looking at them in the wall, no one would suspect that they weren't cemented in like the others. Now they'd be able to get in and out of the Ghetto without being spotted by the guards.

For the first time since moving into the Ghetto, Elżunia came home humming a song, but her mother was pacing around the room like a panther in a cage.

'Thank God you're back. Look at this!' she gasped, and thrust a leaflet into Elżunia's hand. All the residents of the building were ordered to present themselves at the steam baths on Spokojna Street the next morning to eradicate the typhus that according to Nazi propaganda was being spread by the Jews. They had to leave their doors open so that while they were gone the flats could be disinfected.

'But there's no typhus in our building,' Elżunia said. 'And, anyway, it's the Nazis that spread disease by crowding hundreds of thousands of people into a small space.'

'Don't waste your breath,' Lusia said bitterly. 'Any excuse to torment us.'

As soon as Stefan walked in that evening, she demanded, 'You said you'd protect us, so do something.'

He flushed. 'I wish I could, but they've made lists of the occupants in every building so there's nothing I can do.'

'A fat lot of good it did joining the police force, then,' she fumed.

'You don't know what you're talking about,' he shot back. 'The Jewish police don't have much power in here. I tried to get you out of the disinfection but they're adamant that everyone has to go.'

Sensing his frustration, their mother cut in. 'You're not being fair, Elżunia. You know that Stefan's doing his best.'

Elżunia pulled a face and turned away. As usual their mother sided with Stefan and criticised her.

When two guards arrived at their apartment the next day before Lusia and Elżunia had left for the bathhouse, they appraised everything with greedy eyes.

'Your apartment looks very clean,' one of them declared. 'It would be a pity to ruin your things with disinfectant.'

Taking the hint, Lusia rummaged in a drawer and held out a fine gold chain. The older guard picked it up, held it up to the light and pocketed it with a nod.

When Elżunia and Lusia arrived outside the sanitary station, two long columns stretched along several blocks. Men on one side, women and children on the other. Elżunia was wondering how long it would take to reach the entrance when they were surrounded by a ring of SS men and Gestapo wielding leather whips.

'Clothes off! Take everything off!' they screamed. Elżunia looked around. Surely they didn't expect them to undress out in the street in front of everyone?

No one moved until the SS men started lashing people with their whips and smashing heads with rifle butts. 'Hurry up!'

An elderly woman refused to undress, even when an SS man slashed her face and opened up her cheek to the bone. 'I'm seventy-five years old and I've done a lot of things in my life, but I won't take off my clothes in the street,' she said. He pulled out his revolver and shot her.

Elżunia clamped her hands over her ears and shrank against her mother. 'Why are they doing this to us?' she sobbed.

Lusia stroked her head. 'Because they can.'

As Elżunia peeled off her clothes, she wanted the ground to swallow her up. She wished she was dead; anything would be better than this humiliation. She tried to cover herself with her hands and looked at the ground, pretending that if she didn't see anyone, they wouldn't see her. Lusia held her trembling daughter tightly against her to shield her from the whips and rifle butts but the humiliation was worse than the pain. And still they were kept waiting in the cold, until their skin puckered and turned blue. Children cried; some women fainted, while others had to be supported from collapsing.

When they were finally allowed to enter the bathhouse, the water poured over them in an icy stream. There was no soap, and when they emerged shivering from the showers there were no towels. Elżunia's teeth were chattering and she couldn't wait to put her clothes back on, but when she got them back she wept. They were drenched in foul-smelling disinfecting liquid.

Elżunia and Lusia ran home as fast as they could, anxious to throw off the stinking clothes and get warm. But as soon as they opened the door, an acrid smell hit them and almost drove them back on to the landing. They stood in their doorway, unable to believe their eyes. In spite of the bribe Lusia had given the guard, everything they owned had been pulled out of cupboards and wardrobes and soaked in carbolic.

'That disinfection was just an excuse to rob us,' Lusia cried out. 'They've stolen our candlesticks and the silver I was going to sell!'

Overcome by the pungent smell, Elżunia rushed into the bathroom and vomited.

When she emerged, she was white and dry-eyed.

'I will never forget what they did to us today. Never,' she said with an intensity that frightened Lusia. 'Somehow I'll find a way to fight them.'

Nine

Adam swung his rucksack off his back and leaned against the spruce with a sigh of relief. The afternoon spent hiking over the mountains had exhausted him, but if his guide Jacek hadn't set such a brisk pace, he'd still be trudging up the last slope. As a student he had joined a hiking club and climbed the Tatra Mountains, but now that seemed a very long time ago. He and his colleagues used to boast of conquering the peaks; since then, he had realised that the most you could hope for was to conquer your own weaknesses.

While Jacek scrutinised the surrounding area with his field-glasses, Adam slid along the rough trunk until he was sitting on the lacework of light and shade at the base of the tree.

Turning his face up to the late-afternoon sun that slanted between the dense branches and outlined the foliage with a dazzling pencil of light, he closed his eyes, filled his lungs with mountain air and the pine scent of the conifers, and revelled in the freedom of being so far from the city and its tensions. Everything on this autumn day delighted him, and he felt he was rediscovering the beauty of the world like a patient risen from a sick bed he had never expected to leave.

While Jacek collected twigs for a fire, Adam took out a slab of country sausage and a loaf of black bread from his rucksack. A few minutes later, they were sitting in front of a blazing fire, tearing off chunks of bread and sausage, and drinking them down with swigs of vodka.

Anyone who passed them on the solitary trail that threaded along the steep slopes of the Carpathian Mountains would have taken them for friends on a hiking trip.

Their meal over, Adam patted the inside pocket of his padded jacket, feeling for the small cylinder sewn into the lining. He ran through the instructions in his head, even though he knew them so well that he could have recited every detail in his sleep.

It was six months since he'd been inducted into the Underground, and his missions had taken him all over Poland. He had made contact with Underground leaders in Kraków, Lublin and Łodż to let them know about the administrative and military structure of Poland's secret state and to pass on instructions from General Śikorski, the head of the exiled Polish government in London.

While AK members all over the country were derailing trains, blowing up bridges and attacking German posts, Adam, who spoke fluent German, had become a courier. According to his false papers, he was Zygmunt Morawski, an importer of German car parts.

He lit a Klub, inhaled deeply, and went over every detail of the mission once again. Soon they would cross into Slovakia on a route that had proved so reliable for Underground operatives that he didn't expect any hitches. Still, one couldn't afford to be complacent, as he'd recently discovered in Kraków.

He had been instructed to contact the head of an Underground cell near the city's main square and had just left his office when an SS officer stopped him and checked his papers.

'*Ach so, Herr Morawski, sehr gut,*' he said, handing back Adam's *Kennkarte*, satisfied that he was talking to an importer of German car parts. Anxious to get away from him, Adam stopped to feed a flock of pigeons that swooped down on the seeds he scattered but the SS officer stopped, too. Pretending not to notice his close proximity, Adam strolled casually around the ancient square.

He stopped in front of the arcaded Guild Hall, where a crowd had gathered around a group of buskers. The peacock feathers on top of the male performer's hat shook as he played the harmonica while the two women buskers, in white aprons over their striped skirts, and ribbons streaming down their backs, sang traditional Kraków songs in raucous voices that suggested frequent lubrication with vodka.

When Adam turned around, he saw the SS officer standing behind him. He was about to slip through the crowd when he saw an old school friend bearing down on him, hand outstretched. It was too late to dart into the arcades and avoid him.

'Adam Czartoryski! You old devil!' he boomed in a voice that made Adam wince. 'What on earth brings you to Kraków?' He thumped his shoulder and gave a bawdy laugh. 'Let me guess — a blonde or a brunette?'

Adam assumed a politely baffled expression. 'I'm sorry, but you seem to have me mixed up with someone else,' he said.

His friend burst out laughing. 'What are you playing at?' He clapped his hands in sudden delight as comprehension dawned. 'Oh, I get it — her husband's after you!'

Out of the corner of his eye, Adam saw the SS officer looking thoughtfully in their direction. He had to end this dangerous encounter. Taking a business card from his pocket as though in response to a request, he said stiffly, 'Zygmunt Morawski at your service. These are my office hours. My representatives will be happy to talk to you.' And, raising his hat, he strode away, leaving his friend gaping at his retreating figure.

That had been a close shave. Fortunately there was no one in the Carpathian Mountains who could blow his cover.

Adam pulled off his walking boots, took a swig of water from his pannikin and wiped his mouth with the back of his hand. As he lit another cigarette, he felt his whole body settle deeper into the forest floor and breathed in its earthy smell of fallen leaves, mushrooms and wild berries.

Crouching beneath a nearby tree, Jacek chewed on a stalk of grass, casting occasional glances at Adam, who seemed in no hurry to move on. These city fellows were too self-indulgent, Jacek thought. They needed toughening up. He stood up and threw handfuls of dirt over their camp fire. 'Time to go,' he said.

He'd brought many couriers across the border in the past few months but could never relax until they'd reached the inn across the river. So far, these remote mountain trails had always been secure but you couldn't take any chances.

With a sigh, Adam hauled himself up. He wanted to protest that there was plenty of time, but Jacek was striding down the slope so fast that twigs snapped under his boots.

By the time he reached the river's edge, Jacek was already sloshing around on the muddy bank, peering under the bunches of reeds.

'Problem,' he said, still poking about. 'No raft.'

He and the other guide who alternated on this route always left the raft for each other in the same spot, but it was nowhere to be seen.

'Bloody hell,' Adam hissed. 'What now?'

Jacek looked around without replying. He reminded Adam of a woodland animal sniffing the air to detect which foreign species had invaded his territory.

He scratched the back of his neck. 'We should go back.'

Adam couldn't believe his ears. 'Go back because you can't find the raft?'

'Go back because something's wrong.'

Adam was indignant. His mission wasn't a tea party that could be postponed to another afternoon. The Commander-in-Chief of the Polish government in exile, which after the fall of Paris had moved to London, was waiting for the cylinder of microfilm with information about the Underground in Poland. Delays were unthinkable. This was only the first stage of a journey that involved catching trains and boats across Europe. He spoke quietly and succinctly. 'It's out of the question. We have to find another way of crossing the river.'

Jacek shrugged, muttered something to himself, and pointed downstream. 'Six miles further on, the river widens and might be shallow enough to cross on foot.'

The last hour of the hike was the longest and, as they pushed their way through the tangled undergrowth, Adam's pack dragged on his shoulders. Finally Jacek pointed at a spot on the bank and they clambered down the slope to the river's edge, pulled off their boots and tied them onto their rucksacks. Adam stuffed his jacket into the rucksack to protect the microfilm.

The fast-flowing water reached their thighs and, as he held his pack above his head, the current threatened to sweep him off his feet. Several times he would have lost his footing if Jacek hadn't held out a hand to steady him, and he was gasping and shivering by the time he scrambled onto the bank on the other side. Following Jacek up a steep trail, they reached the small inn above the river. The old man who opened the door gave them a suspicious look until he recognised Jacek. He let them in and hurriedly closed the door. From their worried expressions and urgent voices, Adam realised they were discussing the disappearance of the raft.

Jacek turned to Adam. 'He says the other guide didn't come back.'

The innkeeper said something in Slovakian and gesticulated towards Adam.

'He says we shouldn't stay,' Jacek said.

From their gestures and voices, Adam sensed they were convinced some disaster had befallen the other guide. But there were other possible reasons why the man hadn't returned, and Adam wasn't prepared to jettison this vital mission on the basis of mere suspicion.

'We'll leave in the morning as planned,' he said.

The innkeeper poured glasses of homemade *slivovitz*, which was so potent that Adam barely managed to climb the pine staircase to the attic. He was asleep as soon as his head touched the feather pillow.

He dreamed that he was in Kraków again, walking across the square when he suddenly realised he was being followed. He quickened his pace but his pursuer caught up and grabbed his shoulder, yelling 'I know who you are!' Adam looked desperately for a way to escape but the man had him pinned against a wall, yelling louder and louder.

Adam woke with a start. Someone was yelling. He opened his eyes as two arms grabbed him, lifted him to his feet and threw him against the wall, head-first. While one man pinned him to the ground, the other slit open his rucksack with a knife and tipped it upside down.

The room was spinning like a top.

'I haven't got any money,' he gasped, holding his head to stop it from bursting open. 'You can have my watch.'

The huge guy restraining him gave a sardonic laugh, while his companion continued to rifle through every compartment of his pack. Adam involuntarily glanced at the chair where he'd hung his jacket and quickly looked away again but his captor had noticed. 'The jacket,' he hissed to his companion.

Adam's heart sank. He shouted for help. Surely Jacek and the innkeeper would turn up any moment and give him time to grab the film.

But his shouting provoked a hoot of derision, and struggling to free himself only resulted in a tight grip around his throat. 'Go on, shout all you want,' one of the men jeered.

Adam listened for the sound of footsteps on the stairs but all was quiet. It was dark outside. Where could Jacek and the innkeeper have gone at this time of night? The other guy was still going through the pockets of his jacket. Adam prayed he wouldn't feel the small hard cylinder inside the lining. 'I told you you're wasting your time,' he insisted. 'I'm just a hiker; I haven't got any money.'

'Just an innocent hiker, eh?' His captor's voice had a menacing tone as he yanked Adam's arms higher behind him.

'Aha!' The other man uttered a triumphant cry as he ripped the lining of the jacket and the small cylinder fell onto the floor. 'What has our innocent young hiker hidden in there?'

They grabbed his arms, tied them tightly behind his back, and shoved him ahead of them down the stairs. Adam was in despair. His mission was in tatters and his reputation would be ruined. He had no idea who these men worked for or what they intended to do with him, or with the film. If only he could leave a message for the guide.

He supposed Jacek would use his contacts to find out where he'd been taken. As his captors pushed him towards the front door of the inn, he saw an overturned chair. Beyond it, Jacek and the innkeeper lay on the floor, their mouths gaping open like their necks.

'Feel like shouting for help again?' the big guy sneered.

Ten

Lying on his flea-infested pallet in a cell where the only amenity was a stinking bucket, Adam stared at the dried blood on the walls and alternated between self-recrimination over what had happened, and apprehension of what was to come.

Apart from the screams that shattered the night and made the hairs stand up on his arms, the only sound was the regular click of the judas window through which unseen eyes peered at him. Every morning, the turnkey came in, a dour, shifty fellow who never looked him in the eye or answered his questions as he emptied the bucket and banged down a dinted metal dish with a slice of dry bread. In the evenings he would return with a bowl of greasy liquid that turned Adam's stomach.

The previous occupants had scribbled messages on the walls, which oozed black mould. Someone had scratched one wobbly line for each day of his incarceration and Adam wondered what had happened to him after day seventeen. Had he been released, transferred, or bashed to death? His eyes kept returning to the blood stains. Did they belong to the person who had recorded the passing time or to the prisoner who had scrawled a phrase in Czech into the black sludge?

The only word he could make out was *honour*, and each time he read it he recoiled as though it had lunged out of the wall and punched him. Honour was a sore point right now. So was his bad judgment.

If only he had listened to the guide's advice, he wouldn't be in this mess, and Jacek and the innkeeper would still be alive. Shame shot through his body. They had been right all along. The other guide must have been caught and had betrayed the route. Adam felt contempt for him, but most of all he felt disgust with himself. His hubris had caused the death of two men and wrecked the mission.

Time stretched ahead of him, and with every passing minute he felt more apprehensive as grim thoughts and frightening questions churned around his mind. How long would they keep him here? How much did they know? What would they do to him? Although he tried not to think about it, images of hideous torture through the ages flashed through his mind, making it impossible to sit still. He paced around the perimeter of the tiny cell until he was too dizzy to stand up, one thought drumming in his head. No matter what they did, they wouldn't break him.

The hours dragged on until he heard the door of his cell clang open and two guards burst in. One grabbed his arms and hauled him to his feet, then the other gave him a kick that sent him sprawling. They picked him up by his collar and dragged him along an endless corridor where the occasional light bulb cast a dull greenish light.

At the top of a steep flight of stairs, they knocked on a door marked *Lieutenant Otto Hausner*, and pushed him inside.

From the light brown hair combed flat across his forehead like the Führer, whose photograph hung on the wall above his desk, to the grey-green uniform that seemed moulded to his body, and the buffed nails at the end of his soft white hands, the SS officer was such a model of polished cleanliness that Adam had to stifle an impulse to apologise for his unshaven face, unwashed body and crumpled clothes.

'Sit down, sit down,' said Lieutenant Hausner in the jovial tone of someone welcoming a friend. 'I hope you've been treated well. I know our accommodation leaves a lot to be desired and the menu is rather limited, but I'm sure you won't have to suffer this inconvenience much longer.'

Intrigued by this unexpected geniality, Adam waited.

The officer picked up a silver cigarette box and held it out to him. When Adam shook his head, Lieutenant Hausner lit a cigarette and, tilting his head back, exhaled a long column of smoke towards the ceiling. Opening the small cupboard beneath Hitler's portrait, he pulled out a bottle and poured two generous glasses. 'Schnapps?' he asked.

'I demand to know why you've detained me,' Adam said.

The lieutenant drained his glass and uttered a contented grunt. 'We know who you are and why you are in Slovakia.' His smile reminded Adam of an alligator about to snap his jaws around an unsuspecting victim.

'I'm afraid you've made a mistake,' Adam said calmly. 'I'm a school teacher hiking around the mountains on my holiday.'

The SS officer sat forward, his reptilian gaze on Adam's face. 'In that case, we need a little help from you, Herr Professor, and then you can go and hike to your heart's content, *ja*? Although I wonder why a teacher would conceal microfilm in the lining of his jacket.'

Adam started to protest and the smile disappeared from Lieutenant Hausner's face. 'Don't insult my intelligence by denying it. Your microfilm is in code and we don't have the time or the facilities to decipher it. Therefore we require your assistance.'

Adam shook his head. 'I don't know what you're talking about.'

The lieutenant sighed. 'You are very tiresome,' he said in the disappointed tone one might use on a wayward child. 'We could have settled this like civilised men instead of which, I regret to say, things will become rather unpleasant. And in the end you will tell us what we want to know. So, for the last time, what's on the microfilm?'

'I've already told you,' Adam said through clenched teeth. 'I don't know anything about it.'

Lieutenant Hausner picked up his black telephone and a moment later two men entered the room. In the past, Adam had sometimes wondered how he would react under torture, but speculation had failed to prepare him for the reality of seeing two grim-faced Gestapo agents opening a metal box and deliberating which of its instruments would inflict enough pain to make him talk. His imagination had failed to conjure up the terror he now felt as they tied him to a chair and selected their weapon. His heart thumped and he tried to comfort himself with the thought that the anticipation of pain was probably far worse than the reality. He soon discovered his mistake.

The interrogator picked up a rubber truncheon and asked him once more to tell them what was on the microfilm. Adam gritted his teeth. At least it wasn't the rack or the bastinado.

As the truncheon struck him behind his left ear, he leapt up in his chair and heard an inhuman howl rip from his own throat. The world flashed with white light and every part of his body, from his toes to his skull, had become like one enormous tooth whose nerve had been pierced with a drill. The pain tore through him like lightning electrifying every tendon, joint and muscle. The scream was still reverberating through his head when the lieutenant asked him if he was ready to help them. Again he shook his head.

He lost count how many times the interrogator struck him before he fainted. When he woke in his cell, his entire body throbbed and he couldn't hear through his left ear. As he lay doubled up on the pallet, one thought drummed through his head: how long could he hold out? And if he couldn't, he thought grimly, there was always the cyanide capsule.

The following morning, they dragged him out again. He tried not to look at the hooks they fastened to the wall, tried not to envisage what would happen when they suspended him from them. Whenever he lost consciousness, they flung buckets of icy water over him so they could continue.

Anything to stop this. Anything. He had become a wild animal caught in a trap, maddened by pain, an animal ready to gnaw through its own leg to save itself from certain death. As he drifted in and out of consciousness, he could foresee how this ordeal would end. One more session and everything would tumble from his mouth like apples from a barrel. Like snippets of a disjointed movie fragmented by a faulty projector, images of his life flashed before his eyes. His dreams of being a pilot, of defending his country, of making his father proud. All shattered. He saw his life as a chain of bright hopes torn apart by his own defects. And it would end ignominiously, with him betraying everything he believed in and everyone he admired.

If only he could die before he disgraced himself.

Back in his cell, he knew he had to act fast, before they came back for him. Thank God for the cyanide capsule.

Despite the searing pain, he gritted his teeth and groped around for the piece of tape with which he'd fastened the capsule to his perineum. It wasn't there. Covered in sweat, he strained every tendon to bursting point as he tried to locate it. Had the capsule swirled away in the current while he'd waded through the river, or had they removed it while he was unconscious? He cast his eyes around the cell in search of a shard of glass or fragment of razor blade with which he might cut his veins but there was nothing. He fell back onto his pallet in despair. Any minute now they would come for him, and it would start all over again.

The judas window slid back and he started. He'd lost consciousness again. A moment later the cell door opened and his heart lurched. This was it; they'd come for him. But the voice in his ear was whispering.

'Can you stand up?'

He opened his swollen eyes. The shape standing beside his pallet wasn't wearing a guard's uniform. It was the turnkey, and he was speaking Polish.

'Can you stand up and walk if I help you? If you can, I'll get you out of here.'

Adam stared at him. Was this a trap? Who was this man? His head had turned to jelly and the slightest movement shot flashes of pain through his body.

'How long have I been in here?' he gasped.

'Four days. But they're going to start on you again tomorrow morning,' the turnkey whispered. 'Our people are waiting for you outside the gate but you'll have to walk down the corridor, up one flight of stairs and then jump out of a window. Someone will be down there ready to catch you,' he added quickly in response to Adam's horrified expression.

It was too much to take in and Adam sank back on the pallet. Perhaps he was dreaming. But the man's face was close to his and his voice was low and urgent.

'We don't have much time.' He pulled out a grubby cloth from his pocket. 'Bite on this if you have to but, for God's sake, don't make a sound.'

With each agonising step, Adam felt his bones grinding in their sockets. This must be how Christ had felt on the cross, he thought as he bit his swollen lips and groaned while he hobbled along, leaning against the turnkey's shoulder. It seemed to take hours and they hadn't even reached the stairs.

'We have to hurry,' the man urged. 'The morning shift comes on in half an hour.'

Adam leaned against the wall, beads of sweat pouring down his face. 'It's no good, I can't make it.'

The turnkey gave him a stern look. 'Would you rather face another interrogation three hours from now?'

With a groan, Adam shuffled forward.

Soon he stood trembling on the window sill. In the faint pre-dawn light, he saw that two figures had crept out of the shadows and were holding out a blanket like firemen. It was a long way down. 'Quick, jump!' the turnkey hissed.

Adam closed his eyes and forced himself to fall. A moment later his stomach slammed against his spine and he felt the blanket stretch taut under him. Someone hauled him over their shoulders like a sack of potatoes and staggered to a truck outside the prison gate.

As the truck revved up and sped away, the man who had carried him gave a short laugh. 'They've certainly rearranged your face, Eagle. Even your mother wouldn't recognise you. Come to think of it, that's not such a bad thing in our line of work!'

Adam opened his mouth to ask how they had known where he was, and how they'd managed to get him out, but his head lolled towards his chest and he fainted.

Eleven

One bleak November day in 1940, after Elżunia and her mother and brother had been inside the Ghetto for six months, their worst fears were realised. The Ghetto was closed and they were shut off from the rest of the world. It became an island of despair in the centre of the city. Only the slave labourers who worked in German factories or workshops were permitted to leave.

'There's no hope now,' Lusia lamented when they heard the news they'd all been dreading. 'How will your father manage to get us out, now that we're locked up in here?' Her voice dropped to a whisper as though she didn't want to hear her own voice. 'But what if ...?'

The longing for her father was a dull ache that never left Elżunia. Without the hope of seeing him again, she didn't think she could face the rest of her life. Sometimes she dreamed he was standing in the doorway, and she would wake up with a strangled sob of joy in her throat. At night, when she curled up on the bed she shared with her mother, she prayed fervently to the Virgin Mary to keep him safe.

Although only work groups were permitted to leave the Ghetto during the day, the doctor for whom she worked had convinced the German authorities that her help was essential in treating all the patients at the clinic, and her nursing permit hadn't been cancelled. As weeks passed, consumed by the yearning for her father, Elżunia concocted a plan. She couldn't see him but at least she could see their old apartment. On her way to the clinic, she would go there to reassure herself that her home was still there, waiting for them to return. And although she couldn't bring herself to articulate such an irrational thought, at the back of her mind was the fantasy that she would find her father waiting for her.

Sitting by the window of the tram as it clanged along the rails outside the Ghetto, Elżunia shivered. Fine snow was falling but melted as soon as it landed on the collars and hats of the people hurrying by, hunched against the cold. The flakes turned to slush that lay in brown puddles on the pavements.

Elżunia kept her eyes fixed on the street in an attempt to appear nonchalant. Jews were forbidden to ride in the ordinary trams, but having slipped off her armband she was spared the humiliation of riding in those hideous yellow trams with the Star of David on the sides and the sign at the front that said *Nur für Juden*. As long as no one recognised her, she'd be safe. The trick was to look confident and avoid the Polish blackmailers who hung around the tram stops like hyenas ready to swoop on their prey. For a reward of a few zloty, some vodka or a packet of cigarettes, these *szmalcowniks* hunted for Jews. First they took all their money, and then they turned them over to the Gestapo. War brought out the worst in people, Elżunia thought bitterly as the tram squealed to a halt and more passengers got in. Instead of pulling together against their common enemy, they exploited and denounced their fellow countrymen.

Two Germans who were sprawled on the seat in the front of the compartment chatted in loud, confident voices about their posting. Warsaw was surprisingly pleasant, one of them pronounced, and, as for the girls, they were *sehr schon* — very pretty — but tended to be rather standoffish. His companion was surprised to find so many Jews here, but, after all, that's why they'd come, *nicht war*? To cleanse the country of this pestilence. He said he sometimes felt sorry for the stick-thin children wandering around the Ghetto, but his companion corrected his misguided sympathy. 'The Führer knows what he's doing,' he stated. 'Think about Jews the way you would about cockroaches.'

Finally the tram slowed down near the familiar stop, but she forced herself to stay in her seat until it lurched to a halt. She didn't want to arouse suspicion by her eagerness to alight.

Fixing a smile on her lips, she sauntered along Marszałkowska Street as though she hadn't a care in the world. You never knew who was hanging around watching for any sign of fear or uncertainty. As she approached the kiosk on the corner, she started counting. If she got to ten by the time she reached the newspaper stand, it meant he'd be there. She quickened her step to give chance a helping hand.

As she stood under the black branches of the lime tree outside their gate, she became lost in a daydream. Any moment now her father would walk out of that doorway and scoop her up in his arms and she'd realise that the past nine months had been a bad dream from which she had just awakened.

She was about to walk into the building when Pani Stasia, the caretaker's wife, opened the main door and clanged down an iron bucket with a resentful air, splashing dirty water all over the floor. As soon as she went back inside, muttering to herself, Elżunia crept past the caretaker's apartment and ran up the stairs, stroking the polished maple banister like an old friend. She pressed her ear against the door of her old apartment. For a moment she imagined she heard voices but knew that her longing had conjured up these sounds. Elżunia peered over the railing to make sure Pani Stasia was gone, and had just started going down the stairs when the caretaker's door opened and she was standing there, surveying her with unfriendly eyes.

'If you're looking for your father, Miss Elżunia, you've missed him.'

Elżunia stared at her. Had the woman gone soft in the head? It was about six months since her father had been taken away. But, before she could reply, the woman said, 'He dropped in here last week but only stayed a minute. Must have been in a hurry.' There was a mocking gleam in her eyes.

'I think you've made a mistake,' Elżunia said through dry lips.

'Your parents lived here for twenty years. Do you think I wouldn't recognise him?' Her eyes narrowed. 'Nice young lady with him, too.'

Elżunia felt as though every bone in her body had come loose.

'Did he say anything, or leave a forwarding address?' she whispered.

Pani Stasia shook her head. 'He rushed out like the devil was chasing him with a pitchfork. Probably hoped I hadn't seen him.'

She stood there with arms akimbo as she stared pointedly at Elżunia's arm, as though looking for the armband. Elżunia knew she had to get away immediately.

Out in the street, she swayed on her feet. She longed to believe that the woman was lying but something in her tone made Elżunia sense she had been telling the truth. What could it mean? Joy that her father was still alive alternated with anger. How come he hadn't even contacted them, or got a message to them? And that young lady the caretaker mentioned — who was she and what was he doing with her?

If only she could see him and find out what was going on. Although they were living in the same city, they might just as well have been on different planets. For a moment, she contemplated going to the home of her parents' former friends who lived several streets away to ask whether they'd seen him, but she was already late for the clinic, and, in any case, she couldn't risk wandering around the town any longer, in case she was spotted.

She couldn't wait to tell her mother what she'd heard, but upon visualising Lusia's distraught reaction, she changed her mind. It would be a heavy burden to carry alone but she preferred that to coping with her mother's hysteria. As she hurried to the clinic, she felt like crying with disappointment and frustration.

A few patients were already sitting in the tiny waiting room when she rushed in out of breath, hoping that Dr Borowski hadn't noticed she was late. A diabetic patient had come to have the dressing changed on her ulcerated leg, a chain smoker was coughing his lungs out, and a young mother was comforting her son whose arm was in a sling. As Elżunia busied herself preparing bandages and laying out the instruments, the old doctor came in and looked at her over his rimless glasses. 'You look worse than the patients,' he growled. She tried to talk but her chest began to heave and tears splashed down her white nurse's apron. He drew her swiftly into his office. 'Have to be careful. Walls have ears,' he warned, and inclined his head towards Bożena, the other trainee nurse, who was pretending to bustle about while eavesdropping on their conversation. 'You'd better have a vitamin injection. You're as white as a ghost.'

As he drew up the liquid, he murmured, 'Be strong. Our time will come.'

Although the old doctor knew she lived in the Ghetto, he never alluded to the subject. She wondered what lay behind his enigmatic comment, but before she could ask what he meant, he propelled her out of the office and said loudly for Bożena's benefit, 'I don't want to have to tell you again. Kindly sterilise the instruments on the tray as soon as you come in, and lay out the bandages so I don't have to wait.' Out of the corner of her eye, she saw a smirk on the other girl's face.

Bożena made no secret of having a German boyfriend, whose opinions she often parroted. 'Gunther reckons the Jews are to blame for this war,' she told Elżunia while they were dressing the leg of the diabetic patient.

'Then you should be grateful to them,' Elżunia said sweetly. 'Thanks to the war, you've found such a clever boyfriend.' Although she still thought of herself as Catholic and prayed to the Blessed Virgin, people like Bożena made her feel an affinity with Jews.

Back inside the Ghetto, the misery hit Elżunia with new force. Winter was harsher there, and homeless people shivered in the cold. She could never become accustomed to the sight of the emaciated women sitting on the footpaths with dull-eyed children beside them, hands outstretched for a coin or a piece of bread. A man whose cheekbones seemed to protrude through his skin sat propped against the wall, too weak to move. He'd probably be dead soon and would lie there until Pinkiert's black funeral cart took him away in the morning, along with the others who had been released from their suffering during the night. She pushed her way through crowded streets that had become chaotic bazaars. Those who had anything to sell had set up a small trestle, a stool, or simply laid out on the ground whatever they could spare so you could hardly pass by without treading on worn shoes, mended socks, threadbare sheets, or books with bent covers. One woman was trying to sell her little girl's underpants so that she could buy the child a piece of bread.

A tiny girl in a torn sweater and woollen stockings with big holes was standing by herself, singing a sentimental ditty called 'Almonds and Raisins' as she swayed from side to side. Every now and then the words sounded garbled, and whenever the child couldn't remember the next line she chanted, 'I'm hungry. Can you give me something to eat?' over and over in a sing-song voice without losing the rhythm. Occasionally someone would put a coin or a piece of bread into her grubby little hand but most people hurried past without listening. There were too many homeless people and too many hungry children; everyone was overwhelmed and preoccupied with their own misery.

The little girl's impish face and her ingenious way of interpolating her requests into the song touched Elżunia and she knelt down to talk to her. Her name was Gittel and she was three, although Elżunia would have taken her for a two-year-old. Gittel didn't know what her other name was but she lived down that alleyway with her mama, who was very sick.

Whether by chance or cunning, Gittel had positioned herself beside a café whose patrons, the Ghetto's few affluent residents, occasionally dropped a coin in her hand as they went in or out. Whenever the door swung open, bright music poured out into the sad street and the aroma of hot food wafted into the air.

Seized by sudden fury, Elżunia picked up the child and pushed open the door. Immediately, a waiter was at her side. 'Sorry, miss, children aren't allowed in here.'

'But children are allowed to die of hunger outside, right?' she retorted.

Spreading his hands in an exasperated gesture, he told her to wait while he went in search of the owner. She looked around and felt like Alice after she had fallen down the rabbit hole and found herself in a magical world. The café was lined with gold-embossed wallpaper and illuminated by lamps on wall sconces. Through the fug of cigar and cigarette smoke, Elżunia saw that the tables were so close together that the waiters had to squeeze past. A man at a table beside her plunged his knife and fork into his chicken kiev, and the butter spurted in a greasy arc and landed on her blouse. At another table, diners were pulling black Italian grapes as large as plums off luxuriant bunches arranged on a platter. She had had no idea that such a profusion of food existed in the Ghetto nor that there were people who could still afford it.

In the far corner, on a raised platform, a man with a sallow face and hollow cheeks sat at a piano, his long slim fingers trilling a Chopin mazurka, but no one seemed to be listening. She had seen the man in photographs before and recognised him as Władysław Szpilman, the pianist who used to play on Warsaw radio before the war. Elżunia had an impulse to go up to him and tell him it wasn't fair that he was reduced to playing in this club to survive, but there was a cocoon of remoteness around him that discouraged her from approaching him.

By now, some of the patrons had noticed the teenage girl holding the ragged child's hand, and had begun to fidget as though their chairs had suddenly become hard.

The owner waddled towards Elżunia and placed his plump hand on her arm. 'Young lady, I must ask you to leave,' he said smoothly. 'You're disturbing everyone.' He pointed to a small door on the left. 'Go to the kitchen. The cook will give you some food.'

She pulled her arm away. 'I'm not a beggar,' she retorted and stepped onto the raised platform. Szpilman stopped playing and turned his melancholy face towards her. She lifted Gittel up. 'This child hasn't seen a piece of meat or a grape in her entire life! What you're paying here for one meal would save families like hers from starving!'

The diners at nearby tables looked shocked at her outburst.

'Is it my fault that people are starving?' a man's aggrieved voice rang out. 'Did I shut us up in here? You want to be noble at our expense but there are too many destitute people in here. Even if we give them money today, what will they do tomorrow, eh? We all contribute to the Judenrat for the orphanages and soup kitchens and the taxes the Germans keep raising. Anyway, the Germans will finish us off in the end so why shouldn't we enjoy ourselves while we can?'

Elżunia looked around. Among the diners were some of Warsaw's wealthy Jews who had managed to bring their money and valuables with them. Others were wheelers and dealers and entrepreneurs who had found ways of making money in the Ghetto by smuggling, bribing or providing essential services, like the inventors of the *Konnhellerki*, the strange-looking horse-drawn trams that had become the only means of transport inside the Ghetto apart from bicycle rickshaws.

'I suppose you all think you're good people, so how come you don't care about anyone else?' Elżunia burst out. 'What will happen to us if we don't have compassion for each other?'

Gittel broke the silence that had fallen over the café. Pointing to a pile of potato *latkes* on a woman's plate, she asked in a loud, clear voice, 'What's that?'

The woman piled the potato pancakes onto a serviette and handed them to the little girl. Next she removed the fruit from the basket on her table, took out a banknote from her purse, placed it in the basket and passed it to her companions. The basket was passed from table to table while the bewildered owner looked on.

Szpilman resumed playing but this time, instead of the lively rhythm of the mazurka, he played a nocturne. The poignant melody filled the café while its patrons swelled with the pleasure of knowing they had risen above their own self-indulgence. As Elżunia watched the pianist's fingers moving over the keys, she felt that it was the pauses between the notes, rather than the notes themselves, that made her heart ache.

Elżunia left the café with Gittel, amazed at the commotion she had created. She tied the money in a serviette and hid it inside her blouse. Maddened by hunger, small boys often grabbed packages and devoured the contents before the owner could catch them.

Gittel skipped happily along the alleyway, chewing a potato pancake as she led Elżunia to her home. 'I have to keep one for Mama,' she said, looking hungrily at the last one.

Elżunia took her hand as they climbed the dark staircase past people sitting on the broken steps and lying on the floor in the hallway, huddled under coats and rugs. Babies cried and children whimpered. The room they entered resembled a gypsy encampment. Several families lived in the unventilated space, surrounded by their bags and bundles. Gittel weaved in and out between them, stepping over their belongings until she reached the far corner of the room.

'Mama,' she called. 'I got a *latka* for you! And the lady said she'll give you money to buy more!'

The woman lying with her back to them on a thin pallet didn't reply. Gittel shook her mother's bony arm. 'Wake up, Mama, look what I've got!' she squealed.

Elżunia walked around to the other side. The woman's jaw had dropped open and her unseeing eyes were glassy. '*Jesus Maria!*' she said to herself. She looked around. 'Does Gittel have any relatives in here?'

An old woman slumped on the floor looked up. 'Poor Raizel came from a *sztetl* near Radom,' she said, indicating the dead woman and groaning with the effort of straightening her stiff legs. 'She told me she and Gittel hid in a cornfield while all the other Jews were loaded into trucks and driven to the forest. Later she heard the shots.'

Gittel was tugging Elżunia's hand. 'Why won't Mama wake up?' she asked. 'I want to give her the *latka*.'

'She's very tired,' Elżunia said. 'Let's go to my place.'

With a spring, the little girl jumped up and wrapped her arms tightly around Elżunia's neck.

Twelve

Lusia stared at the child clinging to Elżunia's neck like a frightened kitten. 'Who's this?' she said with a frown.

Elżunia took a deep breath. 'Her mother died today and she's all alone in the world.' Gittel's skinny arms tightened around her. 'I couldn't leave her there.' She put her head to one side in a pleading gesture. 'She's so tiny she won't take up much room.'

'How can you just take a child from the street? She's not a sack of potatoes you can pick up and take home,' Lusia protested. 'And how are we supposed to feed her? It's hard enough to feed ourselves.'

Elżunia plunged her hand into her pocket and pulled out a wad of notes. 'Look at this, Mama!' she said. 'I've got enough for us, and for Gittel and for Edek's mother as well.'

Lusia stared at the money. 'How did you get all this?'

As Elżunia described the scene in the café, Lusia looked at her daughter with a mixture of disbelief and admiration.

'I don't know that I approve of you making scenes in nightclubs and collecting money,' she said slowly. Then she smiled. 'I'd have loved to see their faces when you told them off! And we certainly need the money, with the price of food going up all the time. You're always having a go at Stefan but if not for him, I don't know how we'd manage.'

Elżunia nodded. Although she had made fun of Stefan's decision to join the Jewish police, she had to admit he helped them to survive. Sometimes he brought home a bag of dried beans or a few potatoes, and once he'd even brought two oranges and a chicken at which they'd stared in speechless wonder. But whenever they asked how he'd come by such delicacies, he shrugged and mumbled that it came with the job.

They didn't ask any questions. They knew that although the Polish and Jewish policemen were supposed to catch those who smuggled food into the Ghetto, in fact they often collaborated with the smugglers whose bribes exceeded their police earnings. By now, more children had joined Edek's gang and every morning they crawled through the hole in the wall and waited. As soon as the Number 10 tram swung around the curve near Miła Street, as usual, the conductor clanged the bell. This was the signal for them to run into the street and keep an eye out for the Polish boys who stood on the running board ready to toss sacks of potatoes, onions, beans or flour from the tram. Edek and the others rushed forward, grabbed the illicit cargo, sorted it, and delivered it to the entrepreneur in the Ghetto who had financed and organised the deal.

'I hope you never get involved in risky shenanigans like that,' Lusia had told Elżunia when she had described the smuggling process in an effort to cheer her mother up.

Gittel peeped at Lusia through her fingers, then playfully burrowed her face in Elżunia's neck. A moment later, she peeped out again and gave a mischievous smile. Lusia's tone softened, 'She's like a *krasnoludek*, isn't she? A cute little elf.' She gave the child an appraising look. 'I suppose I'd better mend her dress.'

In the weeks that followed, Elżunia was relieved to see that her mother was becoming attached to the child. The longing to confide in her mother what the caretaker's wife had said about her father welled up from time to time, but she always managed to stifle it. She didn't want to rock her mother's precarious equilibrium, but questions that had no answers constantly roiled around in her mind. It couldn't possibly be true that her father had abandoned them and was running around with some girl. He couldn't have abandoned and betrayed them like that. But the doubts, suspicions and uncertainties consumed her.

In an effort to find a distraction, she hurried to Edek's place. His high spirits usually helped to dispel the turmoil.

There were eight boys and three girls sitting on the floor at Edek's place when Elżunia arrived. The Germans were keeping a closer eye on the trams that passed by the Ghetto, so it was necessary for them all to get together and think up new ways of smuggling food.

Edek jumped up and slapped Elżunia's shoulder as soon as she came in. 'Just the person I wanted to see. There's going to be a huge delivery on the corner of Leszno and Żelazna Streets tomorrow, and they'll need lots of people to unload. Want to help? The smugglers are expecting a couple of wagons!'

'Wagons? Coming in here? You're kidding!'

He shook his head in mock amazement. 'Oh boy, I can't believe you don't know what's going on. Listen. They've bribed the Polish policemen and our boys to look the other way until after the delivery. Sometimes they even bribe the German guards. So, are you coming?'

She couldn't help smiling. With his mop of curls and long lashes over his dark eyes, he looked like the innocent hero of a children's movie, not a streetwise schemer organising a dangerous smuggling operation.

Next morning, Elżunia stood beside Edek and his group as they waited for the delivery. She was still dubious until she heard the sound of hooves and wagon wheels rumbling along the road towards the guard post. Her mouth went dry. What if a German guard turned up just at that moment? She glanced at Edek but he was looking towards the gate as excitedly as though St Nicolas himself was about to enter, laden with gifts.

It would soon be Christmas and thinking about it saddened her. Jewish children didn't believe in Christ or St Nicolas. They celebrated Hanukkah, but it wasn't the same. The smell of the pine tree in the lounge room, the fun of decorating it with shiny baubles and silver tinsel, and waiting for St Nicolas to arrive on the sixth of December had always been the most exciting time of the year. And the excitement hadn't palled, even when she knew that it was her parents who placed the brightly wrapped parcels under the tree.

As the wagon approached, one of the Jewish sweepers employed at the guard post raised a broom high in the air.

'Those sweepers are smart guys,' Edek whispered. 'They're the ones that fix the bribes and arrange the deals.' She looked at him in astonishment. She had always thought the men who busied themselves sweeping and cleaning around the guard posts were unfit for anything else. How did he know all this?

'What if the guards take the bribe and then turn up and shoot us all anyway?' she whispered. Thinking of the guards who had double-crossed her and her mother when they'd taken Lusia's gold chain during the horrible night of the disinfection, she started to worry.

Edek shook his head. 'Stop worrying. Nothing will go wrong, as long as we move fast. We've got about half an hour.'

She wanted to ask how they could possibly unload two large wagons in such a short time, but stopped herself. He'd only make fun of her for being a worrywart. She looked at the sweeper again. He was a nuggetty man with short arms and broad shoulders.

Edek followed her gaze. 'He used to be one of Warsaw's top wrestlers,' he said.

The sweeper was still holding the broom up. It was obviously a signal that the coast was clear because as soon as the driver saw it he whistled to the horses and flicked the reins against their flanks to speed them up. A moment later the wagon clattered through the gate and the sweeper ran alongside it, guiding it into the wide entrance to the yard.

Even before the wagon had stopped, dozens of eager hands reached for the contraband as they feverishly began unloading, dragging out sacks of potatoes, boxes of butter, and crates of chickens and eggs. The children tossed them from one to another so fast that their hands hardly seemed to touch them, while the driver, a thin pale man in a crumpled jacket, kept swearing under his breath, urging them to hurry. The second the wagon was emptied, he jiggled the reins and sped out of the Ghetto, as if the devil were on his heels.

As the second wagon moved towards the gate, Elżunia noticed that the horses had become restive. One pricked his ears forward as though ready to bolt, while the other whinnied and pawed the ground. The driver looked around nervously, waiting for the sweeper's signal.

'Ano, co tam?' he shouted, anxious to get inside and get it over with. He took off his battered hat and wiped the sweat from his brow, even though the air was cool. But before the sweeper signalled to proceed, the driver lost his nerve, jumped off his seat and fled, leaving the wagon piled high with forbidden food behind two agitated horses.

Time was running out. Any minute now the guards would return with the Germans. The precious cargo would be confiscated and they'd all be shot for smuggling. Elżunia tore at the skin around her thumbnail. Every cell inside her screamed *Run!* but pride glued her feet to the ground. She'd never be able to face Edek and the other kids if she ran like a coward.

As they stood still, uncertain what to do, a lad suddenly ran forward, leapt onto the wagon, and grabbed the reins. He stood on the driver's seat with his legs wide apart, leaning back to control the horses, his lips partly open and his eyes shining with excitement. He looked like a Roman charioteer, Elżunia thought. He lashed the horses so that they galloped into the Ghetto. As he passed her, she realised it was the boy who lived on the other side of the wall, the one who was always looking at her from his window.

As soon as he jumped off the wagon, they all rushed towards it and turned it on its side to hasten the unloading. Without saying a word, their rescuer rolled up his sleeves and helped them pull down the cartons and boxes, which were whisked away as soon as they were placed in the doorway. He ran back and forth, carrying boxes of carrots, onions and beetroot, and his fair hair seemed charged with energy.

Elżunia was staggering under a crate of butter when he rushed over and took it from her hands. 'You're the girl in the house across the wall. You poked your tongue out at me a couple of months ago, didn't you? I'm Lech. I've been watching you. You brought a little girl home a few weeks ago.'

She bristled. 'You seem to spend a lot of time spying on me.'

He grinned. 'Not spying, just looking. If I like the look of something, I keep looking. Don't you?'

She blushed and pushed her hair back behind her ears. As if she'd be interested in a country bumpkin, even a brave one like him. Her hero was the taciturn airman who had saved her life. The more frightening her existence became, the more she daydreamed about him.

Lech was still grinning at her. Pointing to the wagon, which had only a few cartons left on it, Elżunia said awkwardly, 'That was a really brave thing to do.'

He started to speak, stopped and looked down at his feet. He revelled in her praise and would have liked to take credit for being brave but knew that courage didn't have anything to do with it.

As he stood there, shuffling his shoes in the slush, he had a sudden vision of the person he wanted to be. Then he remembered what he really was, and hoped she'd never find out.

It was his cousin Bolek who had started him along that shameful path. 'Come on, Lech, it's dead simple,' he'd said with that devilish glint in his eyes that Lech had never been able to resist.

'It's easy money. Nothing to it.'

That first time, they'd hung around Gdańsk Station, waiting for a train to come in, and he'd looked over his shoulder a hundred times to make sure they weren't being watched.

Bolek had laughed at him. 'There's nothing to worry about. The Germans won't go after you 'cause you'll be doing them a favour!'

He told Lech to watch people's faces as they got off the train. 'If they look scared or don't seem to know where to go, we'll follow them till there's no one around. Like that one!' he whispered, indicating an olive-skinned man with a worried expression whose dark eyes darted in all directions as he headed for the exit. Before crossing the road, he stood on the kerb, hesitating, trying to decide which way to go, and strolled back and forth uncertainly before asking someone about the tram for Nowy Swiat.

'He's one for sure!' Bolek had hissed. 'Keep close to me and don't say a word.'

The man looked around again, spotted them, and hastened his step, but Bolek had caught up with him. '*Proszę pana*,' he said very politely, 'can you tell me the time?'

As the man glanced at the Doxa with its wide silver band, Bolek said in an insinuating tone, 'That's a very fine watch.'

'It's all I have,' the man had protested. His eyes darted around for a way to escape but Bolek had planted himself in front of him.

'That's a pity because there's a gendarme around the corner looking for people like you,' he drawled.

'You've made a mistake,' the man protested. 'I'm as Catholic as you are.'

But Bolek just laughed. 'Oh really? Let's go to the Gestapo so they can check you out.'

Without another word, the man peeled off the watch, handed it over and melted away into the crowd.

'See, I told you. It's that easy,' Bolek said to Lech, pocketing the watch.

With Bolek's coaching, Lech soon became confident enough to work on his own, thrilled with the money he was making and proud of his new power. His victims beseeched, pleaded and begged. They actually feared him. No one had ever taken much notice of him, not even his parents except to belt him, and now he had all this power over people and they knew it. He had never realised that fear could be exploited so profitably. These people were so scared of being turned over to the Gestapo that they would give you all they had.

Sometimes Bolek would milk his victim and then turn him over to the Gestapo to claim his cigarettes and vodka as a reward, and then Bolek and Lech would spend the night smoking and drinking and bragging about their success. Lech's father, who was still trying to eke out a living growing potatoes, beetroot and corn on his farm, had always told him that he was a hopeless good-for-nothing. It gave Lech a malicious sense of triumph to know that, at the age of seventeen, he earned more money in a week than his father saw in a year. Now we know who's the hopeless one, he thought, smiling to himself.

Lech had never done well at school, had left at age twelve, and had already forgotten the few things he'd learnt, but one thing he remembered was his teacher saying that knowledge was power. It hadn't made any sense to him at the time but now he discovered it was true. In the beginning, he'd thought that all Jews had dark hair and big noses but now he knew that some of them had fair hair, light eyes and noses no larger than his own. But their cocks looked different and they were terrified of the Germans checking them out down there. The other thing he learned was to look at their eyes. The Jews had a different expression, a sad, faraway look, as though their pet dog had just died, and he was proud of his skill at picking them out. It was surer than picking winners at the races.

When that wall had gone up and cut through his courtyard, it improved his business because the Jews still living outside the wall were now more frightened than ever of being caught and were easier to blackmail. From time to time he picked up one of the Underground newspapers that couriers distributed around the city and read that collaborating with the Germans was treason, but he never thought of himself as a collaborator. He was just earning a bit of money that the war had thrown his way. The morality of it didn't concern him. He hadn't started the war and it wasn't his fault that the Germans were after the Jews. Anyway, everyone knew that Jews were loaded.

The girl who moved into the building on the other side of the wall wasn't really his type. The ones he usually went for would show you their boobs and let you do whatever you wanted if you sweet-talked them, while this one looked stuck-up and had hardly any boobs. She wasn't even pretty but there was something about her that made him want to keep looking. He liked her eyes, the way she flicked her hair back, and the expression on her face that said she'd never give in about anything.

He hadn't thought about her being Jewish before, but supposed she must be or she wouldn't be in there. He felt sick at the thought that he might have stopped her or a relative of hers in the street and demanded money or jewellery. He watched her coming in and out. In the mornings, she squeezed through that opening in the wall. He used to follow her to her secret classroom until the Gestapo found out about it. He almost had a fight with Bolek when he found out his cousin had reported the *komplety* to the Germans.

He knew Elżunia still worked at the clinic, and he fantasised about being run over by a car and waking up in there while she was bandaging his head.

Now he took more interest in what was happening on her side of the wall. How did they breathe in there? There were no trees or flowers, just masses of people. It was more crowded than Częstochowa on the day when Catholics from all over Poland came on a pilgrimage to pray at the shrine of the Black Madonna. Most of the people in the Ghetto were so thin that their bones showed, and their clothes were falling apart. And all those skinny children having to beg in the streets made him mad. He had two little sisters back in the village and would have hated to see them begging for a scrap of food.

Once he watched a German guard lining up three small children who had just squeezed through the hole in the wall, pockets bulging with food. With one shot he killed all three, and with a contented expression took out his handkerchief, wiped his pistol, replaced it in its holster and walked away, munching an apple.

It was then that Lech decided that whatever side these Nazi devils were on, he had to be on the other, even if it meant being on the side of the Jews. Bolek would never understand, so he said nothing but promised himself that somehow he would make up for what he'd done, and he'd start by helping the people inside that wall. And that way he'd also help that girl across the way, whose name he still didn't know.

When he'd looked out of his window that morning and seen the wagons approaching the Ghetto, he followed them to see what was going on. He hadn't expected fate to throw him such a golden opportunity of redeeming himself. For the first time in his life, he had done something worthwhile for someone else.

But he couldn't tell Elżunia any of this and, anyway, he didn't have the words. So he kept looking down and shuffling his feet in the slush.

'I've done nothing special,' he mumbled. '*Tata* used to let me drive the horse cart to market on Wednesdays, so I know how, that's all. When we lived in the village, I mean.' He knew how inarticulate he sounded and his ears flamed.

She was looking at him and up close he saw that her eyes were navy blue.

'Catholic Poles aren't allowed in here,' she said. 'You could get into serious trouble.'

He was staring so hard into her face that she felt compelled to drop her gaze. 'I've been watching. Not just you,' he added quickly. 'Watching to see what goes on in here. I can't figure it out.' Not accustomed to long conversations, he paused and then blurted, 'Anyway, my name's Lech. I just wanted to help.' He reddened so much that his scalp flushed under his hair.

As she studied him, an idea came into her mind. 'Well, Lech, if you really want to help, sneak back into the Ghetto tonight.'

As soon as the unloading was finished and the boys had helped to right the wagon, Lech jumped back on it, flicked the reins, and drove it out of the Ghetto, raising a cloud of dust behind him.

Thirteen

In the darkness of a moonless night, shadowy figures stole across the silent Ghetto streets. The Germans had cut off the power and the flickering light that shone from the windows came from carbide lamps. In single file they crept into Elżunia's building and made their way on tip-toe up to the attic where rusty buckets, worn-down brooms and a rickety ladder took up most of the space. As they moved stealthily across the floorboards, they raised so much dust that one of them started sneezing, while the others made frantic signs for him to pinch his nostrils.

Elżunia shivered. She felt responsible for this enterprise. Every detail had been double-checked but, now that there was nothing to do but wait, her stomach twisted like a corkscrew. What if something went wrong, what if someone got wind of their scheme and they were caught? As the tension rose, a small boy on her left let out a high-pitched giggle, and was swiftly hushed with a firm hand over his mouth and a sharp nudge. It was silent once more.

When her eyes grew accustomed to the dark, she saw Edek's bright eyes shining with anticipation and felt a surge of confidence. Like a true commander, he never seemed to entertain any doubts, and, if he did, he made sure it didn't show. Someone was scrabbling on the roof above them. They held their breath. With a slow creak, the flap in the attic roof was raised and a flashlight was shining in their eyes. A moment later, someone appeared through the opening.

'Lech! Thank goodness you made it!' Elżunia whispered.

They rested the ladder against the opening and Lech climbed several rungs at a time to get back onto the roof. A moment later, a sack of barley appeared through the opening. Standing on the lower rungs, Edek, Elżunia and some of the others passed the sack to one another until it was swallowed up into the dark recesses of the attic.

One after another, sacks of sugar, apples, butter, carrots and potatoes were lowered down, the mere thought of which made saliva pool in Elżunia's mouth. An hour later, all the sacks were in the attic. Lech replaced the roof flap and vanished into the night.

Wiping her dusty hands on her trousers, Elżunia stood back and surveyed their haul. She had recently taken to wearing her father's trousers, which she had shortened and secured around the waist with his leather belt. Wearing her father's trousers helped her to transcend her fears. She had packed them on impulse, but now she found that wearing them gave her strength, reassurance and hope. Perhaps the doubts and suspicions were simply a figment of her imagination and at this very moment he was searching for a way to get them out of the Ghetto.

Her mother didn't approve of her new attire. 'Why do you wear those things? You look like a ragamuffin,' she would say, and purse her lips. She had long given up hoping that her daughter would take pride in her appearance but this new affectation was downright perverse. But ever since she had turned fifteen, Elżunia had become more defiant.

'In case you haven't noticed, I've grown out of my skirts and we can hardly go to a shop and buy new ones. Anyway, I feel good in Father's trousers,' she'd told Lusia.

Elżunia was pleased with herself. Involving Lech in the smuggling had worked. How he had organised the delivery of all those sacks to his place and then transferred them from his room up to his attic and then over on to the roof of her building, she had no idea, but, as soon as she'd asked him to help, he had figured out a way to do it.

Elżunia and the group agreed to divide up the food in proportion to the size of their families, and donate the rest to Dr Korczak's orphanage. As a child, she had loved reading the imaginative books of Janusz Korczak, and was shocked when she heard that the popular children's author, who was also the most prominent child educationist in Poland and a passionate advocate for children's rights, was the director of an orphanage in the Ghetto.

Occasionally while walking along the streets of the Ghetto, she passed the doctor, a tall man with a bald head, neatly trimmed brown beard and shiny glasses. He was always on a mission to obtain more help for the children in his care. He was as hungry as they were, but he nourished their spirit by teaching them songs and poems and organising concerts and plays for them to perform. She came face to face with him one afternoon while waiting for Stefan outside the headquarters of the Judenrat, and gathered up the courage to tell him how much she had loved his books, and admired what he was doing for the children. He looked at her with such a penetrating gaze that she was sure he could see into her soul.

'I don't believe in sacrifices, young lady,' he told her in his matter-of-fact way. 'They are nothing but lies, hypocrisy and self-deception. Whatever we do, we do for ourselves to fulfil our own needs. Some people love women or horses. I love children. All my life I've fought for the dignity of children. But who respects the dignity of any human beings these days?'

Before she could think of anything to say, he strode away.

Since that encounter, the Germans had forced Dr Korczak to move his orphanage into much smaller premises, so that two hundred children had to sleep, eat and live in one hall. Every day, increasing numbers of starving, destitute children needed shelter at the orphanage and Elżunia knew it broke the old doctor's heart that lack of space and food made it impossible for him to admit them. She smiled to herself as she anticipated his delight at receiving this food for the orphanage.

Gittel had settled down in their room as though she had always lived there and although she asked about her mama from time to time, she accepted their explanation that mama was sick and needed to rest. But Elżunia and Lusia sensed that deep down the child really knew that she would never see her mother again.

'You know what she said today?' Lusia asked. '"You and Elżunia are looking after me, but when I'm a big girl I'll look after you." Isn't that beautiful?'

Lusia cut up skirts that no longer fitted Elżunia and made them into pretty dresses for Gittel, told her stories, and repeated everything she said as though the child were an oracle whose pronouncements contained great wisdom. Watching them together, Elżunia felt a pang of jealousy. She had never felt such an outpouring of admiration and love from her mother, but she was relieved that her affection for Gittel had roused her from her depression.

'She's as tiny as a sparrow,' Lusia lamented. 'If only we had some milk for her.'

There was no fresh milk in the Ghetto, but Elżunia knew whom to ask. She looked through the window to signal to Lech. As usual, he was standing there, as though waiting for her.

Ever since Elżunia had co-opted him into her smuggling plans, he felt he'd been raised to a higher plane of existence, surpassing anything he'd ever done before. It was like joining an exclusive secret society that valued his skills in a way no one ever had. Instead of being mocked by Bolek, who regarded him as some kind of half-wit who needed to have everything spelled out and repeated a hundred times, these young people trusted him and admired whatever he did. And the best part was that his new role brought him in almost daily contact with Elżunia, whose name he liked to say aloud when he was in bed at night. He'd never met anyone like her, especially now that she'd taken to wearing trousers, which he considered very original.

'Get some cans ready for tonight,' he told Elżunia several days later. As usual, he'd figured out how to solve her problem. He roamed around the Kiercelak Market, a place where you never asked questions but could find anything you needed, from nails and screws to scissors, spades, sheets and even bandages diverted from the German army. Lech wandered around from stall to stall until he found what he was looking for: a length of rubber hose. When he had all he needed, he made a deal with some peasants, who sold him ten litres of milk.

While Elżunia and Edek and his brothers stood beside a collection of assorted cans, jugs and churns on their side of the wall, they watched a length of rubber tubing emerge from Lech's window. He jiggled it around and pushed it until it reached the largest container. A few moments later, a stream of milk cascaded into the can.

Stretched out on his bed that night, Lech thought about Elżunia's excited face as she watched the milk frothing in the cans, and her grateful wave when the containers were filled. The more he thought about it, the more certain he became that her smile expressed more than comradely gratitude. In it, he saw an unspoken promise.

Fourteen

Adam could feel the sun's warm rays through his eyelids. The scent of new-mown hay and the earthy smell of barnyard animals hit his nostrils, and for a joyous few moments he was a boy again, spending the summer at his grandfather's country estate. Left to his own devices from morning till night, climbing the cherry trees and picking plump raspberries off the canes with crimson fingers. Tasting the forbidden chocolates his grandmother kept for special occasions in the heart-shaped Wedel *bonbonnière* tied with a blue satin ribbon. In the attic, where pumpkin seeds were spread out to dry, giving the giggling maid a chocolate each time she showed him her breasts. Hiding behind the haystack to spy on her and her boyfriend, who pulled down his trousers and squatted on top of her, grunting like a pig.

The nostalgia passed and he opened his eyes. This wasn't his grandfather's property and he was no longer a boy. Through the crack in the hasped wooden door, he could see chickens scratching around in the dirt. Nearby, an ugly brown dog with a long muzzle strained at the heavy chain that anchored him to the kennel. Whenever he barked, the chickens scattered but a moment later they wandered back to peck at the grains.

Adam propped himself up on his elbows and groaned. His body felt as though he'd been dropped from the top of a tall building. Where was he, why had his rescuers brought him to this barn, and how long had he been here? He tried to pull himself up but his knees buckled. It took several attempts before he could stand up. Edging along the wall one step at a time, he hobbled to the door, pulled back the hasp and stood outside, blinking in the sunlight.

A man was running up to him, his powerful arms pushed him back into the barn and banged the door behind them.

'Don't ever do that again!' the man shouted. 'We'll come and get you when the time is right. Till then, stay inside and keep quiet. The Gestapo is searching for you. They don't like it when an important prisoner escapes from under their noses.'

He was no older than Adam but there was a menacing toughness about him, although his impassive face gave nothing away.

His aggressive manner irritated Adam. 'I don't think we've met,' he said.

The fellow gave him an ironic look and ignored his comment. 'Remember what I said. Stay where you are. It's for your own protection — and ours.' He shut the barn door behind him.

For the next few days, the only person Adam saw was a slow-witted farm girl with a scarf tied around her hair, an apron with big pockets, and a mouth that hung open, leaving a trail of dribble at the corners. She made strange yelping noises as she scattered grain for the chickens but never looked at him when she brought his food. She shook her head so hard whenever he asked her anything that her scarf slipped off, and the nervous way she kept looking around made it clear that she couldn't get away fast enough.

He assumed he'd been brought to a Polish village near the Slovakian border, but he didn't know where he was or why he was being kept there. The uncouth fellow returned after dark. He said his name was Dariusz, and sat on his heels chewing a stalk of hay, surveying Adam.

After a time he said, 'It's a good thing you were able to walk because we had orders to either get you out of there or kill you.'

'Looks like you rescued me from one jail to put me into another,' Adam said bitterly.

'Think of it as quarantine,' Dariusz said and, without another word, walked out of the barn.

When he'd got over his indignation, Adam realised that this was normal procedure. Any agent who had been captured was always put on ice until his superiors were certain he hadn't talked. Now that he was calmer, he began to think about his failed mission. His future in the Underground didn't look promising. His arrogance had caused the death of two reliable people who'd helped to smuggle couriers across the border. That was a double tragedy because the route was no longer viable either. To rescue him from prison, other agents had risked their lives. If you were in charge, he asked himself, would you trust Adam Czartoryski's judgment? He shook his head. Definitely not.

A week later, when Dariusz told him he could return to Warsaw, he felt partially vindicated. At least they knew he hadn't betrayed anyone or revealed the coded text of the microfilm.

Handing him his new documents, which included a *Kennkarte* made out in a new name, Dariusz shook his hand without changing his expression, and disappeared into the house before Adam had climbed into the back of the horse cart that was to take him to Warsaw.

The driver, disguised as a peasant in an old woollen jacket and a battered hat rammed on his head, covered him with hay. Adam made a narrow space in the hay stalks and looked out as the cart rumbled along the country roads lined with tall, shimmering poplars. It was late June and the yellow fields of rapeseed that rolled towards the horizon reminded him of the paintings by Van Gogh that he'd admired in Amsterdam before the war.

The rowan trees were heavy with the tangerine berries he had used as pellets as a child when playing with the village boys. The memory of their sour taste made the inside of his mouth pucker. Rushing streams bubbled between willows whose overhanging branches swished against the banks, and flights of jays winged across the cloudless sky. How beautiful this country was, even though its fields had been watered by so much blood. He recalled the oath he'd taken in Zenon's office and felt an almost religious fervour to help fight for his country's survival.

But a moment later he became despondent as he realised that his work as an Underground operative was probably over. Perhaps there was another way to serve his country. Some of his colleagues from the air force had fled to England and bathed themselves in glory during the Battle of Britain the previous year. Many of them were now taking part in the Allied offensive against Rommel in North Africa. If the AK didn't want him, perhaps he could make his way to England and take to the skies again.

While he was fantasising about fighting Junkers and Messerschmitts, the driver pulled the reins and with a lurch brought the cart to a sudden stop in a township surrounded by market gardens. Before the war, these growers had supplied Warsaw with its vegetables and it infuriated him to think that now, while Poles were starving, most of their produce was being sent to Germany.

A grey Skoda was waiting by the roadside to take him the rest of the journey to Warsaw. The driver pushed him unceremoniously on to the floor in the back and threw a thick grey blanket over him.

'If they stop me, I'll say I'm delivering tomatoes to German HQ,' he said as he piled some boxes on Adam's chest. 'It won't be a comfortable ride but it won't take long,' he said and stepped on the gas.

An hour later, they were in Warsaw. Through a space between the boxes, Adam saw helmeted soldiers and SS officers striding among the downcast residents. He sighed. Near Marszałkowska Street, the driver slowed down and Adam peered over the edge of the blanket. A man's body was swinging from a lamp-post, his head lolling to one side, a noose around his neck. His face was purple and his tongue protruded from his gaping mouth. The sign pinned to his chest proclaimed that he was a Polish bandit being exhibited as a warning to others.

'He's one of ours,' the driver said. 'They caught him printing Underground papers on his hand-press.'

The Skoda pulled up outside Zenon's office. Judgment Day had arrived and Adam wasn't looking forward to it. Better prepare himself for his *mea culpa* session, he sighed. After all, there was nothing he could say in his own defence. May as well confess his sins and cleanse his soul.

Inside the sparse office, Zenon was sitting at a small table, typing with two fingers. Occasionally he stopped, deep in thought, and smoothed his moustache, but didn't acknowledge the visitor until he'd finished his work. This time however, Adam refrained from making any sarcastic comments. Eventually Zenon pushed away the typewriter and looked up.

'I hear you've had a rough time,' he said.

Adam heard no accusation or recrimination in Zenon's

tone and supposed he was probably being softened up for the verbal punches to come.

Zenon wanted to hear every detail about the doomed mission and like a man sentenced to death, Adam knew there was no point glossing over anything or making excuses. 'It was entirely my fault and I take full responsibility for what happened,' he concluded in a glum voice.

Zenon was looking at him with interest. 'Yes, in some respects it was your fault. But you haven't taken any credit for your courage.'

Adam waited, uncertain how to reply. 'I was lucky the Underground found out where I was and managed to get me out in time.'

'True,' Zenon nodded. He rose and patted Adam's shoulder. 'We're all impressed with your strength during the interrogation.'

Strength? Courage? Adam wondered if he'd misheard. Didn't they realise how weak he was, how close he'd come to spewing out all he knew?

Zenon was watching him intently. 'Every man has his breaking point,' he said. 'That's not a sign of weakness. It's human. Like making mistakes.

'The main thing is, you didn't tell them anything about the organisation or what was on the microfilm.' He went back to his desk and rifled through some papers. 'Enough about the past. We need someone to liaise between our political, military and administrative branches, so their chiefs can be informed about what's going on without having to arrange top-level meetings where they risk getting caught.' He was looking pointedly at Adam. 'That person will need to be detached and objective, and transmit the records of conversations accurately, otherwise there could be serious misunderstandings. We also need someone to listen to foreign radio broadcasts, interpret the news, and prepare reports for our Underground papers. We have to bolster people's spirits, and counter the lies and propaganda of that German-sponsored rag *Nowy Kurier Warszawski*.

'With your background in the diplomatic corps and knowledge of languages, you're the man for the job. Will you do it?'

Adam nodded and swallowed. He tried not to think of the man swinging from the lamp-post.

Fifteen

Their door opened and slammed shut and Elżunia saw Stefan coming in. He threw his cap down on the table, and dropped onto a chair.

'They're having another disinfection the day after tomorrow,' he said.

Elżunia began to tremble. The humiliation of standing naked in public for hours, the mocking laughter of the guards, the screams, the riding crops flailing their bare bodies, shivering outside after an icy shower without a towel, her few remaining clothes drenched in carbolic and ruined ...

She could hardly get her voice out. 'I don't care what happens; I'm not going through that again.'

Stefan looked at his sister with concern. 'I know,' he said. 'That's why I came to warn you as soon as I found out. Maybe you can hide somewhere. They'll be going from room to room, but I've asked around, and, from what I can gather, they're not likely to check every single person, so you might get away with it.'

It was the longest speech she could remember him making.

'I just wish there was something I could do for both of you,' he added, looking despondently at the floor. 'I thought

I'd be able to protect you, but I'm not doing a very good job.'

Lusia stroked his smooth dark hair. 'We know you're doing all you can.' She turned to Elżunia. 'Perhaps you could sneak out to your clinic?' she suggested.

Stefan shook his head. 'They're doubling the number of guards at the gates and cancelling all the passes. Can you think of some way of getting out?'

Elżunia was too numb to think.

But when she ran to tell Edek about the disinfection, he knew all about it and had it all worked out. 'We'll get the little kids out through the hole in the wall the night before the disinfection,' he told her. 'When I was on the other side this morning, I made contact with the rabbi of that church across the road.'

She couldn't suppress a smile. 'The priest, you mean.'

He made an impatient gesture. 'Whoever. Why do girls always quibble? He said we can bring the little ones over tomorrow and he'll hide them until the disinfection's over. At least they won't have to go through that.' He looked intently at Elżunia. 'Next we have to figure out what to do with you, now that you can't fit through the wall any more.'

She blushed and tried to pull her blouse down to flatten her breasts.

'Don't worry, I've thought of a way,' he announced. 'You're going to become an acrobat.'

She thought he was joking but in an excited torrent of words he described his plan for her to sail across the top of the wall in an oil barrel.

'You can't be serious!' she exclaimed when he'd finished, torn between admiration and trepidation. 'No way am I going to do that. It's too dangerous!'

Edek shrugged. 'You're right. Why take risks? You're much better off playing it safe and getting disinfected.'

She stood there, vacillating. Both options were frightening, but she knew which was worse.

'I wish there was some way of getting you out,' she told her mother.

Lusia sighed. 'At least you and Gittel won't have to go through that,' she said.

The following evening, Elżunia's knees knocked together as she stepped on to the balcony of a room at the top of her building. Suspended from the railing by a thick rope, a rusty barrel swayed above the ground. Standing behind her, the occupant of the room tried to hold the barrel while she clutched the rope and stepped inside, dangling in mid-air until the man gave it a push. Lurching and bumping like a cabin in a rollercoaster, she pushed her palms against the sides until she felt herself being hoisted up over the Ghetto wall and on to the other side, where Lech and Edek were waiting. Her face was yellow and she was retching when they pulled her from her metal cage.

Edek gave her a hearty slap on the back. 'I reckon you'd be a hit in the circus with an act like that,' he said.

She glared at him as she wiped her mouth.

It was already curfew, so they crept along the street until they parted company. Edek was going to stay in Lech's room for the night, and Elżunia had decided to hide at the back of the Jewish cemetery. She swung open the creaky wrought-iron gate and tip-toed inside, hoping the sound hadn't aroused suspicion. It was frosty, and icy rain leaked from a grey sky, giving the cemetery a bleak and desolate air. Many of the marble gravestones had been torn out and used for paving, and those that remained had sunk unevenly into the soft loam, like exhausted figures slumped in despair.

In the gloom of the wintry evening, Elżunia walked along the avenues of the dead, past ancient trees that seemed to hold out their bare branches in supplication to the sky. She looked at tombstones whose carved symbolism she didn't understand and whose Hebrew inscriptions she couldn't read. At least most of these people had died normal deaths and been buried according to their traditional rites, unlike those who were killed every day in the Ghetto.

At the far end of the cemetery, she came to a wooden shed. Propped up around its walls were ladders, buckets and hoes. She unbolted the door and looked for a place to hide. The latest change to the boundaries of the Ghetto had excluded the cemetery from its terrain, so being found there would be dangerous. One corner of the shed was piled with empty crates and boxes covered by dusty old blankets and tarpaulins, and a jumble of gardening tools. In the centre, several stone slabs were stacked on top of each other. She pulled a blanket off one of the boxes and curled up behind the largest crate.

Elżunia sat up with a start, her heart pounding. Light slanted through the chink under the shed door. It was morning, and she heard yelling and screaming from the direction of the disinfection station. She squeezed her eyes tight and pressed her hands against her ears to shut out the screams but they shrilled inside her head.

Let Mama be safe, she kept thinking. Let Mama be safe.

Footsteps crunched along the dirt path and there was rustling outside the shed. She covered her head with the blanket. The door creaked open. She held her breath as someone shuffled in.

'I could've sworn I bolted that door when I went out,' an old man muttered. She waited for a reply but the same voice went on. '*Oy yey*, that's what happens when you get to be older than Methuselah. You forget from one minute to the next ...'

Elżunia peeped out from behind her hiding place and saw an old hunchback with a skullcap on his large head, rifling through some of the spades and mattocks on the other side of the shed. She stood up.

'So you're the one who unbolted the door!' he exclaimed.

To her relief, he was smiling. 'So I'm not as senile as I thought!' He peered into her face. 'What are you doing here?'

But before she could explain why she was there, he asked, 'Have you got anything to eat? I haven't got any food left.'

She shook her head. 'Why don't you come into the Ghetto?' she asked 'You might get something to eat in there.'

'And leave them all on their own?'

She looked around, startled. Who else was here?

Pointing to the graves, he said in a quavering voice, 'To a young lady like you, they might seem dead, but I think of them all as my family. I've taken care of them for over fifty years now, ever since I was a lad, sweeping the paths, pulling out weeds, making sure the inscriptions are legible, looking after the *ohel*, keeping the register up to date. Do you think I'm going to desert them now? I'll stay till the Almighty decides it's my time to join them.'

The words shot out of her mouth before she had time to hold them back. 'Do you really think God will decide that? Because it seems to me it's the Germans who make the decisions around here.'

He came closer and shook his bony finger at her. 'Don't blaspheme, young lady. Maybe God has stopped believing in us but we have to go on believing in him. Otherwise, what will separate us from the beasts, eh?'

She didn't know what to say.

'Respect for the dead; that still counts for something in this world, doesn't it? Even animals keep vigil over their dead.'

He shuffled away, muttering to himself, but soon returned with a mug of grain coffee. 'It's freezing in here; you need something to warm you up,' he said. 'This is all I've got but you're welcome to it.'

Elżunia spent the rest of that long day huddled in the shed. She pulled the dirty old blanket over her head to try to shut out the screams and yells, but nothing could shut out the images in her mind.

Unable to get back into the Ghetto at night when all the gates were locked, she waited until the next morning and sneaked back inside while the guard on duty was inspecting the passes of a work group about to leave for one of the German factories. It was always easier to get in than out.

The moment she was inside, she had a sense of foreboding. She ran home, calling her mother even before she had opened the door. She almost cried with relief when she saw Lusia at the table.

'Mama, thank God you're all right! I kept hearing those screams ...'

Lusia was sitting very still, staring straight ahead, her face chalk-white. She didn't turn when Elżunia entered, but swivelled her eyes in her direction and looked past her.

Elżunia took her mother's limp hand. 'It must have been dreadful,' she said.

Her mother looked at her dully. 'I don't want to talk about it.'

They sat in silence until she said, 'Pani Szpindlerowa's gone.'

'What happened?'

Lusia's shoulders shook. 'They kicked her to death while she was saying her prayers. She said God would punish them but it looks as if He punished her instead.'

'What about the others?' Elżunia couldn't stop herself from asking. 'What about Edek's family?'

Lusia gave her daughter a piercing look. 'Don't ask. I'm sure you heard the screams.' She shuddered and turned away. She looked so thin and vulnerable that Elżunia wanted to put her arms around her and comfort her, but she felt inhibited. They had never been demonstrative towards each other and even here her mother seemed to hold her at arm's length.

Elżunia was about to reach out and take her mother's hand when there was a knock at the door and Lech was standing there with Gittel. 'Old ladies in funny black hats gave us milk this morning. Can I go there again?' she squealed.

'She means the nuns,' Lech said, chuckling. 'I don't suppose she's ever seen them before.'

As soon as Lech had gone, Elżunia ran to Edek's place to make sure his mother had got through the disinfection ordeal. When Edek opened the door, his face told her everything. There were dark hollows around his eyes and for the first time since she had known him there was no light in them. She looked around. Edek's mother and baby brother weren't there, and the children sat on the floor, looking blankly into space. Someone gave an occasional harsh sob, while the little ones kept asking for Mama.

She put her arms around Edek and wet his cheek with her tears. He cleared his throat noisily and pulled away. 'I'm all right,' he said, avoiding her gaze. 'I'm not going to blub like a girl. I'm a soldier and soldiers don't cry. They fight.'

Elżunia clenched her fists. 'If only we could,' she whispered.

Sixteen

When Elżunia discovered, soon after the Ghetto was closed, that her Red Cross pass had been cancelled and permission to work at the clinic had been revoked, she was in despair. Now her existence would shrink even further and she would become imprisoned within the Ghetto walls.

Spring showers had already begun to fall that April in 1941, and she was sitting at the window telling Gittel stories about fairies and princesses when Edek came in, whistling a merry tune.

'What can you possibly find to be in such high spirits about?' she asked crossly.

But Edek brought good news. He had discovered a secret passage that would enable her to slip out undetected, if she made sure no guards were around.

She flung her arms around him but he pulled back. Edek didn't like effusiveness. 'Glad to help a damsel in distress,' he said, and giving his scout's salute, ran off.

Under an apartment block close to the Ghetto boundary, a cellar led to a long subterranean passageway that came out at a courtyard in Senatorska Street, which was now in the Aryan part of town. From there she didn't have far to walk to the clinic in Marszałkowska Street.

The route he had mapped out enabled her to sneak out, and, to her delight, Elżunia continued to work at Dr Borowski's clinic. Although he knew she was Jewish, and realised the risk he was taking in employing her, he treated her like any other employee, and spoke to her gruffly so that Bożena's wouldn't suspect the truth. But whenever Bożena extolled the virtues of her Nazi boyfriend, Gunther, the doctor advised her tartly to pay more attention to her studies and less to her social life if she wanted to pass her exams.

Elżunia was applying ointment to a little boy's burnt leg when Bożena flounced into the surgery, cheeks flaming.

'The old crank has it in for me, but if he fails me he'll be sorry.'

Elżunia raised her eyebrows. 'What do you mean?' she asked. But Bożena turned away without another word.

An hour later, when Elżunia was putting away the dressings and bandages, Bożena came in and looked Elżunia up and down in an appraising way. 'Gunther's got a friend who'd love to go out with a Polish girl,' she said. 'You're a bit young but your figure's not bad. Do you want to come? He could do a lot for you if he likes you.'

Elżunia struggled to steady her voice. 'Thanks, Bożena, but I prefer Polish boys,' she said lightly.

Bożena shrugged. 'Your loss.'

Ever since her conversation with the old caretaker at the cemetery, a plan had been simmering in Elżunia's mind. That evening, she discussed it with Edek. Two small candles were burning on the table and the boys sat on the floor barefoot to observe the ritual seven-day mourning period for their mother and baby brother.

'We can't leave your mother and little brother in a mass grave in the street. They have to be buried properly in

149

sanctified ground. So do the others that were killed that night.'

Edek looked up at her.

'It won't be easy but I've thought of some people who might help.'

As Edek and his brothers listened to her plan, the atmosphere in the room lightened. The prospect of taking action and giving their mother and brother a proper burial had energised them.

'We'll need four strong boys, with spades, sacks, long poles, canvas and some sheets,' she told them. 'I'll organise the rest.'

Taking advantage of Bożena's absence one morning, Elżunia had taken Dr Borowski aside and told him what she planned to do. Then, taking a deep breath, she asked for his help. The old doctor listened with growing amazement, and when she'd finished he nodded with admiration and added some suggestions of his own.

'The idea is extraordinary, but you're right, we can't let the bastards drag us down to their level,' he said. 'Let's bury the dead.'

No one who heard the siren screaming as the ambulance sped along Okopowa Street past the Ghetto gate several evenings later could have suspected that the white-haired doctor and his young nurse in her white apron, starched cap and red cape were rushing not to minister to the sick but to bury the dead. Their suspicions lulled by the siren, the guards at the Ghetto gate looked up as the ambulance sped past, and then looked away again.

The ambulance slowed as it turned into Spokojna Street, which was dark and silent. In the small square, shadowy figures were moving around. Elżunia pointed. 'Over there,' she whispered to the driver, who stopped the vehicle. In front of them, Lech, Edek and two of his brothers were pushing something large and unwieldy into a sack. Edek walked over to the ambulance. 'We've almost finished,' he panted, wiping his perspiring brow. 'We've dug them all out, and we've put each of them into a separate sack. Except for Mama and Mosze. We put them in together.'

His lips trembled and he turned away.

'All we have to do now is fill in the grave so they won't suspect anything.'

Elżunia jumped out of the ambulance, ready to grab a spade and help, but Dr Borowski placed a restraining hand on her arm. 'You can't risk getting your uniform dirty in case someone stops us.'

He tapped the driver's shoulder and asked him to help.

When the soil had been replaced and the bodies had been stacked in the back of the ambulance, Lech and the other boys climbed in and the ambulance set off again, siren blaring. Elżunia looked around anxiously and tore at her thumbnail. It was long past curfew. What if a German patrol stopped them and demanded to see inside the ambulance?

A few minutes later they were at the cemetery gate. At a prearranged blare of the horn, the hunchbacked caretaker shuffled to open the gate wide enough for the ambulance to drive in and closed it behind them.

'I've brought you some spades and mattocks but you have to hurry. The SS have been paying us a few visits lately. They've been bringing in slave labourers to dig pits for the prisoners they've killed at Pawiak Jail.'

As he spoke, his gaze fell on Elżunia. 'So you went through with it after all,' he said. 'Burying the dead with the proper ritual is a *mitzvah*.'

Edek saw Elżunia's frown. 'That means a good deed,' he whispered in her ear. He kept forgetting that until she came into the Ghetto, she had been a Catholic girl who knew nothing about Judaism.

The caretaker's eyes lit up when she handed him a packet of buckwheat. 'May the Lord bless you for remembering an old man,' he whispered.

He hobbled around as he directed the driver to a remote part of the grounds where the gravestones thinned out.

The loam was soft and yielding and it didn't take long to excavate a hole large enough for the bodies. They had deposited most of the sacks inside when they heard banging on the gate and loud German voices yelling, 'Open up! Quick!' They looked at each other and the blood drained from their faces.

As the banging and shouting continued, they worked feverishly to lower the remaining sacks into the grave, and covered it with soil, making as little noise as possible. Hiding themselves wouldn't be difficult, but how could they conceal the ambulance?

Gesticulating to the boys to stand behind the vehicle, the driver put it into neutral gear and indicated that they should push it to the back of the cemetery behind some bushes.

In the meantime, the German voices had risen to a crescendo of fury as they cursed the caretaker as he fumbled with the lock on the gate.

'It's the middle of the night. Did you tell me you were coming? How was I to know you'd come so late?' he grumbled.

In the silence of the cemetery, his words carried to the group hiding in the bushes. Furious, one of the SS men struck the old man with the flat of his hand, and sent him reeling.

'We know there's someone in here. We heard noises,' one of them shouted. Elżunia stopped breathing. Now they'd search the grounds and kill them, together with the caretaker.

'You could be right,' the caretaker said, as though considering the officer's words. 'Hooligans sometimes get in here and steal tools from my shed. I'll take you there. I'll be very grateful, sirs, if you catch them. Tools are so hard to come by these days ...'

Ignoring him, the officer pushed him out of the way and Elżunia heard their boots crunching on the gravel away from them. She breathed out again and hoped they wouldn't search the grounds. She heard a bang and supposed it was a rifle butt forcing the shed door open. A moment later, it sounded as though they were knocking over the crates, cartons and buckets behind which she'd crouched the previous week.

'They've been here all right,' the caretaker was saying. 'Some of my spades are missing. The thieving louts! They've probably sold them in Kiercelak by now. A man can't turn his back ...'

Finally, Elżunia heard the creak of the gate as it closed, and the car with the SS officers roaring down the street. A few minutes later, the caretaker returned, panting.

He looked around the group. 'Who are the mourners?'

Edek and his brothers stepped forward. 'With your permission, I'd like to say Kaddish for these poor souls,' the old man said.

While the caretaker recited the traditional prayer for the dead, Edek's shoulders heaved. Sobbing loudly, he put his arms around his brothers and held them close. 'Now Mama and Mosze can rest in peace,' he whispered. Elżunia didn't understand the words of the ancient Aramaic prayer but tears sprang to her eyes as the caretaker's husky voice thanked God for the gift of life, and chanted a plea to the Almighty to grant eternal rest to the dead, and peace to the bereaved.

Lech returned to his room that night, his heart swelling at the memory of Elżunia's gratitude for his help. Inarticulate as usual, he'd mumbled a few words and wished she knew that he would do anything for her. The nuns had dinned into his thick head at primary school that God kept a scoreboard on which He listed everyone's good and bad deeds, something like the blackboard his teachers used. Perhaps by helping the Jews, he was evening up his score, and with each good deed he hoped that God might erase one of the black marks his previous activities had earned. Before falling asleep, he wondered whether it would count against him that he was doing it because he was desperate for Elżunia to like him.

Seventeen

Elżunia was on her way to Edek's place when she became aware of a young man leaning against the building, watching her. He looked around twenty, and the cloth cap rammed boyishly over his forehead accentuated his large ears, which were set so low on his head that they seemed to have slipped down. His stillness was accentuated by the frenetic activity around him as hawkers rushed around, desperate to sell old books, threadbare sheets, spools of cotton, matches and even bits of lining they'd torn from their jackets.

She was about to walk past the fellow when he moved forward and fell into step with her. 'I've been watching you and your group,' he said out of the corner of his mouth. 'Things are starting to move, and when the time comes, I hope you'll join us.'

Before she could ask him to explain, he placed a warning finger over his lips and melted into the crowd.

When she told Edek about her encounter with the fellow with the big ears, he wasn't surprised. 'Sounds like Szmuel,' he said. 'He's with Haszomer Hacair. You know, the scouting group. They've been trying to organise resistance in here.'

How did Edek know these things, she wondered. She was vaguely aware that people inside the Ghetto belonged to different political and religious organisations. Apart from the socialists, Zionists and Bundists, there were many who weren't affiliated with any group. Some dreamed of a Jewish homeland in Palestine while others saw no need for Jews to live outside Poland.

'Resistance!' she exclaimed. 'Let's join them!'

But Edek was diffident. 'All they've done so far is talk and print Underground papers. They can't decide what to do or how to do it and, anyway, they haven't got any weapons. Whenever one group suggests blowing up a Nazi truck or ambushing some officers, another one panics. And the oldies quake in their shoes whenever anyone suggests fighting back. They reckon fighting back will only make things worse.'

'How can they get any worse?' she asked.

Edek shrugged. 'Exactly. But the older people are, the more scared they get.'

'Well, I reckon this lot will get organised soon and, when they do, I'm going to join them,' she said.

On her way to the clinic the following morning, Elżunia's spirits rose, and the more she thought about the idea of resistance, the more excited she became. She saw herself fighting the Germans and was lost in a daydream when she saw the crowd gathered outside the clinic, staring at the smashed windows and broken glass on the pavement.

'*Jesus Maria*,' one of the patients lamented. 'The bloody devils! To think they'd do this to our wonderful doctor.'

Elżunia pushed her way inside. The door was hanging off, a cupboard lay on its side, papers and files were scattered all over the floor, and the table and chairs were in pieces. She climbed over the cupboard and saw that the glass case in the corner had been smashed, the bandages lay unrolled on the floor, and their precious bottles of medicine and phials of vaccines were smashed.

She found the old doctor pacing around his room. 'That slut, Bożena,' he fumed. 'Because of her, they've not only wrecked the clinic, but closed it down. Who's going to look after all these people now?'

He told Elżunia that the neighbours had seen two SS officers break in during the night and smash the place up.

'But what's it got to do with Bożena?'

Hardly able to contain his fury, he spat out, 'She got her exam results yesterday. I failed her.'

Elżunia looked around the ruined clinic. Bożena's vengeance meant the end of medical treatment for the people in this area but it also spelt the end of her own training as a nurse. Without the work she loved, and the clinic where she sometimes forgot her own plight, she was doomed to die inside the Ghetto, whose walls she could feel closing around her.

Eighteen

Lusia was watching her daughter with anxious eyes. Ever since the clinic had closed down, Elżunia had lost interest in everything, and even Gittel's lively chatter failed to raise a smile.

'Play with me, Elżunia,' the child would plead. 'Tell me about Goldilocks and the three bears. Cut out a new dress for my dolly.' But after a few minutes, Elżunia would put down the pencil and scissors and lie with her face to the wall.

To cheer her up, Gittel would sometimes sing 'Almonds and Raisins'. She no longer had to fill in the gaps with her own garbled inventions because Lusia had taught her the words. The traditional Yiddish lullaby took Lusia back to her own childhood when her mother used to sing her to sleep with this song. To her surprise she still remembered the words. More and more frequently these days she thought about her parents, and the resentment she had harboured for so many years gave way to regret. She had thought that she would never forgive them for rejecting her but now she understood that by converting she had rejected their faith and traditions, which meant rejecting them too. It seemed to her that her plight was a cruel form of divine retribution. Although she often asked people whether they had seen her parents, no one seemed to know what had become of them. As life in the Ghetto became increasingly precarious, she longed to see them again and let them know she was sorry for all the heartache, and to tell them that, as they'd predicted, she had become a Jew again, in spite of herself.

The door slammed and Stefan came in.

'Hey, Elżunia, I've got news for you,' he said.

She was lying on the bed and didn't turn around or react in any way. He shook her shoulder. 'Listen. They've just opened the Jewish School of Nursing in the Ghetto. Why don't you enrol?'

She sat up and, for the first time in months, she looked animated.

The following day she rang the bell on the wall of a large stone building on Mariańska Street. The young girl who opened the door wore a pale pink dress with white stripes that reminded Elżunia of the peppermint candy sticks her father used to buy for her at the seaside so long ago. While she waited in the corridor outside the Director's office, she studied a large portrait on the wall. It was a serious-faced woman in a nurse's cap and apron, holding a lamp that lit up the gloom around her.

The door opened and the Director, a tall woman with greying hair pulled into a tight bun, walked stiffly towards her.

'I'm glad you've come to enrol. We need all the nurses we can get, with what's going on here,' she said.

She followed Elżunia's gaze as it flickered to the portrait on the wall. 'That's Florence Nightingale. I hung her portrait there to inspire us. She never let obstacles or prejudice stand in her way, and she never stopped trying to improve conditions for the patients.'

Elżunia nodded. 'She's the reason I wanted to become a nurse,' she said.

She couldn't wait to get started.

On the first day of lectures, the Director walked on to the dais with her stiff-legged gait and held up her hand for silence.

'When you entered this building, you came through a door covered by a heavy curtain.' She spoke quietly but emphatically. 'I want you to know that this is no ordinary curtain.'

They all strained forward.

'This curtain blocks out the outside world. In here, the Ghetto ceases to exist.'

As they absorbed the Director's words, she continued. 'I also want you to know that this course is exactly the same as the one we ran before the war. We will not be restricted by outside considerations. If there's no power, we'll use candlelight. If we have no textbooks, we'll copy notes by hand. Any girl who fails to reach the required standard will be asked to leave. Knowledge is power, excuses are weakness, and the only thing that brings fulfillment is hard work.'

With a curt nod, she swept off the podium, leaving two hundred girls open-mouthed with apprehension and admiration.

Every morning, Elżunia put on her pink-and-white striped dress with the stiffly starched white cuffs and collar that scratched her arms and dug into her neck. Over the dress, she tied a starched apron with straps that crossed over at the back, and, last of all, she pulled a white cap on her head and secured it at the back with elastic. On cool days, she covered her shoulders with a navy-blue cape that swished as she walked proudly along the street. When she wore her uniform, she could feel Florence Nightingale breathing strength into her. She couldn't wait to complete the two-year course and be entitled to sew a piece of black velvet onto her white cap like the graduates.

Lech sometimes sneaked into the Ghetto to walk with her to Mariańska Street, casting sidelong glances along the way at her crisp uniform, and puffing out his chest. He was convinced that all the boys envied him and he hoped they took him for Elżunia's boyfriend. He wanted to tell her that her eyes were the colour of those dark blue flowers that grew wild on his father's meadows, the ones that the village girls used to place at Christ's feet in the wayside shrine, but he was too tongue-tied to say it. Instead, he offered to carry her satchel, but, as usual, she refused. 'Florence Nightingale used to carry her own bag,' she would say.

He had no idea who the woman with the strange name was, or what part of Warsaw she lived in, but he nodded, happy to walk beside Elżunia.

The Director hadn't exaggerated when she said that she intended to continue the prewar regime without compromise. There weren't enough textbooks to go around, and Elżunia's fingers grew numb copying out page after page in the unheated lecture room. The power was cut most days and she strained her eyes to see in the dim light. Sometimes the class heard screams and shots and exchanged terrified looks but none of the doctors or nurses ever interrupted their lectures or gave any indication that they'd heard. Eventually the students took their cue from them and stopped reacting to what was going on outside. There were two worlds now, and, while they were inside, the outside world didn't exist.

*

Elżunia did her practical work in the surgical ward where forty-six beds were separated by small white metal tables. Although there were never enough medicines, the sister in charge insisted on maintaining the regime she had introduced before the war. Two ward rounds each day, records meticulously kept, and everything scrubbed and sterile. She would accept no excuses and terrorised the trainee nurses if she found any lapses. Although Elżunia was awed by this bustling little woman whose tongue could flay the skin off your back, she knew that the sister was always doing battle on behalf of the patients, and constantly begged the Judenrat to provide more money for running the hospital.

'This work is driving me insane,' she told Elżunia one morning, after the doctor on duty had thrown up his hands in a gesture of frustration because he couldn't treat the patients the way he wanted to.

'He prescribes food supplements for the patients but where am I supposed to get them? We only get ten vitamin supplements a day, and there are forty-six patients in this ward alone. I keep begging the Judenrat for more but it's no use.'

Encouraged by Elżunia's sympathetic silence, the sister continued her litany of complaints. 'And we're short of linen as well. How am I supposed to run a surgical ward without clean sheets? We're short of bandages and cotton wool because the pharmacy only sends a fraction of what we need.'

Mulling over the sister's woes as she hurried home, Elżunia almost tripped over an old man whose iron-grey hair hung down over his frayed collar as he teased soulful notes from the violin tucked lovingly under his chin. His eyes were closed and his sallow face had a beatific expression as he played lively *klezmer* tunes with agile fingers that seemed to belong to a far younger man. Even in this sad place where hope was a wistful sigh, his music transported people to an existence they'd almost forgotten, a life with laughter, dancing and celebrations, where there was enough to eat and drink and they didn't watch their parents and children fade away before their eyes.

In front of him lay an upturned top hat with a red silk lining, its brightness defying the spectral figures on this grey street. There was one small coin that lay in the hat like a reproach. Enchanted by the music, Elżunia listened until he removed the violin from his chin and gave her a solemn bow.

'That was terrific,' she said. 'Have you been playing long?'

'An eternity,' he said. 'Fifty-five years to be exact. I used to play with the Warsaw Philharmonic and now I play in the Ghetto.' He glanced at his hat and chuckled. 'Unfortunately the pay here is poor and the conditions leave a lot to be desired.'

The clouds darkened and a fine rain began to fall, which quickly turned to sleet. Elżunia looked at the violinist's thin jacket. 'It must be terrible for you to play in the street for coins like this,' she blurted.

He paused for a moment. 'At first, I thought I'd die of embarrassment. But now I see it differently. You see, I haven't done anything to be ashamed of. Today they think they're lords of the universe but one day they'll stand before the Almighty and have to account for themselves. They're the ones who ought to be ashamed. Not me. And not you. Remember that.'

She drew her cape around her as he placed his violin back in its case.

'Some of us get together sometimes and perform magic in the Library Hall,' he said, and chuckled. 'A dozen starving musicians give concerts for several hundred starving listeners, and two hours later our souls are nourished and our hearts feel full.' He smiled at Elżunia. 'Perhaps one afternoon you'll come and hear us play.'

She was hurrying home when she spotted the young man with the large ears who had accosted her a few months earlier.

He looked at her uniform and nodded. 'So you're training to be a nurse. That's excellent. We're going to need nurses — lots of them.'

'I'll be ready whenever you need me,' she said.

Nineteen

Adam's new role was far more complex and demanding than Zenon had intimated, but he threw himself into it, determined to prove himself and expunge the memory of his failed mission.

To cover his tracks, he rented rooms in three places and used different identity cards in each one. He had spent hardly any time in the only lodging where he was registered under his real name, because this was where he ran the biggest risk of being caught. It was a cramped dusty attic in a house whose façade was pitted with shells fired at the beginning of the war in 1939. The landlady, whose officer husband had been captured by the Russians and deported to Siberia, looked at him askance each time he dropped in to check whether anyone had asked for him, but didn't ask any questions. The day she told him that two Germans in plain clothes had come asking about him, he had moved out.

He wasn't registered at all in the room where he spent his nights. Although it was illegal not to register tenants, and his landlady ran a risk of being arrested if the Gestapo discovered she had an undeclared lodger, he felt he could trust her. Ever since starting work for the Underground, he had increasingly come to rely on his instincts about people. From her sidelong glances, he could tell she guessed why he didn't want a record of his stay. Thanks to her cooperation, he slept secure in the knowledge that no one would come looking for him there.

The third room he rented was his office where he listened to illicit short-wave radio broadcasts and prepared reports for his superiors, as well as writing news items and articles for Underground newsletters and bulletins. Adam was aware that in disseminating genuine information, he was performing a vital service for the nation. People were continually being fed German propaganda, and unless they were willing to risk their lives by listening to illicit broadcasts from London and Washington, the AK publications were one of the few means of finding out what was really going on.

The fall of France the previous year had dealt a terrible blow to Poland's hopes of Allied assistance, but now that Hitler had broken his non-aggression pact with Stalin and invaded the Soviet Union in June, there was a strong likelihood that their former enemy would join the Allies. The AK leaders felt optimistic that 1941 might prove to be the turning point of the war. For one thing, the Polish army imprisoned in the Soviet Union would now be released, and, for another, instead of having two tigers on its back, Poland now had only one.

But Adam had discovered that there was far more involved in his work than sitting in front of a radio listening to broadcasts transmitted from neutral and Allied countries and summarising them for the Underground newsletters. Although the Underground newspapers were printed on small hand-presses or mimeographs, a shortage of paper continually threatened the dissemination of information. As the AK had few legitimate channels for obtaining paper for its publications, Adam hit on the idea of posing as the representative of a manufacturing firm that needed to import it.

Ethnic Germans living in Poland had special privileges, and with his excellent knowledge of German, Adam felt sufficiently confident to pose as a *Volksdeutsche*. He started frequenting the Tatra Tavern in the Żoliborz district in the hope of making useful contacts. The Tatra was one of the *Nur für Deutsche* establishments that the Germans appropriated exclusively for themselves, so in his guise as an ethnic German, Adam was entitled to enter. Downing one vodka after another while a woman in a slinky backless gown crooned a throaty rendition of 'Lili Marlene', he looked around the bar to see if he could strike up a conversation and initiate some contact with a German or *Volksdeutsche* who might be useful.

After a couple of fruitless weeks, Adam was losing patience with his scheme. He was sitting at the bar one evening thinking of giving up, when his eye fell on a short man with sparse brown hair and eyes set into his pale face like raisins stuck into a lump of dough. He was alone and, from his eager expression, seemed to be looking around for company. Adam slipped onto the stool beside him and started a conversation. After he had complained about the ignorant Poles, and rejoiced at the civilising advent of the Germans, their conversation became more animated and, before long, his new friend Horst was showing him photos of his *Frau*, Ilke, in her dirndl surrounded by his three sturdy sons in their lederhosen outside their home in Munich. Horst missed his family and wished he was back home but he'd been sent to *Warschau* by his firm to sell newsprint.

Adam's hand tightened around his glass. 'Allow me to buy you a schnapps,' he suggested. He and Horst toasted each other, clinked glasses and crossed arms as they drank a

Bruderschaft. Several drinks later, the German's face was glowing with bonhomie and brotherhood while Adam kept up with him glass by glass without losing sight of his goal. Before the evening was over, several bottles had been emptied and they shook hands on a deal in which a truckful of newsprint would be delivered to Adam and paid for at market price.

After their third meeting, Adam was ready to spring the trap. Unknown to Horst, someone was standing in the shadowy doorway opposite, taking photographs of the illicit transaction, including the hearty handshake at the end, and the two schemers agreed to meet at the Tatra for a drink the following night.

Horst was already sitting at a table in the far corner of the noisy bar and waved when he spotted Adam. Over their schnapps and vodka, Adam casually pulled out the photos from his inside pocket and held them up. Horst blinked. *'Aber warum ... wersteht nicht ...* I do not understand,' he stammered, staring at Adam in bewilderment. Adam said nothing but continued to hold up the photos like a winning hand of cards. Horst blanched and his eyes widened as understanding dawned.

'Don't worry, Horst, there's no reason not to continue our agreement,' Adam said smoothly as he signalled to the waitress for more drinks.

Horst nodded several times, relieved. *'Ach so,'* he said, looking at Adam uncertainly and mopping his forehead, which was suddenly beaded with sweat.

As they lifted the glasses to their lips, Adam said thoughtfully, 'Except from now on, you will only charge us forty per cent of your original price.'

The German leapt from his chair. 'Forty per cent? *Gott in Himmel*, this is impossible! I cannot! My company will be bankrupt. I will lose my job!'

Adam spread the photos out on the table and pretended to examine them. 'I wonder what the Gestapo will think about a German doing illegal business with a Pole,' he said with the pleasure of a gambler producing his trump card. He almost felt sorry for Horst. The success of this enterprise inspired him to try his luck with German soldiers. His hunch proved right. Always short of cash, they were prepared to sell blankets, belts and sometimes even pistols that the AK desperately needed. And once they had made a sale, the trap was sprung, and they were forced to continue supplying the merchandise for fear of being exposed.

Although Adam was delighted with his success, these transactions left a bad taste in his mouth. Masquerading as a fictitious person, using false papers and carrying out secret missions seemed legitimate ways of fighting the enemy, but he despised the duplicity and blackmail that these business deals entailed, especially when they involved establishing friendly relationships with people in order to deceive them. He felt uncomfortable about duping men like Horst. Although he knew that these deals were essential in the struggle against their oppressors, he couldn't escape the feeling that he was involved in a dirty business that diminished him as a human being. It was a troubling equation and one he was unable to resolve.

He was leaving Zenon's office after being summoned to discuss his progress when he almost collided with Dr Wieniawski in the corridor. It was like going to bed tormented by a problem and waking to find that the solution had sprung into your mind while you slept. The old doctor would help him resolve his ambivalence.

They entered a modest café nearby and sat down at one of the rickety tables near the grimy window where someone had scrawled the words *Niech zyje Polska!* on the dusty pane. Long live Poland! The better quality establishments now displayed the hated *Nur für Deutsche* signs, but this café, with its threadbare curtains, chipped tables, worn-down chairs and penetrating odour of stale cabbage, was at least open to Poles.

As he scanned the dog-eared menu, most of whose dishes were crossed out, Adam noticed that the old doctor had aged considerably since they'd last met. The lines on either side of his mouth had deepened, and the papery skin on his hands was blotched with liver spots. Adam's stomach rumbled but on his modest AK allowance he couldn't afford even these relatively low prices, and he ordered a glass of tea. Dr Wieniawski also confined himself to tea, and, from the way his suit hung on him, Adam surmised that it had been a long time since he, too, had had a good meal.

They talked about the German invasion of the Soviet Union and what it might mean for Poland, and then turned to Churchill's disastrous campaign against Rommel's Afrika Korps in Libya. They agreed that, with the British army stuck in North Africa and Greece, the only hope for Europe was the Soviet Union. With Stalin now fighting alongside the Allies, Germany's grip on Europe might finally be loosened.

When they'd finished discussing the international situation, the conversation took a lighter turn. Adam bided his time for the right moment to raise the issue that bothered him, but his companion alternated between nodding too energetically to whatever he said and drifting off into a world of his own. The doctor was clearly preoccupied with his own problems but, whatever they were, he didn't allude to them.

'There's something I'd like to discuss with you because I value your opinion,' Adam said finally. The doctor looked up. This time he was paying attention.

'I'm good at my work but something bothers me. I feel I'm betraying my values and stooping to their level,' Adam said. 'Can the end really justify the means if we become ruthless in the process?'

The waitress placed two glasses of tea on the table, wiped her red hands on her apron and apologised for not being able to provide sugar. The doctor blew on his tea and took small sips, staring into his cup as though the answer was to be found inside.

'If we win this struggle, when it is over, we'll be able to resume normal life,' he said at last.

Adam shifted in his hard wooden chair. 'But who will we be by then?'

'When a patient stops breathing, you don't worry about setting his broken leg,' the doctor said. 'The only thing you're concerned with is clearing the airways. We're clearing the airways for our nation. You're worried what we will be if we compromise our values, and that's a reasonable concern. But what will we be, what will the future for our children be, if our nation ceases to exist and the Nazis rule the world?'

'But who will we be if we compromise our morals?'

Dr Wieniawski studied his companion. 'I admire your scruples but they're misguided. It's naïve to think you can play by the rules when you're involved in a life-and-death struggle with someone who's determined to destroy you and doesn't recognise any rules. This isn't a dispute over territory: it's a struggle of ideologies, a matter of survival, and it can't be won wearing kid gloves. Would you stop to consider animal rights while a lion was tearing you to bits?' He gave Adam a sympathetic glance. 'We would all like to live up to the moral standards our mothers taught us, but in times like these we have to look at the larger canvas.'

The door opened and a pretty young woman entered. She wore a floral dress that showed off her figure, and a toque secured with a wide band around the back of her smooth blonde hair.

As her gaze fell on their table, she exclaimed with a false laugh, 'Well, if it isn't Dr Borowski!'

Adam looked at his companion, waiting for him to tell the girl she'd made a mistake but, to his surprise, he inclined his head in her direction. 'Well, if it isn't Bożena!' he said in an ironic tone. 'You'll forgive me if I don't get up. I must say I'm surprised to see you here. I would have thought you'd be gracing Warsaw's fashionable cafés with your boyfriend.'

The girl chose to ignore his comment. 'My sister works here,' she said. 'How's life treating you these days?'

'I've been fortunate enough to be forced into premature retirement by the thugs who smashed up my clinic. Perhaps you heard about it,' he said through his teeth.

Adam looked from one to the other, puzzled by the hostile undercurrent.

As soon as the girl pushed open the swing door to the kitchen, Dr Wieniawski placed a few zloty on the table and they left.

At the end of the block, they stopped beside a lamp-post and looked at the sign pinned to it which said *Nur für Deutsche*. All along the street, similar signs decorated each lamp-post.

'I like that!' the doctor chuckled. 'The Germans have appropriated the cafés, and they hang our people from the lamp-posts, so, to return the compliment, someone has stuck these notices up to say we're reserving the lamp-posts for them!'

Adam felt a surge of pride. The signs had been his idea. He knew it would only be a matter of hours before they were all torn down but, in the meantime, they infused some humour and hope into the lives of the Poles, and perhaps a little apprehension into the minds of their oppressors. They watched as two helmeted policemen stopped beside a lamp-post to read the sign and looked around, not sure what to make of it.

'It's a good thing the Germans don't have a sense of humour,' Dr Wieniawski murmured as they turned into a side street.

As they were passing the Prudential Building, Adam was about to comment that at least Warsaw's tallest landmark was still standing when his companion told him what had happened at the clinic.

'One day that bitch will get what she deserves,' he fumed. 'I'll personally shear those blonde locks off her head in public so everyone knows she was a Nazi whore.'

Adam lowered his voice. 'So at the clinic you were known as Dr Borowski?'

The old doctor nodded. 'The clinic was a good cover. I was able to carry on with my Underground work without arousing suspicion, until that little viper got her revenge because I failed her in the exams. I would have liked to fire her but that would certainly have aroused suspicion.' He paused. 'You know I got involved in a strange business at the Jewish cemetery. I had a feisty Jewish trainee nurse who used to sneak out of the Ghetto —'

He was about to launch into the story about Elżunia and the secret burial but Adam had to cut him short. He would have liked to hear about the girl in the Ghetto but it was already late and he had to return to his office. The doctor was right. He had to put aside his personal scruples and keep his eyes focused on the larger canvas to hasten the end of the war. Stirred up afresh, Adam hurried back to his office to listen to the radio broadcast from Turkey so that he could file his next report.

Twenty

'Look at this,' Lusia exclaimed, passing Elżunia a notice from the Ghetto Provisioning Committee. 'I don't know whether to laugh or cry,' she said. 'Now they're publishing recipes for cooking those frozen, rotting vegetables that the Germans dump on us!'

Elżunia started reading aloud. 'Place frozen potatoes in cold water for twenty-four hours and use immediately. Use frozen onions as soon as they start thawing. Frozen meat is safe to use.' She blew on her fingers, which were swollen with chilblains. The January frost seemed more severe than ever that year and she wondered how she would manage to get through the winter. With a bitter laugh, she said, 'I'd like to see some meat, frozen or otherwise.' She scanned recipes for making grain coffee from dried beetroot, lentils and barley. 'Some tips for getting rid of chalk and sawdust from the bread would be useful.'

'Isn't life strange?' Lusia mused. 'We can be murdered any moment at the whim of any Nazi but we still look up recipes and find things to laugh at.'

There was a thump on the stairs outside and they looked at each other in alarm. A moment later, they heard moaning. Elżunia went to the door on tip-toe and opened the door a

174

fraction. A woman was sitting on the stairs, her legs sprawled in front of her like a rag doll, holding her right ankle.

'I twisted it on that wretched broken paving outside, and it's swelling up,' she panted when she saw Elżunia. 'I can't stand on it.'

She was the latest addition to the room across the landing. Elżunia and Lusia had watched with dismay as several families squeezed into the room that had once been solely occupied by Pani Szpindlerowa. To create more chaos and confusion, the Germans were constantly redrawing the boundaries of the Ghetto, and, with each change, its area shrank further, creating more overcrowding. These changes, which took place without any warning, maddened the inhabitants and drove them to despair, because each time the boundaries were redrawn, thousands found themselves out in the street, without a roof over their heads.

Elżunia sat on the landing and palpated the ankle as Dr Borowski had taught her. 'It isn't broken but you've probably sprained it,' she said. 'Come in and I'll strap it for you.'

'Tell her to make a poultice from the frozen potatoes to reduce the swelling,' Lusia called out. 'At least they'll be good for something.'

While Elżunia was bandaging the ankle, the woman said, 'I'm Madame Ramona, the clairvoyant. I'm sure you've heard of me.' She spoke with the regal air of a monarch addressing lesser mortals, and scrutinised Elżunia with her piercing black eyes.

Elżunia pretended to blow her nose as she tried to suppress her giggles. What an ego.

'I charge for telling people's fortunes but come and see me tomorrow and I'll tell yours for free,' Madame Ramona said.

When Elżunia knocked on the door the following day, Madame Ramona was dressed for the part. She wore a floral kerchief over her hair, earrings that hung down to her shoulders, and a long skirt made up of gaudy scraps of material stitched together. She reminded Elżunia of the gypsy matriarch who used to accost passersby in the old market square, offering to tell their fortunes.

Ten or twelve people shared the room, which in normal times would have served as a lounge room. Bundles and boxes were strewn from one end to the other. Some areas were screened by sheets to provide a little privacy, but elsewhere belongings were heaped in untidy piles destined to cause territorial disputes between those who shared this space. Stepping over some of the bundles and weaving between others, Madame Ramona led Elżunia to a corner of the room where a carton covered by a length of black satin served as her table. From the bags that protruded from underneath it, Elżunia saw that this was where Madame Ramona stored her few belongings.

'Give me your hand, child,' she said. She examined Elżunia's palm with close attention, as though deciphering an ancient parchment in a foreign language, and traced each line with firm fingers. Holding Elżunia's hand, she gazed into her eyes with the intensity of a thousand-watt globe.

'I see three lives,' she pronounced in a faraway voice.

'Passages and tunnels,' she continued. She gasped and clutched her throat. 'I can't breathe.' She was coughing now, louder and louder, as if her lungs would burst.

Alarmed, Elżunia wondered whether she should shake her to break this strange episode or bring her a glass of water when suddenly the coughing stopped. Now Madame Ramona leapt to her feet and flailed her arms around as though pushing away invisible flames.

'My feet are on fire!' Her shoulders heaved. 'Ah, light at last!' She sank back in her chair, exhausted.

Elżunia waited to hear more but the performance was

over. Was that all? She had come to find out where her father was and when they would be together again. She also hoped to hear a prediction about the airman who had saved her life.

Madame Ramona stared at her hand again. 'You are searching for someone.'

Elżunia sat forward expectantly.

'You are looking in the wrong places,' the woman intoned.

'Where should I look?' Elżunia whispered.

Madame Ramona shook her head so hard that her earrings bounced against her neck. 'You must find the right path.' She released Elżunia's hand. 'That's all.'

Elżunia couldn't conceal her disappointment. 'I thought clairvoyants could see into the future and find missing people,' she said.

Madame Ramona gave her a shrewd look. 'Sometimes people don't want to be found.'

A good excuse, Elżunia thought.

'How did it go?' Lusia asked when she returned. She was bent over her sewing. When she had heard that people on the other side of the wall needed aprons, she bought used sheets, odd buttons and scraps of material from the hawkers and turned them into pretty aprons that proved popular on the Aryan side and provided them with a few zloty for a piece of sawdust bread and occasionally a few grams of butter for Gittel. As the situation became more desperate, those who still had some furs or jewellery left tossed them over the wall to buy food. In exchange for a fox-fur jacket, the Polish vendors tossed back a pat of butter or a loaf of bread.

Elżunia was hunting in the cupboard for something to eat. Hunger gnawed at her constantly but it was always worse when she came home. She found two army biscuits and a little powdered milk that Edek had brought round. She smiled to herself. That boy was a miracle-worker.

Chewing each tiny mouthful over and over to make it last, Elżunia described the fortune-telling session. 'Waste of time,' she told her mother. 'She rambled on about tunnels, fires, looking for people in the wrong places and finding the right path. Oh, and something about three lives. Not a word about Father. At least I didn't have to pay for that mumbo-jumbo.'

Gittel swallowed the last of her biscuit and climbed onto Elżunia's lap, nestling in like a kitten. 'Can I have some mumbo-jumbo, too?'

The biscuit hadn't satisfied Elżunia's hunger and in an attempt to distract herself from the sudden longing to eat a thick slice of bread spread with cream cheese and covered in thick tomato slices sprinkled with chives, Elżunia picked up *Gazeta Żydowska*. She was scanning the Ghetto newspaper when an item caught her eye. There would be a concert at the Jewish Library that evening.

The large hall was crowded by the time she arrived and as she made her way to a vacant seat, she recognised the stocky man with the fleshy face and bushy eyebrows sitting in the front row. It was Mr Czerniakow, the President of the Judenrat. He was greeting people around him, and he looked surprisingly approachable.

The musicians were already on stage and there was an expectant buzz in the hall as they tuned their instruments. The edge of the stage was piled with small gifts that people had brought in lieu of payment, and their offerings said as much about the poverty of the donors as about the hunger of the recipients. People had brought whatever they could spare from their meagre rations: two shrivelled potatoes, a chunk of black bread, a tiny dish of beetroot marmalade and three blackened onions.

Elżunia looked around for the old violinist but he wasn't in the string section. Perhaps he was ill. A moment later, there was a burst of applause and he walked in front of the orchestra with a slow, proud gait, his violin in one hand, a dazzling white handkerchief in the other. His flag of defiance, she thought.

'That's Juliusz Szajnberg,' the man on her left whispered. 'He's the soloist tonight. He used to play with the Warsaw Philharmonic. My wife and I never missed a concert.' He gave a deep sigh for the gracious days that would never come again.

'Ladies and gentlemen,' the violinist announced in a voice that sounded surprisingly strong. 'This evening we will play Beethoven's Violin Concerto in D Major.'

Shouts of dismay and disapproval erupted among the audience and he held up his wrinkled hand. 'Please. I know some of you are shocked that we want to play the work of a German composer' — here he had to hold up his hand for silence again — 'but we don't believe in discriminating against great music, nor do we adopt a policy of collective responsibility, like our jailers. And, if you recall, Beethoven also lived at a time when a megalomaniac tried to subjugate Europe. That megalomaniac is gone, and this one, too, will eventually be vanquished, but glorious music lives on forever.' With that, Juliusz Szajnberg bowed, tucked his handkerchief under his chin and nodded to the conductor to begin.

From the moment the orchestra struck up the first chords of the familiar concerto, the audience listened in rapt attention as though each note was a delicacy they were determined to savour. Elżunia noticed that all the musicians had written out the score by hand, and wondered how long that must have taken them. As the old violinist swayed in time to the music, his long grey hair brushed against his frayed collar as he played.

As she watched him, it struck Elżunia that he wasn't just playing the music; he was the music. It flowed straight from his heart to his fingers and into the souls of the listeners, transporting them to another realm. Nothing existed apart from the music. The musicians, like their audience, were starving, cold and exhausted but for almost an hour their music transcended hunger, weariness and pain. She looked around. Tears glittered in the eyes of some of the listeners. Swept away by the passionate melody that soared from Szajnberg's fingers, Elżunia felt she was floating on a current of emotion. Gone was the Ghetto, the guards, the war and her missing father. She was running through fields of wildflowers, under a bright blue sky.

There was silence after the final triumphant notes of the concerto, then the hall exploded in applause. Exhausted as he must have been after his performance, the violinist played an encore. It seemed to Elżunia that it was his soul, not his fingers, that played a Chopin nocturne, which he'd transcribed for the violin. It was forbidden to play the works of this composer and she sensed that the whole audience exulted at this defiance. Like a kaleidoscope that forms different shapes when it has been shaken, Elżunia felt as though something inside her had been rearranged into a lighter, brighter pattern. No matter what the Germans did, they couldn't crush their spirit. Suddenly everything seemed possible. As she was leaving the hall, she caught sight of Mr Czerniakow again and an idea began to form in her mind. By the time she reached home, she had a plan figured out.

The next day, after her classes at the hospital were over and she'd finished her shift, Elżunia hurried towards the

Judenrat. At the intersection of Chłodna and Żelazna Streets, she stepped onto the wooden bridge that had recently been erected above the street to relieve the congestion. From the bridge, she saw a view of Warsaw that made her heart stop beating. Outlined against the watery sky were the thin spires of St Karol Boromeusz Church with the statue of the Virgin Mary in the square. It shocked her to see how close that other world was, yet how inaccessible.

At the other end of the overpass stood the guard she had nicknamed Wolfman. He fixed her with his icy expression.

'What are you staring at?' he shouted, tilting her chin with his whip.

Cold sweat ran down her back and she tensed, ready for the blow, when a shot rang out ahead of them. There was screaming and yelling, more shots, and people were running in all directions. Wolfman turned to see what was happening, and, taking advantage of the distraction she slipped away into the crowd.

One day, God will punish you, she thought, and the words comforted her as she ran, her heartbeat vibrating against her throat. But where was God? And why was He punishing innocent people?

She didn't stop running until she reached Grzybowska Street. Before the war, this street had been in the better part of the Jewish district, with wider streets and imposing buildings. This had once been the area of wealthy merchants and wholesale emporiums, where lorries delivered shipments of steel and boxes of exotic fruit from far-off lands. These days, paint peeled off the woodwork of the mansions, which were now coated with grime, and desperate street hawkers replaced the flourishing prewar entrepreneurs.

Through an arched entrance ornamented with Grecian designs, Elżunia entered the headquarters of the Judenrat.

Making her way past the rabbit warren of offices on the ground floor, past the pleading, desperate faces of the petitioners and supplicants who spilled into the corridor to gain an audience with the bureaucrats they hoped would solve their problems, Elżunia started up the stairs.

'Where do you think you're going?' a stern voice shouted after her. 'You can't go up there.'

'I'm from the hospital, I've come to see President Czerniakow,' she said quickly.

The man eyed her suspiciously and his gaze rested on her pink-and-white uniform. Everyone knew that the President suffered from heart and liver problems and lumbago, so perhaps he'd asked the nurse to come. 'Wait here,' he said and knocked on the door at the end of the corridor. A moment later he emerged and beckoned for her to enter.

The man behind the desk raised his thick black eyebrows that met above the bridge of his nose, and looked at her with hooded eyes the colour of burnt sugar. He waved a plump dismissive hand at her. 'I don't know how you got in but you've got no business coming here,' he said sternly. 'I thought it was the sister from the hospital come to badger me again. You'd better go.'

She was about to explain, but, weak from hunger, she felt so light-headed that she began to sway. She would have fainted if he hadn't hurriedly risen and pushed a chair under her.

'Close your eyes and sit there until you feel better,' he said kindly.

When the room had stopped spinning, she opened her eyes and found herself looking at a portrait, and recognised General Piłsudski, the patriotic leader of independent Poland after the last world war.

President Czerniakow followed her gaze. 'That portrait goes with me everywhere,' he said. 'It's a reminder that we are still part of Poland. The rest of Poland — like the rest of the world — may have forgotten us and left us to our fate, but we are Poles just the same.'

His piercing gaze rested on her and he frowned. 'Who are you and what are you doing here? What do you want?'

'I came to ask you to help our hospital,' she said. 'Now that we've merged with the Children's Hospital, things are really desperate. We don't have enough —'

Before she could say another word, he groaned and struck his wide forehead with his large hand. 'Do you know the Greek legend of Sisyphus?' he asked.

She shook her head.

'He spent his life pushing a heavy ball to the top of a mountain, only to have it roll down, so he had to start pushing it up again. Well, I've become Sisyphus.' He sighed. 'I spend my days begging Commissioner Auerswald to reduce the exorbitant sums he grabs from us, pleading with the *Transferstelle* to provide us with decent food and not the rotting garbage they dump on us, arguing with the municipal authorities to give us electricity and water, begging our wealthy inhabitants to contribute more money, and having endless meetings and conferences with everyone else. The Commissioner lies to me, the *Transferstelle* make promises they never keep, the municipal authorities say they'll provide power but they don't, and then the next day I have to go through it all again because the Germans keep imposing bigger ransoms and there are more sick, starving and homeless people.' He passed a weary hand over his fleshy face. 'My dear young lady, I'm an engineer and a poet, not a politician or a miracle-worker. I must have been insane to take on this thankless task.'

'So why did you?' Elżunia asked.

He stared at her for a moment. 'I honestly believed I'd be able to negotiate with the Germans and improve conditions for our people in the Ghetto.' He gave a bitter laugh. 'Some people think I did it for personal aggrandisement.'

Elżunia had heard people revile him as a German puppet. Some even accused him of being a collaborator. He sounded sincere but sincere people could be misguided. It was too complicated to sort out.

'And what about the hospital?' She had to remind him of the reason for her visit. 'If we don't have medicines, bed linen and food for the patients, what's the point of having a hospital?'

When she had finished listing the problems, he looked at the slender girl in her pink-and-white uniform and said sternly, 'For such a young girl, you're very persistent, coming here and haranguing me like this ...'

Elżunia's heart sank but President Czerniakow suddenly smiled.

'I must say, you're a breath of fresh air in this Augean stable. I'll see what I can do.'

She thanked him and felt like skipping out of the office. She was almost at the door when he spoke, as much to himself as to her. 'Sometimes I feel like the captain of the *Titanic*, shuffling the deckchairs while the ship is sinking.'

Twenty-One

Lech looked preoccupied. 'Something's brewing,' he told Elżunia. He'd been pacing outside the nursing school, waiting for her to come out. 'The Germans have brought in special units from the east, and people reckon they're planning something big.'

There were other things he'd heard as well. Like Bolek's story about the death squads. He avoided his cousin these days. He didn't want to be reminded about his past blackmailing activities, and Bolek never lost an opportunity to mock him for being a Jew-lover. But when they'd run into each other in Krakowskie Przedmiescie the previous day, Bolek couldn't resist showing off what he'd found out. He swore it was true because a German from one of those units from the east had told him all about it. He said his squad had been sent to the Soviet Union on a special mission to machine-gun Jewish men, women and children and throw their bodies into pits. *Einzatzgruppen*, the squads were called. Whatever that meant. Bolek had gone into hideous details that made Lech feel sick, but he didn't believe a word of it. Random sadism and violence were one thing, but lining up hundreds of women and children in front of pits and gunning them down in cold blood was too far-fetched. This was 1942, not the Dark Ages. The German had obviously spun Bolek a tale and he'd swallowed it. Still, Lech had noticed an influx of Ukrainian, Litvak and Latvian auxiliary units in town over the past few days and he felt uneasy.

Elżunia looked up, blinked in the sunlight and took in a happy breath of summer. This daily walk from the lecture hall to the hospital was her only chance of enjoying these brilliant July days. She looked up at the cloudless blue sky and felt the sun on her face. At least the Germans couldn't deprive them of the pleasure of a summer's day. She wished Lech hadn't spoilt her mood.

'This place thrives on gossip,' she said. 'The other day I heard someone talking about mobile vans where they're supposed to be gassing people. There's no end to the stories. If you believed them all, you'd go crazy.'

Her eyes today reminded Lech of the sea in Sopot. He'd been about nine years old and it was the only time his parents had ever taken him on a holiday. He could still remember running along the long wooden pier that jutted into the dark blue water. The day had ended with a belting, because he couldn't understand where the waves started and where they ended, and he kept asking questions that his irritated father couldn't answer, but he'd never forgotten the colour of the sea, pools of which seemed to fill Elżunia's eyes. If only he could make her safe. 'Maybe those stories are true and maybe they're not, but you'd be better off in my room than in here. You could sleep on the sofa and I could sleep on the floor. I'd smuggle you inside so no one would know you were there.' He said it all in one breath.

She stared at him. 'What on earth are you talking about?'

'If you came to stay with me, you'd be safe.'

She jumped aside to dodge a bicycle rickshaw. Sweat was pouring down the chalk-white face of the elderly cyclist who coughed and wheezed as he pedalled between the beggars propped up against the buildings and the throng milling in the streets. A shot rang out, and someone screamed.

No longer aware of the sunshine, Elżunia felt that she would suffocate in this oppressive place where shots, screams, yells and curses had become the soundtrack of their lives.

She turned to Lech. 'You're kidding, aren't you?'

He flushed, offended that she doubted his carefully thought-out scheme. 'Why would I joke about a thing like that?'

Elżunia allowed herself to be seduced by the vision of living on the other side of the wall, where people could stroll along normal streets and children still rode on carousels. She tried to imagine what it would be like to live in a place where her heart wouldn't stop beating whenever she heard footsteps on the stairs, and where she wouldn't risk being bashed or killed whenever she went outside.

'That sounds fantastic,' she said with a sigh. 'But what about you? You'd be taking a terrible risk.' She knew that neighbours often reported people who were hiding Jews, and when the Gestapo came, they took the rescuers away as well. Sometimes they shot the whole family on the spot, even the children.

He shrugged. 'I've figured it all out. The only thing is, you'd have to keep very quiet so my landlady wouldn't hear you.'

It sounded so easy. Up in his attic room, she'd be safe at last.

'You'd risk your life for me?' she asked slowly.

For a moment he couldn't speak. She didn't understand anything. She filled his mind every minute of every day and he wouldn't want to go on living if something happened to her. But he'd only make a fool of himself if he said that, and, anyway, the words wouldn't come out right.

He gave a nonchalant shrug. 'Life's a gamble these days, anyway. What's one risk more or less?' Then he added casually, 'So what do you reckon?' He stared at his feet so she wouldn't see he was holding his breath.

Elżunia longed to say yes so that she could live outside the hated wall like a normal person. She was entitled to be free. But just as she was about to agree, her legs began to wobble. How could she have even considered his offer? When she spoke, it felt as though a lump of wood was stuck in her throat. 'What about Mama and Gittel?'

'But your mother would want you to be safe, wouldn't she?'

She sighed. His offer was so tempting. 'There's no point panicking,' she said. 'This might be just another rumour.'

For one crazy moment, he wondered whether he might be able to hide all of them, but knew it was impossible. His nosy landlady even made comments when he flushed the toilet more often than usual.

As they walked side by side through the Ghetto streets, Elżunia tried to still the turmoil in her head. If only there was some way of saying yes and making it right. But however hard she tried to justify her decision to leave the Ghetto, guilt tugged at her mind. How could she abandon Mama and Gittel? And if she put herself first, she wouldn't be the kind of person her father would be proud of. But why should she adhere to principles that he himself had found too inconvenient to maintain? It wasn't fair. If not for Mama and Gittel, she'd be safe on the other side of the wall. Surely at times like these, ideals like loyalty and honour were unrealistic. Lech was right. Mama would want her to save herself. Elżunia looked up at Lech and was about to speak but the words wouldn't come. It didn't have anything to do with her father. The only person she had to answer to was herself.

Outside the hospital, she turned to Lech and, placing her hand on his arm, looked up into his face. 'I wish I could say yes but I just can't. But it was really noble of you to suggest it,' she said. 'I'll never forget it.'

As he walked away, he kept repeating her words in his head like a mantra. He never wanted to forget the look on her face or the feel of her small hand when she touched his arm.

With the sunny July weather, the atmosphere in the Ghetto lightened and Stefan occasionally told them a joke. 'Hitler died and went to heaven but he was shocked when he ran into Christ,' he told Lusia and Elżunia when he dropped in one afternoon. 'What's that Jew doing here?' Hitler asked. 'You have to leave that one alone,' St Peter whispered. 'He's the boss's son!'

Stefan was in an unusually talkative mood that day. 'They're going to resettle some people because the Ghetto's so overcrowded,' he told them.

He had been at the Judenrat that morning and had seen a delegation of SS officers entering the President's office. He didn't know what they'd come to discuss but an ominous silence had suddenly descended over the entire building that had sent a chill down his spine. It was as though everything was in a state of suspended animation, waiting for the axe to fall.

And then they heard music blaring. Some of the SS men downstairs were playing Strauss waltzes on their hand-cranked gramophone. But instead of lightening the atmosphere, these lilting melodies had sounded grotesque and menacing.

Lusia looked up from the lace edging she was stitching onto an apron. She had grown so thin that the skin hung from her forearms and wobbled like empty sacks. Although she frequently lamented about her husband's disappearance, she rarely expressed the hope that he would rescue them, and it seemed to Elżunia that her mother had finally realised that he was either dead, or had abandoned them. As both possibilities were too painful to talk about, Elżunia never raised them, and resolutely maintained her silence about what the caretaker's wife had said.

'What's the difference where they send us,' Lusia said with a shrug. 'They'll finish us off one way or another. It's only a matter of time.'

'All I know is that it's somewhere in the east,' Stefan said. There was something else he had been told. The Jewish police, whose job was to help keep order in the Ghetto, had been told that to speed up the resettlement they'd have to help the Germans round people up and escort them to the departure point. But that was one piece of information he didn't share with his family.

At dawn the following morning, Lusia and Elżunia were woken by the rumbling of trucks that made the whole building vibrate. Gates clanged and voices yelled. They ran to the window and gasped. Their street had been surrounded by German soldiers, the houses had been cordoned off by Ukrainian guards and blocked by a convoy of trucks and carts.

Down in their yard, Jewish policemen were shouting orders. 'Everyone downstairs. You can bring fifteen kilos of baggage, food for three days, and your documents. Leave your doors open. Anyone who doesn't come down will be shot.'

Elżunia and Lusia looked at each other in alarm. Why were the Jewish policemen involved in this action? Were the guards really going to shoot people for not going down? Where were they taking them? Clutching Gittel and their knapsacks, Elżunia and Lusia made their way down the stairs, which were already streaming with dishevelled and disoriented people. Some were throwing on their clothes as they went, while others were still in their nightwear. Everyone carried bundles and valises bulging with warm clothes, shoes, spoons, and pots and pans. Hearts pounding, Elżunia and Lusia stood in the yard and saw groups of frightened people emerging from neighbouring houses.

White-faced, people argued that it couldn't be anything sinister if they were told to bring their essentials and food for the journey. Anything would be better than this stinking hell-hole, even digging ditches or working on farms in Germany. Others sensed impending doom and tried to reassure their frightened children and calm their elderly parents.

The policeman checking papers shouted that doctors, nurses and the families of Jewish policemen should step aside. Elżunia and Lusia breathed out in relief. Thank God they wouldn't have to go.

As they climbed back upstairs, their footsteps sounded eerie in the empty building. They had just returned to their room when they heard boots thumping up the stairs. Someone bashed open a door with a rifle butt and yelled in a language that wasn't Polish or Russian but had elements of both. There was a scream, a shot, and the sound of something heavy bumping down the stairs. When all was quiet, Elżunia ventured out of their room and peered into the room next door. A half-finished glass of tea was cooling on the table and summer flies squatted on a crust of bread. She leaned over the railing and saw a bundle of brightly coloured rags lying at the bottom. It was Madame Ramona. Her black eyes were still open and, for a moment, Elżunia had the impression that she was looking straight at her. She wondered whether the clairvoyant had foreseen her own fate.

Elżunia and Lusia fell silent and even Gittel stopped chattering.

'I don't know where those Ukrainians and Germans are taking people,' Lusia said later, 'but I wish Stefan wasn't involved in this.'

That was the feeling Stefan tried to stifle in himself as the day progressed. At first, he'd felt good striding about in his uniform as he escorted the people towards the assembly point, especially when some of the girls cast admiring glances his way. But, as other groups joined them, they merged into an endless sea of people that clogged the roads and he found the magnitude of the operation worrying.

The SS officers in charge had emphasised the need for efficiency, a request that their Ukrainian auxiliaries had interpreted as a need to smash people with their rifle butts and shoot anyone who tripped or pleaded to be released. Stefan noticed that some of his colleagues had become overzealous and brought their batons down on the shoulders and backs of people who were lagging behind, even mothers carrying toddlers. Keeping order was one thing but mistreating people was another. However, it seemed as though each act of violence released the brake on their consciences a little further.

When the group he was escorting finally reached the gate that led from Dzika Street to the walled area on Stawki Street called *Umschlagplatz*, he was horrified by what he saw. The square was surrounded by a cordon of German guards with rifles. It was mid-morning and the sun was blazing down and there was no shade. More and more people were being pushed into the square, squeezed in like sausage meat into casings.

So many people had been herded into the loading area that they had no room to move, and those who pleaded to be allowed to use a toilet were met with laughter and jeers.

'No one leaves!' one of the guards yelled, and took photos to record the degradation of people forced to relieve themselves where they stood. By mid-afternoon, the stench was nauseating. Stefan gritted his teeth. If only they'd let people get on the train so they could get away from this appalling place.

As the afternoon wore on, the sun beat down on their bare heads but appeals for water were met with the same response as those for toilets. Children's lips were cracking and their eyes became glassy.

A woman near Stefan was holding a listless baby. 'You look like a decent young man,' she whispered. 'Please let me have some water for my child.' He made his way through the throng, trying to ignore the moans and supplications of other desperate mothers, and returned with a mug of water. He was about to hand it to the young woman when it was knocked out of his hand. A Ukrainian had come up behind him, determined not to ease the suffering of a single child. As the precious water spilled on the ground, the woman desperately tried to scoop up some of it in her bare hands before it ran into the excrement and urine. Stefan looked away, unable to meet her stricken expression.

Something was very wrong. If people were to be resettled to ease the congestion in the Ghetto, why were they being tormented like this? But there was no one with whom he could discuss his concerns. The other Jewish policemen were busy keeping order and there was no point expecting compassion from guards who entertained themselves by humiliating people, especially the young girls whose screams made his scalp prickle.

As he tried to make sense of the situation, his attention was drawn to an elderly woman sitting on her valise, staring at him with a gaze like a cut-throat razor. There was something familiar about her face and his glance kept sliding in her direction.

'You remind me of someone I knew a long time ago,' she said, not taking her eyes off his face. 'What's your name?'

A strange expression came over her face when he told her, and she made a small involuntary movement with her right hand.

'And what's your mother's name?'

'Lusia,' he said.

The woman made a strange hollow sound. 'So that's what she calls herself now!' she muttered. Her eyes slid from Stefan's face down to his uniform. She reached into the inside pocket of her loose black coat and held out something. He thought she was about to offer him a bribe so that she could escape, but she pressed something small and hard into his hand and said, 'Give this to your mother.'

Then, looking him straight in the eye, she said in a quiet voice, 'Shame on you.' He was stung and wanted to answer back when the order was given to load the wagons. The officer in charge of his unit called him away before he had time to ask her for her name.

He lost sight of the old woman in the chaos as people were herded towards the train by guards beating them with rifle butts and whips. The wagons, which were used for transporting cattle, had no windows and when Stefan was ordered to push a hundred people into each one, he didn't think they could possibly fit. Mothers were screaming that they'd been separated from their children, daughters were shouting to their frail parents, and husbands and wives tried to clutch onto each other. In that atmosphere of hellish desperation, Stefan broke out into a cold sweat and he pushed them in more forcefully than he'd meant to because he couldn't stand the shrieking and screaming. He hated them but most of all he hated himself for being so helpless.

His throat was as tightly sealed as those wagon doors when the guards slammed them shut and slid the bolts in.

In the white faces pressed against the tiny grille, Stefan saw that these people finally understood that their hopes had been illusions, and all was lost.

Twenty-Two

As soon as night fell, Elżunia crept around the dark streets, jumping each time shutters rattled in the wind. She was pinning sheets of paper to the lamp-posts. She stood back and surveyed them with pride. The notices she was distributing, which were printed on primitive hand-presses in the stinging light of carbide lamps, warned people not to trust German promises of resettlement, and not to go to the Umschlagplatz.

Whenever trucks rolled past their building, she and Lusia blanched, wondering whether this time the trucks had come for them. The ferocity of the Germans to fill the quota of those destined for resettlement had intensified to such an extent that having the right documents no longer guaranteed immunity and even children were being snatched to make up the numbers. Only the day before, Elżunia had seen a young woman standing in the street, tearing out clumps of her hair and howling like an animal because, while she was out, they had taken her little girl away.

The thought of Gittel being snatched like that terrified them. 'If anyone bangs on the door, run and hide under the bed and be as quiet as a mouse. Stay there until you can't hear a single sound,' they told her over and over again.

Gittel understood. She looked at them with her big b
eyes and nodded. 'So the bad men don't find me,' she sa
Then she frowned. 'But where will you hide?'

Elżunia had just come home after pasting all her notices
on the lamp-posts when there was a soft knock on the door.
Four short knocks and two long ones. Edek's signal.

'You'll never believe what happened,' he said. 'Czerniakow
has committed suicide!'

Elżunia's hand flew to her mouth as Edek told them
that the President of the Judenrat had been found slumped
at his desk and there was a faint odour of almonds in the
office. Apparently he had left a note but what was on it
Edek hadn't been able to find out. Elżunia wondered what
Czerniakow knew that had made him swallow the cyanide.
He had compared himself to the captain of the *Titanic* and
she suspected that the ship was about to sink. But whatever
happened, she no longer felt powerless because she had
joined the youth resistance group in the Ghetto.

Several days after the deportations had begun, the young
man with the large ears had sought her out. 'The time has
come,' he'd said. 'Will you join us?'

She couldn't wait.

The summer rains had begun to fall and the sky was as
grey as fate the day that Elżunia and Edek attended their
first meeting to be inducted into the Ghetto resistance.
Elżunia was looking around the hall expectantly when Edek
whispered, 'There must be two or three hundred in here,
every youth group in the Ghetto, and they're prepared to
work together. Things are really happening.'

Just then, a young man with a shock of wavy hair falling
over his forehead and a moustache that needed trimming
rose to speak and Elżunia craned forward for a better view.

'We have to forget our political and religious differences,'
he said and from his tone she knew that he was accustomed

ng attention. 'Some of us are Bundists and
nists, some are from Dror and some from
air, some are Chassids and others are atheists,
e vital thing in common that binds us more
ur differences divide us. We're all determined
to resist and that's the only thing that matters right now.
We have to join together, form a non-political group, and
pool our resources.'

'That's Itzak,' Edek whispered. 'He's one of the leaders.
And see that guy out in front? They reckon he's going to be
the commander.' Elżunia followed his gaze and saw a short
fellow with thick dark hair and heavy eyebrows who looked
more like a student than a military leader.

'Him?' she asked, dismayed. 'But he's so small and
young.'

'So was Napoleon,' Edek retorted.

'We've been waiting for the older people to take the
initiative but there's no point waiting any longer,' Itzak was
saying. 'They're too frightened, so we have to take action
ourselves.'

He was greeted with cheers and applause.

'About time,' voices called out in unison.

Elżunia looked around at the gathering. The air in the
crowded room vibrated with intensity and excitement. They
were pioneers about to embark on a journey into uncharted
territory. They had no money, no weapons and no chance of
success, but the prospect of banding together to take action
against their oppressors was exhilarating. They would take
control of their destiny, whatever the cost. A girl with a
mass of curly hair standing beside Itzak was watching him
with obvious admiration. Pointing to her, Edek said, 'That's
Rahela. She's eighteen. They got married two weeks ago.'

Elżunia looked at Rahela and sighed. How romantic to
defy danger and live together, and, if necessary, die together.

Her mind slipped into her fantasy about the Polish airman whose moody face often invaded her waking dreams. Time had intensified her feelings and endowed him with more heroic qualities. Daydreaming about him lifted her from her surroundings and her terror, and enabled her to envisage a future. She saw herself fighting by his side and earning his admiration —

Edek disturbed her reverie by nudging her. 'You look as if you're in a trance. Why is it that you girls can't concentrate on anything for long?' he hissed. 'They've just asked for a show of hands.'

By the time the meeting ended, they had agreed to form the Organisation of Jewish Fighters. The name alone gave them confidence. They were part of an army now, activists not victims. The revelation that their arsenal consisted of one pistol didn't discourage anyone. That they had no funds, no weapons and no safe way of smuggling arms into the Ghetto were no longer insuperable problems but challenges to be solved. Caught up in the general euphoria, Elżunia's eyes shone. Now she would have her chance to fight back.

Ever since the deportations had begun, Stefan had kept away from home, and on the rare occasions he appeared, he said very little. He felt sickened by what he saw every day and disgusted with his own weakness at not resigning from the service, but he couldn't bring himself to talk about it. He still tried to comfort himself with the thought that his position would protect his family but, as the days passed, he doubted his ability to do this more and more.

He had become less communicative than ever, so Elżunia and Lusia were surprised when he dropped in one evening and told them to listen carefully to what he said.

'Since those notices have been plastered all over the streets telling people to ignore the order for resettlement, the Germans have got tougher. From now on, having the right documents or being related to someone in the Jewish police force won't protect anyone, so you'll have to watch out or you'll be caught,' he said. As he spoke, he realised the futility of his warning. He wished he could say or do something that would help them but knew that in the end there was nothing he could do to even save himself.

He turned to his mother. 'Get a job at one of the German workshops. They're not likely to deport people making uniforms for their soldiers.'

Elżunia was drawing cats for Gittel on the back of one of the subversive notices and slipped it under an exercise book when Stefan looked in her direction. 'And you,' he said, 'you'd better spend as much time at the hospital as you can.'

Lusia's eyes flashed. 'They're hunting people down like wild beasts. Do you really think they're going to respect workshops and hospitals?'

Something in his mother's sharp tone jogged Stefan's memory. Rifling in the pocket of his jacket, he held out the trinket he'd been given.

'I forgot to give you this. It's from an old woman I met a couple of weeks ago. She said it was for you.'

Lusia's hand trembled and the colour drained from her face as she recognised the small sapphire ring she had admired as a child.

'It'll come in handy,' said Stefan who didn't notice the look on his mother's face. 'Everyone's running around in a panic trying to get work in a German factory. You might be able to bribe a factory manager with this and get a job.'

Lusia didn't appear to have heard him. 'What did she look like?'

He shrugged. 'She was old. Grey hair, wrinkled face, that sort of thing.'

'Did she say anything else?' she asked in a voice that was almost inaudible.

'Not that I can remember.'

Clutching the ring, she reached out and clasped his hand. 'Stefan, I have to know. You have to tell me. How did she come to give it to you? Where did you meet her? Where is she now?'

His mother's face was white. Stefan hadn't expected such an emotional reaction, but, thinking back, he remembered that there was something familiar about the old woman's expression. Now he knew why. He didn't know what to say. He couldn't bear to describe the scene in the Umschlagplatz or the one at the cattle train.

His mother was tugging his arm. 'You have to tell me. Where can I find her?'

Stefan swallowed. 'When I saw her, she was in one of those trains heading east.'

Elżunia saw her mother sink into a chair and bury her face in her hands. 'What is it, Mama?' she asked, alarmed. 'Who was that woman?'

Lusia looked up but didn't reply. She had the fixed stare of someone who had seen a phantom materialise in an empty room. The ring was a dying fire that consumed painful memories, leaving nothing but ashes. Without realising it, in one corner of her mind she had clung to the hope that one day she and her parents would be reconciled, but it was too late now and they would never be reunited.

Elżunia saw Stefan looking at their mother with a mixture of compassion and shame, and in that moment she understood who that woman was and why her brother was so uncomfortable. From the upstairs window of the hospital she could see the Umschlagplatz, and was sickened by what she saw. The fact that her own brother was involved added to the disgust and horror she felt whenever she happened to look down.

She looked anxiously at her mother, who was still sitting in frozen silence. So that woman had been her grandmother. Elżunia had never heard her mother speak about her parents, and now she felt a sense of loss that she had never known her maternal grandparents.

With a deep sigh, Lusia passed the ring to Elżunia and clasped her daughter's hand. 'I want you to have it,' she said. 'I hope it brings you luck.'

It was still warm from her mother's touch, and, as it brushed against her skin, Elżunia sensed that it had forged a closer bond between them. She shook her head. 'Stefan's right. You should use it to get work in one of the German factories.'

Lusia nodded dully. While she was staring out of the window, lost in her thoughts, Elżunia walked with her brother towards the door.

'I don't understand why you're still with them,' she whispered. 'It's disgraceful. Why don't you quit?'

They often argued about his role as a policeman, but this time she had an additional reason for drawing him aside. 'Do you realise that the OJF regards the Jewish police as collaborators?'

'Am I supposed to be scared of a mob of kids playing at being heroes?' he scoffed.

She was about to make a stinging retort but something in his expression silenced her. 'Stefan,' she said quietly, 'I'm worried for you.'

He nodded, gave her arm a hasty pat, and walked out the door.

After Stefan left, Elżunia hurried to an urgent meeting called by the Organisation of Jewish Fighters, or OJF as they now called themselves. 'This is Maks,' Itzak said, introducing the speaker. 'He has a very important story to tell.'

'I'm a messenger from hell,' Maks began in a voice that shook so much that his large shaven head wobbled on his thin neck.

Edek and Elżunia looked at each other, not sure how to take his dramatic words.

'I've come back to let you know what's awaiting you at the end of the train journey, so you can stop deluding yourselves,' Maks said. 'If you find it hard to believe, all I can tell you is that I can hardly believe it myself. And I was there.'

For the next hour they listened, mesmerised and incredulous. As he spoke, they heard the wagon doors clanging shut, and felt the searing heat in the cattle truck where people were jammed in so tightly that there was no room to move. They felt the panic as people became hysterical, screamed, wept and fainted. They saw the young father who kept his arm over his small son to protect him from being suffocated by the crowd pressing in on them, but who was unable to keep his arm up any more, passed out and fell forward, suffocating the child with his own body.

Elżunia swallowed. Like a man possessed, Maks described a place called Treblinka with its savage dogs, whip-wielding guards and the smell of death blowing from chimneys that spewed black smoke day and night.

A shudder ran through the silent room. So this was the resettlement they'd been promised. Their eyes were glued to his bony face as they struggled to comprehend the machinery of death he was describing. It was inconceivable that in Europe in 1942 a civilised nation was murdering thousands of innocent people every day with such systematic, cold-blooded efficiency.

Maks had been fortunate. Instead of being sent to the gas chambers as soon as he arrived, he'd been selected to sort the belongings of the doomed, but he soon realised that his reprieve would be short-lived, and hid under a mountain of clothes being sent by train to Germany. 'The last sorter who tried to escape got caught and ripped to pieces by the dogs,' he said, 'but I had nothing to lose. If I stayed, they would have killed me anyway. I could have run away when the train got to Warsaw and tried my luck on the Aryan side of town, but I was convinced that my life had been spared so I could come back to the Ghetto and warn you.'

Exhausted by recounting his ordeal, he sank into a chair, mopping his face. No one wanted to break the long silence that followed. They didn't want to believe him but knew he told the truth. Their ultimate destination was resettlement in the other world.

Itzak rose and faced them. 'Czerniakow must have found out the truth. We have to warn everyone and resist however we can,' he said slowly. 'Somehow we have to get hold of weapons and ammunition. I'll make contact with the Polish Underground. Perhaps they'll help us.'

A week later, Edek smuggled in a copy of the *Information Bulletin*, an Underground newsletter published by the AK.

'Have a look at this,' he told Elżunia. 'It's an open letter addressed to the Ghetto. It says, *Fight them, whatever the cost. Resist the police. Don't wait for them to kill you. Each of your homes should become a fortress.*'

While Elżunia enthused about the article, Edek said, 'That's all very well, but fine words won't fire any bullets. Talk is cheap. I want to see guns and grenades but I can't see the Poles helping us.'

'But listen to this,' she said and read on in an excited voice. '*Whoever remains silent in the face of murder is an accessory.*

The duty of Poles is to help the persecuted Jews. Every day, six or seven thousand Jews are deported to the east. What their fate is, no one knows but it's obvious that the Ghetto is being liquidated. Only scoundrels or fools don't realise that after the Jews it will be our turn to be deported east. Poles must help Jews to resist the hideous plans of our mutual torturers.'

She turned to Edek. 'Whoever wrote that article really understands what's going on and wants to help us,' she said. 'If the AK did supply us with weapons, and the people outside the Ghetto joined us, we'd have a hope of defeating the Germans, wouldn't we?'

Her eyes were shining with hope and he didn't have the heart to tell her that what he had heard gave little ground for optimism.

Twenty-Three

On a sunny August afternoon in 1942, while the deportations were still taking place, Elżunia happened to look out of an upstairs window of the hospital. Down in the Umschlagplatz, a bald man with a neatly trimmed brown beard and round glasses was walking at the head of a long column of children. *No!* she wanted to cry out. *Not him! Not them!* Dr Korczak was walking at the head of his charges, a tall, stately figure, ramrod straight, not looking right or left as he strode ahead, holding two children by the hand. Behind him, accompanied by the orphanage staff, came the rest of the children, some clutching their rag dolls or teddy bears, others waving paper pennants that fluttered in the light summer breeze. One of the older boys held aloft the green flag that Dr Korczak had designed for the orphanage.

The square was already crowded but, as soon as the line of children approached, people moved aside to make room for them to pass. Sitting back in his rickshaw, surveying the scene, was the commander of the Umschlagplatz, who, like a Roman emperor, could spare a man's life or sentence him to die by one casual gesture of his thumb. At a signal from him, the guards surrounded Dr Korczak and the children.

A moment later, one of the Jewish policemen ran up to the doctor and, from the urgent way he was gesticulating towards the man in charge of the deportations, it looked as though he was pleading with the doctor. Dr Korczak listened but his calm demeanour didn't change. He pointed to the children and shook his head. From the gestures and expressions, Elżunia sensed that the doctor had been offered a chance to save himself, but had refused to abandon his orphans.

The matron called her but she couldn't move from the window. It was as though her shoes had been nailed to the floor. She couldn't bear to look at the scene below but she couldn't tear herself away. Surely they wouldn't kill the famous children's author and educationist. Surely not even the Germans would pack two hundred children into wagons and murder them in gas chambers. Surely any moment someone would realise the mistake and turn them back.

Dr Korczak's glasses glinted in the sunlight as he turned to the children and together with his assistant arranged them in rows of four. When they were all lined up, they made their way across the Umschlagplatz towards the train. Ignoring the cordon of guards on either side, the old doctor seemed to be chatting to his charges as though they were on an excursion. The sound of the children's voices floated up to Elżunia and she could hear them mimicking the rhythm of a locomotive as they chanted a poem about a train.

Silence fell over the square. In the weeks since the deportations had begun, over 100,000 people had been deported amid screams, panic and chaos, but there had never been a scene like this.

Elżunia's throat swelled and she couldn't swallow. She watched the children walking confidently with their protector, as though on their way to a picnic. She didn't doubt that he would continue to reassure them throughout the journey, until the very last moments, after the door of the gas chamber slammed shut behind them.

She was still trembling when she went back to the patients. What was happening here was beyond words, beyond tears, beyond human comprehension. No one who hadn't witnessed it could possibly believe it. If only she had a pistol or a grenade to blow up those barbarians. How long before the Polish Underground supplied them with weapons? And where was the rest of the world? Surely they knew what was going on. Why was no one doing anything to stop this slaughter? Where was the League of Nations with all the lofty ideals that she'd learned about in school? Didn't anyone care?

Usually she was able to bring a smile to some of the sad faces in the children's ward but this morning's ward round only deepened her depression. She saw death hovering above the beds. She looked at the swollen, deformed bodies of the malnourished children staring at her with huge solemn eyes in their old faces, and wondered what was the point of trying to keep them alive.

Dr Maryla Sztejn, who was in charge of the hospital, noticed her downcast expression and took her aside. With her frizzy grey hair and a face that was a network of intersecting lines, Dr Sztejn looked like a typical grandmother but her purposeful gait and decisive manner belied her years and inspired her staff.

'One day you'll look back and realise that we practised superhuman medicine here, and you'll feel proud of what you did,' she said.

'I can't see the point any more,' Elżunia said.

The doctor put her arms around Elżunia's shoulders. 'As long as we live, our job is to fight for these children and make their lives as comfortable as possible. That's all we can do. The rest is not up to us.' She sighed. 'Sometimes I have to force myself to keep going. You have to do the same.'

As the day dragged on, the image of Dr Korczak and the children tore at Elżunia's mind. She had to do something, anything, even if it meant saving only one person.

Nurses in their white caps and aprons were usually able to walk across the Umschlagplatz at the end of the day undisturbed by the guards. Perhaps she would be able to take advantage of her uniform in some way.

That evening, when her shift had ended, Elżunia stole into the linen press, pulled out an apron and smuggled it out under her cape. Down in the Umschlagplatz, she glanced around. She spotted a young woman sitting on a knapsack some distance from the guards, walked over to her and held her wrist as though checking her pulse. 'Quick, put this on before they see what we're doing,' she whispered to the startled woman as she whipped out the apron. Her heartbeat was roaring in her ears. If a guard saw what she was doing, they'd both be shot.

'Leave your things here and walk beside me as though we've just finished our shift,' she said as soon as the apron was fastened, and she linked arms with the woman so they looked like two nurses strolling home after a day's work.

Emboldened by her success, Elżunia repeated the deception at the end of each shift. Although she was aware that the reprieve might only be temporary, plucking individuals from under the noses of the guards raised her spirits. She couldn't fight the enemy with weapons, but at least she'd found a way of defying them.

Occasionally she managed to persuade the drivers of the ambulances and funeral carts to pick up some of the old people and speed away with them, but the German guards had woken up to that ploy and were now inspecting every vehicle to check that the occupants were either dead or gravely ill. There was only one way of providing old people with proof of their injury. In a small room behind the square, without an anaesthetic, some of the nurses broke their bones in the hope of saving their lives.

Summer was over but the heat persisted, sapping people's energy and resilience. And still the deportations continued. Day after day, wagons left the Umschlagplatz crammed with people, and returned empty. The ghosts of the Ghetto outnumbered the living. The hunters had grown even more rapacious in their search for prey and people stayed indoors as much as possible to avoid being caught.

Every morning, while the sky was streaked with dawn light, Lusia hurried to Toebbens' workshop. Observant passersby would have noticed something bulging under her coat. It was Gittel whom she smuggled into the factory every day and hid in a cupboard under a pile of the uniforms they were making for the German army. Little as she was, Gittel understood that she had to be as quiet as a mouse all day but she jumped joyfully into Lusia's arms when it was time to go home.

Elżunia never looked down at the Umschlagplatz from the windows of the hospital without holding her breath in case she saw her mother and Gittel among the people being herded towards the wagons. *Don't let them be there, don't let them be there*, she would mutter to herself each time she scanned the square. She started counting in her head. If she didn't spot them by the time she reached ten, they wouldn't be there. Stefan could no longer protect them. Jewish policemen were despised by the Ghetto population, held in contempt by the Germans, and regarded as collaborators by the OJF, who had already shot one of the highest ranking officers and ambushed several others.

Lusia had been right in suspecting that the Germans wouldn't spare the hospitals. Elżunia was spooning watery semolina porridge into the mouths of the babies in her ward one morning when a crash downstairs made her jump and drop the enamel bowl, spilling the precious food.

Something was being smashed, glass shattered and Elżunia could hear bloodcurdling screams. Before she could gather her thoughts, boots stomped up the stairs as a unit of SS men stormed into the adult wards like maddened beasts, rifles in hand. *Jesus Maria*, she thought. There was no way of hiding the infants. She closed the door and murmured a prayer to the Virgin Mary. At times like these, she instinctively reverted to the faith of her childhood. But she had no time to think because her ears were ringing with salvos of gunshots and shrieks that pierced her eardrums. These sounds were followed by dull thuds as patients with bandaged heads, legs in plaster and intravenous drips still attached to their veins were pushed and kicked down the stairs, towards the covered trucks lined up outside. 'Doctor! Sister! Help!' they shouted. Watching through a crack in the door, Elżunia pressed her hands against her mouth to stop herself from crying out.

As soon as the trucks roared away, the nurses and doctors rushed upstairs over the bodies banked up in the stairwell and the corridor. The patients who couldn't walk had been shot as they tried to crawl towards the door.

The following day, Dr Sztejn called all the nurses and doctors together. Her face was almost as grey as her hair and they braced themselves for bad news.

'They're coming back today,' she said. 'I've been given a hundred numbers to distribute among the staff.'

No one moved or spoke.

'Anyone without a number will be deported,' she said and her voice cracked with emotion.

Elżunia's mind was a jumble of panic and dread. So they were holding a macabre lottery in which the prize was life. Until the next time.

There were almost three hundred nurses and doctors at the hospital. What if she didn't get a number? Suddenly she didn't care who missed out, who was taken away, if only she could go on living. The emotion was so powerful that she swayed and someone brought her a chair, thinking she felt faint. She sank into it, and kept her head down for fear that her thoughts were written on her face.

'The Germans are very clever at making us collude in our own destruction,' she could hear Dr Sztejn saying. 'Needless to say, I won't be participating in their ghoulish selection.'

The iron ring around Elżunia's chest loosened and was replaced by a sense of shame. Everyone was talking at once. Some admired Dr Sztejn's resolute stand but others argued that if she refused to follow the order they would all be killed.

The doctor nodded. 'That's quite possible. But following their orders means sentencing some of you to death and that I'm not prepared to do.'

In the end, they decided to draw lots. One by one, with bated breath, they came out to choose the slip of paper that would signify life or death.

Some closed their eyes as they plucked their ultimate destiny from bits of paper fanned out on the table, while others hesitated, their hands hovering in the air as though hoping to divine the contents by supernatural means. Elżunia took a deep breath. Please, please let it be a yes, she prayed as she reached out for the paper that would decide her fate. Slowly she opened it and breathed out. The Blessed Virgin hadn't abandoned her.

As she stood there, coming to terms with her reprieve, Madame Ramona's words floated into her mind. Three lives. She had just received a new lease of life. She felt a rush of exhilaration but almost immediately felt guilty because, all around her, distraught doctors and nurses were staring in stunned silence or weeping, while the lucky ones held their doomed colleagues and cried with them.

Later in the day, Dr Sztejn took Elżunia aside. 'You work in the paediatric ward, so the children know you,' she said. 'Come with me. I need your help.' Elżunia was astonished at the doctor's businesslike manner and the speed with which she had regained her equilibrium. She was even more amazed when Dr Sztejn told her to put fresh sheets on the children's beds, sponge them down, and dress them in clean clothes. It was a strange request to make in the afternoon but she didn't question it. Sensing the sombre atmosphere in the hospital, many of the children were fretful. Some of the toddlers clung to her while she dressed them, while others asked what she was doing. She wondered about that herself.

When the children were ready, Dr Sztejn came in. Elżunia noticed that her usually rapid gait was slow, as though she were dragging herself uphill. 'We don't have much time. They're coming for the children any minute,' she said and her face was the colour of ashes. Elżunia looked down and saw that the doctor was holding glass phials.

'I'm not going to allow them to come in here, and shoot the little ones or toss them into trucks like garbage,' Dr Sztejn was saying. 'The least we can do for them is give them a dignified, peaceful death.'

Elżunia was staring at her. She must have misunderstood. Or had the doctor become unhinged by the day's events? Surely she wasn't planning to kill the children. Then the alternative flashed before her mind. Terrified toddlers being shot in their beds or thrown into trucks with no one to comfort them, pushed into wagons without food or water, and then ... she didn't need to think any more.

She leaned over their cots as she had done so many times before, and told them in a trembling voice that she was about to give them some magic medicine that would make them well again. As they opened their mouths, she and Dr Stejn poured a teaspoon of morphine for each one in turn.

As they waited until all the children had closed their eyes, Elżunia hummed the lullaby that she had heard Gittel and her mother sing in Yiddish to the tiny angels in white, asleep in their little beds.

Twenty-Four

The first winds of winter had begun to blow early through the Ghetto. It had become a ghost town. Spectral figures inched along silent footpaths in empty streets where loose shutters rattled in deserted rooms. Gone was the hubbub and febrile activity that had filled these streets, gone were the hawkers and traders rushing around trying to sell their wares, the desperate people begging for a pass, permit or certificate that would entitle them to get work and food. Apart from the starving and homeless, few people ventured outside.

On her way to the youth group, Elżunia looked up. As in the surreal landscape of a dream, white particles were floating in the air, buoyed by the October wind. Soft and weightless, they fluttered to the ground as soundlessly as snow. Some landed on her head and, as she brushed them off, some stuck to her hand. Feathers from slashed pillows and eiderdowns were falling from the windows of tenants whose heads would never rest on them again. Shreds of bed linen, carefully monogrammed and lovingly embroidered, had been pulled from beds, trunks and valises, and ripped by frenzied hands in their search for Jewish gold.

Transfixed by the strange vision, Elżunia stood watching, as though the falling feathers were a revelation that might illuminate the recent events. Looking around to make sure that no guards or policemen were prowling around, Elżunia moved stealthily from doorway to doorway. The hunt for survivors continued with increased ferocity and the Germans now ordered the Jewish policemen to bring five people to the Umschlagplatz every day or they and their families would have to make up the numbers.

As Elżunia crept along the pavement speckled with the feathers and shreds of bed linen, she thought about Stefan's visit the night before. He was no longer in uniform. 'I've quit,' he'd said in a hollow voice and covered his face with his hands. 'I never thought I'd end up doing some of the things I did. I thought I'd just be helping to keep order, like they said, but somehow one thing led to another. I couldn't even protect you and Mama.' He was shaking his head and sobbing in loud, harsh gulps.

She had knelt beside him. 'I'm glad you resigned,' she said. She wanted to say he should have done it long ago but kept her thoughts to herself. She had her own demons to deal with. The vision of the babies so still in their cots haunted her.

As she walked on, shots rang out and she flattened herself against a wall. The purring sound of a motor drew nearer and she held her breath. Any second now the driver would see her. But the handsome young SS officer, leaning out of the window in the back seat of his Opel, wasn't looking in her direction. His pistol was tilted upwards and he was shooting casually into the windows of the buildings across the road. He laughed each time glass shattered onto the pavement but the driver swore when a shard struck the roof.

The SS man signalled the driver to reverse. Following his gaze, Elżunia saw a small figure in the doorway of a building on the other side of the street. A little boy had run downstairs to pick up a toy that had fallen from the window. The SS man took aim. Suddenly, Elżunia heard herself yelling, 'Halt! Don't shoot!'

Startled, the officer slowly turned around with a look of such loathing on his perfectly proportioned face that she trembled, but something stronger than fear had taken hold of her.

'Did your *Mutti* teach you to kill children? When you go home, will you tell her what you did?'

His finger was still on the trigger.

'And what about God? Your belt says *Gott mitt uns*. Do you think God will reward you for murdering babies?'

From the corner of her eye she saw that the boy had crept inside. Now it was just her and the officer.

She closed her eyes and felt a strange calm filling her veins. So this was how her life ended. Let him get it over with.

An eternity passed. She opened her eyes, expecting to see the pistol trained on her. But the officer was looking past her, as though she didn't exist and he hadn't heard what she'd said. He clicked his fingers and ordered the driver to move on.

Elżunia's knees buckled and she sank to the ground, resting her head against the wall. She had just confronted a murderer with a loaded pistol in his hand and had made an appeal to his humanity while he was shooting people for fun. Her legs were so weak that, when she tried to scramble to her feet, she felt like a rag doll. She was on her way to her youth group, to help them dig and shovel dirt to hollow out a bunker, but she wondered whether she'd manage to hold the spade in her trembling hands.

Every evening, since the deportations had begun, the guards left the Ghetto at sundown, afraid of its accusing ghosts, dark shadows and avenging angels. That was the time the Ghetto came to life, when it resounded with banging, hammering, gouging and digging. Young insurgents working in teams were feverishly building a network of bunkers, passages and tunnels, subterranean dwellings that would link apartment blocks through the cellars so that eventually they wouldn't have to use the streets. They had all thrown themselves into the work, relieved to have a physical outlet for their grief and fury. While they bided their time to rise up and fight their oppressors, the leaders of the OJF were planning ways of obtaining cash for buying weapons. There were whispers of daring raids in which some of the wheelers and dealers had been ambushed and taken hostage until they handed over large sums of money.

Down in the cellar, her colleagues stared in disbelief as she described her miraculous escape.

'Hashem was watching over you,' Beruś told Elżunia. He wore a skullcap and frequently prayed to the Almighty.

'So why wasn't Hashem watching over my little brother and all the others?' retorted Genia, flicking a strand of strawberry-blonde hair from her freckled face.

Beruś had a soulful expression in his pale blue eyes. 'Rabbi Szapiro told us that Hashem himself is suffering and weeping in secret in an innermost chamber of heaven,' he explained.

No wonder, Elżunia thought. Anyone claiming credit for creating a world like this should hide in shame and weep.

Beruś turned to Elżunia, 'You saved that little boy's life.'

'That was pretty irresponsible. You could have got yourself killed,' Genia was flushed and the freckles became more noticeable. 'Your life is too valuable to throw away,' she said. 'You know the Uprising can't be far off now. We need you to help fight them.'

Elżunia felt the blood rushing to her face. 'So are we putting a relative value on lives now? If mine is more important than that child's, whose life is more important than mine? Yours?'

The others were becoming restless. 'This isn't getting us anywhere,' someone interjected. 'Let's just get on and dig this passage.'

They had just picked up their picks and spades when the door opened. It was Szmuel, the young man who had inducted Elżunia into the resistance.

His eyes swept around their faces until he saw her. 'You're to go to Headquarters straight away. The OJF commander wants to talk to you.'

Outside the headquarters of the Organisation of Jewish Fighters, people were standing around or sitting on the stairs, waiting to see the leader. Each time his door opened, Elżunia started, expecting to be called, but messengers came and went, and still she sat there, awed and curious. What could the commander possibly want with her?

Finally she was ushered inside. The commander was short and youthful, as she remembered, but he exuded strength and confidence, and the air around him sparked with energy.

'An Underground courier will be coming into the Ghetto tomorrow. He's going to England to tell them about the situation in Warsaw, and he'll report on the Ghetto as well, so his mission is vitally important to us. We have to smuggle him in and give him a guide so he can see what's going on here.' He was studying her, weighing her up. 'Szmuel says you're keen and capable. Will you do it?'

Elżunia hardly slept that night, and, when she dropped off to sleep, her dreams were filled with terrifying images. She had slept in and missed the guy from the AK. The tunnel caved in on top of her and she was suffocating. The courier she brought in was a German in disguise who whipped out his pistol and shot the commander. After each dream she woke with a start and jumped out of bed, only to see that it was still night.

The guards hadn't yet come on duty when she ran across the quiet streets of the Ghetto to the building on Muranowska Street, as the leader had instructed. She stole down to the cellar. The tunnel through which she had to reach the Aryan side started from here, and she scrabbled under the sacks and boxes in the far corner until she struck something hard and uncovered the concealed door.

She prised it open and took a deep breath. It was dark and musty inside, and the beam of her flashlight disturbed blind, slimy creatures that crawled out of the dirt. Occasionally something scuttled over her feet and she suppressed a scream as she saw a long tail and small bright eyes. The tunnel was longer and narrower than she had visualised, and, as she crept along, showers of dirt fell on her head. The timber roof supports were sagging and she had to control a rising sense of panic. What if the soil collapsed and entombed her?

At the end of the tunnel, old furniture had been piled up to conceal the entrance on the Aryan side, and, after pushing it away, she blinked at the spear of light that dazzled her eyes. She climbed out, brushed herself down, and looked around. Standing on the corner of the street was a tall man in a shabby suit with a workman's cloth cap pulled low over his face. Surely that wasn't him, she thought, and again panic seized her. Perhaps her dream had been prophetic and she really had missed him.

But when he started whistling 'Lili Marlene', she breathed out again. As she walked past him, she whispered, 'Uncle Michał will be late today.'

Without looking up, the man gave a slight nod and buttoned his jacket, as arranged.

'We'd better hurry,' she said, looking around to make sure no one had seen them. 'The tunnel is pretty low, so you'll have to bend over most of the way.' He made a gesture indicating she should go, and followed her into the passage. Apart from an occasional expletive when he hit his head on the timber, he didn't speak.

Finally she came out of the darkness into the cellar and turned to her companion. As he took off his cap to shake out the dirt, she saw his face for the first time. Those heavy-lidded eyes with their bored expression, those gaunt cheeks, that sardonic twist of the mouth. It couldn't be; it wasn't possible. If the Virgin Mary had stepped off the pedestal and stood before her, she wouldn't have been more astonished. She was looking at the airman who had saved her life, the man she had dreamed about during her sleeping and waking hours for the past three years.

Twenty-Five

It was a week since Adam had been summoned to meet Zenon in a location so secret that it hadn't been revealed to him until he was taken there. As their meetings were rare, he had wondered whether this one was connected with that terrible business about Karolinka, his liaison woman. He was weary of Warsaw, sick of the secrecy, subterfuge and duplicity that didn't seem to achieve anything, and fed up with the misery all around. For the first time since he'd become an AK operative, he wished he could throw it all in and find some place where people still lived normal lives. But deep down he knew that what he was really tired of was not Warsaw or the Underground work but himself and his relentless pursuit of women, which always ended in disaster.

It hadn't been Karolinka's blonde prettiness or long slim legs that had attracted him as much as her breathless eagerness to do her bit for Poland. No risk was too great for her. Feeling invincible, she ran around the city from morning till night, carrying dangerous newsletters and documents tucked under the neatly folded laundry in her shopping bag.

Perhaps she had considered him part of the cause she was fighting for, because, although she was deeply religious and unswervingly moral, when he folded his arms around her and kissed her lips she didn't resist, not even when he licked the inside of her soft mouth. Whenever they made love, she seemed to melt into him, and unlike most women he knew, who used sex either as a prize or a weapon, she appeared to delight in it as much as he did. The fact that she didn't know his real name had never bothered her. Sometimes he wondered whether the mystery added to his appeal.

He knew it was unwise and unfair to become involved with liaison women. They had to stay clear-minded and uninvolved because they were the most exposed and least protected members of the Home Army. If they were caught with incriminating documents, they were savagely interrogated to betray the identity and addresses of those whose messages they delivered. The AK watched them all the time to ensure that they were contactable and reliable. They were never told the names of their superiors to ensure they couldn't betray them, but whenever they were caught, their associates immediately moved to new lodgings.

What happened wasn't altogether his fault, but he knew that if she hadn't spent that night with him she would have been more alert. She always left his room after a night of love-making in a daze of euphoria, like a naughty schoolgirl who has got away with a daring escapade. He was standing at the window that morning after she left. As she walked out of the gate, he was smiling at the memory of the lovely pliant body under the demurely buttoned coat when suddenly she tripped over a piece of broken paving and dropped the bag. He let out a string of curses because, before she could scramble to her feet and pick it up, a solicitous plainclothes policeman was at her side, helping her.

Adam could see that Karolinka was flustered and was insisting too nervously that she didn't need help. Expert at interpreting facial expressions and tones of voice, the

Gestapo officer didn't take his eyes off her face as he tipped the bag upside down. Adam dug his nails into his palms as the envelope fell out. He stepped back from the window and his jaw muscles jumped with tension. He hoped she wouldn't look up. She didn't. From behind the curtain, he saw her being pushed into the back seat of a car, which sped off in the direction of Szuch Avenue.

I'll have to find another room fast, Adam thought, dismayed at having to leave his comfortable room and helpful landlady to search for yet another safe place. A moment later he felt ashamed that his first thought had been for himself. In the days that followed, he thought up reasons why Karolinka hadn't been in touch, why he hadn't been able to contact her, and why no one had seen her.

Weeks later, an Underground courier took him aside. He'd met a woman who had recently come out of Szuch Avenue and had shared a cell with a liaison woman called Karolinka. She had told him that, although the Gestapo had interrogated Karolinka for days, she hadn't revealed Adam's address or anything about him. 'I hope he knows she was in love with him,' the woman had said. Adam listened with his head bowed. Women never ceased to surprise him. They were so different from men. He thanked the courier for passing on information about Karolinka but wished he hadn't described in such graphic detail what they'd done to her during the interrogation.

The new liaison woman was a skinny girl with protruding teeth and such a rapid stride that he had stifled the urge to ask whether she was training for the Olympics. The route she took to the meeting with Zenon, through side alleys, courtyards and squares, was so circuitous that he almost lost sight of her, and was fuming at this unnecessary waste of time and energy when she pushed open the heavy wooden gate of a convent and disappeared inside. He stood inside, breathing in the odour of floor wax and furniture polish, when an elderly nun inclined her head to indicate that he should follow. At the end of the corridor, she drew aside a heavy brocade curtain, which revealed a concealed door and then waddled away, her black habit swishing on the wooden floorboards.

As soon as Adam entered, he saw the reason for the secrecy. Sitting beside Zenon at the small oak table was the Commander-in-Chief of the Polish Underground. The Chief rarely left his headquarters, so it wasn't likely that he'd arranged this meeting to discuss the tragic fate of a liaison woman. It was an all-too-common occurrence, a regrettable byproduct of their struggle, but fortunately there was no shortage of women willing to risk their lives for Poland.

The Commander-in-Chief was a middle-aged man with greying hair, a severe expression and the peremptory manner of a military officer.

Without preliminaries, he informed Adam that he was to be sent to London on a top-secret assignment. At the prospect of leaving Warsaw, Adam felt as elated as a prisoner who has just been paroled. False papers had already been prepared for him to travel to England via Spain and Portugal. In London he was to meet with members of the Polish government-in-exile who were based at the Rubens Hotel, and report to them in detail about the activities and problems of the Underground. His stare boring into Adam's face, the Chief said he must impress on them that the Home Army needed cash, weapons and ammunition immediately.

He was also instructed to organise meetings with top English politicians, to brief them about German repression in Poland and the country's desperate need of aid in their lone struggle against Germany. 'Remind them of their obligation to their first ally in this war, and their promise to guarantee our sovereignty.' The Chief's eyes flashed with anger as he spoke. While in London, the Chief continued, he was also to inform as many people as possible about the Jewish tragedy taking place in Poland. 'Let them know that in Warsaw, at this very moment, the Germans are committing systematic murder of an entire race on a scale unprecedented in the history of the world.'

Adam smiled to himself. The Commander-in-Chief was quoting his own words from the AK's *Information Bulletin*, in which he had criticised not only the inhuman policy of the Nazis but also the callous and apathetic attitude of so many Catholics to the fate of their fellow Poles. But although he was outraged at the systematic slaughter of the Jews, it was an intellectual reaction, like the time he had penned indignant letters to stop the hunting of elephants without ever having seen one in its natural habitat.

'If I'm to report to the exiled government about the plight of the Jews in Warsaw, I'll need to get into the Ghetto and see it for myself,' he had told the Chief.

His announcement was received in silence. Zenon stroked his thick moustache. He seemed about to say something but cleared his throat instead.

The Chief studied Adam for a time before replying. 'I've been told it's very dangerous in there, especially with the deportations going on. They're likely to grab you and push you into one of those cattle wagons together with the Jews. I can't allow you to take such a risk.'

'But I put my life on the line every day in this work!' Adam retorted. Zenon's raised eyebrows and the Chief's cold expression calmed him down.

'I understand your concern, sir,' he continued in a calmer tone, 'but I have to see for myself what's going on in there.'

The Chief made a resigned gesture with his hand to indicate agreement.

Arrangements had then been made with the Jewish

Underground for Adam's visit and, as arranged, the guide led him through the tunnel that linked the Aryan side with the Ghetto. As he inched behind her, bent almost double in the dark, he bit the inside of his lip to control the feeling that the walls were closing in on him, and wondered whether insisting on being smuggled into the Ghetto had been such a good idea.

When he finally emerged from the tunnel into the cellar, trembling and covered in dirt, he shook out his cap and noticed that the guide was staring at him as though he were an apparition.

'Is something wrong?' he asked.

She was still staring.

Finally she found her voice. 'You're the airman who saved my life,' she whispered.

Now it was his turn to stare. The girl was either crazy or she had confused him with someone else. He was about to demur when she said, 'That day on the road from Warsaw. Just after the war started. You stopped to give my mother and me a lift. Then there was an air raid and the Stukas were bombing us and you ...' Her voice had become so hoarse it disappeared inside her throat. It had been the most overwhelming moment of her entire life.

'I remember those bloody Stukas,' he said slowly. 'I threw you into a ditch.'

So many times she'd replayed that scene in her mind, and each time her overheated imagination had added details that grew more daring and more salacious. And now to have him standing beside her in the flesh, to be able to see him, and hear him recalling the incident was too improbable to grasp. She knew she was staring like an idiot but couldn't stop. If only this moment would never end. But, at the same time, she fought a sense of disappointment. Ever since that encounter, she had dreamed of seeing him again, and now they were finally together. But she sensed that he hardly remembered her, and he seemed more distant than before. The conflicting emotions were so intense that she felt an impulse to flee to give herself time to absorb this meeting, but she couldn't bear to miss one second of his company.

He eyed her up and down and she blushed under his scrutiny. 'You were a little girl then,' he said. 'You're not a little girl any more.'

She pulled at her blouse self-consciously. 'I'm almost seventeen,' she said. Perhaps he would realise that the gap between them was narrowing. After all, Scarlett O'Hara had been sixteen when she and Rhett Butler had met.

She wanted to thank him for saving her life, to tell him that, ever since that moment, he had been her inspiration, and that the hope of seeing him again had made it possible to endure the past three years. She wanted to say that nothing had turned out the way she'd expected. She had become a nurse so that she could heal people, as Florence Nightingale had done, but instead she had ended up killing babies and watching as they exhaled their last soft breath. She wanted to tell him that all the ideals her father had instilled in her about nobility and courage had turned out to be illusions, and the saddest illusion of all was her father himself.

Her head was bursting with all the things she wanted to say, all the thoughts she'd saved up for this moment that she had been unable to articulate, confide or share with anyone before, but she continued to stand there, as tongue-tied as a peasant girl on her first visit to the manor house.

As he walked beside her through the Ghetto streets, every few moments his legs stopped moving and, when he tried to swallow, his throat closed up. He couldn't imagine that the sun ever shone on these grey streets that exuded an odour of death, damp and decay, and whose inhabitants moved like shadows. Their bodies, sacks filled with sharp bones, reminded him of a medieval drawing called *The Dance of Death* that had haunted him as a boy.

He looked at the tiny children, no bigger than fledglings dropped from their nest, propped up against the walls, their bellies swollen between their stick-like limbs, too weak to sing or even plead. Mothers with breasts like empty gloves stared into space as they tried to suckle their babies. Around the corner, he heard singing. Five children had joined hands and were dancing around in a circle chanting a ditty.

'They're playing,' he said hoarsely.

Elżunia nodded. 'They play until the end,' she said.

Looking sideways, she saw that his square jaw was moving in a strange way.

They walked on in silence, he staring at vignettes of hell, she staring at him. He was drowning in a nightmare while she was immersed in a dream, and neither could believe their eyes.

Something was lying on the pavement under sheets of newspaper and he bent down and saw that it was the naked body of a woman, her face stiff and waxen. A stone had been placed on top of the papers to stop them from blowing away. As he watched, a black funeral cart loaded with bodies pulled up. The undertakers jumped out, put the body on top and, as they bumped over the rough pavings, the heads of the dead banged on the wooden sides of the cart. He stood very still, and horror, pity and disgust mingled on his sallow face.

'Their families can't bury them, so they leave them on the street until the funeral cart takes them away,' Elżunia explained.

'But the newspapers ... she was naked ...'

'These people have nothing,' she began and then stopped, overwhelmed by a sense of helplessness. There was no way

229

to explain this. To him, having nothing probably meant not having money for a new shirt or a glass of vodka.

But he was still waiting for her to explain.

'They don't have any sheets to wrap the bodies in, so they use newspapers,' she said. 'As for the dead woman's clothes, they're no use to her any more, and the living can sell them and get something to eat.'

He shuddered. An irrational feeling had seized him that he'd stepped into an inferno far more hideous than the one Dante's imagination had been able to concoct. When he turned his head in her direction, Elżunia saw the revulsion on his twisted mouth, the disgust in his eyes. Suddenly she felt much older than her companion. The sights that shocked him no longer had the power to shock her. She held out her hand to touch his arm, to comfort him, to say how heroic and compassionate he was to visit this realm of the doomed, but drew back. He might think she was too familiar.

When they had chosen her to guide him around the Ghetto, she had been thrilled that at last someone from the other side of the wall cared enough to risk coming inside, to witness what was happening, and then transmit that information to the outside world. But his expression made her realise that would be impossible. If he couldn't believe his eyes or conceive that such misery and oppression were possible, how could anyone believe it who hadn't seen it for themselves?

She jumped as a staccato of pistol shots rang out. People were screaming, yelling, boots thudded on cobblestones and then there were more shots.

Adam flinched. 'What's that?'

'The German guards are amusing themselves around the corner,' she said bitterly. 'When they get bored, they shoot people. We'd better get off the street.'

They ducked into the doorway of the closest building and ran up the stairs. She was about to warn him not to go near the window on the landing, but it was too late. Grabbing his arm, she pulled him away. A moment later, a bullet flew through the pane where he'd been standing.

They sat on the floor for a long time without speaking, their faces white and frozen. He looked down and saw that her small hand was still gripping his sleeve. He raised it to his mouth and the blood rushed to her face as he pressed his warm lips on it.

His breaths were still coming in gasps. 'Good job you've got such quick reflexes,' he said. 'I don't know how you knew that bullet had my name on it. I think I should keep you as my lucky charm!'

'Perhaps you should,' she said lightly. Suddenly a thought struck her. 'Anyway now we're even!'

'You're a funny girl,' he said, and for the first time she saw a faint smile flickering in the corner of his mouth.

They were back in the cellar again and she had the sensation of sinking, drowning in soft black earth that subsided beneath her feet with every step. Her father used to say, 'Elżunia, if you see someone drowning, take their hand and pull them out.' Well, she was drowning now, but who was going to pull her out? For the past three years her hopes had fed on seeing him again, but this time their parting would be final and there was nothing more to hope for. He would walk out of her life, never knowing that she would have followed him to the ends of the earth if he had asked her.

Before stepping into the tunnel, he turned towards her.

'I'll never forget what you did, or what I saw here today.' He coughed and she realised that his voice was choked with emotion.

The haunted look returned to his face. 'I promise you that when I'm in London I'll tell them everything. They'll have to do something to stop this.'

She took something from her pocket and put it into his hand. 'I'd like you to have this,' she said.

Surprised, he looked down at a sleek silver cigarette case with the initials EO intertwined in acanthus leaves. 'It was my father's,' she said. 'But they're my initials as well.' She didn't dare say that she hoped it would remind him of her.

'That's very generous, but I can't accept it. You should keep it,' he said.

She shook her head. There wasn't enough time to tell him that she had kept it as a talisman, hoping it would bring her father back, but she no longer believed it would.

'I hope it brings you luck,' she whispered.

He was looking into her eyes with his unnerving stare. 'Elżunia, you need luck more than I do.'

She tried to smile. 'What I need is a miracle.' Anger she could no longer suppress welled up. 'Why doesn't the world help us? Doesn't anyone care?'

He didn't reply immediately. Then he said, 'Every country is fighting its own war, but it's up to individuals like you and me to create our own world.'

She sighed. 'That sounds very noble but sometimes I wonder what difference individuals can make.'

'They can save each other. Like us.' He was smiling now. 'And they can show others what's possible. Perhaps that way they can save the world.' He took her hand and held it between his own. 'I hope one day, when this is over, we'll meet again.'

He turned and stepped quickly into the tunnel that divided the living and the dead. Elżunia replaced the boxes and sacks to conceal the entrance to the tunnel and walked slowly back into the Ghetto.

Twenty-Six

It was snowing and large white flakes settled on the rooftops and fluttered to the ground, concealing the grey misery beneath. Standing at the window that faced Lech's room, Elżunia thought of the carefree winters of her childhood. When snow drifts settled onto the slopes in the park, her father would drag the shiny pinewood toboggan to the top and jump on behind her. After she'd given the magic word, they'd slide down, whooping with delight as the slushy snow sprayed around them. As usual, whenever she thought of her father, she uttered a quiet moan and closed her eyes to shut out memories that led nowhere and questions that had no answers.

Gittel had crept up beside her and was tracing patterns on the window with her finger as her breath steamed up the glass. She was bundled up in every scrap of clothing she possessed but kept jumping from one foot to the other to get warm. They had broken all the furniture they could spare for firewood, and Elżunia looked around desperately to see what else they could put into the tiled stove in the corner where her mother sat slumped in a chair.

Lusia looked up. 'I'm thinking of volunteering for the next transport.'

Elżunia stared at her mother. 'Have you gone mad? How can you even think of such a thing?'

'Everyone's been talking about it at the factory. Apparently Toebbens are going to open factories in other towns, and they need workers to move there. They're offering volunteers three kilos of bread and some jam. Why would they waste bread on people they were going to kill?'

Elżunia wanted to shake her. For the past few months she had been running around the Ghetto streets early in the morning, distributing leaflets that warned people not to believe these promises. And her own mother had been duped.

She tried to control her temper. 'Mama, this is just bait to get people to volunteer.' Her voice rose. 'After all that's happened, and all the things Stefan and I have told you, how come you still don't get it?'

Elżunia wished Stefan was there. Mama always took more notice of him than of her. But ever since he'd resigned from the police force, he had become morose, and spent most of his time with his pals who like him had also quit. But she had another reason for wishing her brother was there to back her up. She glanced nervously at her mother, wondering how to break the news.

Lusia looked down at her hands. 'It's all right for you young people; you still have some energy left, but I'm worn out with this constant tension. Will they come for me today or tomorrow; will this be the day they search the cupboard and find Gittel? I can't take it any more.'

Elżunia took a long look at her mother and softened her tone. 'Mama, don't let them fool you. Try to hold on a little longer.'

'Hold on? For what? For my husband to rescue me? For my so-called friends to help me? For the Germans to stop killing us? For the war to end? I've been holding on for nearly three years and it feels like three hundred. How much longer should I wait?'

'Just be patient,' Elżunia said. 'We're going to fight back.' She took a deep breath. 'I've been meaning to tell you. I'm going to move in with my group this evening.'

Her mother's eyes widened with shock. 'So you're moving out? You won't be living here with us any more? Why?'

'We're all going to stay in one bunker so we'll be ready when the commander gives the order for the Uprising to begin.'

Lusia made an irritated gesture. 'Don't talk nonsense. All this talk about commanders and uprisings. What are you going to fight with — slingshots? Even David only had to face one Goliath, not an entire army.'

'So this is your solution, is it? Presenting yourself at the Umschlagplatz to save them the trouble of coming to get you?'

Tears began to run down Lusia's thin cheeks. 'Please try to understand. I'm not strong like you. I've had enough.'

'And what about Gittel?' Elżunia shouted. 'Have you asked her if she's had enough? Don't you think she's entitled to live longer than five years? Do you want her to end up in a gas chamber?'

Hearing her name mentioned, Gittel ran over to Lusia and nestled in her lap. 'You shouldn't shout at Mama,' she said, stroking Lusia's face. 'See, you're making her cry.'

'Not everyone believes those stories about Treblinka,' Lusia argued. 'Why would the Germans kill off hundreds of thousands of people who can work for them? They need labourers and factory workers. It doesn't make sense.'

Elżunia took a deep breath. Something had become scrambled in her mother's head, or else she was deliberately blotting out reality. Either way, there was no point trying to convince her that logic had nothing to do with it. From the

Underground papers, Elżunia knew that a fierce battle was raging in a Russian city called Stalingrad and that it could prove the turning point of the war, but instead of focusing all their efforts on defeating the Russians, it seemed the Germans were still making the murder of Jews their priority.

'As soon as the Uprising begins, in case I don't have time to come and warn you, make sure you and Gittel go straight to the big bunker on Muranowska Street. You'll be safer there.'

Lusia's bewildered expression made her stomach churn. She had to find some way of stopping her mother from carrying out her suicidal plan.

There was only one person she could call on.

As soon as he saw the white handkerchief fluttering from a stick poking out from Elżunia's window, Lech dashed through the labyrinth of cellars, stairs and courtyards he'd discovered, which linked the Aryan side with the Ghetto. Perhaps she'd changed her mind after all and was going to come and stay with him.

She was already waiting, pulling her blue woollen cap more tightly around her face. The January frost was more severe than usual and an icy wind blew across the street, buffeting bits of paper and leaflets from the OJF into the air. Teeth chattering, Lech and Elżunia crept into a nearby cellar.

'I need to ask a big favour,' Elżunia began, and his heart pounded in his ears. 'I have to find a way of getting my mother out of the Ghetto before she does something crazy.' Now that she'd said it, the words shocked her with their bluntness. 'Could you ask around and see if you know anyone who'd let a room to your aunt from the country?'

'But what about the little girl?' he asked, playing for time.

'Edek said a group of Catholic women have been trying to smuggle Jewish children out of the Ghetto. One of them took his youngest brother, but taking boys is risky because it's too easy to prove they're Jewish. He's going to try and contact them and ask them to take Gittel.'

As they stood talking in the cellar, Elżunia shivered and pulled up the collar of her coat. She was looking at him with those navy-blue eyes. Ultramarine, that was the colour. Art had been the only subject he liked at school, and he remembered that strange name in his paintbox.

'When this is over,' he mumbled, 'will you be my girl?'

'Your girl?'

His scalp was on fire. Expressing emotions was like treading barefoot over razor blades. He swallowed. 'You know. Girlfriend. That sort of thing.'

'I've always thought of you as a good friend,' she said carefully. She didn't tell him that there was only one man on earth whose girl she wanted to be, and even on this freezing day, she could still feel the imprint of his warm lips on her hand.

'Well, friends can get married, can't they?' He passed his large hands through his tousled fair hair in frustration, and his usually cheerful face looked downcast.

She touched his sleeve. 'I'm sorry, Lech, I shouldn't have asked you about my mother. I'll have to figure out something else.'

He shuffled and looked down at his feet. If only he could help her. But he lived so close to the Ghetto that the minute he took a stranger in people would guess the truth. Claiming Lusia was his aunt wouldn't fool anyone. Still, everyone was hard-up these days; perhaps someone would be prepared to hide a Jew for money. He wondered if Elżunia and her mother had any cash or valuables. People reckoned that all the Jews had gold and silver stashed away under the floorboards. The trouble was, he couldn't even think of anyone to approach because these days you didn't know who to trust. You could end up with someone like Bolek, or himself, the way he used to be — he forced himself to admit this uncomfortable fact — someone who would take her money one day and turn her over to the Gestapo the next.

'I'll ask around and see what I can do,' he said. If he could convince her of his love, perhaps she'd agree to be his girl.

After he had gone, Elżunia rushed up the stairs and started searching the abandoned building, apartment by apartment, looking for bottles and light globes to make explosives for the Uprising. Since the last deportation, many buildings had become empty and as she opened each door she felt the hair on the back of her neck lift away from the skin. The ghosts of the departed residents seemed to hover in the air around her, watching her with accusing eyes. She forced herself to check every apartment, room by room, then fled, spooked by the sound of her own footsteps.

Clutching the bulbs she had found, she hurried to Nowolipie Street and ran up three flights of stairs without stopping. In contrast to the spectral silence in the rest of the building, it was a relief to enter the attic, which buzzed with activity. This was the OJF's munitions factory, and, as soon as she entered, the pungent smell of chemicals made her eyes water. In the far corner, two older girls were filling bottles with a mixture of kerosene, petrol and sulphuric acid. They were making incendiary anti-tank explosives. After carefully corking them, they took a strip of paper soaked in an explosive solution and glued it to the outside so that when the bottle was thrown and the glass shattered, the two substances would produce a violent explosion.

When they saw Elżunia placing her three bulbs on the table, their faces lit up.

'That's great,' said the girl with the mass of dark curls. It was Itzak's wife, Rahela. Only two days before, Rahela had earned their admiration by smuggling two Brownings and three pistols into the Ghetto. 'We've run out of bottles, but your bulbs will make three more explosives,' she said, giving Elżunia a hug.

Elżunia blushed with pleasure. Knowing that she was contributing to the coming fight energised her and the comradeship of the group gave her a sense of belonging. By now, most of them had lost their parents and grandparents, and they had become each other's family.

Working together for a common cause gave them strength. Resisting the Germans was all that mattered. Whether they lived or died no longer seemed important. They were living together in a bunker under an abandoned building, so that they'd be ready for action the moment the order was given.

By now the Ghetto was honeycombed with subterranean bunkers. Elżunia had heard that the largest ones, which could accommodate hundreds of civilians, had water and electricity connected. The fighters like Elżunia lived in groups of ten in small bunkers hollowed out in the cellars of abandoned buildings. Her bunker had benches around the sides, a few thin mattresses on the earth floor, and a dugout toilet, but the companionship made up for the discomfort. Every evening, they talked late into the night, dreaming and planning a glorious future that they hoped for but didn't dare to believe in.

By day they made weapons and attended training sessions to learn guerrilla tactics; by night they knocked out walls and dug passages to connect adjoining buildings through the cellars and attics, so that when the Uprising began they'd be able to contact each other without having to go outside. In the dead of night, when it was forbidden to move around the Ghetto, they blackened their faces and crept around the silent buildings, dismantling taps, unplugging telephones, and removing pipes and basins to install them in the larger underground bunkers.

'Who'd have thought we'd end up building a subterranean Ghetto!' Rahela joked. She kept up everyone's spirits, and it seemed to Elżunia that if Itzak was the brains of their movement, Rahela was its heart.

'I see us as the first link in a chain of freedom that might include the rest of Poland, perhaps even the rest of Europe,' Itzak had said during one of their discussion sessions. 'We're the descendants of the fighters of Masada,' he continued. 'They defied the Roman army and chose to die rather than be captured. But you have to realise that our path will lead to death. Like the heroes of Masada two thousand years ago, we won't live to see the effect of what we did, but history will never forgive us if we fail to make a stand. I think we all agree that if we do nothing we are lost. All we can do is save our souls and our honour. That way, at least people will respect our memory.'

His words vibrated inside Elżunia like violin strings playing a stirring melody. She saw their resistance as a musical composition being created note by note, and swelling towards its inevitable conclusion. She had never heard of Masada, but the story of the Jewish rebels fired her imagination. That was what Adam had meant when he spoke of the power of individuals. She, too, had made her choice. She didn't expect to survive, but surviving wasn't the most important thing. How you lived, and what you were prepared to die for — that's what mattered.

'It's odd, isn't it, that the old people, who've lived most of their lives, are so desperate to keep living at all costs, while us young ones, who've hardly lived at all, don't care about dying,' Edek mused.

He was sitting at the end of a small table, inserting thin aluminium pipes into tubes with his nimble fingers, and filling the space in between with nails, iron filings and explosives to make launchers. At fourteen, he was one of the youngest in the group but he had overcome the objections of the leaders to be allowed to join. 'When the Germans shoot at me, they won't stop to ask how old I am, so I reckon I'm as entitled to fight for our honour as the rest of you,' he had argued.

'It's not really strange,' said Cesia, taking off her glasses to wipe off the dust. 'The old people have got so attached to living that they can't imagine life going on without them. But we've pressed such faint footprints onto the earth, it's not so hard to tear ourselves away.' Cesia was a shy girl who wrote poems but rarely spoke, and, embarrassed by her speech, she looked down and continued making Molotov cocktails.

Jerzy looked up from the grenades he was making. His eyes looked troubled and his high forehead was creased by a frown. 'I feel terrible saying this, but since my parents have gone I feel freer. They were petrified of something happening to me and I was petrified of something happening to them.'

He returned to his work without saying another word, but the pensive silence that fell over the group indicated that his words had struck a common chord of guilt as they acknowledged the high price of their emotional liberation.

Every morning, news of the exploits of their leaders spread throughout the Ghetto and thrilled the young insurgents with their daring. One fighter had shot a collaborator, while another had shot a prominent member of the Jewish police force. The money they extorted from the entrepreneurs bought arms and ammunition from the Polish Underground. Most inspiring were the stories of heroic women like Rahela, who managed to smuggle weapons into the Ghetto under the noses of the guards. Elżunia envied their courage because, despite her brave words, she was terrified whenever she thought of what lay ahead. As she sewed her two precious grenades into her skirt, she knew that her mother had been right. David was about to confront an army of Goliaths.

Twenty-Seven

It was the Sunday before the Easter of 1943 and the hurdy-gurdy in Kraśinski Gardens ground out jolly tunes as laughing children rode on the carousel. On this pleasant April afternoon, the new buds that swelled on the trees were seen as a symbol of hope. Germany had been defeated in North Africa, the Wehrmacht's mighty 6th Army had been decimated at Stalingrad, and the Allies had finally landed in the south of Italy. Surely the end couldn't be far off.

But behind the gardens, on the other side of the wall, there was an atmosphere of taut alertness. Elżunia and her group were still in their bunker when Jerzy said, 'There's been a huge build-up of German and Ukrainian troops in Warsaw in the past two days. I reckon this is it. They're going to try and finish us off. But we'll spring a surprise on them when they come!'

'I just hope we don't die with any unused weapons in our hands,' Cesia said quietly.

Elżunia was tearing the skin around her thumbnail as usual, too tense to take part in their conversation. Edek hadn't been able to get Gittel out of the Ghetto, and Elżunia wanted to make sure that her mother and Gittel were safely inside their bunker. She was about to run over to their building when Itzak appeared at the entrance, his face taut and stern. 'I want you all in here,' he said. 'This is our last chance to run through everything so you know exactly what to do tomorrow.'

That evening, as the sun was setting, Elżunia looked fearfully at the crimson sky and in it she saw the blood that would soon be spilt and the fires that were about to blaze.

Later that night, Elżunia tossed from side to side, too churned up to sleep. She didn't realise she had finally dropped off until she heard an urgent voice in her ear.

'Quick. Time to go.'

It was still dark. She had slept fully dressed, and, slipping her two grenades inside the deep pockets of her skirt, she sprang up and ran with her group until they reached their post on the rooftop of the building overlooking the intersection of Miła and Zamenhof Streets. There was no sign of activity in the street below, but the scouts had spotted German and Polish policemen staking out the Ghetto wall, so it was clear the assault would soon begin.

'They want to destroy the Ghetto today to give Hitler a nice birthday present tomorrow,' Itzak said.

'It's Seder night this evening,' Rahela mused. She was patrolling the edge of the parapet, scanning the street below. With her unruly hair pulled into a thick plait, she looked like a schoolgirl. Turning to Elżunia with an encouraging smile, she said, 'Whatever happens today, we couldn't have chosen a better time to fight.'

Elżunia knew it was the eve of the Passover festival, which commemorated the liberation of the Jews from slavery in Egypt, but, as Itzak had explained the previous evening, the significance of the Passover transcended the specific event that took place thousands of years before. It symbolised the struggle for liberation from bondage through the ages.

'Our slavery will also end in liberation, even though, like the followers of Moses, we probably won't live to see our promised land,' he said.

Listening to him, Elżunia had felt inspired, but, as she stood shivering in the chilly pre-dawn air, his words brought no comfort. Her chest was so tight that her breaths came in uneven gasps and her thoughts jumped around in her head. Were Mama and Gittel down in the bunker? What would happen when the fighting started? Would they be safe down there?

As dawn broke and streaks of apricot and peach tinted the sky, small groups of Germans started slipping into the Ghetto. Elżunia's hands grew sweaty, her knees shook, and she was certain that the pounding of her heart could be heard on the other side of the wall. Standing beside her, Jerzy could hardly keep still. 'I can't wait for this to start,' he said. Elżunia wiped her moist hands on her cotton skirt and her fingers closed around the precious grenades in her pocket. Would she remember what she'd been taught, would she know when and how to throw them? They had so few weapons — what if she missed her targets and wasted them?

The hours crept by. How much longer would this agonising wait last? A low-pitched hum broke the silence and they turned in the direction of the sound. As it grew louder, they recognised the distant rumble of armoured vehicles and tanks. Elżunia shot an anxious glance at Itzak but his face showed no emotion. How could they possibly fight against tanks?

The convoy came to a halt, and they heard the brisk rhythmic thud of boots on the cobblestones. From their vantage points above the street, they watched the platoon of SS men marching in tight ranks with the arrogant stride of conquerors about to claim a swift victory.

Unseen and unsuspected, in attics and rooftops above the street, the fighters were watching the soldiers as their fingers itched to hurl their Molotov cocktails and grenades. Some of the fighters were as young as thirteen, but they all burned with the desire to avenge the deaths of their loved ones. For once, the arrival of these hated officers with the death's-head insignia on their caps struck no terror into their hearts. This time, they would unleash their own blitzkrieg.

As soon as the Germans had spread out along Miła and Zamenhof Streets, the resistance leaders gave the signal the fighters had all been waiting for.

Explosives sparked, flared and flashed, incendiary bottles shattered, burst and went up in flames, and gunfire stuttered from the rooftops. All along the street, SS men were falling, writhing, running, yelling and trying to see where the attack was coming from. Those who weren't wounded scattered in disarray, confused and shocked by the ambush. Some turned back in panic or tried to shelter in doorways, but they couldn't avoid the Molotov cocktails and grenades that rained down on them from all sides.

It was all happening faster than Elżunia could take it in. Mesmerised by the scenes that flashed before her eyes, she felt disoriented by the explosions, yells and shots, as she tried to grasp the fact that, for the first time, the blood spilt on the Ghetto streets belonged to the Germans, not the Jews. She hadn't thrown her grenades. The right moment hadn't come. She didn't want to consider the possibility that she'd become paralysed with fear.

A threatening roar rose from the far end of Zamenhof Street. 'They've brought in the tanks!' Edek shouted as they watched them roll into view.

He rushed forward and leaned over the edge of the parapet. 'This one's for my mother and little brother!' he cried as he hurled a Molotov cocktail. It struck the side of the first tank near the gunner's turret, exploded, and the tank burst into flames. Elżunia gripped one of her grenades, ready to throw it at the second tank when it advanced, but it stayed back to avoid the fate of the first. Ambulance sirens shrilled up and down the Ghetto streets to take away wounded German soldiers as the fighting raged in Muranowski Square and on the corner of Nalewki and Gęsia Streets.

By early afternoon, the sounds of battle had stopped and a wondrous calm had descended over the Ghetto. The Germans had retreated. For the first time, Jews could walk freely on these streets. It was a victory no one had dared to imagine. The fighters were incredulous.

Edek was jumping up and down. 'Did you see how I demolished that tank?'

Elżunia nodded. 'Now the Ghetto is ours!'

'Listen to this!' Jerzy said. 'Someone told me that a group of AK fellows tried to break through the wall at Bonifraterska Street to help us but something went wrong with their explosives and they couldn't get through. And over on Muranowski Square, some of our fighters put on German uniforms and fooled lots of SS men and captured their machine guns.'

But the leaders were not as euphoric as the fighters.

'Today was a great triumph,' Itzak said, gathering his group around him. 'Ours is the first organised battle against the Germans in occupied Poland, possibly even in the whole of Europe. We've shown what a handful of brave street fighters can do. With hardly any firearms, we've not only won a momentous victory without losing a single fighter, but, more importantly, we've shown the world that the master race is not invincible.'

They all cheered and clapped but Itzak looked sombre as he held up his hand. 'I'm proud of each one of you, prouder than I can say. Today we've written ourselves into the history books. But we don't know what tomorrow will bring.'

On the second day of the Uprising, the Germans, humiliated by their ignominious defeat at the hands of a rabble of *Untermenschen*, sent in huge reinforcements.

'Want to know what I just heard?' Edek asked Elżunia. Even his curls seemed to bristle with excitement. 'The Germans have got rid of the colonel and replaced him with a general, as if they were fighting a proper army!'

Within an hour, every building became a fortress fighting for its life. However hard they fought to repel the Germans, more kept rushing at them from all directions. On their rooftop, a movement to their right caught Elżunia's eye and she saw Itzak motioning them to crouch down, out of sight. She squatted against the parapet and followed Itzak's gaze. Three German soldiers had crept onto the adjoining roof and were setting up a machine gun behind the chimney. Her breath caught in her throat. The only way out was by the stairs but the exit was cut off by the gun that was being trained on them. They were trapped.

Before she knew what was happening, Szmuel sprang from his corner like a panther and threw himself onto the machine gun. The Germans were caught off balance and, for a moment, the path to the stairs was clear. Swiftly and stealthily, they crawled towards them one at a time and ran down, throwing grenades at the Germans trying to get in.

After the Germans had been pushed back from their building, the fighters stole back onto the roof. Elżunia stifled a scream. Szmuel lay sprawled in front of the chimney, his body perforated like a sieve. He had sacrificed himself to give them a chance to get away. But there was no time for tears or gratitude because the Germans intensified their attack, and machine-gun fire stuttered all around. A grenade came flying towards them. Without a moment's hesitation, Elżunia caught it in mid-air and immediately tossed it back, like Jove hurling a thunderbolt.

She ran down the stairs to a less exposed position where one of the older fighters stood near a small window, looking through the sights of a rifle he'd used in the previous war. On the street below, a German soldier was edging along the wall, heading for their building.

'Come on, Grandpa; quick, shoot!' Jerzy hissed from beside her, but the old soldier was in no hurry. Slowly and deliberately, he took aim, fired, and hit the intruder in the chest. But the Germans kept coming. They were almost out of grenades when Edek's Molotov cocktail struck a helmet that sparked and went up in flames. But still Elżunia couldn't bring herself to throw hers.

There was a brief lull and, when they looked down, they were amazed to see three unarmed German officers walking slowly in the centre of the street, with white ribbons pinned to their lapels. In polite voices, they asked to speak to the Jewish commander so that they could negotiate a truce to remove their dead and wounded. 'Stop fighting and we promise all the residents will be resettled peacefully in work camps at Poniatów and Trawniki. They can take all their possessions with them,' the German spokesman announced.

For a moment, the fighters thought they were dreaming. The German general was petitioning them for a truce. A few seconds later, he got his reply. A salvo of gunfire.

That afternoon, the Germans pulled out of the Ghetto once again and, despite their sorrow at the loss of some of their comrades, who had become closer to them than their brothers and sisters, the fighters were jubilant. They had not only held off the enemy for two days, but had forced them to sue for peace and retreat. They'd cheated Hitler of his birthday present.

Twenty-Eight

Elżunia was inside her bunker, desperate to know what had become of her mother, Gittel and Stefan during the past two days, when Jerzy rushed in.

'Come and see the flags flying from the chimneytop at 17 Muranowska Street!' He was so excited that saliva sprayed from his mouth as he spoke. 'There's our blue-and-white flag with the Star of David, and the red-and-white Polish flag with the eagle.'

'How did they get there?' Elżunia asked as she ran beside him. He told her that a Polish boy had crawled into the Ghetto from the Aryan side with the Polish flag and, together with some of the fighters, he'd scrambled to the top of the building and hoisted the flags on the lightning pole on the chimney for all of Warsaw to see.

By the time they reached the building, a large crowd of fighters and non-combatants had gathered to marvel at the two flags fluttering side by side. Elżunia pushed her way through the crowd and heard Edek telling them that he and his Catholic friend on the other side of the wall had hatched the plan. 'We wanted all Warsaw to see these flags flying side by side to show them that we're fighting for our honour and for theirs. Maybe now they'll realise they should be fighting shoulder to shoulder with us.' Standing beside him was someone she hadn't expected to see inside the Ghetto.

'Lech!' She flung her arms around him. 'You're crazy to come here with all this going on. It's too dangerous.'

He gave her a devil-may-care grin. 'Who do you think brought the Polish flag?'

He wanted to say that he couldn't bear to stand by knowing she was in such danger, that every time he heard an explosion, a crash or the rattle of gunfire, his heart stopped beating. The only way to end the torment was to get to the other side of the wall. When Edek had sent him a message to say that the fighters wanted to hoist a Polish flag next to the Jewish one, he was jubilant. Now he had an excuse to cross over to their side of the wall, be part of their fight and perhaps even win Elżunia's love. And from the way she had reacted when she saw him, he thought that she must care about him.

He blushed when she praised his courage in coming into the Ghetto, but, while he was figuring out what to say, she said a hurried goodbye and ran back to her bunker.

That night Elżunia dreamed that the building was on fire and there was smoke all around. The dream was so real that she woke up coughing. But it wasn't a dream; something was burning. The others were trying to figure out where the smoke was coming from when Lech burst in and looked around for Elżunia.

'Get out, quick!' he panted. 'I've just been outside. The Germans are using flame-throwers to set the houses on fire to flush people out, and they're lined up outside with machine guns waiting to shoot them as they leave.'

Panic-stricken, Elżunia and her group bolted into the passageway that connected their building with the adjacent one but the smoke there was even thicker and more pungent. It stung their eyes and choked their throats.

Elżunia clutched Lech's sleeve in terror as they heard the crackle of flames all around.

They ran from building to building, through cellars and attics, but wherever they went the smoke was there before them. Unable to defeat them in battle, the Germans had resorted to setting fire to their houses.

With the glow of burning buildings and thick smoke blackening the air, the light was so murky that they could hardly see one another.

'They haven't got into the central part of the Ghetto yet, so we'll try to break through there, otherwise we'll be burnt alive or machine-gunned in here,' Itzak rasped in between paroxysms of coughing and choking.

As they crept from the burning building, they found themselves standing in the centre of an ocean of flames, surrounded by Germans and Ukrainians waiting to shoot. To stay where they were meant death by fire, but the prospect of going through the flames paralysed Elżunia. They hardly dared to breathe, unable to stand still but too terrified to move. When Elżunia finally forced herself to inch forward, the burning asphalt melted under her feet and she felt herself sinking into a soft mass that stuck to her shoes and seemed to be sucking her in. She looked down and saw that the soles of her shoes were on fire.

A little ahead of her, Lech urged her on. He jumped from foot to foot on the burning ground and grabbed her hand. 'Come on, we'll run together.' She looked at the wall of flames in front of them and shook her head. 'Save yourself,' she mouthed. There was no air to breathe. The heat sucked all the saliva from her mouth and all the moisture from her body, and she had become a brittle shell about to crumble into a thousand fragments.

'I can't do it, I can't do it,' she heard herself sobbing. A thousand hammers pounded in her skull as Lech grabbed her arm and pulled her down into a cellar where some of the group were sheltering. Their faces were blackened with soot and cinders, their hair was singed, and they were almost unrecognisable. There was a crash, and she jumped away just in time to avoid a burning beam that collapsed, missing her by centimetres. Someone bent forward to push aside a chunk of broken sink placed there to conceal the entrance to an interconnecting passageway.

One by one they lowered themselves into it and didn't stop running until they reached the other end. Perhaps now they would be safe. But as soon as they peered out through the chink in the wall, they drew back. Soldiers were wandering all over the place. Two were coming towards them. Any moment they'd be discovered. Elżunia closed her eyes. This is it, she thought. Suddenly Lech motioned for them to stand back and, to her horror, he squeezed into the narrow opening in full view of the Germans. She wanted to cry out, tell him to get away from there, but the words died in her throat. She heard the crack of rifle fire. Inside the passageway, they flattened themselves against the walls and held their breath, waiting for the soldiers to burst in, but Lech's body was so firmly wedged into the opening that the soldiers couldn't pull him out and, after a few kicks and loud curses, they strode off.

Elżunia was numb. She knelt beside Lech and saw that his eyes were open and he was looking at her. 'Oh, thank God,' she whispered. 'Thank God. I thought you were ...'

His lips moved but a bubbling sound came from his throat and a trickle of blood oozed from his mouth. She bent forward to try and catch what he was struggling to say.

'Now will you be my girl?' he rasped.

She clasped his hand and nodded.

A faint smile flitted across his face and the light went out of his eyes.

＊

Wrapping rags around their shoes to deaden the sound, they crept out of the passageway towards the central part of the Ghetto. Bullets were flying everywhere. Several times Elżunia thought she must have been hit and was astonished to find she wasn't dead. They were tip-toeing through the smoke and fire when the Germans shone a powerful reflector on them. Elżunia raised her arm and hurled one of her grenades at the reflector. It shattered, allowing her and the others to disappear into the smoke.

But when they reached the central area, they discovered that fires were raging there as well, and flames enveloped entire buildings. Wherever she looked, wooden beams were cracking and collapsing, red-hot walls and staircases were crumbling, and balconies were crashing to the ground. Such searing heat emanated from the buildings and the ground that it seemed as though the jaws of hell had opened up.

The suffocating smoke was tinged with a strange, sweetish stench. Elżunia sniffed as she tried to identify the peculiar smell. Then her stomach turned over. It was the smell of burnt flesh. On balconies, in window frames, on bits of broken stairs, lay the blackened corpses of those forced from their hiding places by the flames. Dazed, panic-stricken people wandered around aimlessly, not knowing where to go.

Elżunia scanned the faces anxiously for her mother and Gittel. What had happened to them? Surely someone had seen them. But most people either stared at her with dull, uncomprehending expressions or shook their heads and turned away. She looked up and froze. People were leaping from the burning buildings like living torches. Up on the third floor, a couple were standing by the open window. The man kissed his wife, took her hand and they jumped together. A moment later, their bodies hit the ground with a sickening thud. Elżunia wanted to scream or cry, but no sound came as she stared at these apocalyptic visions.

'They remained free to the end,' Edek whispered. 'They chose when and how to die.'

As the days turned into weeks, the weary insurgents fought on, their small cache of arms augmented by captured German weapons. Furious at the Ghetto's continued resistance, and their inability to destroy it, the Germans brought in sniffer dogs to detect the bunkers and flushed out the occupants with flame-throwers. And after each attack, Elżunia waited and held her breath until she checked that the bunker where her mother and Gittel were sheltering hadn't been destroyed. One morning, five weeks after the start of the Uprising, she was in the bunker with the remnants of her group when their building vibrated from an explosion in a nearby building. 'They're throwing grenades into the bunkers now,' Edek said. 'I wonder how long we'll be able to hold out.'

As soon as night fell, and the Germans had left the Ghetto, Elżunia picked up a torch and crept outside. The sky was the colour of bruised strawberries and the street was eerily lit by flames that leapt up and crackled all around her. She darted into a doorway, stumbled along the passageway that had been tunnelled out to connect the bunkers, and felt her way in the dark until she reached her mother's bunker. Something was jammed against the entrance and she couldn't get inside. She called out softly but there was no reply. Picking up a beam of fallen timber, she pushed with all her might until the door gave way and she fell inside.

She shone her torch around the bunker and her knees gave way. When she looked down, she saw she was standing in a pool of thickening blood and the floor was covered with bodies and parts of arms and legs. Grenades. She heard herself moaning as she ran frantically around the bunker, looking at the faces. In the far corner she found her mother, curled up as though asleep. Elżunia almost sobbed with relief. Thank God, she was only sleeping. She tapped her shoulder. 'Mama! Wake up! We've got to get out of here.' She tugged her arm, surprised at how heavy it was. Then she shook her, harder this time. 'Get up, Mama!' she heard herself shouting. She tried to raise her up but collapsed on the floor, panting. 'Mama! You have to get up! Get up!' Her panic-stricken voice made her scalp prickle. Exhausted, she sank to the floor and her sobbing filled the bunker and echoed against the walls. She held her mother's stiff hand and kissed her dead face. Cradling her mother's thin body in her arms, Elżunia thought about the happy days that would never come again, and the life that they would never share. Time had run out. The misunderstandings and conflicts would never be resolved, and the future would not bring her mother peace nor restore her husband. And Elżunia would never have the chance to live up to her mother's expectations, or get to really know her. She looked at her mother's stiffening face and saw a stranger. Forcing herself to remember the woman she had once been, Elżunia saw her sitting erect at the piano, filling their apartment with music that they had all thought would go on forever, and she cried for her mother, for herself, and for all the wasted lives and missed opportunities. Her hand brushed against something hard and, through her tears, she saw that it was her mother's amber brooch. Tenderly she unpinned it and placed it deep into the pocket of her skirt.

She didn't know how long she had sat without moving, cradling her mother while tears flowed down her face, but suddenly she leapt to her feet. Gittel! Where was Gittel?

Swallowing hard, she forced herself to walk very slowly among the bodies strewn all over the bunker, but there was no sign of the little girl. What could have happened to her? Was she hiding somewhere? Had she run away? Had someone smuggled her out of the Ghetto at the last moment? She had to believe that Gittel was still alive. It was the only thing she had left to cling on to.

The sun had already risen in the red sky and the light had begun to dawn when she returned to her bunker. As she made her way to her corner, she avoided her comrades' eyes, and they didn't comment on her swollen eyes and frozen expression. She didn't stir when they heard the rumble of tanks outside. Their weapons were almost used up and there was nothing to hope for except a quick end. Suddenly, Edek rushed out and planted himself in front of a tank. Elżunia rose and saw a Lilliputian with nothing but a grenade in his hand confronting a giant. She closed her eyes.

'Throw it, for God's sake. Throw it, before they see you,' she whispered over and over. 'Oh God, why doesn't he throw it?' But the pin was stuck and he couldn't release it. 'This can't happen, I can't let this happen.' The words were still echoing in her head as she inched out of the bunker and flattened herself against the wall. As though in a dream, she hurled her grenade at the tank with more force than she thought she had. It lurched and exploded.

'Run, Edek, quick, run!' she shouted. He turned and she saw his cheeky grin but at that instant a shot rang out and Edek fell, clutching his leg. The second tank moved forward. Biting her hand until it bled, Elżunia watched in horror as it rolled over her friend's body.

She was slumped against the wall in the corner of the bunker, her face in her hands. Their miracle was over and the end was coming. She'd never get out of there alive and she no longer cared. What was the point of staying alive when the best and noblest souls had died? She thought of her mother, of Lech and Edek, of Itzak and Rahela, and those brave young insurgents, all killed. She paced up and down the bunker, sobbing, muttering to herself, and wondering whether she was losing her mind. How much grief and loss could one person endure? Dying would be much easier than staying alive when everyone you loved was gone. She was seventeen but she had lived through a thousand years of stress and sorrow.

Overhead, she could hear salvos of gunfire and closed her eyes. Soon it would all be over. Then she heard Madame Ramona's voice saying, 'You will have three lives.' In her first life, she'd been a Catholic girl living an indulged existence with a father she hero-worshipped. In the second, she had become a Jewish activist, fighting for her life in the Ghetto. Maybe the clairvoyant was right and she'd have a third incarnation. Curiosity overcame despair. What would her third life hold?

Somehow she had to find a way out because the heat in the bunker was scorching and sucked up all the air. She tried to remember the network of passageways and tunnels that ran underneath the buildings, but most of the bunkers had been burnt out and the passageways linking them had collapsed. Only a few minutes earlier, she'd been prepared to give up but now she felt a spirit of defiance stirring. She hadn't gone through so much to surrender now. If she did, who would be left to tell what had happened here? Who would keep the memory of her mother, Lech, Edek, and all the others alive? If she died, they'd all die with her. Perhaps that was why she had been spared when so many had perished. To describe the indescribable. And what about Gittel? Perhaps she was hiding somewhere, waiting for Elżunia to find her. She had to search for her.

Inside the dark passageway, she gritted her teeth, pushed her hair inside her scout's cap and tucked her skirt into her underpants. Her heart in her mouth, she inched along, holding her hands in front of her to feel for any obstacles. At times she crawled on her hands and knees over craters left by exploded shells and across piles of broken masonry and charred bricks. From the scorching heat, she knew that the buildings above her were ablaze and could collapse on top of her at any moment.

Occasionally a piece of burning timber would crash in front of her and she would leap out of the way just in time. Sometimes she felt something soft underfoot and gagged when she saw she was treading on dead bodies. She whispered an apology. Sometimes she heard skittering underfoot and a rat's smooth fur brushed against her legs.

As she rested in the dark passage, too exhausted to move, she became aware that she was leaning against something that was too soft to be stone or masonry. She turned and ran her hands along its length. At the end of the soft surface, she came to something that felt like polished wood. She climbed on top of it and felt something that resembled a couch. Either she was hallucinating or these were pieces of furniture.

As she groped around in the dark, she wondered whether she'd come to the secret entrance on the Aryan side of town, through which she had led the airman into the Ghetto. She started heaving and pushing the old sofa, tables and cupboards away from the entrance, until a chink of light speared the darkness, making her blink. From here, it was impossible to see what was going on above street level or who was lurking in the shadows or patrolling the block, waiting to catch the Jews who'd escaped the flames. She waited, her ear pressed to the roof of the passageway and shrank back each time she felt the vibration of passing trucks or heard footsteps and snatches of conversation.

When she could no longer hear anything, she climbed onto the table, and reached up. She could feel something hard, and pushed it with all her strength. It was an iron grille covered with leaves and branches, and after a few attempts she managed to raise it. She hoisted herself up with hands that shook so much she could hardly support herself. Her heart drumming in her ears, she scrambled to her feet and looked around to make sure no one had seen her. With her blackened face, tangled hair and blistered hands, it would be easy to tell that she had emerged from the inferno on the other side of the wall.

The bright spring day was drawing to a close and the curfew hour was approaching. Elżunia stood up, straightened her skirt, and tried to brush off the dirt and cinders that clung to her. In the murky half-light, the sky glowed a fierce red from the flames that burned a short distance away. The Ghetto had held out for almost six weeks but all that was left of it now was rubble and ashes. She murmured a few Hail Marys and some half-remembered snippets of the Kaddish prayer, took one last look at the dying Ghetto, and hurried away in the shadows as smoke billowed over the silent city.

Part II

Part II

Twenty-Nine

The gaunt man muttering to himself as he strode along the streets of London, revisiting an internal scenario invisible to others, aroused sympathetic glances from passersby. They took him for one of the unfortunate souls unhinged by the Blitz, who bolted for the shelters jabbering that Hitler was coming whenever they heard the wail of a siren or saw planes darkening the sky.

There were so many ways that war could reshape the landscape of your mind, Adam Czartoryski thought as he rushed on, looking neither right nor left. As a student in London many years ago, he had delighted in its regal buildings and imposing monuments, but now they were merely a blur against the scenes inside his restless mind. He walked along the Thames Embankment, enveloped by the chilly mist that rose from the river, which he considered the dullest waterway in Europe. He was already on the other side of Westminster Bridge before he'd even realised he'd crossed it.

'Cor, you want to watch where you're goin', guv,' the cockney hawker shouted, as Adam walked into his barrow and sent potatoes and carrots tumbling to the ground.

Ever since he'd read in *The Express* the previous morning that an uprising had broken out in the Warsaw Ghetto, he'd been consumed by visions of carnage and destruction, of doomed fighters crushed by tanks and blood streaming down the streets that had haunted him since his visit six months earlier.

He thought about the feisty girl with the elfin face who had guided him around the Ghetto. He wondered whether she was fighting with the insurgents. They didn't have a hope. They were inexperienced street fighters, armed only with defiance and homemade weapons, against tanks, artillery, and an army determined to wipe them off the face of the earth. And yet they'd found the strength to confront the Nazis.

They've shown us the way, he mused. For years we've talked about honour and resistance, but they've actually done it. His thoughts returned to Elżunia. Their paths had crossed twice and each time one of them had saved the other's life. He didn't believe in fate — that was a simple person's way of interpreting life with the benefit of hindsight. But he couldn't find any rational explanation for these coincidences.

There was something appealing about the girl, and, at a different time and in a different world, he would have liked to spend time with her and show her that there was more to life than violence and persecution. He saw himself as her mentor, teaching her about the ways of the world, escorting her to balls and theatres, and watching her blossom into a woman.

As he turned the corner, the Gothic towers and spires of the Houses of Parliament came into view and his fury was rekindled. Ensconced in this bastion of democracy, English politicians planned their strategy and issued their orders, impervious to the suffering of the country that had been their first and staunchest ally. As an idealistic young diplomat, he'd had visions of making the world a better place, but the cynicism of realpolitik made him want to vomit.

It was a cheerless April morning, and he hunched his shoulders against the rain and turned up his collar against the penetrating chill. The weather had been like this ever since he'd arrived four months before, and its greyness reflected his state of mind as he knocked on one office door after another, repeating the same story to people who tried to conceal their incredulity behind a screen of politeness.

Of the members of the Polish government-in-exile he had already briefed about the situation in Poland, he'd been most impressed by the Commander-in-Chief, Władysław Sikorski, whose vision for Europe included the formation of a United Nations organisation to thwart and counterbalance the ambitions of power-hungry dictators. When the time was right, he told Adam, the Home Army would rise up against the invaders and liberate Poland. Adam left his office hoping that one day this statesman would become the head of a democratic Poland.

After meeting the Polish representatives, Adam started doing the rounds of English ministers, secretaries and undersecretaries, whose doors, like their ears, were reluctant to open to him. He was consumed by his mission to convey the situation in Poland, and in particular to give them an eyewitness account of the Warsaw Ghetto so that they'd realise they had to act fast to save the remaining Jews. They were unfailingly courteous and attentive but the almost imperceptible change of light in their eyes signalled disbelief, and the way they averted their gaze while making avowals of support indicated that his mission had little chance of succeeding.

From his student days, he knew that for the English there was a clear distinction between making a diplomatic request and being persistent. By raising his voice and insisting that it was inhumane for the British to stand by and watch while millions of civilians were being butchered in an Allied country, he feared he'd overstepped that line.

He was mulling over the insuperable national differences in communication as he headed to Whitehall for his next appointment. The light was fading and although it was only mid-afternoon it already seemed like evening. It began to drizzle and soon he was coated with a layer of chilly dampness. Inside the draughty building, Adam shivered as he waited to be ushered into the office of a minister who had finally found the time to grant him an interview.

The rain had stopped and the light slanting through the window high on the wall cast a gleam on Sir Ewart Lynn's silver hair. As he motioned for Adam to sit on a straight-backed wooden chair facing him, Sir Ewart continued to suck on a pipe that had discoloured the edge of his neatly clipped moustache. Looking at the impeccably tailored suit with a waistcoat and a tie as understated as his Cambridge manner, Adam thought that he epitomised the stereotypical image of the English gentleman.

'Mr Czartoryski, we understand and sympathise with your passionate concern for your gallant and oppressed country.'

Sir Ewart's manner was urbane and his eyes brimmed with disarming candour, but, from his inflection and his frequent need to adjust his tie, Adam could tell that Sir Ewart didn't regard being passionate as an admirable quality.

There was a deferential knock on the door and a little man bustling with self-importance entered and murmured something. Sir Ewart replaced his pipe in the marble ashtray, pushed back his chair and excused himself.

Adam tapped his shoe on the parquet floor. This was turning out to be another frustrating day. He had just come from an unsatisfactory meeting with Szmuel Zygielbojm, whose manner he had found extremely irritating. A Polish Jew who had escaped from Warsaw, he now represented the Bund political party in the Polish government-in-exile. While Adam described what he'd seen in the Ghetto, Zygielbojm had become so agitated that he paced up and down like a tiger in a circus cage. At one stage, he even spoke of killing himself as a gesture of protest to awaken the conscience of the world to the carnage taking place in the Warsaw Ghetto. He sounded so melodramatic that Adam couldn't wait to get away.

Back in his office, Sir Ewart apologised for keeping Adam waiting and reached for his pipe again. 'We hold our staunch ally Poland in the highest esteem, and it distresses us to see her suffer but unfortunately our resources are stretched to the limit,' he said in a pained voice. 'We must put all our efforts into defeating Germany. The Red Army in Stalingrad has shown us the way. We must defeat Rommel in North Africa, and then turn our attention to Europe. Only when we have defeated Hitler will Poland and the rest of Europe be free from tyranny.'

Pausing, he tapped his pipe and, as he struck a match, his patrician face glowed in the flame. He sucked on the pipe thoughtfully, filling the office with the aromatic smell. Leaning forward, he said in a confidential voice, 'You're a pilot, are you not, Mr Czartoryski? Many of your countrymen are flying with the RAF, you know, and the gallant chaps are making an invaluable contribution to our war effort. We are immensely grateful to them and, after the Battle of Britain, we owe them a debt we can never repay.'

Adam left Sir Ewart's office with a hollow feeling in his stomach, like a starving man who asked for coins but was fobbed off with advice on budgeting. Chilled and dejected, with a roaring headache, he walked past the liveried doorman of The Connaught Hotel, slid into a leather banquette and ordered tea, which arrived in an ornate silver pot along with a jug of milk that he pushed away. As he sipped the black tea, he reflected on Sir Ewart's parting words. When he had returned to Poland after the disaster in Slovakia almost two years before, convinced that his work in the Underground was over, he had considered the possibility of going to England and joining the RAF like thousands of Polish flyers, some of whom flew in the Polish Kościuszko squadron with their own emblem painted on the fuselage. He was fed up with the cynicism of politics and the chicanery of politicians. Perhaps it wasn't too late. Slapping a few shillings down on the table, he walked out of the restaurant with a lighter step.

The paper boy on the corner was shouting, 'Paper, paper, read all about it, Rommel's getting his just deserts in the desert!' A sudden gust of wind almost blew Adam's hat off and sent sheets of newspaper flying along the street. One page fluttered around and came to rest against his shoe and, as he bent down to remove it, a headline caught his eye. Szmuel Zygielbojm had committed suicide.

Adam picked up the paper. Zygielbojm had left a suicide note in which he explained that the only honourable thing to do in an uncaring world was to kill himself, to draw attention to the genocide taking place in the Warsaw Ghetto.

The hollow pit in Adam's stomach deepened. So Zygielbojm hadn't been melodramatic at all. He had taken this shocking action because he believed that he had to take a stand. Zygielbojm had sacrificed his life in the hope of awakening the conscience of the world. Adam gave a mirthless laugh. He had died trying to shame those who felt no shame.

Adam let the paper drop and walked on, his long stride swallowing the stately curve of Regent Street. He had dismissed Zygielbojm and his anguish as theatrical posturing. A man who, as it now turned out, was far more noble and highly principled than himself. He kept walking, oblivious of everything but the failure of his mission.

Thirty

'Jolly good,' the recruiting officer said when Adam applied to join the RAF. 'You Poles are demons in the air. I don't know where we'd be if you boys hadn't come to our aid in the Battle of Britain. And we certainly could do with more airmen right now.'

Adam didn't understand why the other airmen in the squadron burst out laughing when he later repeated that comment. A party was in full swing in the mess hall the evening he arrived, and the sound of clinking glasses, raucous voices and loud music indicated that a great deal of liquor had already been consumed. The air was fuggy with cigarette smoke and every few minutes an outburst of bawdy laughter indicated that someone had told another blue joke.

A few drunken voices were bellowing 'It's a Long-Vey to Tipperary', and 'Roll Out the Barrel' in strong Polish accents, while in a far corner a couple of men were beating out jazz rhythms with their fists on a table.

'So they said they could do with more airmen? That's British understatement for you!' The speaker combed his fingers through thick dark hair brushed back from a film-star face and Adam recognised Romek, whom he'd met in the camp in Romania. Romek roared with laughter and collapsed into a chair while the others joined in. Adam looked from one to the other, baffled.

'My dear friend,' Romek said, slapping Adam's shoulder. 'They've got more Lancasters and Halifaxes than pilots, and that's because —'

A stocky airman cut in. 'That's enough, Romek,' he said, indicating Adam with a motion of his head. 'He'll find out soon enough.'

But Romek had drunk too much to hold back.

'My honoured friend,' he slurred. 'Why do you think you were assigned to Bomber Command? Is it because you are so handsome? No. Is it because you are such a good flyer? No. I'll tell you why. It's because you are DISPENSABLE!' He hiccuped. 'They think the Luftwaffe knocked us out of the air because we lost our nerve. So we're just air-force fodder for our beloved Air Marshal, who wasn't nicknamed Bomber Harris for nothing. He's going to bomb the hell out of Germany, even if he kills every single airman in the RAF in the process.'

His speech over, he slumped into his chair, lifted his whiskey glass and drained it in one gulp.

The laughter stopped, a hush fell over the hall. As Adam looked at the thoughtful faces around him, he realised that Romek was probably right.

'*In vino veritas*, eh?' he said lightly.

The conversation soon turned to a more agreeable topic — English girls, whose appetite for Polish airmen was apparently insatiable.

'The English do everything back to front. Instead of metres, they have yards; instead of litres, they have pints; and they drive on the wrong side of the road. And God knows how they handle their women because they're all crazy about us!' Tomasz's ribald chuckle belied his innocent appearance. With his round face and a lock of almost white hair falling over his forehead, he looked like an altar boy in a village church.

'They're not like Polish girls,' he continued. 'No flirting or playing hard to get. You kiss their hand, tell them how beautiful they are, bring them a few flowers and they can't wait to go to bed! It almost makes war worthwhile!'

'And you can forget those stories you've heard about English girls being cold,' someone chimed in. 'They're as steamy as August in Warsaw!'

Later that night in their hut, Adam took out the silver cigarette case that Elżunia had given him. As he took out a Camel filter, he ran his fingers along the smooth case and traced the finely embossed initials with his fingertips. He thought about Elżunia and wondered what had happened to her. The other men were still boasting about their recent conquests, but his mind was on the Ghetto Uprising and the girl who had sprung forward and pulled him away from the window just before the bullet pierced the glass.

His reverie was interrupted by creaking and rustling on his left. Tomasz, who occupied the next bed, was removing a small package wrapped in brown paper from his kitbag under the bed. He raised it to his mouth, kissed it and put it back. He turned and saw that Adam was watching him.

'That's our sacred Polish soil,' he said. 'I never go anywhere without it, even when I'm in the air. That's the only reason I'm here, fighting this fucking war and bombing the hell out of Germany — so Poland can be free.'

Adam lay on his bunk, watching the cigarette smoke curl towards the ceiling when the door opened and in sauntered a fellow who was beaming and saying something in English that the others couldn't understand. After several attempts to communicate, Romek dragged him over to

Adam's bed and said in a slurred voice, 'This chap, he speaking English.'

'Thank God! A civilised Pole at last!'

Adam sat up and looked into a boyish face splotched with freckles and surrounded by springy hair the colour of a ripe pumpkin.

'You are Scottish, I think,' Adam said.

'Nah, mate, I'm an Aussie, but Dad's family came from Scotland; that's how I got this name. Stewart McAllister. The Poms all think I'm a Scot, too.' He looked around the hut. 'You lot are Poles, aren't you? I reckon I'm a ring-in.' He saw Adam's bewildered expression and grinned. 'Am I going too fast? Or is it the Aussie accent?'

Adam and Stewart talked long after the others had dropped off to sleep, Adam liked the Australian's open manner and Stewart was intrigued by the intensity of the Pole, who spoke little but listened attentively, assessing him with his brooding gaze.

Stewart rifled in his pocket and pulled out an official-looking card with gold lettering. 'Strewth, I almost forgot. I've been invited to a party in London tomorrow.' He looked at Adam. 'I reckon I could get you in. Wanna come? There'll be some big-wigs going. Might be good for a laugh.'

Adam shook his head. 'I don't like those — what do you call them — big-wigs.'

'Listen, mate, you want to get away from the base as much as you can. Once they get you up in the air, God knows when you'll have the chance to get away again.'

Amused by the fellow's infectious enthusiasm, Adam promised to go to the party. He could always slip away if it became boring.

When he finally fell asleep, he dreamed that someone was ordering him to bomb Berlin and shouting that he was dispensable.

Thirty-One

Judith McAllister's sharp gaze swept over the gathering like a searchlight, resting briefly on each group before moving on. The scene was typical of so many official English receptions she'd attended since arriving in London. The men, masters of the art of understatement, murmured noncommittal pleasantries over their whiskey, while the women smiled vaguely as they sipped sherry.

Above the murmur of polite conversation, glasses clinked as waiters in tails with starched white napkins over their arms offered drinks and crackers decorated with gherkin slices and rosettes of mayonnaise.

'I'd like a beer, thanks,' she said. The waiter's eyebrows jerked up towards his brilliantined hair. A few minutes later he returned with a single glass of lager on his large tray.

'Here you are, madam,' he said. His tone implied that females who drank beer weren't ladies.

Judith took a mouthful and pulled a face. The English had conquered countries all over the world and imposed their laws and customs everywhere, but they'd never got the hang of serving beer cold.

Placing the glass on a mahogany console, she checked her wristwatch and looked around. Bloody Stewart was late as usual. She hated these staid, boring functions, but he always managed to get round her. She shuddered to think of all the times she'd lent him money he never returned or covered up for scrapes he'd landed into. Each time she vowed never to bail him out again, but each time she had succumbed to her younger brother's entreaties. Ever since he was small, she hadn't been able to resist that innocent smile of his. Everyone had their Achilles' heel and she supposed Stewart was hers.

'Hi, Sis. How's tricks?' At the sound of his voice over the phone the previous day, she'd let out a sigh of relief. The sorties across the Channel had intensified, and casualties were increasing, but because of wartime censorship she never knew when he was flying out, or when he'd returned. 'How about coming with your brother to a shindig the War Department are giving at Admiralty House?' he had asked. Before she could refuse, he said, 'Oh come on, Jude. I haven't seen you for ages. It's time to get out of those hospital corridors and see how the better half lives. They reckon your hero might even put in an appearance.'

She took the bait. 'You think Mr Churchill will be there?'

'Bloody oath, the old war horse himself.' Pushing his advantage, he continued, 'Here's your chance to get out of that starched bib and tucker you're always wearing.'

She let out a long-suffering sigh. 'I suppose it's going to be one of those la-di-dah functions then?'

'Just la,' he said, chuckling.

Judith usually paid little attention to fashion, but she noticed that the women at the reception were dressed to the nines. From their ankle-strap shoes to their gloved hands and smoothly coiffed hair, these women looked a million dollars, as the Yanks would say. As she was marvelling at all the time, expense and effort it must have taken to achieve this elegance, she looked up and caught sight of herself in the gilt-framed mirror above the Regency fireplace. She felt like a weed in a rose garden. Her face had too many angles. Picasso rather than Renoir, she chuckled to herself. The beige houndstooth suit she'd bought because it was serviceable now seemed too long and dowdy, the flat-heeled shoes made her look like a schoolmarm, and her crinkly red hair, which she had tried to coax into a roll around the nape of her neck, was already beginning to unravel.

'You'd be quite good-looking if you did something with your hair,' her friend Nancy had told her recently, surveying her with an appraising look that wasn't flattering. 'And your figure's not bad either, if only you'd stop hiding it under those loose blouses and frumpy skirts. As for those clompy shoes ...'

But Judith wasn't interested in crippling her back or feet in a quest to catch a man. Might as well face facts. At thirty-six, she was a confirmed spinster, mostly by choice, although if she'd ever come across a man who didn't feel diminished by a professional woman, she might have considered a relationship. The only men she encountered were her patients who regarded her as a dragon, and the doctors who thought she was a dyke. The medicos weren't above seducing the giggly young nurses who were impressed by their status, but they had no interest whatsoever in women with positions of authority.

Throughout her nursing career, which spanned almost twenty years, Judith had heard the disparaging way physicians and surgeons referred to hospital matrons as being unfeminine — certainly not marriage material. That was fine by her because she was married to nursing.

'Damned if I'm going to be any man's subservient wife,' she told Nancy and chuckled. 'If anything, I'm the one that could do with a little wife to take care of all those tedious everyday chores.' While Nancy shook her head, Judith continued, 'I'll just concentrate on mending broken bodies and leave charmers like you to break men's hearts.'

The English born-to-rule voices around her sounded affected and the conversations shallow. How did people sustain such enthusiasm when they had so little to say?

Her mind kept wandering back to the training course she was giving at St Bart's, and the young nurses whose minds these days were on their sweethearts in the armed services, rather than on their lectures.

The bitter smell of cigar smoke and a sudden buzz of activity made her turn towards the far end of the reception hall. A stocky man with bulldog features, round shoulders, and a belly that seemed to balloon from his neck had entered the room. Winston Churchill was shorter than she had imagined but he exuded power. She always listened with admiration to his forceful broadcasts on the BBC but sometimes wondered whether he felt equal to the task that his ambition and world events had thrust upon him. The Prime Minister was soon surrounded by an entourage of politicians and bureaucrats, and the guests resumed their conversations, tactfully avoiding looking in his direction.

On her right, a tall woman in silk and pearls was lamenting about her nanny. 'One never really knows what foreigners are thinking, does one?' she was saying. 'The French nanny we engaged for Rupert and Jane upped and left after three years. Said she wanted to be with her own people. I told her we needed her, and, anyway, she was much better off here because our Mr Churchill' — she stole a discreet glance in his direction — 'would soon make mincemeat of the Jerries, but she wouldn't listen. My mother always said you couldn't trust the Frogs.'

Sympathetic nods and assenting murmurs encouraged her to continue complaining. Bored, Judith moved on and joined a group of men in striped suits and waistcoats. At least they wouldn't be complaining about nannies. But she didn't find their conversation about the relative virtues of race horses, the appalling condition of the golf course at St Andrews, and a scandal concerning a highly placed bureaucrat any more interesting than the women's chatter. You'd never guess there was a war on.

She was relieved when someone introduced a new topic. 'I'm not sure what to make of those Mitford sisters,' one man said. 'And, as for that Oswald Mosley character ...'

One of his companions, a short man with a shiny bald head and long teeth looked thoughtful. 'You're absolutely right, of course, but one can't entirely discount some of his views. After all, one wouldn't want Britain to lose its character and become a dumping ground for colonials of all colours, would one?'

Judith turned to the speaker. 'In case you haven't noticed, we colonials are helping you fight this bloody war,' she blurted in a voice that sounded more Australian than usual. The man's expression reminded her of a fish that has just been reeled in and can't figure out how it came to be dangling on the end of a hook.

'Watch that temper, Jude,' she muttered to herself as she walked away. The sooner she got away from these pompous bigots the better. If Stewart didn't turn up in ten minutes, she'd leave. She walked towards the long window and gazed at the smooth baize lawns of Pall Mall. It was a calming view that proclaimed that no matter what chaos there was in the rest of the world, there would always be an England and it would always have impeccably manicured lawns. Taking a deep breath, she turned back towards the assembled guests.

Leaning against the wall on the other side of the room was a gaunt man with an air-force cap set at an angle. His jacket was nonchalantly draped around his shoulders in a way that was decidedly un-English, a cigarette dangled from his hand and a sardonic expression twisted his mouth. Judith heard him ask for a vodka and chuckled at the waiter's effusive apology. Vodka, like cold beer, was in short supply in London.

He had high cheekbones from which the flesh fell away into deep hollows and in his pitted complexion her trained eyes recognised the residual scars of smallpox.

She didn't realise she'd been staring until his mocking glance met hers. He bowed, raised the glass as though toasting her, swallowed the contents without pausing, placed the empty glass on a passing tray, picked up another whiskey and walked towards her.

Bowing stiffly, he said, 'Adam Czartoryski. I think I should not be speaking because we are not introduced, but I think you and I are what you English call strange man outside.'

She smiled. 'You mean odd man out. And I'm not English, I'm Australian.'

'Is same, no?' He spoke very precisely, sounding every consonant.

Before she could enlighten him about the ocean of difference between the two nations, he waved his arm to indicate the gathering. 'These people are very happy with themselves, isn't it?'

His sardonic tone made conversation difficult but she sensed he wanted to talk. 'What made you come here?' she asked.

'I am messenger from small nation, begging for crumbs from rich man's table.'

She was surprised how well he spoke English, apart from dropping the indefinite article, which she found quaint. She was about to ask what he meant when he raised his arm to silence her. From his frown, she saw that he was listening to the conversation of the group nearby.

'Our so-called allies in Europe are a dead loss,' a man was saying, and, when she looked around, she recognised the man with the long teeth who had made the disparaging remark about colonials. 'I don't suppose anyone was surprised when the French fell over themselves to surrender. They're always brave with words but damned cowards when it comes to action. But they've all crumbled like a pack of worn-out cards — Belgium, Holland, Norway. No bloody use at all. Damned collaborators, the lot of them.'

'It sounds as though the Poles are still struggling on,' someone commented.

'The Poles? Don't make me laugh. They're primitive. Back in the Middle Ages. Going to battle with horses and lances. And their pilots threw in the towel after three days. It's pathetic. They haven't got a clue.'

Tamping his cigarette out with two jabbing movements, Adam stepped forward and stood in front of the speaker, fists clenched, his face taut and white. 'You are not fit to clean boots of Polish soldiers.' He spat the words out through clenched teeth. 'And Polish airmen helped you win Battle of Britain, no?'

'Steady on old chap,' the speaker protested. 'Do calm down. In this country we're entitled to voice our opinions. But if I happen to think that another nation is backward, then I have the right to —'

Before he could say another word, Adam had swung his arm back, his fist clenched. There was a sharp intake of shocked breath and sounds of consternation. Suddenly Adam's arm was stopped in mid-air by a man behind him, who gripped it to restrain him.

'No doubt about you hot-headed Poles; always spoiling for a fight!'

Adam shook himself free and turned to see Stewart McAllister giving the group around them the disarming smile of a parent come to collect a naughty child from a party. Judith stared at this unlikely duo and realised that her brother must have befriended the Pole at the RAF base. Adam had stepped back but he was still glaring at the man whose comment had offended him.

Speaking in a low hoarse voice, he said, 'Poles are primitive and backward people on horses, yes? For three years Poland has been fighting Hitler. We don't have Vichy, we don't have Quisling, we don't collaborate. We fight Germans. And where is brave ally England? Our people are tortured and killed, our children are starved and shot and we still wait for help from your Prime Minister.' He shot an angry glance towards Churchill and the VIP group on the other side of the room. 'And you laugh at us!'

By now he had the attention of the entire hall. Everyone's eyes were fixed on him, appalled yet fascinated, as his voice rose and his face contorted with fury.

'Backward people are your politicians who don't do anything. And when we are dead and war is finished, your politicians will say they saved Europe!'

Two guards appeared on either side of him. 'You must leave at once, sir,' one of them said in a polite but forceful tone. They yanked Adam's arms behind his back and began to hustle him out of the room when Winston Churchill blocked their way.

'Please release Mr Czartoryski,' he growled. 'I'm sure he will find his own way out.'

'Let's go,' Judith said quickly. She had taken Stewart and Adam by the arm and was propelling them towards the door. She shook her head at Adam. 'And I thought I had a temper! You certainly know how to turn a posh gathering into a political bunfight!'

Stewart grinned. 'Now you know what I have to put up with. This temperamental Pole's my flying mate, worse luck! I just hope no one upsets him when we're up in the air!' He gave Judith's arm a playful punch. 'I'm not going yet, Sis. That glamourpuss in the slinky red dress is giving me the once-over. Sure you don't want to stay a bit longer?'

She shuddered. 'Couldn't bear it. I'll meet you at Lyons Corner House for tea later.'

Judith and Adam walked down Pall Mall. She had listened to several broadcasts on the BBC about Poland and had been distressed by the reports. It sounded as though terrible things were going on there and her blood boiled to think that the Germans were getting away with such savagery. One of the reports had been by a man called Śikorski, who was apparently the Commander-in-Chief of their government-in-exile, a concept she had never been able to understand.

Judith stole a glance at Adam's stormy expression. She wanted to tell him how angry she was that his country was suffering so much while the rest of the world was doing nothing to help, but decided against it. They continued their stroll in awkward silence.

Turning into Hyde Park, they walked along the banks of the Serpentine. It was peaceful there and the war seemed far away. The long winter was over. Swans glided in the lake and beds of daffodils brightened the park. Nature always boosted her spirits but from Adam's preoccupied expression she sensed he was in no mood to exult in the beauty of spring.

Her mind filled the silence with questions. Who was he? What had he been through that had etched such bitterness onto his face? The papers were always full of stories of the fearless Polish airmen who were pursued by women and fêted by the press. She knew that thousands of them had joined the RAF but the things Adam had said hinted that he'd had some other mission in England. His brooding expression didn't encourage conversation but there was one question she had to ask.

'How come Mr Churchill knew who you were?'

Adam gave a short, bitter laugh. 'I came to England to give information that could change the course of this war, maybe even history. But it was useless. They didn't think the fate of their ally was important.' He paused and the muscles in his jaw twitched. 'Now it is too late. Germans have crushed the Ghetto and Warsaw will be next.'

Bewildered, she waited for an explanation but, without saying another word, he abruptly raised her hand to his lips and bowed without taking his eyes off her face. As Judith watched him stride away, she felt the blood rushing to her cheeks, and she wondered what it would take to bring a smile to that haunted face. It was too early to meet Stewart, so she sank onto a park bench facing the lake. In its dark waters she saw only the image of Adam Czartoryski as his strange prediction resounded in her head.

Thirty-Two

Outside the dispersal hut, Adam was sitting in a sagging armchair with broken springs, eyes closed, face turned up to the sky, trying to focus on the weak sunshine instead of dwelling on his grievances. For several days now he'd watched enviously as his colleagues donned their yellow mae wests, grabbed their goggles and kitbags, and rushed off to the airfield. Half an hour later, the engines of the Lancasters would rev up, and the planes would roar down the runway and lift off. At the end of the day the airmen would stagger back to the base and discuss the dogfights and their narrow escapes.

During his training on the twin-engine Beech 16s, Adam had found it difficult to contain his impatience. He couldn't see the point of doing exercises in planes so different from the powerful four-engine Lancasters he'd be flying, and he was fed up with the condescending manner of some of the British officers. Now that the training period was over, he couldn't wait to get started. He hadn't met the Group Captain who had been on leave when he arrived, and he chafed at the incompetence of the RAF commanders who were so short of pilots yet left him there to stew.

Shifting around in the chair to relieve the pressure of

the springs, Adam had just closed his eyes again when he was summoned to see the Group Captain, who had recently returned to the base.

He sprang up, smoothed down his hair and, as he sprinted towards the office, he went over in his mind how he would let his superior know he was keen to start flying without making it sound like a criticism. When he entered, the Group Captain was standing with his back to the door, pinning markers on a large map of Germany. Adam was about to make his prepared speech when his superior turned around and the words died in his throat.

'Mr Czartoryski, isn't it? I believe we've already met.'

Adam swallowed and nodded. It was Charles Watson-Smythe, whom he'd met at the Europejski Hotel the night the Englishman's fiancée had thrown a glass of champagne in his face. The recollection of that night, and the humiliating conversation that followed, was still vivid in his mind.

As on the previous occasion, Sir Charles had the upper hand. He took advantage of it by prolonging the uncomfortable silence, giving Adam ample time to reflect on his misfortune in having the man he'd cuckolded as his commanding officer. There was nothing Adam could say so he waited, looked down at his shoes, and wished he'd never set eyes on his superior's vindictive fiancée.

'I seem to recall that when we met in Warsaw, Mr Czartoryski, you had joined the Polish Air Force, whose career was unfortunately cut short by the Luftwaffe. So now we've come full circle. You've joined the RAF in England and I've been appointed to this squadron because of the Polish flyers.

'Perhaps you recall that I speak a little Polish. Life is quite wonderful with its twists and turns, don't you agree?' His voice was mellow but his eyes threw darts.

Adam nodded. 'Yes, sir. Absolutely wonderful.' The words almost choked him.

Watson-Smythe stroked his chin. 'Everyone says that Polish airmen are daredevils. Do you think recklessness is a national trait, Mr Czartoryski?'

The conversation was about to become a minefield. Adam replied carefully, 'We think that the sooner Hitler is defeated, the sooner Poland will be free, sir.'

'They say you Poles know how to die but you don't always know how to live.'

Adam bit the inside of his lip to suppress a retort. In the circumstances, it wouldn't be wise to react to the provocation.

Watson-Smythe was flicking through a log book. 'The Polish chaps certainly seem to chalk up a lot of successes. More than the British crews. I find that very strange, given their, ah, less than distinguished performance in 1939. How do you account for it?'

Adam pulled at his tie, which suddenly felt very tight. He wanted to say that their training made them sharper and more alert. Their loose formations, spread wide at various altitudes, gave each member of the squadron a clear view of the sky, instead of being hemmed in by the close formations that the British air force favoured, which risked collisions with their own planes. And they were taught to fly right up close to the enemy. He could still remember his instructor reiterating, 'Don't fire till you can see the whites of their eyes.'

Struggling to keep his voice even, he said, 'We had weak planes, sir, not weak pilots. They were outmoded and didn't have sophisticated equipment, so instead of relying on radar and radio, we had to use our eyes and concentrate on what was going on around us.'

'So the Polish airmen are good at using their eyes, are they?' Watson-Smythe said in an insinuating tone. 'From what I hear around the village, that's not all they're good at. I hear they're rowdy troublemakers, and no female is safe with them around. The local high school has warned its girls to keep away from gin and Polish airmen!'

Adam looked down to conceal a malicious smile. If Englishmen knew how to court their women and make them feel desirable, they wouldn't lose their sweethearts to the Poles. But, as he was well aware, after the incident at the Europejski Hotel, Watson-Smythe had a score to settle.

Finally the interview was over and he was curtly dismissed with a sharp glance that warned him to watch out. As he walked away, he wondered whether he had any future in the RAF.

He was mulling over his prospects over a glass of whiskey that evening when pandemonium broke out in the hut. The airmen were shouting and one of them grabbed the *Daily Mirror* from someone's hands, tearing several pages.

Romek leapt up on a table, his face brick-red with anger. 'The sons of bitches! The fucking bastards! And they're supposed to be our allies! I knew we couldn't trust them!' He spat in disgust.

'You're a bloody moron,' Tomasz was shouting. 'It's just German propaganda and you fell for it!'

Several others joined in the fracas, punches were thrown, and beer glasses shattered on the floor.

'What's all the fuss about?' Adam asked Romek. 'Did someone run off with your girlfriend?'

Romek had fallen in love with the dimpled village girl who served their meals. Betty had resisted the other airmen but she hadn't been able to resist Romek. He boasted about his conquest at every opportunity, which irritated the others and often led to fights.

Before Romek could reply, Tomasz thrust the tattered pages of the *Mirror* into Adam's hands. 'You must be the only one who hasn't heard. Here, look for yourself.'

As Adam read the news item, he raised the paper closer to his eyes, as though to ensure that not a single word escaped his attention. According to German Radio, the bodies of about four thousand Polish officers had been discovered in mass graves in Katyń Forest, near Smolensk, and they accused the Russians of their murder.

'You can shout and break all the glasses you like, but you'll never convince me it was the Bolsheviks.' Tomasz was standing over Maciej, who looked as though he was about to hurl another glass into the fireplace. 'Wake up, for fuck's sake; why would they murder our soldiers? It's obvious that the Germans would blame the Russians. Surely you don't expect them to own up and say they did it?'

Maciej's face was contorted with emotion. 'You're the one that should wake up! Have you forgotten how they marched into eastern Poland like a bunch of hyenas in 1939? While they were spouting propaganda about brotherhood and equality, they were deporting hundreds of thousands of Poles to Siberia. Reckoned they were subversive elements or bourgeois intellectuals or such like. They're devious bastards. Just ask anyone who ever lived under Russian occupation.'

They were all shouting at Tomasz. Like Maciej, most of the men in the hut had become Russian prisoners when Russia invaded eastern Poland in 1939 and had been deported to remote parts of Siberia where they starved, froze and suffered at the hands of their Russian captors.

Maciej banged the table with his fist and his voice rose above the others. 'People died like flies in their stinking gulags. If Hitler hadn't broken his pact with Stalin in 1941, we'd still be rotting in those camps. They only let us go because circumstances turned them into our allies. They hate our guts. Polish bourgeois pigs, pimples on the arse of humanity — that's what they called us. First chance they get, they'll grab Poland by the balls — just wait and see.'

While the arguments raged back and forth, Adam was deep in thought. When he had given his report to the Polish government-in-exile, Śikorski, the Commander-in-Chief, had impressed on him that it was vital for the Allies to remain united in order to defeat Hitler. What would happen to that unity now, if it was discovered that Russia had murdered thousands of Polish officers in cold blood? From his insights into politics, he surmised that, in blaming the Russians, the Germans were putting the cat among the Allied pigeons to weaken the alliance. Would the British risk offending Stalin by giving credence to the German report?

Like Maciej and most of the others, Adam had no illusions about Soviet methods either, and was familiar with their ruthless quest for domination, which masqueraded as benevolent ideology.

He knew that hundreds of thousands of Polish academics, priests, businessmen, military and government personnel had been arrested and shot, or deported to Siberia during the Russian occupation of eastern Poland in 1939.

Adam sat bolt upright. Perhaps that's what had happened to his father. From the moment he'd heard that his father had disappeared, he had assumed that he'd either been killed in battle or captured by the Germans. But it was possible that his father was one of the Polish officers shot by the Bolsheviks in that birch forest near Katyń. If that was true, he knew that his father would have died with dignity and without regrets, content that he had done his duty for Poland. Although he and his father had never seen eye to eye on most issues, he had a grudging admiration for the old warrior's uncompromising principles. Adam sighed. He had always longed to discuss things with his father as an equal, to have his ideas taken seriously and respected, instead of being dismissed as puerile. But that would probably never happen now.

He felt a sense of loss rather than grief. His father would have died with his honour intact, knowing that he hadn't disgraced his noble lineage. Adam wondered whether when his turn came he'd be able to say the same.

Thirty-Three

Elżunia didn't know how long she'd been stumbling along unfamiliar streets, brushing against buildings for support. Only one thought spurred her on: to put as much distance as possible between herself and the smouldering Ghetto. As though in slow motion, her knees buckled and she leaned against a large plane tree, shivering in the cool May evening. Plastered to a lamp-post nearby, large black letters proclaimed that any Jews caught outside the Ghetto, and those who sheltered them, would be shot. She broke into a cold sweat. So she had merely exchanged one set of dangers for another. She had thought that if she could dodge the bullets and the flames, avoid being buried alive in collapsing tunnels, and get to the other side of the wall, she'd be safe. But now she realised that this had been an illusion. No matter where she was, her life was still in peril.

Her limbs were heavy and she wanted to crawl into a dark corner and sleep, but she knew she had to keep going. Gritting her teeth, she forced herself to move on. Warsaw had become an alien, hostile city where dark buildings threw malevolent shadows and people cast suspicious glances as they hurried to reach home before the curfew hour.

Home. Elżunia swallowed hard to hold back the tears. She had no home, no parents, not even a roof over her head. Her identity card! Where was her identity card? She plunged her hand into her skirt pocket. Thank God, it was still there. But a moment later she realised the card was useless on this side of the wall, worse than useless. She had to get rid of it and fabricate some plausible story to explain how she'd lost it in case a policeman or Gestapo agent stopped her. She had to get off the street. But where could she go?

Think, quick, think, she urged herself, but the more panic-stricken she felt, and the faster her heart raced, the more paralysed her mind became. There must be someone she could trust. She recalled all the parties, dinners and happy occasions they'd celebrated with her parents' friends, including her own name day. Surely someone would shelter her. She thought of couples she had particularly liked, and visualised the delight on their faces when they opened the door and saw that she'd survived. She could almost feel the warmth as she fell into their arms.

Then she remembered that some of them had turned against her mother when they'd discovered she was Jewish, while others made sympathetic noises but had done nothing to help. Perhaps her father was out there somewhere, longing to tell her how desperately he'd tried to get the three of them out of the Ghetto, but she knew that was a fantasy.

Her girlfriends — how could she have forgotten Gosia and Lydia; surely they'd persuade their parents to take her in. Then she remembered. Her friends had no idea she was Jewish, and she doubted whether they would help her when they found out.

The acrid smell of smoke mingled with the cloying stench of burning bodies wafted over the street, and as she looked up and saw the smoke billowing above the city she thought about her mother down in the bunker and blinked away the tears. And Gittel. What had become of her? She hadn't seen any trace of her in the bombed-out bunker. Was she wandering around, scared and hungry, in the burnt-out streets of the Ghetto? At the thought of the child being frightened and alone, Elżunia choked back a sob. She should have stayed in the Ghetto and died with all the rest. Unable to walk any further, she sank into a doorway. Let them arrest and shoot her. She was too exhausted to care.

Elżunia fell into a slumber as deep and dark as a well. She heard someone demanding to see her papers, calling her a thief and a murderer. I'm only waiting for my father, she kept saying. He said he'd come, he'll be here any minute now. But the voice grew louder and more insistent and a hand was shaking her shoulder. Her eyelids fluttered open.

Someone was leaning over her. She sat up. Her father had come! But the dream faded as she saw an old crone with a hunched back and quick dark eyes leaning on a walking stick. Elżunia shrank back in fear. With her sunken mouth and jutting chin, she reminded Elżunia of Baba Yaga, the witch who kidnapped and ate children in fairy tales.

The old woman was peering into her face. 'What's the matter, dearie? You were tossing around and moaning. Are you ill?'

Elżunia shook her head, still dazed by her dream and repelled by the Baba Yaga in front of her who was clucking her tongue.

'You're as skinny as a fieldmouse. How long since you've had something to eat? Come upstairs and I'll give you a bowl of hot soup.'

Elżunia's eyes darted around for a way to escape but the old crone seemed to read her thoughts. 'Don't look so worried. I only want to help you. You'll get picked up if you stay out here.'

Elżunia hesitated but the light was fading and soon the curfew would start. She couldn't remember when she had last eaten something, and the prospect of hot soup and a place to sleep was too strong to resist.

'I'm Granny Koszykowa. You can call me Granny. Everybody does,' the old woman panted as they climbed the dusty staircase. Finally they were on the top floor and Elżunia almost fell inside with exhaustion as soon as Granny turned the key in the door.

She caught sight of herself in the small pitted mirror on the wall and screamed. Looking back at her was a blackened face streaked with tears and covered with blisters, and singed, matted hair that stuck out in clumps all over her head. Granny's appearance had scared her, but she looked even more frightening. It wouldn't have been necessary for anyone to inspect her *Kennkarte*; one glance would have told them who she was and where she'd come from.

Granny placed a steaming bowl of soup on the table but Elżunia was so exhausted that without touching the soup she crumpled onto the bedding that the old woman had made up on the floor, and fell into a dreamless sleep.

When Elżunia opened her eyes, she felt the sun shining on her face. The window was open and shafts of light were streaming in between little pots of scarlet geraniums lined up on the sill. She looked around the room. Every surface was covered with ornaments: flowered dishes with scalloped edges, wooden statues of priests and peasants, jugs with fancy handles, pottery elves with red hoods, and porcelain dogs with pink tongues lolling out. There were snow-storms from Zakopane, gilt-edged saucers from Sopot, and watercolours from Gdańsk. One shelf was filled with dolls. Polish china dolls with braids, red boots and head-dresses trailing ribbons; Dutch dolls in clogs and aprons; and

Japanese dolls in kimonos and obis. It seemed that Granny never discarded anything. The effect was so cheerful and homely that Elżunia's spirits rose.

The old woman had gone out, but she'd left a plate of buckwheat *kasza* on the worn oak table. As Elżunia started spooning it greedily into her mouth, suddenly such sadness overwhelmed her that tears rolled down her cheeks and salted the *kasza*, which stuck in her throat. Unable to eat, she walked over to the window. Birds were twittering in the plane tree as they hopped around among the large leaves that had begun to unfurl. In a nest, wedged into the fork of two thick branches facing the window, three fledglings opened their beaks as their parents flew back and forth, dropping insects into their waiting throats. As Elżunia watched, she felt something quicken inside. She hadn't struggled so hard and endured so much to give up now. Facing the smoke that was still billowing from the Ghetto, she made a vow. 'Gittel, wherever you are, I promise I'll never stop looking for you, as long as I live,' she whispered, fighting back the tears.

As she stared out of the window, she thought she heard a skittering sound in the ceiling and looked up. The noise stopped but a few moments later it started again, and this time it sounded like scurrying feet. Perhaps a cat with kittens. She strained to listen but the noise had stopped and she returned to the view out the window. A strong breeze shook the branches and with a sharp flap of their wings the birds flew away.

The key turned in the lock and Granny hobbled in, puffing. After looping her cane over the back of a chair, she took a heavy metal pannikin from her string bag and placed it on top of the tiled stove.

'So you're awake at last, dearie,' she said. 'Did you know you slept for two whole days? I was getting worried but I suppose after what you've been through, you needed rest more than food.'

While Granny bustled about, chattering as she put away her parcels, Elżunia felt her stomach twisting. Soon she'd have to leave this safe haven, but where would she go and how would she live?

Granny was standing by the window, looking in the direction of the Ghetto, shaking her head until her jowly chin wobbled. 'There's nothing left of it now but rubble and ashes. Those poor souls. But one day God will punish the evildoers, you'll see.'

Her wrinkled mouth was working as though she were whispering to herself. After a pause, she asked, 'Do you have anyone you can go to, child?'

Elżunia shook her head.

Granny lapsed into a thoughtful silence again. 'I could do with a bit of help around the house,' she said. 'If you can do a bit of dusting and washing, you can stay with me.'

Elżunia threw her arms around the old woman's neck and promised to do whatever she asked, although she couldn't understand why someone living alone in one small room would need help with the housework.

'There are lots of busybodies in this building so keep yourself to yourself,' Granny cautioned her. 'But if anyone asks, you're my great-niece from Białystok. You ran away from home to stay with me because your stepfather was a drunkard and used to belt you.' She gave Elżunia a searching glance. 'Anyway, until those blisters heal, and your hair grows back, you'd better stay out of sight.'

That night, while she lay on her bed on the floor, she heard faint noises again and glued her eyes to the ceiling. How did cats get in there, and how would they get out?

It was still dark when she woke up and saw a shadow moving across the room. Without making a sound, she propped herself up on her elbows. The old woman was tip-toeing to the bathroom. Elżunia lay down again but heard two distinct taps. She sat up. A few moments later she heard the skittering sound again, before drifting off to sleep.

'I've heard some funny noises up in the ceiling,' she said the next morning while she was sweeping the wooden floor.

The old woman nodded. 'Mice, probably. Or rats. These old buildings are infested with them but with everything else that's going on these days, who's going to bother about rodents?' She picked up her worn handbag. 'I'm off,' she said. 'Can you cut these vegetables up while I'm out?'

As Elżunia peeled a few soil-encrusted potatoes and turnips and cut up the cabbage, she wondered what had become of yesterday's barley soup. Granny certainly had a hearty appetite.

Thirty-Four

Elżunia looped the eiderdowns and pillows over the railing at the back and was bashing them with a bamboo carpet beater, raising fine puffs of dust with each blow when she heard voices in the yard and looked down. Two women with scarves over their hair and black rubber boots halfway up their calves were gossiping as they leaned over large metal basins while they scrubbed their sheets. One of them straightened up, arched her back and waved a soapy arm towards the landing where Elżunia stood.

'You have to be careful these days. You never know who your neighbours are,' she said. 'They're all over the place now. They change their names and learn to recite the Lord's Prayer, but I can tell them a mile off.'

Elżunia stopped beating the bedding and flattened herself against the wall.

The other woman placed her hands on her wide hips. 'Franek says it's good riddance; we'll be much better off without them. He and his pals keep going on about their houses, and the gold and silver and stuff that we'll end up with. I won't say no if any of it comes my way, but I can't help thinking that God might punish us for gloating over them.'

The other woman waved a dismissive hand, sending a stream of iridescent bubbles floating over the yard. 'If you ask me, God meant it to happen. Anyway, the Germans will let us have it if they catch any of them in here, so we'd better keep a lookout.' Her gaze swept around the yard and lingered for a moment on the back stairs, where Elżunia had been standing a minute before.

Back inside, Elżunia heard the door of the adjacent room open and close. High heels clicked down the stairs. Curious, she peered through the window in time to see a tall brunette in a loose navy coat, a beret set at a jaunty angle on her smooth hair, and a small basket over her arm. She had just turned the corner when two men in trenchcoats banged on the door downstairs. Gestapo. Elżunia's heart pounded. She couldn't make out what they were saying. Were they looking for someone in particular or hunting for Jews? Any minute now, they'd bash the door down and find her. If they asked tricky questions about her supposed family in Białystok, she'd be lost. She heard a key turning in the lock and jumped.

'Quick,' Granny whispered. 'They'll be here in a minute. Lie down on the sofa and don't move. I'll throw the eiderdown on top of you. Thank God you're skinny.'

Several moments later, there was banging on the door. Feigning an exasperated sigh, Granny opened it, looking older and more stooped than ever. 'What on earth are you people looking for in a poor old woman's home?' she complained as they pushed past her.

'We know there are Jews hiding in the building,' one of them snapped, his eyes hard as hammers.

'Jews? Do you think I'd risk my life hiding Jews?' Granny scoffed, and sat down heavily on the sofa. 'If I thought any of the vermin were hiding here, I'd be the first to let you know.'

Groaning, she stretched out on the sofa. 'I'm that worn out. The doctor says, if I don't rest, I'll cark it. With all the hours I spend in queues trying to buy a bit of food, my poor old legs can hardly hold me up.'

On and on she grumbled while Elżunia hardly dared to breathe, terrified that at any moment they'd notice the bulge under the eiderdown. They stomped around the little room, looked in the bathroom, peered over the balcony and then stomped out, slamming the door so hard it almost fell off its hinges.

Elżunia didn't budge for a long time. When she finally emerged from under the eiderdown, she was still shaking.

'That was quite an act you put on, Granny,' she said. 'But you're risking your life having me here. I think I should go.'

Granny took her hand. 'If we can't help each other, what's life all about?'

That night, on her bed on the floor, Elżunia thought about the conversation of the two women in the yard and wondered whether one of them had contacted the Gestapo. But how could they have known she was there when she'd never stepped out of the building?

When Granny returned the following afternoon, her whole body seemed to sag and her chin looked more prominent than ever. And for once she hadn't brought any bags. Although she didn't say what was on her mind, it was obvious that something was worrying her. Elżunia wondered where she went every day and why she was so upset.

When Elżunia peered into the mirror a week later, she was relieved to see that her blisters had healed. Finally she would be able to stretch her legs and feel the late spring sun on her face. Granny had thrown out Elżunia's torn and charred clothes, and had altered one of her old dresses to fit her.

Looking at her reflection, Elżunia felt confident that she could merge with the crowd without attracting attention.

Intrigued by Granny's mysterious comings and goings, she decided to follow her the next morning. As soon as the old woman had closed the door behind her, and Elżunia heard her limping down the stairs, she ran to the back door to check that the women were too busy beating their rugs and eiderdowns over the back railings to notice her, and slipped out of the house.

Once outside, she realised how debilitated she'd become and how often she had to stop to catch her breath. Luckily Granny hobbled along, and stopped to rest from time to time too, leaning on her cane. The journey seemed interminable, and the further away from the house Elżunia walked, the more apprehensive she became.

Eventually she saw Granny's bent figure turn into Nowy Swiat Street, near the Four Seasons Café. Long ago, back in the long-distant days when life was happy and predictable, her parents would sometimes take her there for tall glasses of iced coffee heaped with scoops of luscious vanilla ice-cream, but now the sign in the window said *Nur für Deutsche*.

A tram was clanging along the road, and she was wondering why Granny hadn't boarded it instead of walking so far when she noticed the sign on the front. *Germans Only*. Nowy Swiat was a good name for this area, she thought bitterly. It certainly was a new world, where trams, shops, cafés, cinemas and restaurants were reserved exclusively for German use.

Granny hobbled on until she came to the Square of the Three Crosses, a large tree-lined plaza with its familiar landmark, the baroque dome of St Aleksander's Church. As soon as she saw the church, Elżunia's throat constricted. It was here that her mother had undergone her conversion, and, to their misfortune, it was here that Madame Françoise's cousin had been the parish clerk. Three elderly women in headscarves were entering the colonnaded portico, and Elżunia wondered whether this was where Granny was heading.

But the old woman walked past the terminus where the tram drivers were calling out to each other and cursing while they shunted the carriages and hooked up the cables. Elżunia felt uneasy. She had strayed into the heart of the German district, the forbidden zone of the city that no longer felt like Warsaw.

The sound of hob-nailed boots reverberated through the square. Elżunia flattened herself against a recessed gate as a detachment of SS men emerged from their barracks and marched towards Ujazdowskie Aleje. They passed the German soldiers' home, where a Beethoven symphony was blaring from the upstairs windows, and disappeared from view.

Now that the parade was over, Elżunia ventured into the square again and saw some street urchins hanging around outside the soldiers' home. Some proffered loose cigarettes from their grimy hands, and others held up entire packets, while here and there the young hawkers swaggered around with an assortment of packs displayed on trays suspended around their necks. A German official emerged from the building and was immediately beset by the youngsters vying for his attention as they waved their merchandise in his face and shouted its praises.

'Egyptians, Klubs, Mewas, roll-your-owns, best prices!' they shouted.

Elżunia noticed that they weren't frightened to approach the soldiers, or to argue with them about the price.

'Those others are crap; that's why they're so cheap,' she heard one girl say in a shrill voice as she sidled up to one of the Germans. 'If you want quality, you have to pay for it.'

Elżunia looked around for Granny and spotted her in the corner of the square that led to Jerozolimskie Aleje. She was surrounded by some of the cigarette sellers who were all talking at once. In the centre stood a small boy, shuffling in his broken wooden clogs, and from the way he hung his head as the others pointed in the direction of Konopnicka Street, where the SS barracks were located, she guessed he was the subject of their discussion.

Every few moments, he hitched up his trousers, which were fastened with a big safety pin, or adjusted the piece of mangy fur that was wrapped around his thin shoulders with a piece of string. From the way Granny was bending over the boy, it looked as though she was trying to talk him into something. She didn't smoke so what possible business could she have with these young cigarette sellers, Elżunia wondered. But a few moments later, the old woman walked away from the youngsters and, to Elżunia's astonishment, entered the soldiers' home.

Intrigued by the boys and their business dealings, Elżunia edged a little closer. Their clothes looked as if they hadn't been taken off in months. From their torn and stained jackets and trousers, she could see they were homeless. The tallest boy's trousers were frayed and reached halfway down his calves, as though he'd outgrown them several years before. Standing next to him was a smaller boy with fair hair and light-coloured eyes. Despite his colouring, something about his features and worried expression reminded her of a kid she'd seen around the Ghetto. Could he and some of the others possibly be Jewish? But a moment later she dismissed the idea as preposterous. It was absurd to imagine that Jewish children would risk plying their trade under the noses of the Germans.

The boys noticed her watching them, nudged each other, whispered something, and moved to the other side of the square. Common sense urged her to move on, but she had to find out whether her hunch was correct. Perhaps they, too, had escaped from the Ghetto. It was a long shot, but perhaps they had come across Gittel or Stefan.

As she walked towards the oldest boy, whom the others called Toughie, he tossed back a lock of fair hair and stuck out his chin, looking at her defiantly.

'I'd like to buy one of those cigarettes.' She pointed to the individual ones spread out in a row on his tray.

He gave her a knowing look. 'Your favourite brand, is it, miss?'

Ignoring the sarcasm, she whispered, 'Where are you from?'

'What's it to you?'

The others had moved closer and were looking at her suspiciously.

'Who's the nosy dame?' one of them muttered. 'Why's she hanging around and asking questions?' He turned to Elżunia and waved his arm as if to shoo her away. 'Clear off! Beat it!'

Elżunia realised that they suspected her of being a *szmalcownik*. She was offended that they thought she was snooping around to blackmail them, but their reaction told her what she wanted to know.

'Don't worry, I'm not spying on you,' she began, and hesitated. She was trying to figure out a way of letting them know that she was one of them. Perhaps they had seen Gittel or knew something about her. If she could win their confidence, she might be able to ask them if they knew where the little girl was. But before she could speak, she saw two SS officers striding across the square, and the boys rushed towards them, holding out their cigarettes.

Seeing the SS men, Elżunia was shocked. Distracted by the cigarette sellers, she had forgotten the risk she was taking, wandering around without any documents. It was getting late, and she had to do her chores before Granny returned. She wanted to run but forced herself to slow down, so as not to attract attention. Although her heart was pounding, she held her head high and tried to look confident. Several times she weaved in and out of side streets to avoid Germans who were patrolling the streets.

As she walked, she thought about the feisty young entrepreneurs who managed to make a living on the streets of Warsaw, dodging local extortionists, SS officers, Gestapo, Polish policemen, and Hungarian auxiliaries who had been co-opted into the German militia. She supposed that they were homeless orphans who were desperate enough to earn a living in this dangerous way.

Back home, she almost collided at the gate with the young woman in the beret and trenchcoat she had seen the previous week. She had the same small basket over her arm and Elżunia noticed that it was covered with a fringed white cloth, like Little Red Riding Hood about to take her grandmother some food.

'I'm Marta,' the woman said. 'I don't think I've seen you before.'

'I haven't been here long,' Elżunia said. 'I'm Granny Koszykowa's niece. I ran away from Białystok because my stepfather was bashing me and ...'

Marta was watching her attentively. 'I see,' she said. 'That's very interesting, but I wouldn't volunteer so much information all at once if I were you.'

Before Elżunia could reply, Marta gave her a friendly wave and hurried off.

Upstairs, Elżunia turned the conversation over in her mind, upset that Marta had seen through her story and had known she was lying. Was she giving her a warning or just well-meant advice?

That night, while Granny snored softly in her bed, Elżunia was washing herself over the wobbly sink in the corner of the kitchen that served as a bathroom when she heard the scrabbling noise in the ceiling again. This time she'd find out what it was. She picked up the broom, climbed up on a stool, pushed aside the manhole in the ceiling and poked her head inside.

At first she couldn't see anything but after a few moments, when she became accustomed to the dark, she saw something gleaming and held her breath. She was looking into the terrified eyes of a tiny boy wrapped in a mangy fur jacket.

Thirty-Five

'So now you know!'

Startled, Elżunia almost fell off the stool. Behind her, in a loose flannel nightgown, her sparse hair pulled into a skimpy pigtail at the back, Granny Koszykowa stood clasping and unclasping her gnarled hands. The old woman hobbled to the table and sat down heavily on a chair, while Elżunia chewed her thumbnail, bracing herself for rebukes and accusations.

'I suppose you had to find out sooner or later.' Granny held up a warning finger. 'I'll tell you why he's here, but don't breathe a word to any of the neighbours.'

For the past year, Granny had been working in the kitchen of the German soldiers' home. Each day, while walking across the Square of the Three Crosses, she had noticed growing numbers of cheeky cigarette sellers accosting passersby. With the Germans burning and razing the Ghetto to the ground, she realised they must be Jewish orphans who'd managed to escape.

'I felt sorry for those kids so sometimes I bought the odd packet of cigarettes from them, and traded it for food in the soldiers' home,' she said.

As time went on, the cigarette trade in the square had flourished, and more youngsters joined them.

'I couldn't believe how young some of them were, like Zbyszek here.' Granny inclined her head towards the loft. 'He's only seven.'

Elżunia looked up and saw a little face with a mop of tousled hair peering through the open manhole.

'It warmed my old heart to see the way the older ones took the younger ones under their wing and shared everything with them. They say war brings out the worst in people, but those kids made me feel there's hope for us yet.' Granny's eyes grew moist, and, pulling out a large handkerchief she'd stuffed into her sleeve, she trumpeted into it.

'But the Square of the Three Crosses swarms with Germans, so why on earth aren't those kids picked up?' Elżunia asked.

'I wondered about that too at first. But I don't think it would occur to the Germans that Jewish kids would have the nerve to run around the city and do business with them. Anyway, the Germans want cigarettes and don't care who sells them. They probably think they're just ordinary Polish kids.'

'But how come the Polish cigarette sellers don't dob them in?' Elżunia asked.

'They'd like to get rid of the competition, but they don't know for sure whether they're Jewish or not, and besides, what they're all doing is illegal, so they don't want to draw the attention of the Gestapo to themselves. Whenever the Polish boys start bullying and threatening them, Toughie and the older boys soon show them who's boss. They've learned to use their fists and protect themselves.'

Elżunia nodded. From what she'd observed, Toughie and his gang could be very forceful. 'You were going to tell me about Zbyszek,' she said.

For the next few minutes, Granny told her how Zbyszek had come to be in her loft.

Because it was so easy to find out whether boys were Jewish, the older boys had tied Zbyszek's trousers with a piece of cord and fastened them with safety pins instead of elastic to make it harder to pull them down, but he clung to the moth-eaten fur because it used to belong to his mama. They'd drummed into him that he had to stay close to them, never mention his parents or the Ghetto, and, if anyone asked, he was to say that his father had died in Siberia and his mother had died of pneumonia. They kept telling him to stay close to them, but Zbyszek was a bit of a dreamer and kept wandering away.

One day, while he was dawdling around the square, picking up scraps of coloured paper and small pebbles, two Catholic kids gave him a caramel. Thrilled with his new friends, Zbyszek told them a secret. His real name was Srulek.

As soon as he realised he'd given away his Jewish name, he bolted, weaving in and out of the crowd until they lost sight of him. But when he told the other boys what he'd done, they were aghast, and, as soon as they saw Granny the following morning, they rushed over and begged her to take him before the Catholic kids or the Germans came looking for him, and for them as well.

'I've helped them out in the past when some of them were in trouble and had nowhere to go,' Granny said. 'It's warm up in the loft and quite safe, as long as they don't make a noise. I can't leave them down here. You know what little boys are like — they'd run around, make a noise, and the other tenants would soon know I was hiding Jewish children.

'So I brought Zbyszek here but that little monkey just can't keep still. That was the day before you arrived. I just tap the ceiling to let him know food's ready and I slide it in through the manhole.'

They heard sniffling above them. 'It's not fair. I don't want to stay here on my own. I want to sell matches and be with the other kids,' Zbyszek wailed. 'I promise I'll never talk to strangers again. Not even if they give me two caramels.'

Elżunia looked at Granny. 'You're taking a terrible risk, having both of us here, you know.'

'Don't worry, dearie.' She chuckled. 'You only die once and at my age I can't die young!'

Then in a serious voice, she added, 'One day we'll all have to give an account of ourselves, and I don't want to say that I turned away little children who needed help. Anyway, my dear mother always taught me that if you see a drowning man, you have to stretch out your hand and pull him out.'

Elżunia sighed. That's what her father used to say, but he hadn't pulled her and her mother and brother out when they were drowning. Although it hurt to think about her father, and she tried to push the painful thoughts away, he was never far from her mind and she wondered how long it would take for the wound to heal. She looked gratefully at Granny and her thoughts turned to Gittel. If only she was still alive; if only she had found a kind soul like Granny to look after her in some warm corner of Warsaw. Perhaps the cigarette sellers knew something. If only she could win their trust.

In the days that followed, Elżunia returned to the Square of the Three Crosses several times and watched the cigarette sellers from a distance. Within a week, she knew their names and nicknames, but, whenever they looked her way, their wary expression warned her not to approach them. One morning she watched a sharp-faced girl of about twelve, whose name was Basia, as she stopped a German official striding towards Jerozolimskie Aleje. Thrusting a pack of cigarettes in his face, she said, 'Look, American filtertips. Only thirty-five zloty for the lot.'

He examined the pack with narrowed eyes and handed them back. 'Thirty-five? I can get them for thirty over there.' He pointed in the direction of the gangly kid the other cigarette sellers called Giraffe.

'His are cheap because they're fakes,' she scoffed. 'If you want cheap cigarettes, take the Mewy or Egyptians. I've got some German Junos as well, but if you want the best, you have to pay for them.'

Without another word, he whipped out the notes from his bulging leather wallet and pocketed the cigarettes. As the girl skipped away laughing, she caught Elżunia's eye.

'That was smart work,' Elżunia said. 'How long have you been selling cigarettes?'

But the girl gave her a suspicious look and hurried off. As she disappeared from view, Elżunia felt like screaming with frustration. She admired these youngsters so much, and longed to establish contact with them, but they rebuffed her advances and misconstrued her intentions. She had to find some way of breaking through their mistrust.

For the next few days, Elżunia kept away from the square. There was no point exposing herself needlessly to the risk of being asked for her papers. But when Granny suggested one morning that she should go with her to the market for bread and cottage cheese, Elżunia jumped at the opportunity. Walking beside the old woman in the warm June sunshine, she felt safer. They were crossing the square when some of the cigarette sellers ran towards their old friend. A moment later they surrounded her, all talking at once, but when they noticed Elżunia, they fell silent and started edging away.

'She's all right,' Granny said, pushing Elżunia forward. 'You can trust her.' She glanced around to make sure no one was eavesdropping and lowered her voice. 'She's from the same place as you lot.'

Being Granny's protégé was Elżunia's passport to acceptance by the cigarette sellers. 'I'm looking for a little girl called Gittel,' she blurted out. 'She's five, but very tiny. Curly brown hair.'

They shook their heads. No one had seen or heard of the child. She thought the older boys might have come across Stefan, but they didn't know him either.

Elżunia walked home with a heavy heart. Her last hope was gone.

From that day on, the cigarette sellers treated her like one of their own, and in between darting around selling their cigarettes, they told her their stories.

After escaping from the Ghetto, they had wandered around Warsaw trying to find somewhere safe to stay. Many people refused to open the door, while others took one look and threatened to turn them over to the Gestapo.

Occasionally, someone took pity on them and let them spend the night in a cellar or attic, until a comment from a neighbour shrivelled their kind instincts. In their nightly hunt for a safe place to sleep, the kids sneaked into basements or curled up in doorways, and covered themselves with doormats until dawn when the caretakers shooed them away. Zbyszek had found a warm corner at the gasworks where he huddled on top of a floor vent, until the cleaner had found him and chased him out with a broom.

'When we're really desperate for something hot to eat, we go to the soup kitchen near the square,' Giraffe said, 'but we always have to be on the lookout in case someone recognises us and calls the Gestapo. Sometimes we go and clean up at the public bathhouse, but it's nerve-racking for us boys because we have to make sure no one sees us naked.'

Every day Giraffe walked several miles to the allotments where Warsaw residents had small plots of land. The owner, who didn't know he was Jewish, let him sleep on a pile of straw in the shed in return for digging the vegetable garden. Basia and three of the boys had found cheap lodgings in an attic on the other side of Warsaw.

'Our landlady has guessed we are Jewish and she keeps raising the rent. If we don't pay, she'll throw us out and maybe even report us to the Gestapo,' Basia said, casting her sharp eye around the square for prospective customers.

On the way home, Elżunia thought how lucky she was that she had a safe place to stay, not like the cigarette sellers who lived in constant danger on the streets, struggling to find a roof over their heads, and scrounging and hustling to survive. But in a way, she envied their camaraderie. At least they had each other. She had no one.

She had just stepped inside Granny's flat when she heard muted voices coming from the room next door. One was Marta's, but the deeper one belonged to a man. So Marta had an admirer! Elżunia remembered her mother saying that only cheap girls invited men to their rooms, but she didn't think Marta was cheap. She was so attractive — no wonder men fell in love with her. Elżunia sighed and thought of that courier from the Underground she knew only as Eagle. If he ever wanted to visit her at night, she wouldn't hesitate. She strained to hear what they were saying on the other side of the wall, but the voices had dropped to whispers. A moment later she heard muffled sounds, like kissing. The door opened and she heard soft footsteps going down the stairs.

Elżunia lay on her bed but couldn't sleep. She was wondering where the cigarette sellers were sleeping that night, and whether Eagle's mission had been successful. If only the Allies would come to Poland's rescue so that the war would finally end and life would be more than just a struggle for survival.

Thirty-Six

Adam cycled along the winding country lane on a warm July twilight, his hands sticking to the handlebars and his face streaming with sweat. He cursed each time he came to a hill and had to dismount and push, but, engrossed in a newspaper article he'd been reading, he'd missed the truck that had ferried the others to the village pub. Still preoccupied by what he had read, he had to swerve to avoid a small boy in a knitted sleeveless pullover who was meandering in the middle of the road.

More alert now, Adam bumped along the small stone bridge over the stream, past the old mill, and between the yew and hawthorn hedgerows where dog roses, daisies and campions flashed past like an impressionist's canvas. Past the hedgerows, small baize-green fields and market gardens were enclosed by low fences. Everything was neat and pretty here, and made him feel nostalgic for the small chequerboard fields and dark forests of Poland where wolves and bears still roamed.

Away from the airfield, which hummed with engines and throbbed with adrenalin day and night, life in these villages rolled at a slow pace and there was nothing to indicate that, for the past four years, this country had been fighting a war for its very existence.

Adam dismounted and wiped his neck and forehead, trying to catch his breath as he leaned the bicycle against the mock Tudor façade of the Red Lion. After pedalling for five miles, he realised that he was even more out of condition than the bike.

He pushed open the door of the pub. It was crowded and, through the fug of pipe and cigarette smoke, he saw that the buxom waitress was run off her feet, balancing four tankards of beer in each hand as she squeezed past the tables to a large group of villagers in the corner, bawling out a song he recognised as 'Roses of Picardy' at the top of their voices.

Some of Adam's colleagues were slouching at the bar, downing glasses of scotch as they flirted with the barmaid, whose face was half hidden by a cascade of peroxided waves in the style of Jean Harlow. Romek was hanging over the bar and looking soulfully into the girl's eyes.

'You are beautiful,' he said. 'Romek is my name.'

The girl didn't bother looking up from the beer she was drawing from the cask. 'Romeo, more like,' she retorted. 'And don't get your hopes up neither, 'cause my name's not Juliet.'

The others slapped their thighs and cheered, glad to see Romek get short shrift for once. They gave Adam a drunken wave and called him over, but he shook his head and kept walking. He didn't feel like listening to their flirtations, and their high spirits irritated him.

He sat down at a small round table wedged between the raucous merrymakers and the dartboard where two men with damp semicircles under their arms burst into triumphant cheers whenever one of them scored a bullseye. Adam stared moodily into his whiskey. How much longer was Watson-Smythe going to keep him hanging around? He'd joined the RAF to fly planes, but he was being kept in cold storage. Perhaps this was Watson-Smythe's way of settling scores. He drained the whiskey and signalled for another. What with his vindictive Group Captain, and the pugnacious Air Vice-Marshal Harris with his obsession to bomb the hell out of Germany, the RAF seemed in a pretty sorry state. In spite of their appalling losses, Harris had pressured the war ministry to let him send an aerial armada to pulverise Germany into submission, so no planes could be spared, and all air drops with supplies for the AK had been stopped. And, to make matters worse, even the Polish Parachute Brigade, which had been created expressly for the purpose of dropping supplies in, was being deployed elsewhere. Too restless to sit still, Adam took out the silver cigarette case, which felt as smooth in the palm of his hand as a lover's cheek, and lit a Camel filtertip.

The news he had read that morning had shocked him. He was astonished that, despite all that he and the world had endured in the past four years, he hadn't lost the capacity to be shocked by the death of a single individual. General Śikorski's plane had crashed in Gibraltar. Adam felt the death of the Commander-in-Chief of the Polish government-in-exile as a personal loss as well as a blow for Poland. Adam was convinced that General Śikorski would have been the ideal leader for the new Poland that would emerge after the war. There was no one of his vision or stature to replace him.

The mirth over the barmaid's rebuff had died down and the voices at the bar rose as the airmen discussed the crash in Gibraltar. They were a cynical lot, always looking for conspiracies, ulterior motives and underhand plots but for once Adam agreed with them. Although engine malfunction could have been responsible, he didn't believe the crash was an accident. He saw the discovery of the bodies of the murdered Polish officers in Katyń, the allegation that the perpetrators were Russians, and Śikorski's insistence on a Red Cross investigation, as a related chain of events that had culminated in his assassination. An inquiry would have exposed the Russians as the murderers of the Polish officers, diminishing their moral authority in their alliance with Britain and the United States.

Adam had thought it strange at first that the British and American leaders hadn't pressed for an inquiry themselves, and had even encouraged Śikorski to drop his demand, but suddenly he understood. The Allies had caved in because they were afraid of confronting Stalin, in case he made another pact with Hitler. He had done it in 1939 and he could do it again. He had only joined the Allies in 1941 because Hitler had invaded Russia, but there was nothing to stop him from deserting them and changing sides again. If he did that, the alliance would be in tatters, and so would their hope of winning the war.

The more Adam thought about this scenario, the more depressed he became about the future of his country. Who knew what promises had been made and what secret deals had been negotiated behind closed doors when Roosevelt, Churchill and Stalin had got together, and which countries would become the disposable pawns in their global chess game? From what he'd heard about Stalin, he had no doubt that under the benevolent avuncular façade he was as cunning as a fox, a devious poker player who could out-bluff his gullible allies and win the game, even if he held the weakest hand. When the stakes were so high, and alliances were built on shifting sand, how significant would the fate of Poland seem, and how staunchly would Churchill uphold its rights and keep his promises to uphold the sovereignty of Poland?

The carousing villagers were halfway through their boozy rendition of 'The White Cliffs of Dover' when a man with a red face veneered with sweat staggered to his feet, raised his foaming glass of Guinness in the direction of the airmen at the bar and shouted in a slurred voice, 'I'd like to propose a toast to the gallant Polish gentlemen who fly our planes and steal our women.'

The middle-aged woman beside him tugged at his sleeve to make him sit down. She was glaring at her husband but some of the other men slapped him on the back and nodded agreement.

A couple of the airmen were already pushing their way past the crowded tables with tense jaws that indicated their intention to settle the issue with their fists. They headed for the speaker who, along with two of his cronies, had already picked up chairs, ready to lash out.

Adam kicked away his chair and stepped between them. 'Piss off,' he told the airmen, signalling them to back away. Turning to the belligerent locals, he said, enunciating each word slowly and carefully, 'If you want to fight, join the air force and fight the Germans, not us.'

The uncertain lull that followed was enough to calm the combatants, who gave each other dirty looks but resumed their seats, fists clenched.

'Hey, Adam, I'm shouting you a scotch for restoring peace,' Tomasz called out. As Adam slipped onto a stool beside him, Romek half turned and muttered, 'Ungrateful peasants. We're getting our arses shot off defending their country and all those buggers can think about is that we're screwing their women.'

The others were nodding, and, sensing an imminent escalation of anger, Olek broke in.

'Can someone explain this to me? We've been dropping cookies on German cities, bridges and industrial areas for over a year now, losing men and bombers, but the Jerries still haven't surrendered. How long is Harris going to keep up this so-called Operation Millennium?'

'At least you're taking part in it and not just sitting around like me,' Adam said bitterly.

'Don't worry, your turn will come,' Tomasz said with a chuckle. 'And when those bastards come at you in their Me 109s, and the flak turns your plane into a sieve, you'll wish you were just sitting around!'

Adam's turn came sooner than he'd expected. As he entered the mustering hall the following day, the officer in charge, a jovial fellow with a veined bulbous nose nodded to him and said, 'Welcome aboard!' Then he turned to the others. 'Off you all go, lads, and get yourselves sorted.'

As they organised themselves into crews and collected their kits, Olek, their bombardier, pointed at Stewart. 'You'd better watch this navigator,' he warned Adam. 'He attacks pilots!'

Stewart grinned. 'Only when they try and bail out while I'm still inside.' He turned to Adam. 'We got coned by their searchlights last time,' he said. 'I thought we'd had it, and cold sweat was pouring into my daks till I thought I'd pissed myself. Then the bloody pilot panicked and started reaching for his parachute and jabbering that he was going to bail out, so I tackled him and threw him on the floor. The other guy flew the plane till the pilot calmed down enough to take over again.'

Adam was laughing. The Australian's flattened vowels and strange expressions never failed to amuse him. 'I give word of honour I'll never *jabber* as you call it, about my parachute, as long as you don't get us lost.'

For once Stewart wasn't smiling. 'Listen, mate, it gets pretty hairy up there at times. You never know what you'll do, fair dinkum.'

Adam's heart was racing as he walked into the briefing room and saw the map of Germany pinned to the wall.

There was an air of taut expectancy and the only sound was the rustling of the airmen's large celluloid pads. Watson-Smythe sprang onto the dais and tapped his pointer on the map.

'The plan is on,' he said in his clipped way. 'This is the night. Your target is Germany's third largest city, Cologne, and you're going to bomb the bejesus out of them.'

As he spoke, Watson-Smythe's gaze rested on Adam, who sensed a mocking light in his pale blue eyes. He looked down at his pad. Without realising it, he'd scrawled the word 'Cologne' on his pad and underneath he'd sketched a cathedral with two spires. He'd passed through the city as a student and had admired the Gothic spires soaring above the large *Platz*.

After the weatherman had given his report — full moon, good cloud cover — the intelligence officer estimated how much heavy artillery, how many ack-ack guns, and how many searchlights they might encounter, and explained that a new system of flares used by pathfinders would mark out their targets.

'Air Vice-Marshal Harris believes that a concentrated bomber stream is the best way to win this war,' Watson-Smythe concluded. 'So stay close together, lads, and good luck.'

Lurching in the lorry ferrying them over to the airfield, Adam lit a cigarette and inhaled deeply to control the butterflies in his stomach. It was twilight, and the sight of the lumbering Lancasters stationed on the tarmac made his heart pound. This was it. He tossed his half-smoked cigarette on the ground and looked up. The pale moon hung low in the silent sky that would soon throb with the sound of hundreds of aeroplane engines. Adam climbed into the cockpit and, as he adjusted his goggles with shaking hands, Tomasz touched his packet of Polish soil for luck, while the others kissed the crosses their mothers or sweethearts had given them to keep them safe. Stewart pulled on a wide-brimmed khaki hat with one side turned up, which looked so comical above the goggles that, despite the tension, the others laughed.

'I never fly without it,' he said. 'Dad's digger hat from Gallipoli. It brought him luck, so I reckon it'll bring me luck, too.' Seeing Adam's horrified expression, he added, 'Don't worry, mate, I'll take it off as soon as we're in the air. Just like to keep it close by.'

Adam's hand tightened around the cigarette case. That would be his talisman. Sitting high above the tarmac, he switched on the powerful engines of the Lancaster, thankful that it could fly faster, higher and further than the other bombers.

Behind him, squadrons of Lancasters, Halifaxes and Stirlings were about to lift off. He felt proud to be participating in the biggest concentration of air power in history and, as the huge plane vibrated, he recalled the pioneer aviator he'd hero-worshipped as a boy, and couldn't wait to get started.

He rolled the plane to the end of the runway, waited for the green light to flash, and lifted off, marvelling that such a huge machine could rise so smoothly. As they climbed into the sky, Adam looked down and caught his breath as he saw lakes of blood. It was the crimson glow of the setting sun reflected on the clouds but the apocalyptic vision seemed an omen. A moment later, the unnerving sight dissolved into luminous castles and golden mountains, a world of ethereal beauty of clouds above the earth.

They were flying high over the North Sea and the air had become so thin that they were all using their oxygen masks. Adam had an exhilarating sense that time was standing still when, in the darkness, he saw showers of sparks, as though thousands of lighters were flickering in the sky. The sparks crackled. 'Flak ahead,' he said. Instantly the atmosphere inside the Lancaster changed from relaxed camaraderie to taut watchfulness. In a way he couldn't explain, Adam felt that the crew had instantly drawn closer together, as though they were no longer individuals but parts of one body.

Around them, he saw the greenish vapour trails of other Lancasters. Focused on the same goal, it felt as though they were all part of one gigantic organism. In the distance he heard volleys of ack-ack fire. The thick dark clouds that had covered them until that moment had turned white and Adam knew that the Lancaster would now be a black sitting duck moving across a white screen, an easy target for the searchlights.

Suddenly they were flying into hell. The whole sky was lit up by vivid fighter flares, yellow, red and green, like a lethal fireworks display. Every few seconds, one of their planes became engulfed in orange flames and plummeted from the sky. Adam tried to keep the plane steady as they flew through a hail of tracer fire, heading for the centre of the pyrotechnic show. Flak guns spat great lumps of shrapnel and steel that thumped into the fuselage, and the acrid smell of cordite filled his nostrils as they were buffeted about.

A Lancaster on their starboard beam was caught in a cone of searchlight. A moment later, an eerie white light flooded their plane and Adam's voice, dead calm, spoke through the intercom.

'We've been coned. Hold tight.'

With all his strength, he pushed the control column forward and to the left, went into a steep descent, then, with a violent lurch, dived, twisted and corkscrewed up again, away from the deadly searchlights, flinging them around like a shuttlecock in a gale. Stewart's voice broke the silence. 'Good job I didn't have much for dinner. I've got to find the bloody target.'

He lay on his belly to line up the target ready for bombing. 'Four minutes to target,' he said. Adam knew he had to fly straight and level until the drop. His knuckles ached with the tension because they were at their most vulnerable in this flight position.

He heard sharp pinging sounds as flak shells struck the fuselage and he gripped the wheel so tightly that his hands seemed welded to it. He wondered whether they'd make it.

'Can't you drop the fucking thing?' he hissed at Stewart, who merely replied, 'Two minutes to target.' Adam shot an appreciative glance at his navigator. Underneath all that light-hearted bantering, Stewart had nerves of steel.

'Steady, steady, left, left, right,' he said, directing Adam to the target. It was hard to hear the words above the roar of the engines, the explosions and the bursts of fire all around them, and Adam had to strain to make out what Stewart was saying. Every six seconds, the bomber dropped payload and four-thousand-pound explosives burst like evil stars, their white fires spreading and joining up in the burning city below them.

When Adam looked down at the blazing city and saw the spires of Cologne Cathedral, something stuck in his throat and he had to clear it several times. He wanted to say the Lord's Prayer, but although he had lisped the words from the moment he could speak, hands clasped together as he'd knelt at the foot of his bed every night, this time his mind was numb and no words came.

'Cookies gone,' the gunner announced, and, with a sigh of relief, Stewart called out the new course that would take them home. Suddenly they were flying into a hailstorm of metal. Another succession of thumps rocked the plane.

Shells. They held their breath waiting for the explosion. Another shell pierced the fuselage and missed Stewart's seat by inches.

His face was white. 'Strewth, this must be my lucky day,' he said. 'Good job I brought my digger's hat.'

The hits had made holes in the fuselage and almost immediately the aircraft felt like a freezer. 'I do like a nice cool breeze on my back while I'm working,' Stewart quipped.

'Good job I'm flying this low,' Adam muttered. 'At least the shells aren't set to explode at this altitude.'

The plane shuddered. As he checked the instrument panel, he set his jaw. It was worse than he'd suspected. One engine was over-revving, another had had its propeller shorn off and the third had been struck and had lost oil. This left him with only one engine that worked, but if he used it for more than a few minutes at a time it would overheat.

The controls were almost impossible to handle because the lines for the trim tabs for the ailerons had been cut. It was a pilot's worst nightmare. Adam felt as if he were riding a wild bronco at a rodeo, expecting to be hurled off any second.

The plane had dropped to five thousand feet and he sensed that they'd crash any moment. 'I'm pressing on the control column as hard as I can, but it's no good,' he told the crew. 'Get ready to bail out.'

'Are you bailing out?' Olek asked.

Adam shook his head.

'If you're staying, so am I,' Olek said and the others nodded in agreement.

'I don't know what you're worrying about, mate,' Stewart said. 'We've got three dead engines, an unmanageable control column and no hydraulics, but apart from that we're doing fine.'

'Shut up and help me put more pressure on the control column,' Adam snapped. Standing behind him, Stewart practically climbed onto his back, and their combined weight helped to move the controls.

'Ditch everything fast to get rid of excess weight,' Adam said. 'Everything!' he repeated as the men hesitated before tossing out oxygen cylinders and parachutes. The die was cast. They'd made their decision and would live or die with the plane.

As soon as they saw the English coastline, their spirits surged. Almost home. But Adam knew that a crucial test remained. Somehow, he had to land this crippled machine.

He called 'Darkie, Darkie' repeatedly until a wireless operator at an airfield in Kent responded. 'You have to get to another airfield; you must,' she insisted. 'Our runway isn't long enough for a Lanc.'

'Can't you understand? There's no choice. I must land now!' he shouted.

He could hear muffled sounds and realised the girl was panic-stricken. Unable to use his flaps, he lowered the wheels. The Lancaster hit the ground with a sickening lurch that ripped the wings off. They bumped over some obstacles until they finally stopped.

The men emerged from the broken aircraft, white-faced and shaken. Some of them were limping while others had blood streaming down their faces. The medic waiting on the tarmac looked at them as though he'd just seen Lazarus rise from the dead.

'I've never seen anything like it! You've just taxied across a row of fuel tanks!' he cried.

Stewart, whose left arm was broken while his right hand was pressing against his broken clavicle, pointed to the digger's hat with his good arm. Turning to Adam, he said, 'Told you this'd bring me luck!'

Adam reached into his shirt pocket for a handkerchief to wipe the blood streaming from a cut on his forehead and patted the cigarette case.

Adam was writing his report about their mission a little later when Watson-Smythe strode into the briefing room.

'I'll thank you to bring the Lancs back in one piece in future, Czartoryski,' he said. Adam was wondering whether this was a criticism or an example of dry English humour when his superior gave him a brief nod and said, 'Well done.'

Thirty-Seven

As the months went by, Elżunia often saw her neighbour Marta hurrying from the building, always with the little basket that exuded the yeasty smell of freshly baked bread. Marta was a mystery. She couldn't be going to work at such irregular hours, so where was she taking the bread, and how did she manage to support herself? Apart from her man friend, whose murmurs Elżunia sometimes heard late at night, Marta had no visitors. It was unusual for such an attractive young woman to lead such a solitary life, unless she came from the country and had few friends in the city, but, with her jaunty beret and belted trenchcoat, Marta looked far too sophisticated for a country girl.

Intrigued, Elżunia watched out for her, hoping to draw her out, but, whenever they passed each other on the stairs, Marta gave her a bright smile and friendly wave and kept walking. It was clear she intended to keep her distance.

Elżunia was mulling over this while thrashing the dust out of Granny's eiderdowns and pillows. There was an autumn chill in the air and by the time she'd finished the daily ritual, she always felt warmer. Calmer too, as though beating the bedding helped to exorcise her anger and her desolation.

Down in the yard, the two women were gossiping over their washing as usual.

'One of these days that hussy will get what's coming to her,' the fat one said. Her little eyes were darting all around the yard. 'Who does she think she is? Miss High and Mighty. Too busy to pass the time of day, always running around.'

Her companion had been bending over the metal basin, wringing her sheets, and now straightened up with a groan. 'The Lord only knows what she gets up to,' she said, and added with an insidious smile, 'and who with.'

That was the question that had been on Elżunia's mind as well. The visits had become more frequent and she often heard Marta and the mysterious caller whispering in tones that sounded hoarse and intimate late at night. She picked up the unwieldy bedding and carried it inside. She swept the floor, dusted the furniture, wiped the window sill and wondered what to do with herself. For the first few months after her ordeal in the Ghetto, Granny's place had been a haven of rest and peace. But lately she felt she had lost her spiritual centre, as though a black hole had opened up inside and was threatening to swallow her up. With all hope gone of finding Gittel, and no trace of Stefan, there was nothing to live for. Nothing even to die for.

At night, when Granny knelt by her bed, saying her rosary, an irrational anger seized Elżunia. Didn't the old woman realise that her prayers floated into a cosmic indifference? One night, after saying her prayers, Granny turned and saw Elżunia watching her, and with her uncanny instinct for divining her thoughts, said gently, 'We have to pray harder than ever now, dearie, to make sure He hears us. You can see what happens to the world when people are left in charge.'

Elżunia had too much time to brood. Violent images from the last days of the Ghetto flashed constantly into her mind, and the sense of loss she felt each time she thought of her mother and Gittel, her brother and all her friends, was so overwhelming that she wanted to howl, hurl herself against the walls and bang her head on the floor so that the physical pain would dull the anguish in her mind.

The pressure continued to build so much that she thought she'd explode. All she could do was bash the eiderdowns and pillows each morning, and in between she tore at her nails until the skin around them was raw and bleeding.

In the Square of the Three Crosses, the cigarette sellers sometimes asked Elżunia about Stefan and Gittel.

'Your brother sounds like a smart fellow,' Giraffe said, stamping on the ground to warm his feet. 'He might have got away. You might find him one of these days.'

'But I don't like your chances of finding the little girl,' Toughie said gruffly. 'Even if she got out of there, how would she survive? She'd get picked up by the police in no time.' Noticing Elżunia's dejected face, he asked, 'Who is she, anyway? Is she your sister?'

Elżunia swallowed. 'Sort of. She's very tiny ...' Her voice trailed off and she pretended to look for something in her pocket.

'Someone might have felt sorry for her and taken her in,' he said, 'but they'd probably change her name, stick a cross round her neck, take her to church and you'll never find her. But at least she'll be safe.'

Elżunia walked away from the square, kicking the stones with her shoe. Her heart ached at the thought that she might never see Gittel again, but perhaps Toughie was right. She would certainly be better off living as a Catholic than wandering around the streets, hungry, cold and in constant danger. But what if someone cruel had taken her and she couldn't get away? Wherever Gittel was, whoever had taken her, however long it took, she had to go on looking for her.

She was walking towards St Aleksander's Church on a chilly December day when a convoy of open cars full of SS men and armed police drove into the square. She sighed. It would soon be New Year but 1944 held no promise of joy or freedom. The cars came to a halt in front of the church and the officers jumped out and rushed inside. Elżunia's heart was pounding with dread. They hadn't gone inside to pray.

A hush fell over the square. All eyes were on the church. They didn't have long to wait. They heard screams and yells and then the SS men and police were herding the worshippers from the church. Most were elderly women still gripping their rosaries. All the worshippers were lined up in front of the church wall. Just then, a covered truck roared up. Four armed police jumped out, pulled back the khaki canvas, and pushed out thirty prisoners, whose hands were tied behind their backs. Elżunia looked at their faces and almost screamed. Their mouths had been taped with plaster.

A deafening salvo of shots rang out, and a few seconds later the captives as well as the worshippers lay on the ground.

Elżunia's legs were trembling and she would have fallen if someone standing next to her hadn't reached out and gripped her arm. She looked up into bright blue eyes beneath a broad-brimmed felt hat.

'Dr Borowski!'

He looked around and placed a finger on his lips. 'No names,' he whispered.

When he felt it was safe to leave the square, he took her arm. Around the corner in Żurawia Street they slipped into a drab little café, whose occupants, like themselves, were shaken by what they'd just witnessed. Dr Borowski removed his hat and his thick white hair sprang around his face, like a nimbus. Still unable to speak, Elżunia looked at her trembling hands and listened to the conversations around them.

'Why did they shoot those poor people who'd been praying in the church?' the waitress asked as she placed two glasses of tea and some plain biscuits in front of Elżunia and Dr Borowski. 'What did they kill them for?'

'Just wait, they'll finish us off like they finished off the Jews and they'll flatten Warsaw like they flattened the Ghetto,' said a man at the next table, and added, 'At least the Jews fought back.'

When Elżunia finally picked up her glass and started sipping the scalding tea, the doctor leaned forward. 'I'm so happy to see you, Elżunia. I've thought about you so many times and wondered whether ...' He left off because tears were streaming down her face. Seeing him again evoked all the tragic events that had happened since they'd last met. She covered her face in her hands and cried.

'Don't hold back; get it all out,' he said soothingly, patting her hand.

She tried to speak but choked on the images in her mind before the words could come. Lech being blown up trying to save her, Edek's body crushed by the tank, Szmuel being machine-gunned, Itzak and Rahela probably torn apart by grenades or suffocated by smoke. Her mother dead and probably Gittel and Stefan too, and the living torches leaping to their deaths from the windows of blazing buildings. She still had a vision of the curtains in deserted houses blowing about in the breeze like spectral figures performing a ghostly dance.

'I don't know what it was all for.' Her voice came out as a hoarse rasp she hardly recognised. 'All those lives lost, all those great ideals, gone up in flames. What was it all for?'

'Never underestimate the value of what happened there during the Uprising,' Dr Borowski said. 'It was a noble stand for human dignity. For the right to choose.'

'The choice to die in a hundred hideous ways,' she retorted.

He shook his white head. 'The choice to die on your own terms, not theirs. That's true freedom. You rose against them and fought them for nearly two months. You've inspired us.'

She studied him. 'Us?' she asked. 'Who do you mean?'

He put a few zloty on the table and stood up. 'Let's go,' he said curtly. 'This isn't a good place to talk.'

As they strolled along Jerozolimskie Aleje, he threaded her arm through his and drew her closer so that he could speak softly.

'Those people were dragged from the church and shot because someone tipped off the SS that there were members of the AK inside.' He was looking at her as though he'd said something significant and expected her to show some reaction. She waited.

'Elżunia, thousands of us all over the country are working secretly to free Poland. You said you don't have a goal in life. Join us and you'll be able to continue the fight you began in the Ghetto.'

Elżunia felt sick. All she wanted was a quiet life in Granny's room as far away from the chaos and carnage as possible. Her courage was all used up.

'You're a nurse,' Dr Borowski continued. 'A very good nurse. Before long, we're going to need nurses. Lots of them. Especially brave ones like you.'

Elżunia wanted to tell him that she wasn't brave any more. That she was exhausted and apprehensive, that the scene she'd witnessed that morning had terrified her. But she couldn't turn away from his gaze. 'I don't think I'd be any use,' she murmured. 'I'm not strong enough.'

'None of us are strong enough,' Dr Borowski said. 'There are no heroes in resistance movements. Just ordinary people, like you and me. People who don't want to live on their knees.' He gave her a shrewd look. 'Join us and you'll have a reason to go on living.'

A wind sprang up, blowing sheets of newspaper along the pavements. Men held on to their hats and women struggled to keep the hems of their billowing summer dresses from flying up. Head down, Elżunia turned the corner into Nowy Swiat Street. A crowd had gathered and their heavy silence and the horrified looks on their upturned faces made her follow their gaze. Hanging from the balcony of a large ruined building were bodies swinging slowly by their hands with each gust of wind. Their ghostly figures reminded her of the curtains that swayed in the empty rooms of the blazing Ghetto. Among the bodies swinging from the balcony were three young women and a boy of about ten. Anger choked her. Dr Borowski was right. Something had to be done to stop this barbarism.

She knew little about the AK except that all over Poland its members were blowing up railway lines and bridges to prevent German supplies reaching the front. They spied on the Germans and occasionally shot key figures, and published illegal newsletters like the *Information Bulletin* that she'd read so eagerly in the Ghetto.

The bodies swayed in the wind above the street and in their staring eyes she saw a challenge. Something had led her to this spot. A gauntlet had been thrown at her feet. Was she going to walk on and ignore the message of those mute lips or join the cause her hero, Eagle, believed in?

*

Two weeks later, trembling with emotion, Elżunia took an oath to guard the honour of Poland and fight for its liberation from bondage with every ounce of her strength, even if it meant sacrificing her life. She promised to obey without question all orders of the *Armia Krajowa*. As she walked home elated after being sworn in, she felt that the third life Madame Ramona had predicted was about to begin.

334

Thirty-Eight

As the train rattled along the tracks, Elżunia stumbled through the narrow corridor with her straw basket until she found a seat. She squeezed in between a burly man with the shoulders of a carter, and a bird-like woman wrapped in a threadbare shawl who conducted a long conversation with herself in a dull monotone. Elżunia placed her basket in the overhead rack. She would have preferred to hold it, but that would merely draw attention to it, and that was the last thing she wanted. This was the most important mission she had been sent on since joining the AK six months before, and she was determined to prove herself.

The burly man fixed his inquisitive gaze on her, so, to avoid being drawn into conversation, she kept her eyes fixed on the windows. They were so thickly encrusted with grime that the cornfields were blurred and the sunflowers looked faded.

The train chugged along at an agonisingly slow pace with frequent stops between stations to let trains pass that were carrying German soldiers and supplies to the Eastern front. Each time the engine lurched to a halt, throwing the passengers forward, Elżunia glanced up at the basket and prayed it wouldn't fall.

The stations all resembled one another, dismal waiting rooms on grimy platforms crowded with dejected people gripping their bundles and baskets.

Shortly before they reached her destination, the little market town of Ozarów, the train screeched to a halt. Elżunia was wondering whether she should risk getting off when the compartment door slid open, revealing two Gestapo agents standing there.

'*Papiere, bitte*,' one of them snapped. Elżunia fumbled in her pocket, and hoped they wouldn't notice that her hand was trembling as she held out her *Kennkarte*. They scanned the identity card, which stated that she was Anna Wilczek, a trainee nurse working at the Infant Jesus Hospital in Warsaw.

'Why are you going to Ozarów?' one of them demanded, staring hard at her.

She didn't drop her eyes. 'I'm going to see my grandparents,' she said. 'They're too old and ill to look after the farm so I help them out whenever I get a bit of time off.' She hoped her voice sounded strong and confident.

The other agent's eyes rested on her basket. 'Is that yours?' he barked.

She hoped he couldn't hear her heart thumping as she nodded and said breezily, 'Mama always bakes them some bread. She says they don't eat properly. I'll get it down if you'd like to have a look.'

Her nonchalant manner paid off because, making an impatient gesture with his hand, he turned his attention to the other passengers. After a perfunctory check of their papers, they left the compartment and she closed her eyes in relief.

Several minutes later, the train crawled into the station at Ozarów. As Elżunia was getting off, she caught sight of the two Gestapo agents leaning against the wall at the far end of the platform, talking and smoking with another man. She took a deep breath, and, swinging her basket, controlled her urge to quicken her step. As she drew closer, she could hear the three of them laughing together. Just as she was passing, the third man raised his hand to his mouth to puff on his cigarette. She noticed the mangled red stumps where two of his fingers used to be, and averted her face as he blew the smoke in her direction.

The long summer's day was coming to an end and it was twilight by the time she reached the Janowskis' farmhouse. A curved gravel path between straggly lilac bushes led to the old gabled house, a solid building that looked as though it had withstood battles, invasions and uprisings.

'I hope you'll enjoy the bread,' she told the couple with a conspiratorial smile as she placed the basket on the table.

Ryszard Janowski was a hard-grained man of few words. With a curt nod, he took the basket and went out into the yard. From the small kitchen window she watched him remove the contents and lower them quickly into a deep hole.

After filling it in, he placed a large wooden barrow on top and heaped it with chopped logs.

His wife bustled around the large country kitchen, wiping her plump face on a corner of her apron. Placing a glass of buttermilk and a bowl of steaming potatoes in front of Elżunia, she urged her to stay the night. 'The Germans patrol the roads at night searching for Underground activists from Warsaw,' she said with a sigh. 'They've caught quite a few of the partisans lately. Get some sleep and leave early in the morning.'

Elżunia had been instructed to return to Warsaw as soon as she'd delivered the revolvers intended for the partisans in the forest near Ożarów, but with all the delays, the journey had taken much longer than usual and she was exhausted.

As she followed the farmer's wife up to the attic at the top of the stairs, she felt a surge of long-forgotten pleasure. As a child, she had often stayed at her grandparents' estate in summer and as her head sank into the goose-feather pillow it seemed as though nothing had changed and she was back in the innocent days of her childhood, unaware that her hopes and dreams would soon be swallowed by a black void.

Something woke her and she sat up and peered through the small dormer window. It was a moonless night and she couldn't see anything, but there it was again, a tinkling sound. When her eyes had become accustomed to the dark, she saw a man under the cherry tree. He bent down and a moment later she heard the tinkling sound again. He was tossing handfuls of gravel at the downstairs window to wake the owners.

Elżunia paced around the room. She should have left straightaway. But as she stood shivering by the window, consumed by self-recrimination, she realised that this visit couldn't be sinister. Anyone coming to arrest or kill them would have burst into the house instead of using such a delicate method of attracting attention.

A moment later the front door opened a fraction and the man looked around before making a dash for the house. The door closed silently behind him.

Elżunia crept to the top of the stairs, wondering who the visitor was and why he had come in the middle of the night. From what she'd been told, the Janowskis arranged the delivery of weapons to partisan groups in the forests nearby, organised false papers for those on the run from the Gestapo, and helped to hide people who escaped from the transports heading for the camps.

She supposed the visitor was connected with their clandestine work. They were speaking in hushed voices, too muffled for her to make out. Instead of using their kerosene lamp, which might attract the attention of their neighbours, they had stuck a candle inside the neck of a bottle, which cast elongated shadows on the floorboards.

As she leaned over the railing to overhear the conversation, Elżunia dislodged a loose plank, which crashed onto the floor below. The trio downstairs leapt to their feet, and the farmer was already pointing a pistol at her, while the visitor had backed into the darkest corner of the kitchen.

As she mumbled her apologies from the top of the stairs, Elżunia was relieved they couldn't see her flaming face. She was mortified to be caught eavesdropping.

'Go back to bed,' Pan Janowski said gruffly.

The visitor seemed to draw back into the furthest recesses of the room and it seemed to Elżunia that he wanted the darkness to swallow him up. 'I've got to get going,' he mumbled. 'Show me the stuff.'

So the midnight visitor had come for the weapons she had delivered. Just as the farmer raised his arm to unbolt the door, the light from his candle fell on the visitor's hand and Elżunia saw that the last two fingers of his right hand were missing.

Back in bed, she tried to make sense of the situation. This was the man she had spotted chatting cosily with those Gestapo agents, yet he was supposed to deliver the weapons to the insurgents in the woods. She wondered whether to tell the Janowskis what she had seen at the station, but didn't want to make a fool of herself. There was probably some logical explanation.

The sun was already streaming in through the open window when she woke, and she sat up with a start. She had overslept. The noise that had woken her was the sound of loud German voices in the yard.

With trembling fingers she started pulling on her jacket when Pani Janowska ran into the room holding out some clothes. 'Quick, they're looking for AK people from Warsaw. Put this apron on, pull on the rubber boots, plait your hair like a country girl, and stick this scarf over your head,' she panted. 'Then run down to the kitchen and start peeling potatoes. Pretend you're deaf-mute and backward.'

Elżunia barely had time to pick up a knife when two SS men with savage dogs at their heels burst into the kitchen and started yelling that there was an activist from Warsaw staying there. Pani Janowska stared at them in amazement. 'Here?' she asked. 'Are you sure?'

'Bring the girl here immediately or we'll string you and your husband from that cherry tree,' one of them snarled.

'You can look around the whole farm,' she said. Indicating Elżunia, she added, 'The only girl here is poor Ola, who's as deaf as a post and can't say a single intelligible word. She can hardly figure out which end of a knife to use to peel the potatoes, so I can't imagine her doing intelligence work.'

One of the officers strode over to Elżunia and wheeled her around. She went white. They were the officers who had checked her papers on the train. Any moment now they'd recognise her. Thank God Pani Janowska had told her to change her hairstyle and had disguised her in peasant clothes. Averting her face, she started twitching, making incoherent sounds, and dribbling saliva from the corner of her open mouth. Repelled, the officer pushed her so hard she fell against the sink and flopped onto the floor, her limbs flailing. She covered her face with her hands.

'Disgusting,' he spat. 'When we have won the war, there will be no more Slav idiots like this.' He reached towards his leather holster.

Elżunia held her breath and closed her eyes. She was about to be killed for being an imbecile instead of an insurgent. The incongruity of her predicament suddenly struck her as so comical that her shoulders started to heave. I must be hysterical, she thought calmly as she watched the officer taking the revolver from its holster. Any second he's going to shoot me and I'm actually going to die laughing.

Just then, Pan Janowski strode into the kitchen. 'Good morning, officers,' he boomed in a jovial voice. 'I hope that stupid girl hasn't caused any trouble. I'd get rid of her myself but my wife can't find anyone to help around the house.'

The SS man lowered his weapon and looked uncertainly at Elżunia, whose knees were trembling uncontrollably at her last-minute reprieve. Having managed to distract their attention from Elżunia, Pan Janowski said, 'Now that you know we're not hiding any activists, don't waste your time up here. I've got some cherry brandy in the cellar that will curl the hair on your head. It's better than that schnapps of yours. Come down and, if you like it, I'll give you a few bottles.'

At the prospect of homemade cherry brandy, they lost interest in Elżunia and followed the farmer down the cellar steps.

After the SS men had gone, Pan Janowski sat brooding at the big oak table in the kitchen. 'They've caught a lot of our boys in the forest lately, and now this. Someone must be tipping them off,' he said to Elżunia.

Her face was still white from her narrow escape.

'I have an idea who it was,' she said quietly.

They listened intently as she told them what she had seen at the station. 'Those SS officers who came here, they were the ones I saw talking to your guy at the station,' she said.

The Janowskis discussed the situation for a long time. Finally Pan Janowski pushed back his wooden chair, took a firearm from the recess behind the stove and walked out of the house with a purposeful expression.

It was late afternoon when Elżunia returned to Warsaw. The city was sweltering in midsummer heat that seemed to rise from the footpaths and envelop passersby in vapour that beaded their foreheads and ran down their necks. On her way to her group leader to report on her mission, Elżunia reflected on her narrow escape. You couldn't trust anyone. Life was a succession of punches that came at you from all directions without any warning. All you could do was keep fending them off and hitting back, and hope that with each punch you grew stronger and more confident.

After giving her superior officer a detailed report about the mission in Ozarów, Elżunia couldn't wait to get back to Granny's. In the thirteen months she had been living there, she had come to regard the old woman as her grandmother. It was the only place where she felt safe and wanted.

She was about to turn the key in the lock when she noticed that Marta's door was wide open. There were sounds of a scuffle coming from inside, a piercing scream that made the hair on the back of her neck stand up, and then two Gestapo agents were hustling her neighbour towards the landing. As Marta tried to pull away from them, Elżunia saw that her mouth was swollen and blood was trickling from her left nostril. Shocked, she stepped forward but one of the agents shoved her aside so violently that she fell.

They were dragging Marta down the stairs. She turned to Elżunia and gasped, 'Take the bread.'

Shaken, Elżunia went into Marta's room and looked around, wondering what she meant. The basket she always carried was lying on the floor, empty, its lining ripped away. Obviously they'd found what they were searching for. Suddenly, everything became clear. Marta must be a liaison girl in the Underground, and under the lining of that innocent little basket she must have concealed maps and plans that she delivered to the AK. The room was austere, with nothing to reveal the occupant's personality, interests or taste. A small table and two chairs, a hard sofa, a few unmatched cups and plates. Not a single photograph, picture or ornament.

Elżunia rummaged around in the kitchen drawers but they contained only basic items of cutlery. She pulled out the paper that lined the drawers in case there was something concealed underneath, but found nothing. Not even stray crumbs. She picked up the wicker basket again. As she turned it over, something scratched her hand. At one end of the handle, a strand of rattan had begun to unravel. As Elżunia began to unwind it, a scrap of brown paper fell out. At first she thought it might have been inserted into the handle by the weaver as a base, but she noticed that it was perforated with tiny pin-pricks. Back at Granny's place, she turned the paper this way and that to work out what these perforations signified. At first they looked like random marks but eventually she realised that she was looking at numbers. Perhaps a telephone number. The other dots were letters that formed one word.

Elżunia's heart was hammering as she dialled the number. It rang several times, then cut out with a click as though someone had lifted the receiver and replaced it. She dialled the number again, but this time, the instant she heard the receiver being picked up, she blurted out the name on the paper.

'Zenon? It's about Marta,' she said, but the man at the other end cut her short.

'Come to the corner of Jerozolimskie Aleje and Nowy Swiat Street at twelve tomorrow. I'll be reading page four of the *Nowy Kurier Warszawski*.'

Long after he'd hung up, she couldn't get his voice out of her mind. Was this the voice she'd heard whispering late at night when the man left Marta's room?

The busy corner in the heart of the city at midday was a good place to avoid suspicion. All morning, Elżunia had been on tenterhooks, intrigued at the prospect of coming face to face with the man she believed was Marta's lover.

She was hurrying towards the meeting place when she noticed a man striding one block ahead of her. Something about his measured gait and the way he held his head made her heart race. It couldn't be. It was impossible. She was imagining it. But when he moved his head, she bit her lip and crossed her fingers.

He turned to glance at something and all her doubts vanished. She couldn't believe her eyes. At last. After all this time. A miraculous coincidence had brought her here just as her father happened to be passing by.

Any moment now he'd fold her in his arms and all the questions she had about him would finally be answered and she wouldn't be alone any more.

Elżunia glanced anxiously at the corner of Nowy Swiat Street. Marta's lover hadn't arrived yet. She quickened her step, feeling that her heart would burst from her chest. Nothing mattered except that in one moment she would run into her father's arms. She could already smell his cologne and feel his moustache nuzzling her cheek. She was almost sobbing with anticipation.

She craned her neck through the crowd, to make sure she didn't lose sight of him. He was only a few metres away; she was catching up to him. She glanced nervously at her reflection in a shop window. As she smoothed down her hair and tucked the worn blouse into Granny's old skirt, she hoped her father wouldn't be disappointed in the way she looked. She hadn't yet turned fifteen when he'd last seen her; now she was nearly eighteen. What if he didn't recognise her? Only a few steps separated them now. Her heart was pounding against her throat. Another few seconds. She took a deep breath to try to compose herself because she was trembling so much she could hardly stand.

She saw him reach the corner and glance at his watch. Then he leaned casually against the wall and Elżunia's mouth went dry as she watched him unroll the *Nowy Kurier Warszawski* and turn to page four.

She doubled up and vomited into the gutter and retched until there was nothing left but bile and the bitter taste of betrayal.

Thirty-Nine

Adam handed his heavy overcoat to the liveried attendant and crossed the foyer to the draughty lounge where a smoky fire was giving off some grudging heat. It was impossible to keep warm in a city where a penetrating chill rose from the ground and a malevolent yellow fog swirled around the streets. He found London particularly bleak and dispiriting in winter. 1943 was drawing to a close but although it was only November, the cold had already set in with the usual sleet, slush and icy drizzle. Soon it would be December, but for him, London's yuletide, with its phony red-suited Santa Claus and cheerless tinsel looped over store windows, lacked the true spirit of Christmas, which made him ache for Poland.

Stewart was already there when he arrived, his feet sprawled out in front of the fire. 'How on earth did they ever manage to build an empire when they can't figure out how to make doors and windows fit?' he said.

Judith's invitation for Adam to accompany her to a ball being given by the British Association of Nursing had arrived at an opportune moment. He had just completed his last tour, and was entitled to a short break. The attrition rate was so high these days that the airmen rarely completed more than six sorties.

The idea of getting away from the base and the world of bombers and airmen had appealed to him at the time, but now that he'd arrived at this function with its haughty attendants and draughty halls, he regretted accepting her invitation.

Stewart, who'd been asked to partner Judith's colleague Nancy, had no such qualms. 'They'll put on a good spread and Jude reckons Nancy's a good-lookin' sheila,' he'd said, noticing Adam's glum expression.

Adam had another reason for his misgivings. Although he'd enjoyed talking to Judith, interesting conversation had never been his criterion for an exciting evening with a woman. She was too direct, too matter-of-fact for his taste. He wondered whether this was an Australian trait. Even the English girls, who lacked subtlety, knew how to dress in a provocative way and liked to tease and flirt, but Judith seemed to know as little about being seductive as the nuns at his high school in Warsaw.

He heard the click of heels and looked up. A statuesque redhead in a gown of jade green was walking towards him and, with every step, the silky material clung to a different part of her body.

'Sorry I'm late,' Judith was saying. 'I had a bugger of a time getting away. We had an emergency admission. Seems you airmen are determined to keep us busy.'

'You look so different,' Adam said. He liked the cat-like greenness of her eyes and the way her thick red hair, worn loose, curled down to her shoulders.

'I can thank Nancy for that,' she said with a laugh. 'She said it was time I stopped looking like a schoolmarm. I haven't got a clue what clothes are fashionable or where to buy them, and I can never do anything with my hair, so I just did what I was told.'

Adam was amused. He'd never met a woman so refreshingly devoid of vanity.

As he took her gloved arm and led her into the ballroom where the band had struck up a lively foxtrot, she leaned over and whispered, 'I'd better warn you, I've got two left feet.'

He looked down at her slim ankles wobbling slightly in the unaccustomed ankle-strap shoes and said, 'They look all right to me.'

Although Judith made deprecatory comments about herself, she was delighted with his admiration. It had been a very long time since any male had looked at her that way; not since Pete Arnott had escorted her to the high-school dance years ago. She had been an ungainly girl with unruly hair, and the idea of going to a dance had horrified her, but in the end she asked the boy next door. He was the only one she was sure wouldn't refuse. Pete was a head shorter than she was and had no sense of rhythm, and as they struggled to keep time to the music, stumbling over each other's feet, she stared over his head while he told corny jokes. Whenever she looked around, she saw her sophisticated school friends sashaying past with their handsome beaux, whispering as they cast pitying looks in her direction. Sick with embarrassment, she walked off and left Pete standing on the dance floor while the band played 'Charmaine'. To this day, she couldn't hear that tune without feeling sick.

It was Nancy who had pushed her to invite Adam. With her nose for romance, she'd noticed that Judith mentioned his name far more often than the conversation warranted.

'Ask him,' she'd urged. 'What have you got to lose?'

'What if he won't come?'

Nancy stood back, put her hands on her slim hips and cocked her head to one side. 'Listen, lovely, you've got to go for what you want while there's still time.'

That made Judith think. She was close to thirty-seven and, from the cases she saw in the wards every day, she knew how precarious Adam's life was. Every day, airmen were admitted to the hospital with their faces burnt off or their limbs blown away. And they were the lucky ones who survived.

Adam's hand felt pleasantly firm on her back and he was looking into her face but didn't interrupt her reverie. She looked over and saw Nancy's smooth fair hair bouncing around as she jumped around the dance floor and kicked up her heels in a lively rendition of the quickstep, while Stewart laughed and tried to keep up with her. As they twirled past, Nancy gave Judith a conspiratorial wink.

'Go on,' she mouthed at her with lips painted into a scarlet Cupid's bow. 'Go for it.'

Nancy had hooked her arm around Stewart's neck and Judith could see that her brother was entranced. She envied Nancy's ability to act on impulse; as for herself, she always thought too much and felt self-conscious. Being captivating like Nancy probably gave you confidence. But Nancy was right. She should go for it before it was too late.

After the dance bracket was over, she and Adam were walking towards the buffet table when she surprised herself by blurting out, 'You can't breathe in here; it's too stuffy. Let's go outside for a bit of a walk.'

Adam looked puzzled. 'Go for a bit of a walk?' he repeated. 'But it's very cold outside.'

She blushed so deeply that her décolletage turned bright pink.

'I just thought, we could ... that it might be ...' She would never get the hang of this. Better stick to what you know, Jude, she told herself, mortified at her gaucheness.

Adam stepped a little closer. 'Are you suggesting a romantic stroll?'

She was so embarrassed that she was about to deny it but changed her mind. 'That's exactly what I'm suggesting,' she said.

'I don't understand you,' he said as they strolled along the Embankment, their collars turned up against the wind. 'You are two different people in one skin.'

'Isn't everyone?' she retorted.

He gave her an appreciative look. 'Well, I like this woman,' he said. 'The one who invites men for romantic walks.'

'Not men,' she corrected, emboldened by his remarks. 'Just you.'

The cold damp air rose from the river and in the darkness the Houses of Parliament and Big Ben had become transformed into shadowy silhouettes, their outlines blurred like charcoal drawings smudged by an artist's hand.

They stopped and leaned over the railing, gazing at the glossy blackness of the water.

'You must be devastated by what's going on in Poland,' she said. 'I've read what Mr Churchill said in the House of Commons about the terrible situation in Warsaw.'

'Talk is cheap,' he said, and the lines around his mouth deepened.

'You mean they talk and do nothing?' she asked.

He nodded.

'After all your airmen did to help save England during the Battle of Britain, it's disgraceful that they're not doing more to help,' she said.

He shrugged. 'They're not even sending air supplies at the moment.' He flung a pebble into the river and watched the ripples widening in the blackness.

'I heard an English politician on the wireless the other day,' she said. 'He said Poland was being crucified.'

He looked at her with interest. 'You know so much about Poland.'

She reddened. Since they'd met, she scoured the paper for news about Poland and had read enough to know that lately admiration for Russia had increased in the press, while sympathy for Poland had decreased.

'It's a bloody disgrace,' she said. 'The Allies seem to have forgotten that Poland was our reason for declaring war on Hitler. Ever since Stalin came into the picture, they've pushed Poland further into the background. I wouldn't even be surprised if someone had bumped off that General Korski or whatever his name was, the one who was the head of the Polish government in London, because he was annoying Stalin and making a nuisance of himself. If I were you, I'd be hopping mad.'

Adam hadn't spoken to anyone in England who was so well informed and so aware of the underlying issues. She was looking straight into his eyes with her direct gaze and he was touched by her empathy and the warmth in her green eyes. The weak light from the wrought-iron lamp beside the river lit up her red hair which shone like burnished copper. Standing behind her, Adam gently rubbed the back of her neck.

She was startled. 'What are you doing?' she asked, but, without answering, he continued the massage. No one had ever touched her so sensuously before and the light pressure of his hands seemed to exert a slight electric charge that thrilled and disturbed her. What did this mean? What would it lead to? She ought to stop this. It was the sort of thing student nurses did on their nights off. What would he think of her?

In the meantime, the pressure on her neck intensified until the warmth spread to her shoulders, which seemed to be dissolving under his hands. He turned her around, looked into her eyes and kissed her very gently on the cheek.

'Is this what you had in mind when you suggested walking in the dark?' he asked.

She didn't reply.

'Because what I had in mind was this,' he said, and, pulling her close to him, kissed her again, on the lips.

Confused by the intensity of her feelings, she pulled away. 'Goodness, it's late. I have to be back before they lock the gate for the night,' she murmured, avoiding his eyes.

He whistled and a moment later a large London cab pulled up beside them. As she climbed in, Adam leaned inside.

'If I survive my next tour and get more leave, can we go for another walk?'

'Yes, let's do that,' she said, and blushed at her own eagerness.

As the cab drove towards the nurses' home, it seemed to Judith that the streets of London no longer looked bleak, and the air had lost its chill. She was tingling with possibilities.

On the last day of his leave, Adam went into the Lyons Corner House in Oxford Street, chose a table in the far corner of the restaurant, scanned the menu, and, in his halting English, ordered sausages with beans and mashed potatoes but pushed the plate away when he saw that everything was doused in a thick sludge of brown gravy.

'I suppose our English food isn't good enough for the likes of you,' the waitress muttered as she removed the plate with a sweeping gesture. He was about to order coffee when he remembered how bad it was and asked for a pot of tea instead.

He checked his watch again. Feliks was late. He was on to his second cup of tea when the door swung open and his friend rushed towards him, full of apologies.

As he placed his briefcase on the chair beside him, Adam saw that Feliks was as dapper as usual. Ever since they had met during their training in the diplomatic corps, Adam joked that the apocalypse would find Feliks immaculately attired in a fashionably cut jacket and an Italian silk cravat tucked inside his tweed coat. But in the past year, Feliks had become thinner and his hair had receded so far from his wide forehead that he was almost bald.

Adam couldn't wait to get to the point. 'So what's the news from Poland?'

Feliks shrugged. 'Executions, round-ups, arrests, interrogations and murders. But of course that isn't news.' He stared moodily at the table.

Adam clenched his fists. 'If only the English government would get moving and send the AK more supplies.'

Feliks looked up. 'I do have some news. Don't expect any help from the Allies. Politics is like fashion and we're not in fashion any more. We're yesterday's people.'

Adam sat forward. It wasn't like Feliks to sound so discouraged and cynical.

'Today's people are the Russians. They're the heroes who repelled Hitler at Stalingrad and they're the ones who will rescue Europe from the Germans. In the process, they'll swallow up Poland and Eastern Europe. We're out of favour because instead of being grateful to them, we are unreasonable enough to insist that our nation be left intact, and we won't agree to hand over our eastern lands to Stalin. But Stalin has to be kept happy at all costs, so the Allies will force Poland to accede to his demands.' He gave an exasperated sigh. 'I'll tell you something, Adam, I can see what's coming and it makes me sick.'

Adam couldn't conceal his shock. 'How do you know all this?'

'There was a secret meeting in Teheran a few months ago, and I spoke to one of the attachés who was there. It seems that Churchill and Roosevelt have made certain promises to Comrade Stalin and they've decided that Poland is disposable.'

'But we're their oldest ally in this war! In fact, they declared war because we were invaded! After the fall of France, Churchill made a promise to Prime Minister Šikorski. I was so stirred up by his words that I still remember them. *We shall conquer together or we shall die together.* And his foreign secretary, Eden, was even more emotional. He said something along the lines of, "We'll never abandon your sacred cause. We'll continue this war until your beloved country is returned to her faithful sons."'

Feliks made a rueful face. 'Full marks for recall, but zero for realism. My dear fellow, it's obvious you've been away from politics for too long. You sound like a naïve schoolgirl. That was yesterday. Today all they care about is having Stalin on their side at all costs. At our cost, actually. He wants a chunk of Poland so that's what they'll agree to. Our Prime Minister in London did his best to present our case but they regard him as a nuisance. That's what it's all come to. Meanwhile the AK, which is the biggest resistance movement in Europe, is still fighting, and still waiting for help from our Allies!'

Feliks downed his tea in a few quick gulps, rammed his hat over his large head and stood up. 'I have to run. An RAF plane is taking me to Brindisi tonight and from there I'll be parachuted back to Poland with my good news. That's the fortunate life of a courier for the AK. See what you're missing?'

The duplicity that Feliks had revealed embittered Adam as he stared moodily at the bare trees and brown hedgerows on the way back to the base. He considered himself politically astute, and he'd suspected that the alliance with Stalin would be against Polish interests, but nothing had prepared him for such treachery by the British and Americans after the noble sentiments Churchill and Roosevelt had expressed about standing by their gallant ally Poland.

As soon as he returned to the base, he was summoned to a briefing in the hall. Watson-Smythe strode across the room, sprang onto the dais and tapped his pointer on the map of Germany.

'You're going to bomb Berlin from here to kingdom come,' he told them in his crisp way and Adam felt the Group Captain's chilly glance lingering on his face.

Watson-Smythe's announcement was greeted by a sharp intake of breath. Berlin was the most important target and the one the airmen dreaded most. It meant they'd have to fly their lumbering giants for ten hours into the very heart of the Third Reich, through the best organised defences in the world, which included anti-aircraft guns ready to fire tonnes of flak, and a sky swarming with night-fighters to shoot them down.

'We'll be as hard to spot as a herd of elephants trying to sneak into a fortress,' Tomasz whispered to Adam with a rueful grin.

'You'll have to fight all the way there and all the way back,' Watson-Smythe was saying. 'But if you don't wipe Berlin off the map today, you'll have to go back and do it tomorrow, and tomorrow they'll be waiting for you!

'Stay alert,' he warned. 'Flying for so many hours, it's easy to lose concentration. And that's what you can't afford to do, not for a second. As you know, German night-fighters are armed with powerful cannons assisted by radar, and, together with searchlights, they've formed a lethal barrier right across Northern Europe. Once you're spotted, you'll be like flies caught in a spider's web. Good luck.'

Flying the Lancaster past Dover and across the Channel, Adam wondered whether he'd ever see those white cliffs again and the nostalgic refrain of Vera Lynn's popular song resounded in his head with new meaning.

But the nostalgia evaporated with the appearance of the first Ju 88s and Me 109s. As he dived and rose and spiralled to avoid them, he recalled watching the aviator whose aerobatics inspired him as a boy, so long ago. He'd never imagined that one day he'd be emulating his hero, not for the joy of flying but for sheer survival.

They were approaching Berlin when, with a calmness that astonished him, Adam thought, We're flying straight into hell.

Bands of dazzling searchlights ringed the city and chunks of burning metal cascaded from the sky like scalding missiles from an alien planet. Suddenly a fighter flew underneath them. Adam corkscrewed crazily to avoid it but a Halifax nearby didn't get away in time. The fighter unleashed its upward-firing machine guns and ripped open the Halifax's underbelly from nose to tail. It plummeted from the sky in a column of black smoke. Adam closed his eyes. There but for the grace of God and the vigilance of his gunner. But he didn't have long to enjoy his relief because almost immediately Stewart spotted night-fighters on their tail. If they hit the Lanc, it would go up like a fireball.

Adam plunged in a spiral dive at thirty degrees to the left, then climbed to the right, pushing the plane to its limit, past its limit, making loop de loops so the fighters couldn't catch them. Thankful for the Lancaster's manoeuvrability, he wondered how long his luck could possibly last.

The air inside the plane crackled with tension as they approached the target. Once they'd dropped their payload, the toughest part of the mission would be over and they could head back.

Adam listened to Stewart's flat-vowelled Australian

voice. 'Steady, steady, right, right,' he directed. 'Bloody hell,' he exclaimed a moment later. 'We missed it.'

Everyone was shouting at once. 'You fucking idiot,' Tomasz hissed.

'Now we'll have to turn round and do it all over again,' Romek complained. 'Now the Jerries can have another go at us.'

Adam's jaw ground back and forth but he said nothing. He needed all his strength to focus on flying the plane.

The second time around, the gunner discharged payload and hit the target but as Adam looked down at the smoke and firestorms rising from the explosions, he was convinced that their missions were based on a false premise. Bombing Berlin wouldn't end the war because, no matter how much they pulverised Hitler's capital, Adam couldn't see him surrendering. So much effort, so many lives lost, at such a cost, for so little gain.

Before leaving German airspace, they had to get through massive radar-guided searchlights that striped the sky with vertical blue beams. Suddenly the lights swung around and coned them in a terrifying band of dazzling light. It seemed as though all the lights were focusing on their Lanc and Adam's hands felt clammy under his gloves. He felt naked and exposed. Then the flak opened up and they were flying through a sea of red-hot shells. He tried not to think of the Cologne mission. He still didn't know how he'd managed to fly and land the plane with only one engine and no hydraulics, but it wasn't a performance he wanted to repeat.

'*Matka Boska*.' He could hear Tomasz's murmured invocation to the Virgin Mary over and over again as he pushed the Lanc far beyond its limits, higher and higher into the sky until they were out of reach of the flak.

Forty

Elżunia walked along the streets of Warsaw, trying to imprint every detail on her mind to fill the emptiness she felt. A small girl in red woollen stockings was holding her mother's hand as they crossed Jerozolimskie Aleje. An elderly man with red-rimmed eyes wiped his face on a large checked handkerchief. A young woman in a floral dress turned towards her companion, who pulled her into a hungry embrace. But instead of taking her mind off her own unhappiness, each vignette was petrol splashed onto the bonfire of her despair.

What had it all been for, all the years of suffering, starving and struggling? Now that she had seen her father in the flesh, she knew that his devotion was nothing but a sham, and the reunion she had longed for was a mere fantasy. Ever since hearing Pani Stasia's story, she had hoped it was false, but now she had no doubt it was true. Just as she now knew that it was he who had been Marta's nocturnal visitor. All those sentiments about honour and heroism that her father had drummed into her throughout her childhood were a farce, a mockery. While they'd been struggling to survive in the Ghetto, he'd abandoned them and carried on with another woman, as though they didn't exist. At least she had spared her mother that disillusionment. Tears filled her eyes. She had no mother or father now, and her hopes of finding Gittel and Stefan had faded. It seemed that you needed the combined strength of a hundred people to get through a single lifetime. Elżunia felt that her strength had run out.

A tram was bearing down on her, its harsh clanging reverberating in her head. It would be so easy; all she had to do was close her eyes and step in front of it at the last minute, before the driver had time to stop, and then it would all be over. She heard the gut-twisting squeal of brakes and felt a shove that sent her sprawling onto the roadway.

Blood was pouring from her knees and she looked up to see the driver shaking his fist at her. 'Cholera psia krew! What a bloody idiot! Why don't you look where you're going?'

A large woman with a flabby double chin wobbling inside her blouse was leaning over her, dabbing her knees with an embroidered handkerchief that was now splotched with red.

'Are you all right? You would have ended up under that tram if I hadn't pushed you out of the way!'

Elżunia stared at her. The woman obviously thought she'd done a good deed. The idea of oblivion, of putting an end to all the suffering was so seductive that she closed her eyes, wishing she was dead.

'She needs an ambulance,' the woman was saying excitedly, in the tone of someone accustomed to giving orders. 'There must be something wrong with her that she didn't see the tram.'

By now a curious crowd had gathered around Elżunia, and everyone offered an opinion about her accident. An elderly man with a shock of white hair under his trilby stepped forward. 'Is somebody ill?' he asked.

Elżunia opened her eyes and found herself looking into Dr Borowski's concerned eyes. He helped her up and took her by the elbow like an old-world suitor. As she hobbled along the avenue leaning on his arm, a small figure bolted from a side street and skidded into the entrance of an apartment building. For a moment she thought it was Zbyszek, but knew that he was under strict instructions not to leave Granny's loft.

When they reached the Square of the Three Crosses, Dr Borowski sat her down on a bench under a lime tree.

'What was all that about?' he asked, watching her with eyes that missed nothing.

She shrugged, unable to speak.

He sat forward and looked straight into her eyes for a long time. 'I know things sometimes look so hopeless that there seems no way out, and no point going on, but we mustn't give in to that feeling. There's always something or someone worth fighting for and living for.'

She tore savagely at her thumbnail. She wasn't in the mood for lofty sentiments. 'It's all pointless,' she burst out. 'Those missions, risking our lives to deliver a few arms or blowing up a train or two, that's not weakening the Germans or affecting the course of the war. We're wasting our time.'

He tilted her chin so that she had to meet his gaze.

'Listen to me,' he said sternly. 'This isn't the time to wallow in personal grievances. We've reached a crossroads in our history when we have to stop thinking of ourselves and be ready to fight for our common cause. When you and I met up again a few months ago, I urged you to join the AK and I'm glad you did. I told you we'd need nurses. Well it won't be long now before we rise up and show them what we're made of. And we'll need every single person to join the fight. Don't waste your anger and your strength. Use them to create a free Poland.'

Despite her distress, Elżunia listened and was impressed by his fervour. So an uprising was being planned. She wondered when it would begin, and whether the liberation movement would be a national one or restricted to Warsaw. But Dr Borowski had planted a stake in the ground for her to cling to and she felt her resolve returning. She would fight back to avenge the lives of her mother and her friends, to continue the struggle that had cost them their lives.

As she climbed the stairs to Granny's place, she tried to blot out the image of Marta's battered face when the Gestapo had hustled her from her room and what had followed. It sounded as though her father was also involved in the resistance and she wondered whether Marta had betrayed him under interrogation. It would serve him right if she had, she thought, but a moment later felt ashamed of her childish vindictiveness. I have to find some equilibrium, she thought. I'm like a weather vane spinning out of control with every twist of my emotions.

As soon as Elżunia closed the door, Granny hobbled towards her and grabbed her arm. 'It's Zbyszek,' she gasped, wringing her gnarled hands. 'He's gone.'

Zbyszek had often complained of being bored in the loft. He missed his pals and the activity in the square. Granny and Elżunia had explained repeatedly that he had to stay there, not only for his own good but for theirs as well, so he wouldn't accidentally betray them. Each time he nodded so hard that it looked as though his head would fall off his neck, but the following day he would nag them again about going to the square.

He must have sneaked off while Granny was out.

She had found out about it on her way home with her pannikin of soup that afternoon. She had stopped to cross herself in front of St Aleksander's Church when Basia ran up to her, pulling at her sleeve with agitated fingers.

'That little devil; I knew we couldn't trust him. Now he's gone and done a bunk and God knows what'll happen,' Basia said.

By then, Toughie and some of the other children had gathered around Granny, all gabbling at once. They had been horrified to see Zbyszek rushing towards them that morning. Basia had told him he could stay with her for a while, but he had to go back to Granny's that afternoon. Her attention had been distracted for a moment, and, when she looked around, Zbyszek had disappeared. The cigarette sellers searched all over the square, distraught in case he'd been caught by the *szmalcowniks* or the Germans.

'Poor child. He's only seven! How will he manage out there? What will become of him?' Granny lamented.

So the small figure she'd seen darting into the doorway had been Zbyszek after all. 'I spotted him this morning,' she said, and described what she had seen. If only she had followed him and brought him back.

Granny nodded with relief. Looking up from the soup on the stove, she asked, 'How come you were near the square today?'

Before Elżunia could think of a reply without mentioning her aborted meeting with her father and her botched attempt to throw herself under the tram, the old woman was peering into her face. 'You look pale, child. Here, get some of this into you,' she urged, ladling the steaming broth into a bowl.

Elżunia's eyes followed Granny as she moved slowly around the kitchen. Although she was frail and crippled, she was like a gnarled oak with roots that ran so deep and true that no storms could shake or topple it. It's what people do that counts, Elżunia thought, not their noble sentiments and beautiful-sounding words.

Forty-One

Elżunia hurried along the street, checking her watch every few minutes. There was still time before the siren sounded. She shivered. The first day of August was marked Sunflower Day in the calendar but there was nothing bright or sunny about this drizzly, grey afternoon in 1944. It was almost four o'clock and the streets were full of young people who, like her, were heading for their posts. Many of them wore loose coats to conceal whatever weapons they had been able to lay their hands on: antiquated revolvers, pistols from the last war, hunting rifles or homemade *filipinki*. For the first time since the war began, the streets of Warsaw were charged with a sense of purpose and a feeling of exhilaration. The Uprising was about to begin. Only a few days more and their capital would be free.

Ever since they heard the boom of Russian artillery from the other side of the river the previous week, they had sensed that the Uprising must start soon. In the evenings, they pointed to Russian reconnaissance planes and bombers that flew over the city, lighting up the summer sky with rockets that sparkled like chandeliers. By day, Soviet broadcasts and leaflets exhorted the people of Warsaw to take up arms and join with them to expel the Germans.

'Poles! The time of liberation is at hand! There is not a moment to lose!' they urged.

Now that General Rokossovsky's victorious Red Army had stopped on the left bank of the Vistula outside Praga, the people of Warsaw exulted that they'd soon oust the Germans. It wouldn't be long before Poles were finally in control of their capital.

To add to the optimism, the Germans had started retreating. The people of Warsaw rejoiced as dejected German soldiers, civilians and officials headed west, their belongings tied onto the roofs of cars or heaped on trucks that raised clouds of dust in their wake as they left the city they had occupied for five years. Smoke emanated from offices all over the city, as the invaders destroyed incriminating documents. The day of liberation was approaching.

But as Elżunia neared Kierbędz Bridge, she felt uneasy. There were more German patrols circulating around the city that afternoon than she had seen in the past week, and tanks had been rumbling along Jerozolimskie Aleje. The trucks that rolled slowly across the iron girder bridge were filled with soldiers who looked strong and arrogant, not like the demoralised ones who had slunk away like mangy dogs the previous week.

She was mulling this over in her mind as a German truck screeched to a halt beside two youths on the other side of the road. Judging by their loose coats and bulging pockets, they were also hurrying towards their posts.

Watching from the other side of the road, Elżunia held her breath. One of the Germans jumped down from the truck, scrutinised their papers as though memorising every word and pointed to the coat pocket of one of the lads with a commanding gesture.

The boy put his hand into his pocket as though to empty it, but, before she realised what was happening, he had raised his arm and thrown a grenade. The soldier jerked backwards and lay on the roadway in a spreading pool of blood. A moment later, shots rang out from the truck and the two youths lay sprawled on the road, dead.

Elżunia forced herself to keep walking but the exhilaration she had felt a moment earlier changed to a sense of foreboding. There was still one hour to go. What if this incident alerted the Germans to the Uprising and removed the vital element of surprise? Perhaps the increased patrols indicated that they already suspected that the revolt was due to begin and had prompted them to send in the tanks and reinforcements.

At her post near the Warsaw power station, in the riverside district of Powiśle, she reported nervously to her commander. No one had heard about the incident near the bridge and morale was high. Singing the stirring words of 'Hey Lads, Grab Your Bayonets!' scores of insurgents were milling around, laughing and bursting with pride as they pulled their red-and-white AK armbands above their elbows. Some of the men wore their fathers' army trousers from the previous world war or the Polish–Russian war, while others wore ordinary trousers tucked into their boots. On their heads they wore field caps, peaked caps, the four-cornered caps of the Polish army, and some even wore tram-drivers' caps. Like most of the girls, Elżunia wore a skirt and blouse. Only their armbands revealed that they belonged to the insurgent army.

After pulling on her armband, Elżunia made her way to the chief nurse, who was distributing first-aid satchels. She felt excited and sad at the same time. Sixteen months had passed since she had joined the Ghetto insurgents in a fight that was doomed from the start. If only the AK had joined forces with the Ghetto fighters then, how different the outcome would have been for them all. The Ghetto and its inhabitants might have been saved, Warsaw might have been freed, and this battle might not have to be fought. But there was no time for reflection. As she joined her group preparing splints and dressings, there was a buzz of nervous chatter in the room.

'*Oy yey*, I wish I had trousers like the boys,' the girl beside her lamented. 'What if I have to climb a ladder or go up a hill and they see my panties?' Janka covered her wide mouth with her hand in anticipated embarrassment.

Elżunia couldn't help smiling. 'I don't think that in the midst of battle the boys will be looking at your panties.'

Janka was braiding her ash-blonde hair and pinning it on top of her head in a coronet. Taking two bobby pins from her mouth, she gave a loud snort. 'If you think that, you don't know boys. All they ever think about is what's inside our panties and how to get into them. Believe me, I know. I've got four older brothers!'

The other girls were all talking at once now, but Elżunia fell silent. She felt very young and naïve, and was shocked by their crudeness. Ever since she had met the airman who turned into an AK courier she knew only as Eagle, she had daydreamed of having an intimate relationship with him, but what that might actually entail was veiled in vague fantasies and romantic yearnings.

'Hey, girls! Look outside!' one of the nurses shouted. They pushed past one another in their rush to get to the window. A Polish flag fluttered from the top of Warsaw's tallest structure, the Prudential Building. Across the road, a young boy had clambered up to a balcony and ripped off a German poster. In the apartment above him, a toothless old man was leaning from his window, triumphantly waving a Polish flag. All over the city, flags that had been concealed for five years were finally being unfurled.

Janka started singing the Polish national anthem at the top of her voice, and the others joined in. '*Jeszcze Polska nie zginęła,'* they sang, and their eyes glistened with tears. They were still singing when the siren sounded, long and shrill, and the hair on the back of Elżunia's neck stood up. It had begun, the moment they'd been waiting for.

Together with the other nurses she followed the route they'd been given towards the power station, through back alleys and dusty underground passageways, until they reached the barricade. Along the way, people cheered and blessed them. 'Look at our brave youngsters, going off to win our city back for us,' Elżunia heard someone shout.

'May God bless you!' another called out and others made the sign of the cross over their heads. Elżunia felt her heart swelling. This was how heroes felt when they marched off to war.

When they were all gathered at the barricade, behind sandbags, planks of timber and broken furniture that people had hurled into the street, the commander explained that their objective was to capture the power station, the source of Warsaw's electricity. Elżunia tried not to jump each time the stuttering salvo of machine-gun fire rang out from the direction of the power station. It was obvious that the Germans were attacking, and the fighting was already intensifying. Fighters carrying wounded comrades on stretchers or slung across their shoulders brought them to the barricades and ran back to continue the assault or bring back more wounded. Elżunia tried to stay calm as she bandaged ripped flesh and splinted broken bones, but many of the injuries were too severe for her limited first-aid kit. As she looked at a boy's chest that had been ripped open, she reassured the grey-faced soldier that he'd soon be fixed up in hospital, and hoped she sounded more convincing than she felt.

She looked up and froze. Two insurgents were carrying a wounded comrade on a stretcher towards the barricade when shots rang out. They dropped the stretcher as they fell to the ground. The Germans had deliberately fired on the men bringing a wounded soldier to safety. The injured soldier and one of the carriers lay motionless on the ground about fifty metres from the barricade, but the other stretcher-bearer was writhing in pain and she could hear his moans.

While the nurses watched in horror, the unit commander discussed the situation with his deputy.

'Two of the nurses should go and get him,' the commander said. 'It's their job.'

'You can't send them out there under fire,' the other protested. 'They wouldn't stand a chance.'

The commander shrugged. 'We can't spare the fighters. Anyway, I haven't got time to stand here and argue. Let them decide,' he said and strode away.

The nurses looked at each other helplessly. You couldn't leave the man out there to die but it was suicide to go and get him.

Janka was fiddling with her braids. Finally she said, 'I'm game. Anyone coming with me?'

Without a second thought, Elżunia sprang up to join Janka. In her mind was an image of Szmuel, Edek and Lech who had given their lives to save their colleagues. To save her as well. She had to live up to their example.

Clutching the stretcher between them with one hand, and their first-aid kits over their heads with the other, they crouched down and started across the road. Almost immediately, bullets started whizzing around them.

'We'd better crawl on our stomachs,' Elżunia hissed. 'Keep moving! Not in a straight line!' she warned Janka who had slowed down. 'Don't worry, no one can see your panties.'

That struck her as so comical that she forgot the danger they were in and started laughing while Janka kept repeating

'Hail Mary' in a voice verging on hysteria, like a record stuck in a groove. The sniper didn't let up but by some miracle he missed them. Covered in perspiration and shaking all over, they reached the wounded soldier, and, exhausted, lay flat on the ground beside him.

Assuming from their motionless bodies that he'd killed them, the sniper stopped firing. Elżunia fumbled in her first-aid kit for a syringe and managed to inject the insurgent with morphine without sitting up. She and Janka lay on the ground, exchanging terrified glances while they encouraged the wounded soldier to hold on. As soon as it was dark, they placed him on the stretcher and staggered back with him, trembling so much they could hardly stand. Janka touched her cheek and saw that her hand was red.

'*Oy yey!*' she exclaimed. 'I'm wounded! I'm bleeding!'

Elżunia shook her head. 'That's iodine, you dope. The phial probably broke when you were holding the first-aid kit over your head.'

Janka lit a cigarette with trembling fingers. 'Is this what they call baptism by fire?' she quipped and they both burst out laughing.

Forty-Two

Adam was lounging outside the mess hall popping blackberries into his mouth. He had picked them from the bramble bushes near the base, nostalgic for the pleasures of childhood, but as he examined his scratched arms, he realised he'd forgotten that those pleasures came at a price. The thorns had made deep welts on his skin. He settled back in the sagging armchair to read *The Express* at leisure. Half of 1944 had already passed, and perhaps it was the exhilaration of having survived so many tours that made him so keenly aware of the blueness of the sky, the sweetness of the lark's call and the coolness of the breeze that ruffled the hairs on his scratched arms that August morning.

As he unfolded the newspaper, he sat up so suddenly that the dish fell off his lap and the berries rolled onto the cement, staining it crimson with their juice.

A moment later, his colleagues were crowding around him, tearing the pages from his hands in their eagerness to read every word. An uprising had broken out in Warsaw. Their pride that Polish honour would finally be vindicated was mingled with envy and regret that they couldn't fight shoulder to shoulder with their countrymen to liberate their capital.

Romek lined up a row of glasses and poured the whiskey. 'Let's drink to their success,' he said in a voice hoarse with emotion.

'May it come quickly,' Tomasz added.

Several hours later, Adam was in a lorry speeding towards London to meet Feliks, who had recently returned from Warsaw. He could hardly wait to see his old friend to discuss the news.

As a courier between the Polish government-in-exile and the AK leaders in Poland, Feliks had access to the top people in London and Warsaw, as well as to the British politicians. No one was as well acquainted with what was going on behind the scenes in both groups as he was. This was the post Adam would have held if he hadn't joined the RAF and at times like these he felt frustrated at being so far removed from the corridors of power.

Most of the tables in the restaurant of the Savoy Hotel were already taken when he arrived, and the warm smell of roasting meat permeated the dining room. As the maître d' showed him to his table, Adam suddenly felt a yearning for *pierogi* stuffed with mashed potatoes and cabbage, or *bigos* stew with smoky sausage and sauerkraut, and he ached for his mother, his home and his country.

Inside the restaurant, waiters leaned over the starched tablecloths listing the day's specials — roast lamb from the carvery, accompanied by mint sauce and roast potatoes, followed by apple-and-blackberry pie. Looking at the menu and the diners — men in their pin-striped suits and women in little hats turned down at a saucy angle on their marcelled hair — it seemed as though the war and the Uprising were taking place in another world.

He looked up expectantly when he saw the maître d' ushering Feliks to their table and noticed with amusement that, as usual, his friend was dressed in the latest fashion, a double-breasted jacket with long lapels. He was about to make a facetious comment, but without any preamble Feliks said, 'I'll give you the short version. Confusion, conflict and chaos.'

Adam felt as though he'd turned on a hot-water tap and been showered with ice cubes. Out of the corner of his eye he could' see the waiter hovering in the background with a large leather-bound menu, and waved him away. Feliks propped his large, bald head on one hand and drummed the table with his long fingers.

'Tell me,' Adam said.

Feliks raised his eyebrows until his high forehead resembled a washboard. 'How much time have you got?'

For the next hour he spoke in a rapid staccato that resembled a salvo of machine-gun fire, accompanied by sweeping hand gestures. It appeared that there had been dissension in London, disagreement in Warsaw, misunderstandings between the exiled government and the Home Army leaders and even confusion about when the Uprising should begin, whether it was to encompass the whole of Poland or just Warsaw, and even whether it should break out at all.

In London, the Commander-in-Chief and Prime Minister of the government-in-exile mistrusted each other and disagreed about practically everything, including the timing, extent and location of the Uprising.

'The Chief didn't think the time was right for an uprising, but he was like the girl who didn't say yes and didn't say no,' Feliks said. 'You wouldn't believe it, but just before they were to decide whether to give Warsaw the go-ahead or not, he went off to Italy.'

In reply to Adam's puzzled look, he said, 'No one knows for sure why he did that. There are all sorts of rumours, as you can imagine. My feeling is that he got away from

London so he wouldn't have to take responsibility for the decision. Some of the representatives of the Polish government-in-exile warned against the Uprising. They said that without Russian cooperation and Allied support, it couldn't possibly succeed, and were convinced that the insurgents couldn't count on the Allies.'

Adam was frowning. 'But wasn't that why the government-in-exile sent you to Warsaw, to let the AK know exactly how things stood?'

Feliks gave a sarcastic laugh. 'You would think so, but the obstacles they put in my path at every turn make me wonder. First they couldn't find a plane to take me to Warsaw. And when I finally got to Warsaw, it was four days before they let me speak to Bór-Komorowski, the Commander-in-Chief of the AK.'

'I suppose there were powerful elements in the AK who wanted to start the Uprising and didn't want you near him in case you put him off the idea.'

After they parted, Adam was so furious that he couldn't calm down. He walked the length of Regent Street to Oxford Circus, then along the Thames, and, before he knew it, he'd reached Greenwich. He was seething at the duplicity Feliks had described, and felt that unless he kept moving he'd explode. From what his friend had said, the Uprising wouldn't stand a chance without Allied help. He clenched his fists. He had to do something.

Over the past few months, whenever Adam was on leave, he had come to London to see Judith, whose forthright manner and guileless nature he found more intriguing each time they met. But although he had intended to stay in London that night and have dinner with her, after his conversation with Feliks he decided to return to the base immediately to talk to his superior. Charles Watson-Smythe was staring out of the window of his small office, deep in thought, tapping his fountain pen on the desk. The knock on the door, which sounded more peremptory than Adam had intended, roused him from his reverie.

'Ah, Czartoryski,' he said with a marked lack of enthusiasm. 'What is it?'

'Sir, if I can have a minute of your time. I'm sure you're aware that an uprising has broken out in Warsaw. How soon do you think we can drop supplies to Poland? I know the other men are also keen to get going.'

Watson-Smythe gave an irritated sigh. 'Our mission is to bomb Germany, not send supplies to revolutionaries in Poland. As you know, we can't spare the planes, the pilots or the fuel. Flying to Poland involves too great a distance and an unacceptable level of danger.'

Adam opened his mouth, closed it, and took a deep breath. He would have liked to comment about the unacceptable level of danger they faced each time they bombed Cologne, Berlin or the bridges in the Ruhr, but stifled the retort. Of all the RAF officers he'd come across, Watson-Smythe was the most arrogant. 'Sir, with respect, the 1586 Special Duties Flight and the Polish Parachute Brigade were formed expressly to drop supplies to Poland, and they're urgently needed right now.'

His commanding officer placed the fountain pen in the marble inkstand and gave him a hostile look. 'I wish you'd leave the running of the air force to the RAF, Czartoryski,' he snapped. With that, he picked up a dossier on his desk and began reading it as though Adam wasn't there.

Resentful for being dismissed like a schoolboy, Adam strode back to the hut where the others were in the midst of a heated discussion.

'We're going to boycott dinner tonight, in protest,' Tomasz said.

374

Adam found it difficult to control his irritation. 'Do you think they'll change their policy just because you go to bed without your dinner?'

Romek pounded his fist on the table. 'We've got to do something to make these sons of bitches change their minds.'

'The Russians encouraged us to rise up against the Germans, so they're bound to come to the aid of the insurgents,' Tomasz mused.

At this, pandemonium broke out. 'You're an idiot!' Olek shouted. 'Don't you remember the leaflets they dropped in '39 saying our Russian brothers were coming to help us against the Germans? The next thing they were invading and deporting us in our thousands to Siberia.'

Like Olek, Romek had also been deported. 'Help from Stalin?' He was tapping his temple derisively at Olek.

'You need to get your head examined. The Russians are devious bastards. You can't trust a word they say.'

Tomasz looked thoughtful. 'We could write a letter to King George and Queen Elizabeth. Remember how they walked around the East End talking to ordinary Londoners during the Blitz? Let's appeal to their sense of honour. After all, Polish airmen helped save Britain in 1940. Now it's their chance to show their appreciation.'

The arguments continued and, listening to them, Adam felt old and cynical. These men saw the world in black and white, and believed in notions like justice and gratitude, while he knew that politicians had short memories, and debts were only repaid when it suited their agenda.

'It will take ages to get a reply from Buckingham Palace,' Tomasz was saying. 'I still think we should boycott the mess tonight. As a gesture.'

✱

The following afternoon, while the sun was still high in the summer sky, they were summoned for an urgent briefing.

'A situation has arisen that has made it necessary to modify our plans,' Watson-Smythe announced in a voice as dry as tissue paper. 'This evening, instead of bombing Germany, you'll be dropping supplies to Poland.'

A spontaneous cheer went up. With a curt nod, he stepped off the dais and the information officer took over. They all craned forward as he pinned photographs of Warsaw's General Post Office to the board. 'That's where you're to drop the containers,' he told them. He explained that they would overfly the Russian zone but, despite repeated requests made to the Russian High Command, permission for British planes to land on their territory had been rejected. Recalling Feliks's comments, Adam wondered what game Stalin was playing and why he'd refused permission for his allies to land so they could deliver supplies to another Allied nation.

As the briefing continued, they were warned to expect enemy fighters along the entire route. 'If for some reason you can't locate the General Post Office, don't waste time and fuel but head straight for Krasinski Square, make the drop and get the hell out of there.'

Unlike their usual bombing missions, when they were given the exact route, this time they had to do their own navigating. The supplies they were carrying, which included PIAT anti-aircraft weapons, were so heavy that some of the equipment had to be removed to decrease the load. The officer concluded with the usual warning. 'Fly as high as you possibly can over enemy territory. You won't survive more than a minute below twelve thousand feet.'

Before they were dismissed, the officer read a message from the Prime Minister. Churchill stressed the grave importance of their mission because of the desperate situation in Warsaw where insurgents needed weapons and supplies. Adam wondered about his change of heart. Perhaps the Polish government-in-exile had been more persuasive than usual.

In the long summer twilight, Adam and his crew jumped into a truck, which bumped along the uneven ground to the airfield. It was still hot and they brushed away the sweat that ran down their foreheads and stung their eyes, but inside the Lanc the air around them palpitated with quiet determination. This time they were bringing not destruction to the enemy but aid to their countrymen. Weighed down by the heavy wooden boxes and metal containers stowed in the recess usually reserved for the bombs, the engine took longer than usual to rev up, but as Adam gripped the column and the plane rose into the cloudless sky, he breathed out. He always felt calmer when he heard the comforting hum of the engines.

Stewart sat beside Adam, the map in his hands. As they flew, he gave exact coordinates and Adam steered their course. After flying over the Adriatic, avoiding the heavily fortified towns of Vis and Dubrovnik, they flew above the mountains of Yugoslavia, dropping altitude then rising steeply over the peaks of the Carpathians. As artillery fire flashed and sparked all around them, Adam saw another Lancaster turn into a fireball and spin from the sky. He raised his hand to his top pocket, and felt for the cigarette case, which always comforted him. They flew on unscathed.

It was a moonless night and in the darkness it was impossible to identify any topographical features as control points to aid their course. Adam turned to Stewart, unable to conceal his anxiety. 'Where the fuck are we?'

For once, Stewart looked rattled. 'How the hell am I supposed to know when it's as black out there as inside a bear's arse?'

Eventually he spotted a narrow ravine and suggested flying through it to avoid making a steep ascent later, but Adam shook his head.

'If you can't give me an accurate position, I'm not going to risk it. I'll keep flying over the peaks till we get closer to Warsaw. At least we're heading in the right direction.'

On their descent to Warsaw, they were flying into an area with the biggest concentration of German planes in the world. No one spoke. They were south of Kraków, flying dangerously low, when Stewart pointed to the left. Illuminated by bright reflectors, they could see an area enclosed by barbed wire, with watchtowers looming above low barrack huts. Stewart whistled between his teeth and noted the position of the towers. 'Strewth, it looks like a prisoner-of-war camp — maybe a concentration camp. I reckon we should tell them about this place at the debriefing.'

Before long, they saw a red glow on the horizon. There was no need to consult the map. Warsaw lay about a hundred miles ahead and it was burning. When they were only a few miles from the capital, Adam opened the bomb recess, ready to make a quick drop and disappear into the darkness.

Stewart was peering down, trying to make out landmarks through the smoke. 'I can see the main road but where's that bloody post office?' he hissed. The city centre was ablaze, and flames flickered through the smoke, leaping almost as high as the plane.

No one spoke and the sandwich Adam was chewing tasted like sand in his mouth. 'We can't make the drop here,' he said through clenched teeth. 'The parachute lines will catch fire and the containers will be smashed to smithereens. It's too dangerous to hover so low and we can't waste fuel. We'd better head for the other drop-off point.'

Past columns of black smoke they spotted the Vistula River, a winding ribbon that gleamed faintly in the light of the flames. Adam lowered the flaps and undercarriage. They were flying slowly now and recoiled each time trails of lighted bullets flashed past. Their eyes blinded by flashes, they scanned the ground for the drop-off point.

Stewart waved his arm excitedly in the direction of a large red cross. As they approached, they saw that it was made up of people lying on the ground, holding hurricane lamps to guide them. The bomb recess was released and seconds later sparks flew on the road from the impact of the metal containers.

The plane shuddered, the engines roared, and they flew into the sky again. Everything had calmed down and they passed round the large thermos of black coffee. Stewart poured some for Adam and himself, but, before they could drink it, someone shouted 'Fighter!', and shells were exploding all around them.

A dazzling blast made them jump. Adam looked down. One of the Halifaxes had been shot down. 'At least it was over quickly,' he said.

But he didn't have time to reflect on the fate of his colleagues because enemy planes were already pursuing them, and he corkscrewed and spiralled until he lost them.

They were flying above the peaks of the Tatra Mountains now, and beneath them, wrapped in darkness, lay mountain hamlets like Zakopane where he'd spent carefree holidays skiing on Mt Gubałowka and seducing the young women he met on the slopes.

The radio operator sent a Morse message that they'd made a successful drop, and they began to relax.

The rest of the flight passed without incident and with a sigh of relief they saw the familiar airfield below. Home at last. Adam released the undercarriage and checked his watch. It had seemed a lifetime but it was only ten and a half hours since they'd taken off. He cut the engines and they jumped onto the tarmac. It was unusually quiet. There was no personnel around, and they had to wait for half an hour before a truck arrived to take them back to base.

The operations room was deserted when Adam went inside to report on the mission. He glanced at the blackboard that listed the names of the ten planes and their crews that had flown out at the same time as his. Beside every single name, including his own, the officer in charge had chalked the symbol they all dreaded, a hatchet.

All the other crews that had set out for Warsaw the previous evening had perished, and as they were so late, Adam realised that the officer must have assumed that his plane had also been shot down.

He looked at the hatchet again and shivered. It was like looking at his own gravestone.

Forty-Three

As Elżunia changed the dressing on a young woman's leg, she dreaded the moment when the patient would wake from her morphine-induced sleep. The beds in the ward had been pushed so close together that the nurses and doctors had to squeeze through a narrow space to get to the patients. More patients were being brought in all the time, civilians as well as insurgents, children as well as adults, many of them horribly burned by incendiary rockets or maimed by bombs.

As she straightened the sheet over her patient, Elżunia reflected on the turbulent progress of the Uprising, which had led to her being removed from the field and posted to this hospital. Only five days had passed since the Uprising had begun, intoxicating days of great hope. First came success that surpassed all of their dreams. Their surprise attacks had won control of the power station and the water board, and left much of the administration of the city in their hands. Red-and-white national flags fluttered everywhere, and the atmosphere was euphoric. It seemed as though the secret state had finally emerged from underground. All they needed now was for the Russian army to join the fight and for the Allies to send desperately needed supplies.

But the exhilaration of those first days soon evaporated into the sultry air. Instead of withdrawing, the Germans had brought in reinforcements. They were pounding the city with heavy artillery, setting fire to it with incendiary rockets, smashing it with bombs and killing civilians and insurgents indiscriminately. It was clear that they intended to raze Warsaw to the ground and bury all its inhabitants under the rubble. And no one could figure out why the Russian guns on the other side of the Vistula had fallen silent. Some said it was because of the ferocity of the German counterattack, while others saw it as a sinister communist agenda.

The young woman's eyes fluttered open and rested on Elżunia. She struggled to sit up but fell back onto the pillow. 'Why am I here?' she asked.

'Your house was bombed,' Elżunia said. 'Don't you remember?'

The woman shook her head. She was as pale as the fair hair that hung loosely around her bloodless face.

Several patients were moaning or calling for a doctor while someone kept shouting, 'Watch out!' in a frightening voice. 'I shouldn't be here,' the woman was saying. 'I'm just taking up a bed you probably need for someone who's really ill.'

Elżunia swallowed. 'You'll be here for a few days. Until your leg heals.'

'My leg?' The woman's eyes widened. She looked down and closed her hand around Elżunia's wrist. 'What's wrong with it? It'll be all right, won't it? I'm a physical education teacher.'

Elżunia sat on the edge of the bed and took her hand while she explained that a shard of glass had severed her right calf and part of the shinbone so that her leg had had to be amputated below the knee.

The woman stared as though unable to grasp Elżunia's words. Then she let out a despairing cry and buried her face in her hands.

Elżunia was still thinking about her as she headed for the adjacent ward where a German soldier had been admitted. Her blood was boiling. No matter how often the matron explained that their job was to heal the sick, regardless of nationality, she couldn't come to terms with having to nurse the enemy.

'It's outrageous,' she fumed to Janka when they met in the corridor. 'We're healing them so they can go and kill more of us. And we've hardly got enough medicine for ourselves as it is.'

Janka nodded. 'It's insane. Why do we have to be so stupidly noble? Can you imagine them looking after us if we were wounded? But there's one good thing about having their soldiers in here. At least they won't attack a hospital that's looking after their men.'

That morning they had draped a huge Red Cross banner on the roof, so the German bombers would see that this was a hospital, but Elżunia didn't feel safe. She knew they didn't respect hospitals, but having German soldiers there would probably protect them. As soon as she stepped into the next ward, her gaze was drawn to the man lying in the bed nearest the door. There was a blood-stained bandage on his head but the eyes that met hers were hard and cold. She stopped breathing. It was Wolfman, the SS officer from the Ghetto. Although their situations were now reversed, and he was in her power, her hands trembled so much that she had to leave the ward to compose herself.

He was staring at her with that terrifying expression when she returned with a basin of warm water, iodine and bandages. Unable to bring herself to look at his face, she removed the stained bandage and proceeded to clean the gash that looked as though someone had taken a cleaver to his skull. As she worked, she could feel his eyes boring into her.

'*Du bist die Jüdin von Ghetto, Fraülein, nicht wahr?*'

She pretended not to hear.

Assuming she didn't understand German, he said in halting Polish, 'I soldier. I orders obey.' He winced as she swabbed the wound with iodine.

She didn't reply. There was no point getting into a discussion with a sadist who thought it was his duty to murder children.

'Why this hospital is German soldiers taking?' he asked suddenly.

'Because we also obey orders,' she retorted. 'Our orders are to heal the sick, even barbarians who murder women and children.'

He shrugged. 'But that is war, *nicht wahr?*'

'Your country gave us Beethoven, Schubert, Schiller and Goethe,' she blurted. 'Aren't you ashamed to stoop to such barbarism?'

He looked amazed. '*Du liebst Schubert? Die Winterreise, ja?*' And before she could reply, he began to sing the organ grinder's plaintive song in a melodious baritone. Gone was the icy stare; the hard features had softened and he was a music-lover paying homage to his favourite composer.

When he'd finished, he sighed. 'I to my *Mutti* listen and to *Gott* pray every day. I good man. Germans good mans. *Mein Führer* says we must to Polen go to help the Vaterland. We must liquidate Jews and Slavs to make Germany safe. War makes bad mans.'

Furious at his justifications, she turned to leave when she heard screaming, yelling, gunshots and boots clattering in the corridor. The ward door swung open and a unit of SS officers burst in.

'*Hande hoch!*' they yelled. '*Alles raus!*'

'These people can't walk,' she protested. 'Most of them can't even get out of bed!'

Their leader, a stocky man with a swarthy complexion, who didn't look German, raised his pistol and shot the patient closest to him through the head. '*Alles raus!*' he screamed. '*Alles!*' He glared at Elżunia. '*Du auch.*'

'Halt!' Wolfman called out in German. 'Some of us are German, and the Polish nurses and doctors are looking after us. They are good people. Leave them alone.'

'We have orders from Berlin,' the officer snarled. 'All Polish bandits are to be eliminated, along with their city. If you don't like it, tell Himmler.'

Terrified, the patients staggered, limped and crawled from their beds, while Elżunia tried to support the ones who trailed intravenous drips. Those who stumbled or fell were shot, and the floor became slippery with blood, the thick metallic smell making Elżunia's stomach rise into her throat. As she passed the other ward she saw the physical education teacher lying across her bed, unconscious. The sheet had been thrown aside and blood trickled between her thighs. Elżunia pressed her hands to her mouth to stop herself from screaming. They were in the jungle now and wild beasts were in charge.

They were herded into the basement, the patients, nurses and doctors. A key turned in the door. They were locked in.

'Holy Mother of God, what are they going to do to us?' Janka whispered. She was shaking so much her teeth were chattering.

Elżunia put her arm around her friend. She had faced death so many times she no longer felt afraid. As long as it was over quickly.

Someone was turning the key in the lock. The door opened and one of the SS men was standing there, revolver in hand, and beside him stood Wolfman.

'I'm ill. I need someone to look after me,' he barked to the other officer. He pointed at Elżunia and Janka. 'These two will do!' Elżunia's knees shook. She didn't fear death, only what might precede it.

They walked in front of Wolfman along the corridor, past the eerily empty wards, and were almost at the entrance when he tapped her on the shoulder. '*Schnell!*' he said, and with a nod of his head indicated that they should run for it.

Hearts in their mouths, they crept along the passageway past the entrance and glanced outside. SS officers were milling around the forecourt, looking as pleased with themselves as guests at a wedding.

Elżunia and Janka bobbed down and kept going until they came to a window. Janka raised it, biting her lip as it scraped against the weathered frame. They jumped down and, without looking back, reached a clump of bushes just before they heard an explosion. Through a pall of dust and smoke they saw that the lower part of the hospital building had been blown away and the wall was sliding down as though in slow motion, until it collapsed into a heap of broken masonry.

They crouched there for what seemed an eternity, hands over their ears until Janka tugged convulsively at Elżunia's arm. 'That explosion came from the basement. They must have thrown grenades in there.' Tears were rolling down her cheeks. '*Jesus Maria*, they've killed them all.'

'So much for the Red Cross banner,' Elżunia said harshly.

Janka looked at her questioningly. 'That Nazi saved us. He must have taken a fancy to you.'

Elżunia didn't reply.

'I feel guilty,' Janka whispered. 'I want to apologise to all the nurses and doctors and patients because I got out and they didn't.' She dropped to her knees and put her hands together. 'I'm going to pray for us all.'

Forty-Four

After their escape, Elżunia and Janka were transferred to a makeshift hospital that was being set up in the basement of an apartment block in the Old Town. To equip the wards with the bare essentials, they and the other nurses had to run up and down the stairs, knocking on doors and begging the tenants to contribute mattresses, sheets, blankets and pillows, and whatever else they could spare. Some helped willingly, others grudgingly, while some refused outright, even after Elżunia explained politely that the way the Old Town was being pounded by artillery, they themselves might one day benefit from their own generosity. All they needed now was for a doctor to arrive.

From the moment the new doctor loped into the hospital, Elżunia thought he was too casual. Lanky as a beanpole, with a tram-driver's cap perched on the back of his head, she was convinced he'd never command respect. For one thing, he was always cracking jokes, and, for another, he didn't want the nurses to address him as Dr Zawadzki, but to call him Andrzej. How could he expect to be taken seriously if he insisted on being treated like one of them? Dr Zawadzki — Elżunia still couldn't bring herself to call him by his first name — operated on an oak refectory table donated by the nuns at the convent nearby, and he worked by the weak light of a small generator that hummed so loudly they could hardly hear themselves speak.

He often whistled or told jokes as he removed chunks of shrapnel or amputated crushed limbs, and seemed as cheerful as though he were working in the best equipped operating theatre in the world.

'Who's first on the list?' he asked, and rubbed his hands as if anticipating a joyous event although his eyes were red-rimmed from lack of sleep and long hours spent in the musty cellar.

Even before they saw Captain Wajda being brought in on a stretcher, they heard him let fly a string of curses that made Elżunia blush. He propped himself up, glared at the doctor and shouted, 'I will not permit you to amputate my leg!'

Before Dr Zawadzki could respond, the captain whipped out a revolver from his military jacket and pointed it first at the doctor then slowly swept it around in an arc that encompassed the nurses, who shrank back against the wall. His face was ashen and beads of perspiration bubbled on his forehead. 'You're not going to knock me out with an anaesthetic either,' he said through tightly clenched teeth. 'I don't trust any of you. I want to be conscious so I can see what you're doing. Just fix the leg.'

Shocked, Elżunia glanced at Dr Zawadzki, but, as usual, he looked as if he were enjoying a good joke.

In a cheerful voice, he said, 'I can see you're very good at giving orders, Captain Wajda, but I'm the one in charge of this hospital.'

'Well I'm the one in charge of my leg,' the captain retorted, 'and no one's going to cut it off.'

The doctor raised his eyebrows. 'Just tell me, do you intend to shoot me and my nursing staff now or later?

Because I'm not going to waste my time patching you up if you're going to put a bullet through my head.'

'Make no mistake about it,' the captain barked. 'I'll shoot any nurse the minute she tries to stick a needle into my arm or you if you pick up a saw. Remember, I'll be watching every move.'

'Let's have a look at that leg,' the doctor said.

The knee was shattered and the thigh bone protruded through the skin as though it belonged to someone else's leg and had accidentally become attached to this one. But, despite the intense pain, the captain continued to hold his revolver in both hands, pointed at the doctor. 'I know you doctors like to amputate these days,' he said through his teeth.

'That's because we love the sound of saws grinding through bones,' Dr Zawadzki said with a pleasant smile. 'But it's also because we don't have the facilities for prolonged medical treatment, and amputating limbs saves lives. But, if you're willing to risk gangrene, I'll see what I can do. Only we have a rule here: the doctors use the scalpels and the patients don't carry firearms. So if you'll kindly put that aside, we can proceed; otherwise, you can leave and start praying.'

Elżunia stepped forward. 'We have a special locked cupboard where we deposit the weapons.' She spoke briskly, as if this was a common occurrence. 'I'll give you a receipt and you can collect it when you're discharged.'

Captain Wajda hesitated for a moment and dropped the revolver into her hand. As she placed it in the bottom of their increasingly depleted medicine chest, Dr Zawadzki gave her a knowing wink.

Their next patient was a sapper whose arm had been blown off. After Dr Zawadzki had cauterised the stump, Elżunia dressed and bandaged him, chattering to distract him from the pain. He was a dour man with deep lines that disillusionment had carved into his long face. He stared into space and didn't react to Elżunia's conversation. She assumed that his silence was due to pain and stoicism, so she was taken aback when he suddenly spoke.

'Before the Uprising started, the chief promised I'd get so many explosives, I'd be shitting dynamite — pardon the expression, miss. But you know how much they gave me? Fifty kilos of explosives. Fifty kilos. For the whole of Warsaw. And I had six hundred sappers under me! You know what our military chief told me when I said I had to have more explosives? He said, "Don't worry about it. In three days' time, either we'll be dead or we'll be free."' He sighed. 'Well, miss, it's been ten days now, and those murdering bastards are knocking Warsaw down building by building. I reckon we'll be dead long before we're free.'

Elżunia was mulling over his words as she plunged the instruments into a metal saucepan of water boiling on a primus stove, when Janka's bright face appeared in the doorway. 'Quick, come outside! Our boys have captured a German tank!'

As Janka started running up the stairs, she caught her skirt on a nail. 'Bloody hell!' she cried, examining the strip that had torn off. She turned to Elżunia and called out, 'Come on! Don't be long!'

Dispirited by the sapper's words and what they implied for the future of the Uprising, Elżunia couldn't summon up much enthusiasm over a captured tank. 'I'll come in a minute. I'll just finish up,' she called back as Janka ran off.

She had just finished sterilising the instruments when a powerful blast rocked the building and she heard glass shattering. For a moment there was deathly quiet, far more terrifying than the explosion. Then she heard screams that raised goose pimples on her scalp and she rushed outside.

Thick black smoke poured from the tank and unfurled in the sky like evil flowers. She looked around and her throat closed up. Through the smoke and dust she saw that the pavement and roadway were littered with bits of bodies, as though a stage manager had arranged a grotesque tableau. Arms, legs and long coils of intestine were scattered everywhere, and the faces on the severed heads were twisted in terror. Some people were wandering around dazed, silent, with vacant eyes and hands covering their mouths, while others moaned or screamed hysterically and kept asking if anyone had seen their loved ones. A young woman beside her was searching frantically among the bodies, her lips moving in an agitated prayer. She bent down, picked something up from the pavement and let out a howl so visceral that Elżunia could feel it vibrating inside her body. The woman was holding a baby's foot, still wearing its tiny white leather shoe.

The Germans had booby-trapped the tank.

A woman with blood running down her face noticed Elżunia's armband and planted herself in front of her.

'Take a good look around, miss. This is what you AK people have got us into.' She spat each word out. 'Go on, have a good look. Let this be on your conscience!'

Elżunia felt sick. She leaned against the wall of the building, her head in her hands, when she felt an arm around her shoulders and turned to look into Dr Zawadzki's face. He didn't comment on the carnage or try to console her but kept his arm around her while she sobbed.

'We'd better go inside,' he said quietly when her shoulders had stopped heaving. 'We'll have a lot of work today.'

Suddenly her stomach twisted into a tight coil. 'Janka?' she murmured through dry lips.

He shook his head.

'I have to find her,' Elżunia whispered.

She stumbled among the dead and dying, a handkerchief pressed to her mouth. Only one thought pushed her on, to find Janka. She tripped on something, looked down and caught her breath. The woman lying there with her face contorted in a silent scream was Madame Françoise. This was the woman whose malice and jealousy had caused all their misfortunes. For years, Elżunia had fuelled her hatred of this woman with hopes of revenge as she envisaged ways of making the woman pay for what she had done. But now, looking down at her lifeless body, she felt no triumph, only a hollow sense of the transience of life.

She forced herself to keep moving until on the far side of the road she saw a scrap of white apron stained with blood, and beneath it a shred of skirt with a long rip. Her knees buckled and she sank to the ground. Janka's body had been torn in half by the explosion, but she couldn't find the upper part.

Gritting her teeth, Elżunia took off her cape and covered her friend up. 'Now no one will see your panties,' she whispered.

She wanted to lie down in some dark corner and weep, but when she returned to the hospital Dr Zawadzki was already tending to the crowd of bleeding, broken people lining up to be seen.

Taking a deep breath, she walked towards the operating table on unsteady legs. They worked hour after hour, and there were times when she swayed on her feet and could hardly see, and still the patients kept coming. She had never longed for anything as much as an hour to put her head down somewhere and sleep, but the doctor kept going, always with a smile and a quip to relax the patients. Ashamed of showing her weakness, she gulped strong black coffee and kept working.

When they'd done what they could for the last patient, they flopped into chairs. Elżunia was certain she'd never be able to get up again.

'Thanks,' Dr Zawadzki said. 'You did a terrific job. But I wonder how you'll cope on a busy day!'

Her eyes filled as she thought of Janka. 'That could have been me. If I'd gone out a minute earlier, I'd have been blown to bits out there as well.'

He nodded. 'It's a matter of chance, isn't it? Being born is a zillion to one chance, and staying alive is an even bigger one these days. Still, there's no point dwelling on it, so I just keep working.'

'The people hate us now,' she said. 'They blame the AK for all this. Don't they realise we're doing it for them?'

He was shaking his head. 'But we're not doing it for them. We're fighting because we want to be free and live with honour and dignity, and we're prepared to fight for it.'

'How many lives are honour and freedom worth?' she asked in a hollow voice. 'And what's the good of honour when you're dead?'

He shrugged. 'You can only answer that in hindsight. In the meantime, you and I have a job to do.'

Elżunia thought about booby-trapped tanks and shook with rage. 'How can they do this? It's inhuman.'

'Unfortunately it's all too human. It's war.'

His reply reminded her of Wolfman's words and she bristled.

'That's just making excuses for their barbarism. We'd never do anything like that,' she protested.

'We never know what we're capable of,' he mused. 'For good or evil.'

She wondered how to articulate a question that had been nagging at her ever since she'd listened to the sapper. 'Dr Zawadzki, do you think we can win?'

He didn't reply and she looked up. He'd fallen asleep standing against the wall with his tram-driver's cap tipped over his eyes.

Forty-Five

Elżunia was clambering over mounds of broken masonry on her way to the water pump when the shelling started again. She crouched behind a wall with her hands over her ears while bricks rained down, burning timber beams snapped off, and façades of apartment blocks slipped down and collapsed as though in slow motion, sending up sprays of cement and dust as they crashed to the ground.

She didn't venture out until the shelling stopped. The narrow cobbled streets of the Old Town, once so quaint with baroque buildings with their illustrated façades and open-air cafés, now resembled a surreal lunar landscape of dust and rubble. A broken street sign hung crookedly from a metal pole, creaking as it swung overhead. It was impossible to identify any landmark apart from the occasional church spire poking into the sky like a reproach.

A few people had already gathered at the pump with their basins, jugs and buckets, complaining about the shortage of water and the risks they took dodging the shells to fill their containers.

'The devil take them and their uprising,' an old man was grumbling. 'Now that the filtration plant's been hit, they're telling us to dig wells. Next they'll be telling us to grow our own barley.'

Elżunia headed back to the hospital with her pail of water. She walked slowly to avoid spilling it and changed hands every few seconds.

A small crowd had gathered near the Royal Castle. It had become an empty shell, gutted and robbed of its treasures, but in front of it stood Warsaw's landmark, the Sigismund Column. This marble monument, which had been erected three hundred years before to commemorate the king who had moved Poland's capital from Kraków to Warsaw, now soared above the devastation around it, a symbol of hope for the city. In the centre of the crowd lay a dead horse that was still twitching while people crowding around it were feverishly hacking off chunks of flesh with knives, hatchets or axes — whatever they could lay their hands on. They were pushing and jostling and abusing each other in their frenzy to obtain a larger part of the animal, now a bloodied mess. The thought of tasting meat again made Elżunia salivate but the gleam of bloodlust in their eyes repelled her and the thick smell of blood made her gag. It was better to keep eating barley soup than be reduced to such primitive behaviour.

As she walked, she heard solemn voices chanting Latin prayers. Walking slowly along the street, a straggling group carried a medieval wooden cross. At their head came a white-haired priest, his cassock raising clouds of dust as it swished along the ground. He paused for a moment to mop his perspiring face and then spoke in a voice palpitating with spiritual revelation.

'It's a miracle, that's what it is,' he said. 'It's a sign. My church caught fire and everything went up in flames, but this crucifix was untouched.'

She gazed after them curiously as they walked on, still chanting, bearing the crucifix like a coffin. It looked like a funeral procession on its way to bury Christ.

Ever since the Uprising had begun three weeks before, she'd noticed an upsurge in religious feeling. In courtyards, cellars and hospital wards, crowds knelt to pray while priests performed Mass as solemnly as though they were inside cathedrals. Tragedies that she expected would have shaken their faith seemed instead to have strengthened it. Perhaps faith was all they had left, Elżunia mused. Or, like Granny, they believed that prayers were now more important than ever. She sighed, wondering what had become of dear old Granny, alone on the other side of the city. Her mind went back to the morning when they had parted. Granny had cried when she had told her that she was going to join the Uprising, and made the sign of the cross over her head and blessed her, wiping her eyes on her apron.

Now that raging fires and intense fighting had cut communications between the Old Town and the city centre, Warsaw had become a number of isolated districts, and the only safe way of crossing from one to another was through the sewers. One of the fighters in her ward had told her that the wireless operator in his unit had to radio London in order to get through to Żoliborz, which was only three kilometres away.

As she ducked into an underground passage that connected the cellars of several buildings, Elżunia noticed that people had scrawled the names of the streets above ground to guide those below. Although it was safer to use the network of cellars to get around the Old Town these days, Elżunia had mixed feelings about doing so. When the occupants of the overcrowded stuffy cellars saw her armband, they often launched into streams of invective and abuse. Her heart ached as she looked at the swollen bellies of the hungry children and the gaunt grey faces of their parents. Most people huddled in the cellars to avoid the bombs and incendiary rockets that usually hit the upper storeys of buildings and within seconds reduced them to rubble. After each strike, Elżunia dreaded seeing the charred little bodies of children being brought into the hospital, and was happy for them when they died quickly.

'Could you give me some of that water to wash the children's clothes?' a young woman whispered, eyeing Elżunia's bucket. Two dull-eyed children clung to her skirt as she spoke. On the verge of tears, the woman pointed at the dirt that coated everything in the cellar. 'I'm going insane living in this filth. It's even worse than the hunger.' But although Elżunia wished she could help her, she couldn't part with even a drop of the precious water that was needed for the patients and for sterilising the medical instruments.

She came to a deserted building. Several days earlier, a bomb had ripped through the roof and destroyed the upper storeys before becoming lodged on the floor of the first storey without exploding. The floors and ceilings of the upper apartments had been torn down and the staircases hung suspended in the air.

Tormented by the hunger that gnawed at her most of the time, Elżunia wondered if anyone had left food in those apartments, and her mouth watered as she imagined the delicacies that might be stored in their cupboards and pantries. She could already taste the velvety sweetness of cheesecake and the smoky flavour of sausage. Even a slice of stale bread would satisfy her hunger.

Salivating, she placed the bucket against a wall, covered it with a plank of wood, and climbed over the pile of broken bricks blocking the entrance. Clinging to a fragment of the staircase, she hauled herself up to the small wooden platform that was all that remained of the first-floor landing. She stopped to catch her breath and regain her balance when she heard a noise and looked around. Perhaps she'd imagined it. But a moment later, she heard it again. Tip-toeing in the direction of the sound, she inched across a plank of wood and peered behind a door that hung open.

Lying entwined on a rug on the floor, surrounded by fallen paintings, broken china and shattered chairs, were a man and a woman. Her skirt was rucked up around her waist, her legs were wide apart, and she was moaning and gasping, but whether it was with pain or pleasure, Elżunia couldn't tell. Lying on top of her, the man was making rough rasping sounds and violent movements as though pushing a plough through unyielding soil. Her mouth dropped open. So that's how they did it. Her breath came faster and she felt something warm and moist between her thighs.

Suddenly aware of the intruder, the couple separated and sprang up, red-faced, and hurriedly adjusted their ruffled clothing.

'Jesus Maria!' the girl exclaimed, pulling down her skirt while her boyfriend rolled away and hitched up his trousers. 'What are you staring at? Go on, beat it!'

Flustered and confused, Elżunia backed out, retraced her steps, grabbed her bucket and walked back to the hospital.

Unsettled for the rest of the day, she couldn't get that scene out of her mind. It looked disgusting but, although she was ashamed to admit it to herself, it excited her. She wondered how it felt and whether it hurt, and wished there was someone she could ask. Now that Janka was gone, there was no one she could discuss these things with.

'You've looked preoccupied all afternoon,' Dr Zawadzki said after they'd sunk into their chairs at the end of the day. 'Anyone would think there was a war on.'

She was irritated. 'How come you're always so cheerful, Dr Zawadzki?'

'We can't control the wind but we can adjust our sails,' he said. 'I can't do anything about the war, so I concentrate on what I can do. And I've never found that being depressed improves the situation or my mood.'

He glanced at her and added, 'But if you don't start calling me Andrzej, I will get upset.'

She hesitated for a moment, wondering whether the question she was about to ask was impertinent. 'Why do you insist on being called by your first name?'

He smiled. 'That bothers you, doesn't it?'

She struggled to explain her disapproval. 'It's just not done. It's like not having enough respect for yourself. It's bringing you down to the level of ordinary people.'

He burst out laughing. 'But I am an ordinary person. I can't claim any credit for being born with a retentive memory and parents who supported me while I studied. Having a degree in a profession I chose doesn't make me any better than a nurse or a street cleaner. And if the respect I get is on account of my title, then it's not worth having.'

She stared at him, trying to absorb his ideas.

'I can see you find this strange,' he said. 'But isn't this part of what our struggle is about? We want to be independent but we also want to establish a more democratic Poland, where everyone will be represented and all people will be treated equally.'

She looked at him in dismay. 'Are you a communist?'

He shook his head. 'I hate categories that put people into boxes. Most of the problems of the world are created by people who add "ism" to their beliefs. Look at Catholicism. They'd have us believe that we should give up everything we enjoy — our desires, our passions and our pleasures — so we can go to heaven. They want us to be dead while we're alive, so we can be alive after we're dead! I'd rather live now and take my chances later. But if you must give me a label, you can call me a humanist.'

What an unusual man he was, she thought, with his tram-driver's cap, devil-may-care manner and strange ideas. Although she didn't agree with everything he'd said, the idea of a real democracy where everyone was accepted and regarded as equal appealed to her. It sounded like the Utopia she'd once read about in the classics at school. Perhaps if enough people believed in it, and wanted it to happen, it could come true.

She thought of the doctor's quiet authority and self-control, his good-natured humour, the confidence he gave the patients to whom he was so dedicated, and she felt mortified about what she'd said about respect.

That evening, in the cellar she shared with nurses and runners, she spotted Pola, the girl she had seen with her lover in the abandoned building.

'Sorry I told you off up there,' Pola said. 'It's just that you gave me such a fright, appearing out of nowhere like that.'

She saw Elżunia's expression and shrugged. 'That's just how it is nowadays. I can see you're shocked, but everyone's doing it. What am I saving it for? I might be dead tomorrow.'

Despite her exhaustion, Elżunia couldn't sleep. All around her, the girls were giggling and confiding secrets, probably about their sexual adventures. Even the sixteen-year-old who had recently joined the AK as a runner shared confidences with them, but Elżunia, who was almost nineteen, was unable to take any part in these whispered conversations. Although she felt excluded and immature, she was shocked that, like Pola, these girls had dropped their moral standards without a qualm. But Elżunia knew that there was one man she longed to make love with and that was the AK courier — Eagle. With him it wouldn't seem immoral. But what if she never saw him again? What if she died without ever doing it?

Forty-Six

Elżunia counted out the six grinding roars that sounded like the agonised bellowing of a cow in labour, and waited for the explosion to find out whether she was alive or dead. As soon as she heard the deafening booms that followed, she breathed out. Of all the weapons that the Germans had unleashed on them, the mortars they called 'cows' terrified her most, with their long flames like the burning tongues of prehistoric monsters.

What with the roar of the 'cows' that turned buildings into infernos and people into charred statues, the stuttering of artillery and the hail of machine-gun fire, it seemed to Elżunia that she was living out a nightmare from which there was no awakening.

At the same time, remote-controlled Goliath tanks crashed into houses, armoured trains spewed shells so huge that they sliced through buildings like drills, and Stukas peppered them with bombs. Fires often raged unchecked because of the shortage of water, but over twenty thousand fighters sent to defend the Old Town still hung on. They fought street by street, corner by corner, and building by building, armed with pistols, rifles, hand grenades, insufficient explosives and ammunition, and a grim determination not to

403

surrender the ancient heart of the capital. For the third time since the war began, Warsaw was fighting for its life.

'I don't know why we haven't gone crazy in here,' Elżunia said, looking helplessly at the endless line of insurgents and civilians who hoped to be admitted to the hospital, even though they knew there was nowhere to put them all and no medicines with which to treat them.

'Because we're far stronger than we realise,' Dr Zawadzki replied. 'And we're too busy to think about ourselves.'

He was telling his small patient to keep watching out for the fairy that lived behind the door while he extracted splinters of glass from her face. As Elżunia handed him the tweezers and disinfectant, she listened to his stories about hobgoblins and princesses that distracted his young patient from the pain. His audience included the first-aid workers and other staff who hovered around to hear his tales.

'Got any of your spitting soup left?' he asked Elżunia as the orderlies brought in the next patient.

She couldn't help smiling at his description. Every morning she made a big pot of soup from barley that hadn't been husked, so that as they ate they had to keep spitting out the chaff. To her dismay, even the barley ration had recently been reduced.

With the ever-increasing number of patients, there wasn't enough soup to go round, but no one was keen to volunteer to go to the warehouse, which could only be reached by a route above ground that was right in the firing line.

'I had a funny dream last night,' she said as she covered a patient with a sheet, exposing only the ripped abdomen through which his slippery intestines were showing. 'I dreamed that I'd made a big vat of barley soup, and, when I went to ladle it out, it turned into a huge sausage.'

Dr Zawadzki chuckled. 'It could be a sign of meat deprivation. Of course, Freud would have interpreted it differently.'

She blushed. Next time she'd keep her dreams to herself.

But right now she didn't have time to think about soup, sausage or dreams because it was time to select the most urgent cases for him to see. This responsibility always weighed her down. What if she made a mistake and someone died while waiting to be seen? As she walked briskly among the stretchers, trying to comfort and reassure the patients without becoming involved in discussions, she noticed a young man whose head was bowed as he pressed one hand against his shoulder. She walked towards him and stopped, hardly able to believe her eyes.

'Stefan!' she cried and flung her arms around him. 'Oh thank God! Thank God you survived.'

He was squeezing her hand as he cleared his throat and tried to speak. 'Lucky they brought me here,' he said finally.

The stain under Stefan's arm was spreading and he bit his lip. 'It's my shoulder. I've been shot,' he said.

As she motioned for the first-aid boys to bring him in to see Dr Zawadzki, she noticed that he was thinner and taller than she remembered. More manly. His bored, spoilt expression had been replaced by a steadier, more focused gaze.

He winced as Dr Zawadzki examined his shoulder.

'I'll have to remove the bullet,' the doctor said. 'Unfortunately we don't have any anaesthetic. All I can give you is a swig of moonshine.'

'Make it a big swig,' Stefan said through white lips.

❋

Elżunia was leaning over her brother when he came to. 'You fainted while Dr Zawadzki was getting the bullet out,' she said. 'Probably just as well.'

His face was contorted with pain. As she handed him a glass of water, he whispered, 'Mother. Where is she?'

When she told him how she had found their mother in the ruined bunker, a strange, harsh sound, more like a cough than a sob, tore from his throat. They sat in silence for a long time.

'What about Father? Have you heard anything?'

She pulled a face. 'He's all right,' she said brusquely, 'but it's a very long story.' She sat down beside her brother. 'First I want to hear all about you. How did you manage to get out of the Ghetto?'

'After two weeks, I joined a group of fighters. We didn't have any Molotov cocktails or grenades, so we used to ambush Germans or Ukrainians and take their uniforms and weapons. In the end, our bunker got hit. It was a miracle I got out alive. By then, most of the Ghetto was on fire and there was only one way out.' Stefan winced as he described his journey through the sewers.

After wandering about town, avoiding the round-ups and hiding from the Germans, he'd found work on an allotment on the outskirts of the city. Determined to fight the Germans, he'd joined the insurgents, and, when the Uprising broke out, his unit was sent to the Old Town. They'd been fighting hand-to-hand battles in the streets when he was shot.

'Our ammunition's running so low now that we can't fire on the Germans until we're up close so we don't waste any bullets,' he told Elżunia. 'I'll tell you how bad things are. Our major had a revolver of one calibre but ammunition for another. He had to run around begging for someone to give him the right ammunition. I don't know what the bloody Russians are up to on the other side of the river, but if they don't come and help us soon, and if the Allies don't drop us some more weapons, I don't know how long we can go on defending the Old Town.' He gave a mirthless laugh. 'Talk about history repeating itself!'

His eyes darted around the ward. 'Gittel. Where's Gittel?'

'I can't find her. I've looked, I've asked people, but no one knows anything.' The desperation made Elżunia's voice rise. 'I don't know what's become of her.'

He shook his head and said, 'Poor little kid.'

She saw the tears in his eyes and was surprised. He had never shown any interest in Gittel before. They sat for a while without speaking, and from his expression she sensed he wanted to get something off his chest.

'I wish I'd never joined the Jewish police,' he said. 'I got conned by German lies. They said that joining up would protect us and our families, but I didn't protect you and Mama, and, in the end, the Germans deported most of the Jewish policemen like everyone else.'

He tried to sit up but fell back against the lumpy pillow donated by one of the tenants of the apartment building. 'I never thought it would turn out like that, or that I'd end up doing what I did. Somehow one thing led to another ...' He trailed off, looking at her as though expecting absolution. 'I made the wrong choice, that's all.' He paused for a moment. 'And you chose the right side, you brat. You always do.'

There was affection mingled with resentment in his voice. As a child, she had always envied what she saw as his privileged status in the family. He was a boy, and older, so he was treated more indulgently by their mother, whose favourite he was. Now it occurred to her that perhaps he had envied her as well.

407

She was overjoyed to see him, to know that he was still alive, that she wasn't alone any more. The resentment and anger she had felt towards him for the past few years evaporated in the thrill of having him with her, and her mind was flooded with nostalgic memories of their childhood, when he was her adored older brother whose approval and affection she had sought but never received.

Promising to come back and see him as soon as she had finished her work, Elżunia returned to the operating theatre with a lighter step but for once Dr Zawadzki didn't make any quips, and the look he gave her was decidedly cool. While scrubbing up for the next patient, he said, 'I don't approve of what you did.'

She stopped pulling on her gloves and looked up at him, startled. 'What do you mean?'

'Bringing your brother in to see me ahead of people who were more seriously injured was unprofessional.'

'But he's my brother, I thought he was dead —' she stammered, but he cut her short.

'I understand your reasons but I don't approve of your action. Did you know that when the Uprising began, the Commander-in-Chief's wife was seven months' pregnant? He could have warned her and sent her to their country estate but he didn't. You know why? Because he felt it wasn't fair to all the other pregnant women who couldn't be warned in time.'

Elżunia's eyes blazed. 'Well I don't approve of *his* action.' She could feel the blood rushing to her head, and the words burst from her mouth before she could stop them.

'There's nothing admirable in putting ideas ahead of people. That's what fanatics do, the ones who add an "ism" to elevate their ideas and spread their beliefs. And here's something else for you to disapprove of!'

She peeled off her rubber gloves and flung them to the ground, sobbing. 'I can't stand this place. I'm sick of the blood and pain and screams. I've had enough of this war. I wish I could get away from here and never come back!'

She expected another rebuke but his voice was full of concern. 'You've been working too hard. I'm sorry. I should have realised. It's just that you seemed so calm and competent —'

'Well now you can see I'm not competent. I'm unprofessional, remember?' She glared at him like a defiant child, pushing the limits of his patience, challenging him to a duel of words. Until that moment, she hadn't realised how much his opinion mattered, or how stung she was by his criticism.

He folded his long arms around her, held her without speaking, like an understanding uncle, and she felt his warm breath on her head.

Suddenly she was telling him about the Ghetto Uprising and about her mother and Gittel. When she pulled away, the lapels of his white coat were wet with her tears.

That evening, she looked up at the pale moon and thought it looked cold and hostile. She heard footsteps and turned.

'Lovely maid in the moonlight,' Dr Zawadzki said and started humming a slow, sweet melody in a deep voice.

'What's that?' she asked.

'It's an aria from *La Bohème*. Rodolfo has just seen Mimi for the first time and he's smitten.'

'How does it end?'

'Tragically. But for a time they find love.'

She stole a glance at him. In the pallid light of the moon, with his face in shadow and his tall, lean body in silhouette, she could imagine Rodolfo serenading his beloved Mimi.

'It's my name day tomorrow,' she said suddenly.

'That's a very special day,' he said. 'I'm going to prepare a feast for you.'

She chuckled. 'Spitting soup?' Then she stopped smiling. Name day or not, tomorrow she would have to go to the warehouse for more barley. When the Uprising had begun, the civilians had carried the sacks but now that the area was under fire, several men had been wounded on the way, and they stopped volunteering. No amount of pleading or cajoling could persuade them to change their minds, so now it was left to the AK nurses and fighters.

There were wisps of lollipop pink in the dawn sky when Elżunia set out for the warehouse with three first-aid workers and an insurgent soldier as their guide. Every few seconds, as artillery fire crackled around them, they crouched down until they were lying still on the broken pavements, and then inched along, praying they wouldn't be hit.

After several hours, she sniffed the sharp, burnt smell of roasting grain. They were almost there. A row of people sat outside the storehouse, waiting their turn. As the flash of artillery fire lit up their faces, Elżunia froze. They were all dead.

Her heart in her mouth, she clambered up the ladders that rested against the storehouse wall and slid down a ramp into an Aladdin's cave filled with mountains of golden grain that shimmered in the light slanting through the windows. In a querulous voice, the old storeman told them to hold their sacks wide open as he filled them with a river of barley.

On the way back, the sacks grew heavier with each step. Elżunia felt as if her arms were dropping off, and carrying the sack alternately on her back, by the corners, or against her chest gave only momentary relief. She longed to leave the accursed sack and lie down but forced herself to keep going. So many people were depending on it. That barley was more important than her tiredness, even more important than her life.

Almost numb with exhaustion, she tripped and sprawled on the ground, clutching the sack to make sure the precious barley didn't spill. As she waited to catch her breath, she noticed a spindly stick poking out of the ground and was astonished to see that it was the offshoot of a lilac bush, most of which had been ripped away. Part of its root still clung to the soil of the devastated street, determined to bloom again.

Dr Zawadzki was standing at the door when she staggered in, his face taut with anxiety.

'I hope you're hungry, because I've made you a celebration dinner.'

She longed to fall onto her mattress and sleep but she was touched that he'd remembered her name day, and didn't want to disappoint him. He led her to the table and, with a mysterious smile, placed something in front of her. She breathed in an unfamiliar smell and closed her eyes.

Meat! It was years since she'd tasted meat. She tried to chew slowly to make it last but ended up devouring it, licking every morsel and sucking the marrow from the bones. It didn't matter that it was tough. It was meat.

He watched like an indulgent parent as she ate. After she had licked her plate clean, with a flourish he produced a pear. She cupped it in both hands and stared at it in wonder. The innocent greenness of the small leaf attached to the short woody stalk brought tears to her eyes.

'It almost seems sacrilege to eat it,' she whispered. She turned to him with shining eyes. 'Where on earth did you get hold of a pear?'

'A patient from Żoliborz gave it to me.'

It seemed incredible that pear trees still grew in Warsaw. Żoliborz was only a few miles north of the Old Town but it seemed as though it must be in another country.

'And the rabbit?' she asked. 'Did she give you that too?'

He shook his head, relieved that she hadn't asked what kind of animal they were eating.

'I never imagined I could have such a wonderful name day in this place,' she said. Without realising it, she had devoured the whole pear and he had watched her without saying a word. She flushed with shame at her greed.

'This has been a fantastic evening,' she said.

He raised her from her chair, put his hands on her waist and looked straight into her eyes. 'I can think of an even better way to end it.'

Confused by the intensity of his words and the intimacy of his tone, she pulled away and lowered her eyes. It hadn't occurred to her that he might be interested in her as more than a colleague and she didn't know what to say.

'It's perfect just as it is,' she said lightly, avoiding the unspoken subject.

'Are you sure?' he asked gently. 'Life is such a brief gift. I believe in seizing happiness with both hands. Especially now.'

Her heart was beating faster as the scene in the deserted building flashed before her eyes. What was it that Pola had said? Why save it when you could be dead tomorrow? She could have been killed that afternoon hauling the sack of barley. Tomorrow she could be dead. This could be her last chance to be initiated into the mystery that she'd thought about for so long.

She stole a glance at Dr Zawadzki. Without his tram-driver's cap, his thick fair hair fell across his forehead, accentuating the intense gaze of his grey eyes. She had seen the admiring looks some of the nurses and first-aid workers had given him and she'd heard them whispering about him. None of them would hesitate if given the chance. But the gap between her heart and her mind was too great.

'Quite sure,' she said trying to steady her voice.

He kissed her cheek lightly and went inside, humming Rodolfo's aria.

She felt a stab of regret. But it was the airman, not the doctor, she wanted to hear serenading her in the moonlight.

Forty-Seven

August was drawing to a close, but, apart from the stifling heat, there was nothing to remind them of the last luscious month of summer.

'Will we ever see a golden August again?' Elżunia sighed. She cast a dispirited glance at the ward, which was a jumble of beds, stretchers and mattresses on which some patients were mumbling in feverish voices while others screamed for something to take away the pain.

'Instead of corn stalks, sunflowers and the scent of new-mown hay, we've got war, hunger and the stink of death,' she said to Dr Zawadzki, who was amputating a fighter's shattered arm.

Ever since her birthday, when she had rebuffed his advances, she'd found it awkward to work so close to him. Whenever she brushed against his white coat or touched his arm, she shrank back in case he thought it was intentional. At the same time, she felt put out that he gave no indication that anything of a personal nature had ever passed between them. Although she had rejected him, she would have liked to see desire and disappointment in his eyes, but his glances never lingered on her, and his voice, whenever he asked her to pass a scalpel, syringe or bandage, was politely impersonal.

It irritated her that Krystyna, one of the first-aid workers, a pretty girl who reminded her of a porcelain doll, had been finding too many excuses lately to come and talk to Dr Zawadzki. Even more annoying was the admiring expression that appeared on his face whenever his eyes rested on Krystyna.

I didn't want him, so why should I care? she reasoned with herself, but it riled her that he'd switched his affections so quickly to someone else.

Now that Stefan's shoulder had almost healed, he was keen to return to his unit. 'They thought the Uprising would only last a few days, but we've already held out for almost a month,' he told her proudly.

'Almost as long as the Ghetto,' she said. Out of the corner of her eye, she noticed Krystyna sidling in to see Dr Zawadzki again.

'If only the Allies would drop more supplies,' Stefan said. 'We spend most of the day looking up at the sky, hoping to see them. With more weapons, we'd stand a chance.'

He paused and frowned. 'That story you told me about Father. I still can't make any sense of it.'

Ever since Elżunia had told him about their father's betrayal and his affair with Marta, he had been mulling over it. He had never been close to their father who, he felt, had always been too hard on him, while, in his eyes, Elżunia could do no wrong. But he found it difficult to believe her version of events.

'How do you know they were having an affair?' he asked for the third time. 'You said they were both in the AK. Maybe it was quite innocent. Maybe they met to talk about their work. You were always his golden girl, so I'm amazed you could jump to that conclusion.'

While Stefan was speaking, Elżunia realised that he had probably envied her closeness with their father just as she had envied the fact that he was their mother's favourite.

'People in the AK don't meet in their lodgings to discuss their work, especially when one of them is quite junior. Anyway, he always came at night. I used to hear them murmuring.' She blushed. 'It sounded very intimate.'

Stefan wasn't convinced.

'That doesn't prove anything. The man who came at night might have been someone else. And, even if it was him, they could have pretended to be having an affair to put people off the scent.'

Elżunia tried to stay calm. 'I told you what the caretaker's wife said. It all adds up. We have to face facts. He met this attractive girl, got involved with her, and abandoned us. That's why he didn't get in touch or try to get us out of the Ghetto — just left us there to rot.'

'I still think there must be some other explanation,' Stefan persisted. 'I can't imagine Father doing that.'

She shrugged, irritated. 'War changes people. You don't know what anyone's capable of until they're tested.' Her eyes rested on him for an accusing instant, then looked away.

As the fighting in the narrow streets of the Old Town intensified, more and more patients flooded into the hospital, which had spread from the underground shelter to the basement apartments and to the landings as well. Armed with lanterns, Dr Zawadzki and Elżunia, together with three of the first-aid workers, including Krystyna, made their way to an adjoining cellar to see if it could be used to accommodate patients.

Dr Zawadzki swept his flashlight around and shook his head. The cellar was used for storing coal and wasn't suitable. They bent over to squeeze through the low entrance when Elżunia felt the floor shift under her feet. There was the deafening crash of a bomb exploding nearby, and the walls shook. The bombardment had raised so much coal dust, that, as they breathed it in, they were seized by violent paroxysms of coughing. Elżunia felt as though the next cough would rip her lungs out.

'Quick, pee into your handkerchiefs,' Dr Zawadzki said.

Doubled up with coughing fits, the girls stared at him, then at each other.

'For heaven's sake, this is no time to be coy,' he said. 'I won't look.'

But whether from anxiety or embarrassment, none of them could do it. As they continued to gasp and cough, he grabbed their handkerchiefs and turned away. Several moments later, he handed them wet handkerchiefs to place over their noses and mouths.

'That was disgusting,' one of the girls said when they'd returned to the hospital, their faces and hands streaked with black. She shuddered. 'I feel sick. I'll never be able to stop spitting and rinsing my mouth out.'

'He saved us from choking to death,' Krystyna said, loudly enough for Dr Zawadzki to hear. 'I think he's wonderful.'

Elżunia glared at her.

Suddenly they could hear a commotion near the entrance. Someone was running down the stairs and shouting for help in a panic. 'There are people trapped down the road. Hurry!'

Elżunia and the other girls rushed out with their first-aid kits, but, as soon as they stepped outside, they saw the bombers still circling above.

'*Jesus Maria!*' Krystyna's hand flew to the cross around her neck. Her voice was teetering on the edge of hysteria.

'I'm going back! They're going to bomb us! We'll all get killed!'

Elżunia laid a restraining hand on her arm. 'Imagine you're with Dr Zawadzki,' she whispered. 'Would you want him to see you running for cover?'

Her words had an immediate effect. Elżunia took her hand and together they made a dash for the bombed house.

The rescue squad had already arrived and the men were carefully removing the rubble with their spades, but the front of the building had collapsed and the entrances were blocked, making access to the cellars impossible. A distraught woman was wringing her hands and sobbing as she spoke to the emergency workers. 'Can't you dig faster? Most of them were sheltering down there. They'll suffocate before you get to them at the rate you're going.'

One of the men flung down his spade and held up his blistered hands in her face. 'You try it!' he yelled at her. 'See how fast you can go!'

Elżunia raced to the back of the building where people were wandering around in shock. As the nurses and first-aid workers feverishly cleaned wounds, applied compresses, gave injections and placed the seriously injured victims onto stretchers, more planes flew past.

Elżunia's grip on the stretcher tightened and she and Krystyna exchanged grim looks but they kept working until they'd taken care of the people above ground. 'We may as well go and have a rest until they break through to the cellar.'

It seemed that she had just lain down on her camp bed when Krystyna was shaking her arm.

'Wake up, we've got to go,' she was saying. Elżunia rubbed her eyes. It was still dark. She staggered to her feet, slung her knapsack over her shoulders and picked up her torch. They had knocked out an opening in the wall and rescue workers were digging people out by the faint light of a torch someone had suspended overhead.

Those at the back of the cellar were clamouring for help, demanding to be taken out before they were all buried alive. In a panic, some of them surged towards the opening, pushing others out of the way.

Suddenly Elżunia heard herself shouting above the melee. 'Hold it! We're doing our best to get you out but you'll leave one by one, in an orderly way, not in a stampede. Stay where you are and I'll tell you when it's your turn.'

It was four o'clock in the morning when she crawled back to the hospital. Dr Zawadzki, who was already in the operating theatre, removing a crushed spleen, looked up as she came in.

'I heard that you frightened the life out of those people in the cellar,' he said with a chuckle. 'You should have been a sergeant-major.'

Too exhausted to reply, she walked on. She had reached the end of the corridor when he called out, 'Great news! I heard on Radio Błyskawica that Paris was liberated today!'

Elżunia couldn't sleep. Although her body was exhausted, her mind leapt from one disturbing thought to another, as images of the day's events raced through her brain. She ached with loneliness. She doubted whether she and her brother would ever become close, but, even if they did, fraternal affection was no substitute for intimate love. If only she mattered to someone, if only there was someone to share her life, so that if she died, somebody would care enough to grieve.

Without stopping to think, she jumped out of bed and ran along the passageway until she reached a door at the far end, tapped on it and entered. Sitting on his camp bed, reading, Dr Zawadzki looked up at her.

'Andrzej,' she whispered.

In two strides he was beside her, and, without speaking, he cradled her against him.

Like a sleepwalker who has woken with a jolt in a strange room, she fought an impulse to run back to bed, but the moment passed. She looked into his eyes and knew why she had come.

Shocked at her own audacity, she said, 'I feel as though I've jumped off a cliff without a parachute.'

'I'll make sure you have a soft landing.'

She wrapped her arms around him, laid her head on his chest and let out a deep sigh. Cupping her face in his hands, he kissed her lips so gently that his touch felt like the brush of butterfly wings.

He was looking into her eyes. 'Are you sure?'

She nodded.

They lay on his narrow camp bed, their arms around each other. He stroked her hair and kissed her eyelids.

'You're like a delicate porcelain figurine wrapped in brown paper,' he said, kissing her collarbone as he unbuttoned the worn blouse. 'I'd like to put you up on a mantelpiece and gaze at you.'

His breath grew hot and urgent and she stiffened with apprehension.

'I'll try not to hurt you,' he whispered. 'Tell me if you want me to stop.'

She clung to him, excited, curious and nervous, but she didn't tell him to stop.

Afterwards, they lay with their arms around each other. It hadn't been the thrilling experience she had envisaged — there were no epiphanies, no fireworks and no bolts of lightning — but she felt warm, secure and connected.

He was nuzzling her earlobe. 'I've wanted to make love to you from the first day I saw you,' he said. 'It must have been your stern, disapproving look.'

'I thought you were too casual and flippant,' she retorted. Then she pulled away and looked at him. 'I thought you fancied Krystyna.'

He burst out laughing. 'So do I have jealousy to thank for your change of heart?'

She reached up and playfully boxed his ear.

'We'll always remember the night Paris was liberated,' he murmured.

'Paris wasn't the only one that was liberated,' she said with a mischievous smile.

Forty-Eight

Although the evening was cool, Adam didn't seem to notice that Judith was shivering as they strode along the Embankment. He didn't even seem to notice that she had loosened her hair or that she wore a short floral dress that showed off her legs. They had arranged to meet at The Connaught but he was too restless to sit in a restaurant. She had dressed for a romantic dinner, and had forgotten to throw a coat around her shoulders before running out of the nurses' home, but as soon as she saw his drawn face, she suggested going for a walk instead. Dinner with him in this state would be neither romantic nor relaxing.

The trouble with Adam was that she never knew until the last moment whether he would keep any of their arrangements. Sometimes he broke their rendezvous because his leave was cancelled or because he had to meet someone to discuss the situation in Poland or rush back to the base for some emergency. Although Judith regarded punctuality and reliability as essential, and reprimanded nurses who were even a minute late, she always made allowances for Adam.

She felt confused and troubled because she didn't understand him. That unexpected kiss after the ball had been followed by disconcertingly casual behaviour. Nursing was straightforward. You had a problem and you dealt with it by applying the appropriate treatment. But relationships with men had no set guidelines to reassure you. Nancy, on the other hand, always seemed to know what was acceptable and what wasn't. 'Don't tell me he's stood you up again?' she'd say, her blonde curls bobbing indignantly under her nurse's cap. 'I don't know why you put up with it.'

No matter how often Judith explained Adam's commitment to Poland, Nancy dismissed the excuses. 'I don't know politics but I know men, and he's messing you around,' she said. 'Give him the flick.'

Judith was too embarrassed to tell her friend how often Adam's gaunt face figured in her thoughts and dreams, or how minutely she still examined every detail of their walk along the Embankment when he had kissed her.

'I wouldn't be putting my shoes on just yet,' Nancy had said acidly that evening when she saw Judith dressing for dinner. 'He'll be calling any minute to tell you he can't make it.'

But on this occasion, Nancy's predictions proved wrong, and as Judith shivered in the breeze that blew up from the river, she walked so close to Adam that the woollen fabric of his jacket scratched her bare arm. From his set jaw, she could tell he was brooding over something, so she decided to break the silence.

'Isn't it wonderful that Paris has been liberated?'

He shot her a sharp look that made her flinch and she added quickly, 'Surely it can't be long before Warsaw is liberated too.'

Adam gave a cynical laugh. 'Who gives a shit about Warsaw? When we begged them to let us drop supplies for our resistance, they couldn't spare the planes or the fuel. But we had to give them air support on D-Day, so Paris could be liberated.'

Five years had passed since the war began, and Poland, Britain's oldest and most loyal ally, was still fighting the Nazis, while France, which had surrendered in 1940 and set up a collaborationist government, had been rewarded by having its capital liberated. While he vented his anger about this latest instance of Allied duplicity, he walked so fast that Judith wished she'd worn sensible shoes. She was relieved when they stopped near Tower Bridge and leaned over the parapet.

A fine mist had risen from the river and swathed the Tower of London in a soft, ghostly light. 'Looking at it now, you wouldn't believe all the bloodthirsty things that have happened here,' she said.

He looked amused and she wondered whether she sounded like a naïve colonial. Although she'd been living in London for several years, its palaces, towers and domes still excited her. 'In Australia, we reckon a building that's a hundred years old is pretty ancient, so it's incredible to see landmarks that are over a thousand years old,' she said.

He put his arm around her shoulders and, for the first time that evening, he looked straight at her. 'I think you are cold and hungry. We go for dinner, yes?'

Over their consommé, which was tasteless and lukewarm, she studied his face. In her company, its deep lines had softened and his mouth looked less bitter than usual.

'What are you going to do after the war?' she asked.

He shrugged and pushed away the half-eaten soup. 'I don't know. War has taken so many years of my life, I wonder if I will fit into a peaceful world.'

'Will you go back to Poland?'

He looked down at his long fingers. 'Life outside Poland I cannot imagine. If a democratic government is set up, I'd like to be part of it.'

'You said if.'

'I hope that will happen but who knows? Stalin has stacked the provisional government in Lublin with his supporters. They call themselves the Committee of National Liberation, but whenever the communists talk about liberation, I wonder about their real motives.'

She looked thoughtful. The London newspapers were full of stories extolling the sacrifices made by the Soviet Union, and of the heroic Russian soldiers who were about to liberate Eastern Europe.

'I keep reading articles that praise Russia and the Red Army,' she said. 'They glorify Stalin and criticise Poland for not giving in to his demands.'

His face darkened. 'Yes, it's true, we are very unreasonable people.' He spat the words out. 'We don't believe that letting an enemy cut off our arms and legs will make him our friend. The commentators have backed the wrong horse, as you say in English. One day they will regret it, but by then it will be too late.'

At the next table, a man was holding his companion's hands, gazing at her lovingly. He said something that made her blush and look down, and Judith wondered what it would be like to receive such ardent attention, and to indulge in intimate chitchat instead of discussing global politics. Although she suspected it wouldn't be stimulating like her conversations with Adam, she couldn't help stealing envious glances at the amorous couple.

'What about you?' Adam was asking. 'What will you do after the war? Will you go back to Australia?'

'Eventually I will. I miss the sunshine and the friendly faces. But for now I'm hooked on Europe. There'll be a lot of reconstruction going on, and they'll probably need nursing sisters to set up health services and train nurses and so on,' she said. 'That's what I'd like to get involved in.'

He was looking at her closely but whether it was friendly interest or something more intense, she couldn't tell.

'You are an interesting woman,' he said after a pause. 'I have never met anyone like you.'

She took it as a compliment but decided not to repeat it to Nancy, who was bound to find some negative interpretation.

Outside the hotel, he leaned against a street light and lit a cigarette. As he exhaled, he said, 'I look forward always to seeing you.'

A wave of impatience swept over her. She'd had enough of this pussy-footing around, enough of all the talking, guessing, interpreting, analysing and playing games. It was wartime, they were adults and every sortie could be his last. She placed her hand on his arm, pushed her hair back from her flushed face and looked boldly into his eyes.

'If you'd like to spend the rest of the night with me, we could go back inside and get a room.'

She held her breath. Would he be shocked at being propositioned? But he said nothing. Putting his arm around her, he squeezed her shoulder and led her through the portico towards the reception desk.

From the smirk of the clerk whose insolent glance noted their lack of luggage as he watched them sign the register in different names, Judith wasn't surprised that he'd allocated them one of the rooms at the back of the hotel. It was at the end of a long corridor that smelled of stale cigarette smoke and looked out onto the rear of grimy buildings crisscrossed with fire escapes.

The room was small and dark, and the gold fringes at the base of the curtain pulls were worn from decades of handling. In the weak light of the lamp, which cast shadows on the ceiling, the burgundy bedspread looked blotchy.

'This must be their worst room,' Adam said. 'I'll tell them to change it.'

Judith raised her eyebrows. 'Why bother? We didn't come here to admire the décor, did we?'

He was looking at her with that amused expression again. 'I'll ask them to send up a bottle of something. What about champagne?'

'I've never been keen on champagne,' she said. 'I think it's overrated. Why don't we have your national drink?'

When the bottle of Wodka Wyborowa arrived, he poured out two glasses. 'Do you know the right way to drink vodka?' he asked.

She nodded and they clinked glasses.

'Let's drink to Poland,' she suggested. 'How does that national anthem of yours go? "Poland hasn't perished and never will"?'

'I'd like to drink to you,' he said. 'You're such ...'

'An interesting woman?' she prompted with a touch of sarcasm.

'A very interesting woman.' He raised his glass, drained it, and leaned over to kiss her.

She kept up with him glass for glass, but, when she pealed with laughter at everything he said, he took the glass from her hand, placed it on the coffee table and took her in his arms.

Several hours later, he was lying on his side, his head propped up with one hand while he caressed her with the other. 'That night at Admiralty House, you looked so crisp and starched, like the typical matron who frightens everyone in the hospital.'

She looked at the damp, rumpled sheets, shook her tousled hair, and burst out laughing. 'I'm certainly not crisp or starched now!'

The morning sun shone weakly through an opening in the curtains, and, when Judith opened her eyes, Adam was already pulling his shirt over his head. She lay very still, not wanting to dispel the memory of the previous night. He saw that she was awake, sat down on the edge of the bed and kissed the palm of her hand.

'You were right about the décor,' he said. He folded his arms around her and kissed her so passionately that the fragment of her mind still capable of rational thought started concocting an excuse to be late back to the hospital.

But he was already dressed. 'I'd better get back to the base,' he said.

'That's a beautiful cigarette case,' she said as he picked it up from the bedside table and placed it inside his shirt pocket.

'A girl in Poland gave it to me,' he said. 'I never go anywhere without it.'

'An interesting girl?' She hated the archness of her question but it was out before she could stop herself.

He thought for a moment. 'An extraordinary girl.'

Judith swung her legs onto the floor and reached for her dress. She wished she hadn't asked.

By the time Adam returned to the base, the briefing officer was pinning photographs and maps on the wall.

'Our intelligence people in the Thames Valley have been studying photographs taken by a reconnaissance flight over Poland recently. They're photos of the IG Farben industrial plant at Monowitz, and they've identified a power station, carbide plant, and synthetic rubber and synthetic oil plants,' he said. 'Monowitz is two-and-a-half miles east of a place called Auschwitz.' He tapped his pointer on the map.

Adam craned forward. That was where they'd spotted the watchtowers and barbed-wire fences.

'Today your task is to bomb the IG Farben plants at Monowitz,' the officer went on. He was about to step off the dais when Adam spoke up.

'Sir, that plant is part of Auschwitz–Birkenau. It's a concentration camp.'

'What's your point, Czartoryski?'

Adam tapped the photograph. 'Thousands of people are still being transported there every day by train to be gassed and incinerated. While we're bombing the plant, why don't we bomb the railway line that leads to the camp? That will delay the transports and save thousands of lives. And maybe by the time they repair the line, the war will be over.'

The officer looked dubious. 'Quite a scenario you've created. The trouble is, you've got things back to front. Look here, I have nothing against bombing the bastards' death camps and making it harder for them to murder people, but that's not our immediate concern. Our priority is to bomb the Monowitz plant to stop them expanding because, as you're well aware, the German war machine depends on oil and rubber production.'

In a more sympathetic tone, he added, 'Once we cripple the German war machine, they'll have to surrender. And that's when they'll stop killing people in those ghastly camps.'

As they were walking to their lockers for their parachutes and mae wests, Stewart muttered to Adam, 'Just like we're getting them to surrender by bombing their cities. How many sorties do you reckon we've made over Cologne and Berlin?'

Half an hour later, Adam swung the Lancaster around the perimeter track to the end of the runway. The green light flashed and they took off. Soon they were flying over the North Sea towards the enemy coast. The atmosphere was so relaxed, they might have been on a pleasure flight, until Stewart pointed to the starboard beam. 'Flak ahead.'

From the jets of red tracer all around them, they realised they were in the middle of an aerial battle. Adam gripped the controls and hauled the plane around, twisting and turning to escape the fighters. It rocked wildly from side to side, there was a powerful upward thrust, and they rose above the flak, high among the clouds.

Adam looked down through a break in the clouds and clenched his teeth. Below them stretched the railway lines that carried entire communities to their death. It would be so easy to drop a few bombs and halt these obscene transports, and he chafed at his own powerlessness, and the apathy of the entire world.

Forty-Nine

'I think I'm getting addicted to this,' Elżunia said as she snuggled against Andrzej in his bed. She delighted in the secret glances they exchanged across the operating table by day, and couldn't wait to sneak into his room at night. In his arms, the harshness of the world receded. There was no Uprising, no suffering and no terror. At last she had something solid to hold on to.

'I'll probably be arrested for corrupting minors,' he said, and chuckled. 'Come to think of it, you're the one who corrupted me.'

After they made love, he kept his arms around her and nuzzled the nape of her neck. It was his tenderness she craved as much as the sexual intimacy, but this time his gaze slid away, as though to conceal his thoughts.

He sat up. 'There's something I have to tell you.'

She felt the air squeeze from her lungs. He was going to tell her he was married, or that he didn't want her any more.

'The AK fighters are pulling out of the Old Town.'

He told Elżunia that one of the military commanders of the Old Town district had come to see him at the hospital that morning. German attacks had intensified, and the AK fighters had lost about seven thousand men and couldn't continue defending the area. The remaining units were to be evacuated to the central district along with some civilians, and that included patients from the hospital.

Elżunia found it difficult to listen as Andrzej described the situation. 'That's insane,' she burst out, recalling her recent expedition to the warehouse. 'They'll never make it. They'll be shot on the way.'

'They're not going above ground,' Andrzej said. 'They're going through the sewers.' He was squeezing her hand so hard that she winced. 'Elżunia, we have to evacuate the hospital.'

She stared at him. 'Evacuate the hospital? How?'

He told her what the major had said.

'Listen, Zawadzki, I'm not going to mince words,' he had barked. 'There's going to be one hell of a bloodbath here once the fighters pull out. Pick out all the patients who can walk, get your staff together, and be ready to leave the day after tomorrow. No stretchers or stragglers. It's a tough journey even for able-bodied people but if anyone collapses in there they'll endanger everyone else.'

The next day, an unusual quiet hung over the hospital as word of the evacuation spread among the patients. They all knew why Dr Zawadzki was pacing up and down the cellar corridors, scrutinising each of them in turn. They knew from the doctor's haggard face and the dull look in his eyes that he was assessing them and weighing up who could make it through the sewers, but although their lives hung on his decision, no one made his task harder by pleading their case.

'Don't take it so hard, Dr Zawadzki,' one of the patients said. 'We know you'll make the right decision. God bless you for all you've done.' Andrzej nodded briefly and turned away to hide his tears.

At the end of the ward round, he flung himself onto a chair and buried his head in his hands. 'This is the hardest thing I've ever had to do,' he told Elżunia. 'They're like people on death row hoping for a last-minute reprieve. My job is to heal people, not condemn them to death. I don't want to play God.'

Elżunia tried to console him but she was struggling with her own anguish. Stefan's harrowing account of his escape through the sewers was still vivid in her mind and the prospect of having to make that journey herself made it difficult to concentrate on anything else.

That evening, when she crept into Andrzej's room, he wasn't stretched out on the narrow bed as usual. He was standing up, fully clothed, a flashlight in his hand.

'Let's go,' he said. 'We're not staying here tonight.'

Intrigued, she followed him up the broken stairs and into the street. By night, the streets were eerily quiet with the sinister silence of a volcano about to erupt. Without speaking, they held hands as they ran into a jagged shell that had once been a building. Mounds of pulverised bricks and broken slabs of stone filled the courtyard, which had once connected the neighbouring apartment blocks.

Andrzej stopped and looked around to get his bearings. A moment later they crept through a small cave-like opening in a collapsed wall and climbed one step at a time to the top of a flight of stairs that swayed under their feet.

They were standing in an apartment with no window panes. The blast had hurled pictures from the walls and books from their shelves, and the floor was covered with chunks of plaster and smashed glass. Elżunia bent down and picked up a copy of *War and Peace* with its cover torn off.

'If Tolstoy were writing today, he'd have to call it *War and War*,' she said.

In the eerie silence of the devastated apartment and the debris of family possessions acquired over generations, she saw shattered hopes and broken lives. Suddenly a clock struck with a deep, sonorous tone that made her jump. At the far end of the apartment, behind a wall that had crumbled like a stale biscuit, stood a handsome grandfather clock in a walnut case, its brass pendulum swaying from side to side.

Andrzej's face lit up. 'That clock has been part of the family,' he said in a hushed voice. 'I remember it striking the hour and half-hour since I was a small child. Sometimes I hid inside the case. I can't believe it's still ticking. But for how much longer?'

He sounded so sombre that she looked anxiously into his face but he said no more.

'Is this why you wanted me to come, to meet your family?' she asked, moved that he wanted to make love to her in his family home, surrounded by the spirits of his ancestors. It was as though he had brought her here to obtain their blessing. As he folded her in his arms in front of the grandfather clock, she imagined that she could hear the heart of this abandoned household beating.

'I wanted us to spend our last night here,' he whispered.

He pushed away the fragments of portraits and porcelain from the Persian rug, shook it out and they lay in each other's arms. After the explosions and artillery fire during the day, the quiet of the evening lay like a balm on their anxious souls.

'Listen,' she whispered. 'Can you hear it?'

He held her more tightly and nodded.

Across the courtyard, someone was playing a Chopin nocturne. She closed her eyes. Grandeur and intimacy, nobility and grace, poetry and passion were all mingled in each exquisite phrase and, as she listened, she stroked

Andrzej's hand. 'The last time I heard that,' she murmured, 'Szpilman was playing it in a café in the Ghetto.'

The music stopped but its magic hung in the air. Without speaking, Andrzej bent down and kissed her. Gently at first, then more passionately. Instead of the comforting and affectionate sensations she usually felt, this time his kiss sparked an unexpected rollercoaster ride that started slowly but became wilder and more intense. She heard herself moaning in a voice she'd never heard before, as her body arched and rocked with a primal rhythm of its own until it ended in a shuddering rush of joy. For the first time, she hadn't imagined that it was the airman making love to her.

'I thought my head was going to blow off,' she said.

'You should always keep your head.'

'I suppose I should, now that I've lost my heart.'

She recalled later that he didn't smile at her quip.

'I wonder where we'll be this time tomorrow,' she mused.

'You'll be safely out of the sewers, in the Centre,' he said.

'So will you.'

He shook his head. 'Elżunia, I'm not going.'

She thought she must have misheard but a drum was already pounding a warning beat inside her chest. 'What do you mean, not going? Are you leaving later?'

'I'm not leaving.'

Her eyes widened in alarm. 'You can't mean that! It's crazy! You can't stay here after the fighters pull out!' She was shouting and he took hold of her hands.

'I can't leave knowing that the patients I've left behind will be at the mercy of the SS.'

She tried to control her rising panic. 'Andrzej, that doesn't make sense. You can't save them by staying. You'll just get killed as well. What's the point? You can't stay here! It's not heroic, it's suicidal!' She didn't realise she was shaking him.

He stroked her hair. 'I'm not trying to be a hero. No one knows what will happen here, but I can't abandon my patients.'

'What about me?' She was shouting and sobbing at the same time. 'You're abandoning me! How come your noble conscience lets you do that?'

'Elżunia, believe me, I want to live. I want to be with you. But sometimes our worth as a human being is distilled into a single choice. I couldn't live with myself if I abandoned the patients. Please try to understand.'

'Then I'm staying too! I won't go without you! '

He placed his hands on her shoulders and looked into her eyes. 'Elżunia, listen to me. That's out of the question. You must go.'

She shrugged. 'I'm tired of trying to survive.'

'You must,' he insisted. 'Being alive is a unique gift; that's the real blessing — not the rituals and myths concocted by priests. You can't throw it away. The patients you'll be accompanying tomorrow are counting on you.'

She turned away from him. There was nothing more to say and she had no emotions left. Everything inside her had been scooped out and only a hollow shell remained. She should have known that there was nothing to hold on to, that there was no one she loved who wouldn't die or leave her. She couldn't even cry.

Fifty

Stefan rushed into the hospital early next morning, looking for his sister. Her face was expressionless and she moved like an automaton as she washed and dressed the patients who would be leaving that evening.

'Are you ill?' he asked

She shook her head, not trusting herself to speak, not even to ask why he'd come.

'Krasinski Square's under fire and some of us will be escorting you to the manhole at ten tonight. Our unit's going down there as well and they've asked me to be their guide for the evacuation because I know the sewer system.'

He seemed proud of being entrusted with this mission, but all she could do was nod.

All day, time had stood still and every hour had lasted a lifetime, but suddenly it was time to leave. During her fitful sleep the previous night, she had dreamed that Andrzej was telling her he'd be leaving with her after all, and she'd almost burst out of her skin with joy. But when she woke and realised it had been a dream, she felt such paralysing despair that she could barely find the strength to get up.

437

Throughout the day, the wild hope evoked by her dream tantalised her. Dreams were sometimes prophetic. Perhaps he really had changed his mind; perhaps she could still persuade him to leave. But there was so much to organise and prepare that they hadn't spent a moment together, and time was running out.

Shaking all over, Elżunia swung her knapsack onto her back and led her group towards the stairs. She felt as though each part of her body was disconnected from the rest, and was being pulled in different directions. Andrzej was standing near the entrance, his tram-driver's cap perched on the back of his head as usual as he chatted with the patients to lighten their spirits and defuse the anxiety.

'Make sure you don't run too fast along those sewers or the fighters won't be able to catch up with you,' he told a lad hobbling around on an injured leg.

At last the moment she had dreaded arrived. She clenched her fists and looked straight ahead to avoid breaking down, but when she looked into Andrzej's face, her strength melted away.

'Andrzej,' she cried and fell into his arms. 'Oh, Andrzej. Please, please, come with me. Please. I can't live without you.'

He held her tightly for a moment, pressed his cheek against hers and looked deep into her eyes.

'Remember the grandfather clock,' he said in a hoarse voice. 'You have to keep ticking. For both of us.'

There was so much she wanted to tell him, but she couldn't gather her thoughts and the words wouldn't come. The patients behind her were becoming restless and the moment passed. Blinded by tears, she stumbled up the stairs and out of the hospital.

The manhole in Kraśinski Square was so close to the German positions that the group was under constant attack as grenades exploded and machine guns stuttered around them. Although it was evening, and a new moon as thin as a fingernail paring hung in the sky, the blaze from surrounding buildings brightened the square like daylight.

As they waited behind a wall for the signal to run to the manhole, Elżunia looked around for her last glimpse of the Old Town. There was nothing to remind her of Sunday afternoons spent in the old part of Warsaw, of the *doroszka* rides with her parents along the quaint cobbled streets, their visits to the royal palace, or afternoon teas at outdoor cafés where she drank iced coffee piled with whipped cream and ate sugary doughnuts filled with rose marmalade. Even the Sigismund Column, that proud symbol of the old city, now lay in fragments on the ground. Smoke and dust rose from the rubble of the ancient buildings. Here and there a forlorn red-and-white flag hung in shreds from a splintered window frame.

Over in the ruined courthouse on Bonifraterska Street, the Germans were setting up machine-gun posts and she couldn't bear to think of the fate awaiting Andrzej and those who had stayed behind. Domes and towers had been ripped off churches and cathedrals, and, instead of pavements and roads, there were piles of rubble and deep craters. Six hundred years of Warsaw's history lay in ruins. Like her life.

The manhole was well concealed by sacks of sand and paving stones but every few minutes shadowy figures broke away from the waiting column, dashed across the open space and disappeared among the sandbags.

Stefan had emphasised the need for total silence inside the sewers. The Germans were patrolling the streets overhead and if they heard anything they'd hurl grenades and poison gas into the sewers.

Finally it was Stefan and Elżunia's turn. Bent over, they bolted across to the manhole. She looked down and froze. She was looking into a deep, black, bottomless well.

'Lower yourself down by the metal hooks,' Stefan whispered.

Her legs trembled so much that her feet could hardly find the slippery metal hooks that were so far apart that she had to stretch to reach them, terrified each time that she'd slip and plunge to the bottom. Finally there were no more hooks and she was standing in mud that gleamed in the sickly greenish light.

She was in a low vaulted tunnel with black mould on the walls and an overpowering stench that made her gag. It was the fetid odour of rotten-egg gas mixed with the rank smell of excrement, rotting plants and slime. The sewer was so low that she had to bend her head as she crept along. She longed to straighten up and thought her neck would snap off. Occasionally the current of muck flowed faster, and she had to grit her teeth and cling to those slimy, stinking walls so she wouldn't fall.

Behind her, someone was moaning and she looked back in alarm. The lad with the injured leg had fallen over and was being dragged along by his companions. Overhead, she heard the grind of metal and the crunch of loose stones, and felt the vibration as a tank rolled overhead. Germans. Elżunia's heart pounded as she noticed the open manhole above her head. Stefan held up his arm for them to stop moving. Even a splash could betray their presence.

Ahead of her, sewage had banked up over the wire entanglements that the Germans had erected during the Ghetto Uprising to stop the Jews from escaping. Somehow they'd have to crawl over the obstruction. Every cell in her body screamed to keep moving, to get out of this hellhole as fast as possible and get into the fresh air, but she knew that many of the patients would need help to get through, and she forced herself to swallow her terror and wait for them to catch up.

Past the entanglements, something ran across her feet and scurried away. A moment later her feet sank into something soft and she covered her mouth to muffle a scream. She was standing on a body, on several bodies. These people had tried to get through the sewers but had drowned. A little further on, the passage was barely a metre high and they had to crawl on their hands and knees, or double over, gasping. A new terror gripped Elżunia. If it rained, and the water level rose, they'd drown in a river of filthy sludge. The nuns at her school had spent a great deal of time warning them against sin and describing the torments of hell. If I survive this, I'll be able to tell them what hell is really like, she thought.

Stefan was pointing to something small and dark dangling above their heads on a string. A grenade. Even brushing against it would be sufficient to cause an explosion. Hardly daring to breathe, they crept under it, one by one.

'I'm going to see what's happening further back,' Stefan whispered. 'Some of the people are having trouble. I'll go and help.'

Seeing the alarm on Elżunia's face, he added, 'Don't worry. It's quite straightforward from here on. Just follow the main sewer until you come to the third manhole. When you see the sign that says *Ulica Warecka*, go up. Our people will be waiting. See you there.'

Before Elżunia could say a word, he was clinging to the edge of the sewer wall as he made his way towards the back of the column of terrified people inching step by step behind her.

Elżunia's heart pounded with every tentative step. What if she missed the manhole? The current was stronger here and carried not only excrement but bits of stone and large gravel that tore the skin off her legs. It was impossible to dodge them, and each time they struck her she bit her lip so hard that she tasted blood in her mouth.

Stefan had said to keep to the main sewer but suddenly it divided, and she wasn't sure which branch to take. There was a commotion behind her and she smelled gas. People were screaming, surging forward, panicking. 'We can't breathe!' they were shouting. 'We've got to get out or we'll suffocate!' They were pushing and trampling over each other in their panic and confusion. It was impossible to calm them down. The Germans must have thrown poison gas through the last manhole after she'd gone past. Someone was laughing hysterically and behind her she heard someone say in a clear, resonant voice, 'I'll just sit down here a moment and have a glass of tea.'

She was weak and dizzy but something drove her on. Like the insistent ticking of a clock, a voice in her head kept repeating, 'Don't stop, keep going. Don't stop, keep going.' The street sign below the next manhole looked blurred and she couldn't read the street name, but she had to get out of the poisoned sewer. With the last of her strength, she hauled herself up the metal rungs and tried to push the manhole cover. It was too heavy. She wasn't strong enough.

Was she dreaming or had all this happened before? All she wanted to do was sleep. She could feel herself slipping away when she felt a draught of cool air and saw a chink of light. Someone was raising the manhole cover. She wanted to laugh with relief. Our people are waiting for us, she thought, just as Stefan had said.

Someone was lifting her out. She blinked in the sudden dazzle of morning light and looked down at a pair of shiny black boots. She sank onto the ground but the hands pulled her to her feet.

'Over there, you Polish bandits. Go and join your friends!'

On the other side of the street, against a wall, stood a group of fighters who had entered the sewers ahead of her.

'*Hande hoch!*' the SS officer yelled.

So this is where the clock stops ticking, she thought, amazed at her calmness. She might as well have stayed with Andrzej. At least they could have died together. As they stood with their arms raised, a car pulled up and an SS man got out. She watched him stride towards them with a disdainful expression on his thin lips and wondered whether Wolfman would recognise her in this state.

'So, *Fraülein*, we meet again,' he said. The wound on his forehead had healed, leaving a crescent-shaped scar.

She looked straight at him, unafraid, and waited.

He turned to his colleague and shouted, 'Don't waste my time with this filthy rabble. We're fighting insurgents, not troglodytes.'

He waved a dismissive hand in their direction. 'Let them go!'

He met Elżunia's gaze and clicked his heels. 'It is almost finished,' he said, but whether he meant the Uprising, the war or the city, she didn't know.

He walked back to the car and drove away without looking back. Elżunia stood on the road, dazed. She knew she would never be able to untangle the twisted events that had brought her to this moment in her life.

Fifty-One

At her new hospital in Warsaw's central district, Elżunia kept her distance from the staff. Her reserve was a safety net that held the fragments of her mind from disintegrating. Never again would she allow herself to become close to anyone. Attachments ended in disappointment and grief.

Ever since starting work in this hospital a week after she had escaped through the sewers, Elżunia had been desperate to find out what had happened to those left behind in the Old Town, but all her inquiries proved fruitless. Communication with other parts of Warsaw had been cut and she might as well have tried to contact a foreign country. She knew that Stefan had got away after their flight through the sewers, but no one knew the fate of the hospital, its patients or their doctor, and the most common response was the one she dreaded. In the bloodbath that had followed the pullout of the AK fighters, thousands of civilians had been slaughtered. She couldn't bear to contemplate Andrzej's fate, and her longing for him was like the relentless ache of phantom limbs that so many of her patients suffered.

'I know it's not there any more but it still hurts like hell,' said Witek, whose right leg had been amputated. He was fourteen and, like most of the young fighters, he couldn't wait to get back to his unit.

He looked pensive one morning when she came to change the dressing. 'I was wondering what they did with my leg,' he said. 'It's because of what I saw at a field hospital in a forest outside Warsaw when we were near the front. They kept bringing more and more bodies on stretchers and tipping them out onto the ground, and we had to hose them down to see if anyone was still alive. If they were, we'd take them to the doctor inside the tent. All he had was a tree saw — they're not very good for amputating because the teeth are too far apart.' He paused to make sure she understood the implication, then went on. 'Next morning, when I looked outside the tent, there was this pile of arms and legs just lying there. I wouldn't want my leg to end up like that. This might sound silly, Miss Elżunia, but, if I die, I'd like my leg to be buried with me.'

She nodded. 'I'd feel exactly the same way.'

The following day, one of the nurses handed her a crumpled note. 'From your bashful admirer,' she said.

Elżunia unfolded the paper and read:

ODE TO NURSE ELŻUNIA
On the corner of Szuch and Unia,
Lived a nursie called Elżunia.
She's so gentle, she's so smart,
Nurse Elżunia won my heart.

Witek's poem continued in a similar vein for eight more stanzas. Touched by his verses, Elżunia was still smiling when she stepped outside. Although it was September, the heat was oppressive and the air in the basement was stale and clammy. But compared to the Old Town, life in the centre of the city seemed almost normal. In between mortar and artillery attacks, people ventured from their underground shelters and it seemed to Elżunia that, despite the hunger and chaos, they hadn't altogether lost hope. Like her, some of the occupants of the shelters nearby had also emerged into the street. While they commiserated with each other about their problems, the children ran around searching for spent shells, whooping when they found them.

As usual, at the sight of children playing, Elżunia's throat constricted and her thoughts turned to Gittel.

She was leaning against the wall feeling the warm sunshine on her face when she felt the road vibrate and heard a rumbling sound. A moment later, a tank lumbered into their street. An old man puffing a hand-rolled cigarette pointed at it. 'It's one of those panzers,' he said. 'We've got nothing to touch them. Our bullets just bounce off them like dried peas; they don't even make a dent. Lord knows how we've managed to hold out for five weeks.'

The tank rolled towards a jumble of overturned tram carriages, sandbags, chunks of masonry and broken tables, crushing everything like a boot grinding an ant. Now there was nothing between the people in the street and the tank advancing towards them. Just then, a boy rushed out from a doorway, leapt up and pushed something into the tank-driver's visor. There was a flash as the petrol bomb exploded. The old man whistled through his tobacco-stained teeth as the tank veered to the side, lurched off the road and became wedged in a crater. The more desperately the driver tried to reverse and free himself, the deeper the tank became embedded.

Another lad suddenly appeared in front of the tank and shouted, '*Alles aussteigen!* Everybody out!'

Elżunia and the bystanders watched and waited. Surely German soldiers wouldn't take any notice of an unarmed Polish boy. But slowly the tank's upper cover was raised and its occupants clambered out, arms raised above their heads.

To the approving murmurs of the onlookers, the boys jumped onto the tank and disarmed the Germans. As they swaggered off with their haul of revolvers, carbines and a crate of anti-tank mines, Elżunia saw their faces clearly for the first time.

'Toughie! Giraffe!' she shouted.

Giraffe was at her side in two bounds and threw his arms around her, but Toughie held back. 'We're insurgents now,' he said gruffly.

In an awestruck voice Giraffe added, as though unable to believe it himself, 'Guess what! We just captured a German tank!'

The boys came to see Elżunia at the hospital an hour later, after they had handed over their haul to their superior. She couldn't get over her delight at seeing them again. It was like finding long-lost relatives.

'What's happened to Granny?' she asked, bracing herself for bad news. 'Is she all right?'

She breathed out when Giraffe nodded. 'She's a tough old bird,' he said. 'Her building was shelled but she was down in the cellar at the time. I think she swallowed some soot and went deaf for a while but she's all right now. We drop some food in for her from time to time. She's living in one of the downstairs rooms but she'll have to move soon because the building is bound to collapse.'

Elżunia had tears of relief in her eyes. 'Thank God she's safe,' she kept saying.

'What about Zbyszek?' she asked. 'Any news of him?'

The look on their faces gave her the answer. Zbyszek had vanished without a trace.

It only took a few days for the relative calm of the central district to be shattered. Having pulverised the Old Town, the Germans turned their attention to the city centre. Ever since running into Toughie and Giraffe, Elżunia couldn't wait to see Granny, and, despite the increasing ferocity of the shelling, she set off as soon as she was able to get away from the hospital. Most of the journey was through a passage of cellars that connected apartment buildings and stretched beneath several streets. On the corner of each cellar, arrows and signs indicated the streets above, and she felt she'd entered a surreal subterranean world. Inside the shelters, people sat huddled with listless faces, while others quarrelled with their neighbours for taking up too much space, or allowing their children to run riot.

'See what we're reduced to?' a woman called out to her. 'What did we need this wretched Uprising for? We're the ones that are copping it. Those that brought it on our heads should come and see what they've done to us.'

Elżunia couldn't get out of the labyrinth of underground passages fast enough. But once above ground, she craved the safety of the cellars as bullets whistled overhead and bursts of artillery exploded nearby. Every few metres she had to find shelter in a doorway, under a clump of shrubbery or behind a pile of rubble. A journey that should have taken twenty minutes had already lasted three hours and she still hadn't reached Granny's street.

She ran into another doorway, and leaned against it, panting. It was crazy to risk her life like this. As soon as the shelling stopped, she'd go back to the hospital. As she stood there, trying to catch her breath, she heard something that made her scalp shrink and tighten around her skull. Somewhere nearby, children were singing a familiar tune but she didn't recognise the words. Then it hit her. The song was 'Almonds and Raisins' but the children seemed to be making up garbled Polish words to fit the tune. Intrigued, she crept forward in the direction of the sound, and found herself in a large courtyard. At the far end of the yard stood two small children. They sang at the top of their voices, occasionally missing out words but keeping the melody going, as they swung their arms in time to the rhythm. The little boy in broken clogs and a piece of fur wrapped around his skinny shoulders was holding the small girl's hand. Before she realised it, Elżunia was racing across the courtyard.

'Gittel!' she said hoarsely, as she cradled the child's head against her shoulder. 'Gittel! I've found you!'

The little girl wriggled from her embrace and hid behind her companion.

'Gittel, don't you recognise me? It's Elżunia!'

The little girl peered from behind Zbyszek and pushed her tousled curls from her face. 'Elżunia,' she repeated uncertainly. Her huge dark eyes rested on Elżunia's red-and-white armband.

'What's that?' she asked, and, without waiting for a reply, she added, 'Where's Mama Lusia?'

Zbyszek hadn't let go of Gittel's hand and clutched it as he stepped forward.

'Me and Gittel sing together,' he said.

Some of the people from the surrounding cellars stood in their doorways, watching.

'That's right,' a woman called out. 'Those two go round the courtyards together every day, singing. That funny little kid with the fur, he seems to take care of the little girl.'

Emboldened by the woman's words, Zbyszek raised his voice. 'I don't want you to take her away,' he said defiantly.

He was already pulling Gittel away when Elżunia knelt down and put her arms around them both. 'I wouldn't take her away from you,' she said. 'I'd like both of you to come and stay with me. You'll have a safe place to sleep and something to eat every day. Will you come?'

Zbyszek hesitated and Elżunia saw that he was weighing up her offer. After a pause, he nodded. 'All right,' he said. 'But we want to stay together.'

The cold, hollow feeling that she'd had in the pit of her stomach for the past few weeks was gone and she couldn't stop hugging them, but when she tried to pick Gittel up, the child scrambled from her arms like a scalded kitten.

'I'm not a baby,' she said, pouting. 'I'm a big girl now.' Then she put her thin arms around Elżunia's neck and said, 'You can give me a kiss if you like.'

As they walked towards the hospital, Elżunia suddenly asked, 'That song you were singing. Did you forget the words?'

Zbyszek gave her a withering look. 'We couldn't sing in Yiddish out here, so we made up Polish words.'

She looked at the children with admiration. Life had made them wise, far beyond their years.

The firing grew louder as they approached Marszałkowska Street. Elżunia edged slowly towards the main street and flattened herself against a wall, keeping the children behind her. A tank stopped in the middle of the road and two German soldiers climbed out. The afternoon sun glinted off their helmets as they pointed their rifles at a group of terrified women on the pavement and motioned for them to climb up onto the front of the tank. One of the women, who was wrenched from her small son, grabbed hold of his hand and scrawled something on it.

'That's your name; never ever wash it off,' Elżunia heard her say as the tank rumbled off with its human shields, leaving the bewildered child crying on the roadway for his mother. Elżunia let out a sigh of relief as an elderly woman stepped from a doorway and picked up the boy. She drew Gittel and Zbyszek closer and walked on. Whatever happened, she was never going to let them out of her sight again.

Fifty-Two

Adam leaned across the bar counter at the Savoy and clinked glasses with Feliks. 'Let's drink to the success of the Uprising,' he said.

Feliks downed the vodka and motioned to the barman to refill their glasses. 'I don't think it can last much longer,' he said. 'Even if Rokossovsky's army makes a move now, it'll be a Pyrrhic victory at best.'

He had just returned from another clandestine visit to Warsaw, and the words of a friend in the AK were still ringing in his ears. When he'd asked how the Uprising was going, his friend had replied with one chilling word: *Thermopylae*.

Feliks told Adam that the German commander had recently issued an ultimatum to the Commander-in-Chief. Either the insurgents capitulated at once and laid down their arms, or he'd raze the entire city, together with its inhabitants. 'Bór-Komorowski didn't even bother replying,' he said. 'He knew what would happen to the insurgents if they accepted those terms. Besides, he was counting on the Russians to start their offensive any minute.' He stared into the bottom of his glass. 'Unfortunately, that's where he miscalculated.'

'I wonder if Stalin is hanging off because of the strong German counter-offensive,' Adam mused.

'Or because he'd rather wait for the Germans to destroy Warsaw and the AK so that he can take over a ruined city with no rebels, and start with an empty slate,' Feliks retorted.

After discussing Stalin's possible motives for withholding aid, they agreed not to talk about the Uprising any more.

There was a long pause, then Feliks spoke. 'How's that girlfriend of yours — the nurse?'

'Judith is a very unusual woman,' Adam said.

Something in his tone made Feliks wag a finger at him. 'Do I smell romance in the air?' he asked playfully. 'Don't tell me you've finally succumbed? She must be something special. What's she like?'

Adam suppressed a smile. 'She'll be here soon; you can see for yourself.'

After they had ordered another round of drinks, Feliks sat forward and from the gleam in his eyes, Adam sensed that he was about to tell one of his stories.

'I came across a bizarre situation in Warsaw last week that seemed straight out of a Kafka novel,' he said.

Adam gave a short laugh. 'So much for keeping off the subject! All right, go on.'

Feliks lit an American filtertip, sat back, and launched into his story, embellishing it with sweeping hand gestures.

'One day, my old pal Rybacki asked me to go with him and retrieve a wad of dollars he'd hidden for the AK High Command after one of the Allied air drops. A lot of places where they'd hidden cash had been burnt down or blown up, so they were pretty desperate. You've seen Warsaw from the air, but I can assure you, on the ground it's a hundred times worse. Anyway, the whole idea was so preposterous that I agreed straight away. We'd almost reached the house where he'd stashed the money when the Germans suddenly opened fire and all hell broke loose. We nearly bought it. We kept lying down and getting up again like ninepins.

'When we finally staggered into the house, there were these four old codgers around the kitchen table, so intent on playing cards that they hardly looked up. Before I knew it, Rybacki had plonked himself down on a stool to kibbitz as though he had nothing better to do.'

Feliks was shaking with laughter. 'You wouldn't believe it. That house was right on the frontline but those guys played bridge there every afternoon. "Why should we worry?" one of them said. "If the Germans bombed us, they'd hit their own men."

'While Rybacki was kibbitzing in the kitchen, I decided to check things out. And sure enough, the floor in the front room was covered in gravel and at the window stood one of our fighters holding a rifle, but when I peered over the sandbags, I could see that those old geezers were right. There was no one on the German side of the street at all!

'Back in the kitchen, I reminded Rybacki that we hadn't risked our lives going there so he could watch a card game. So he went into the next room, measured out three paces from the door, counted five tiles to the left, raised one with a bit of wire, and took out three bulging leather pouches. We were almost at the door when the host called out to Rybacki, "Why don't you drop in one afternoon for a few rubbers?"'

Adam and Feliks were still laughing when Judith arrived. Feliks rose as Adam introduced them, and taking Judith's hand, put it to his lips.

'Delighted to meet you, Miss McAllister.'

Judith looked questioningly at Adam. It was their first rendezvous since the night at the hotel and she had looked forward to an intimate tête-à-tête. Adam might have told her that his friend would be joining them.

As though reading her mind, Feliks said, 'I hope that you don't mind the intrusion. I told Adam — '

But Adam waved away his apologies with a dismissive hand. 'I wanted Judith to meet you so she'd know I had at least one friend in the world.'

As they were ushered to their table, Judith wondered whether it wasn't the other way round and Feliks had been invited to give his seal of approval. Conscious of being appraised, she felt gauche and resentful, and felt that whatever she said sounded lame and forced.

Stop being childish and pull yourself together, she told herself. A woman in charge of five hundred patients should be able to cope with one unexpected person at the table.

'I think the best profession is one that is always needed.' Feliks was making wide sweeping arcs with his large hand as he spoke. 'You made a good choice, Miss McAllister. Nurses are always in demand.'

'So are undertakers.' The retort was out before she had time to think. There was a surprised pause, then Feliks burst out laughing.

'Adam told me you always say what you think.'

She wondered what else Adam had told him.

'You people are so formal, even among friends, with your hand-kissing rituals and the way you address people in the third person,' she said, and immediately regretted sounding so critical. 'Why don't you just call me Judith?'

Feliks nodded. 'You are right. We belong to the old world, and you, Miss Judith, belong to the new.'

'Judith knows more about the situation in Poland than just about anyone else in London,' Adam cut in. 'Probably more than Mr Churchill.'

454

Her momentary glow of pleasure at the compliment was replaced by irritation. Was it her interest in Poland that Adam found attractive? Surely when men discussed the women they were involved with, it wasn't their political acumen that they boasted about.

She caught Adam looking at her but turned away. She wasn't going to exchange glances that implied intimacy in front of a stranger. That was the trouble with Adam, she suddenly thought; he was so elusive and taciturn that she never knew what he was thinking.

Feliks looked from her to Adam, and, as neither of them spoke, he turned to Judith. 'Many hospitals in Warsaw have been bombed, and we've lost many doctors and nurses,' he said. 'When this is over, we will need people like you to help us organise our health system.'

Judith nodded. This was a topic she could discuss with confidence and she found Feliks an attentive listener. But whenever she glanced at Adam, he was looking at them with such a dour expression that she wondered whether the conversation bored him.

Over dinner, Feliks entertained them with anecdotes about politicians and generals, and several times she burst into such hearty laughter that people nearby turned and smiled.

'Your friend is great company,' Judith said after Feliks had gone. 'Never a dull moment with him around.'

Adam was staring into his glass. 'So you like him?' he said without any enthusiasm. 'When you came in, you didn't look happy, but he cheered you up in no time.'

As he took out the cigarette case he always carried, she wondered why she was wasting her time with this uncommunicative man whose moods she could never read and who was obviously attached to someone he'd left behind in Poland.

'If you didn't want me to like your friend, why did you ask him to join us? Make your mind up what you want.'

Adam leaned across the table and seized her hand. 'I know what I want.'

She surveyed him for moment and a smile broke over her face. 'I'm no good at these games,' she said, 'but you wouldn't be jealous, would you?'

Not taking his eyes from her face, he said, 'Shall we go?'

Her palm was burning and it wasn't just from the pressure of his hand. For once, she knew what he was thinking.

Fifty-Three

On the first Sunday in October, when rain leaked from a sky the colour of wet cement, the front-page item in the AK's *Information Bulletin* made Elżunia's heart race. Warsaw had capitulated. The Commander-in-Chief's desperate pleas for Britain to send weapons and ammunition had gone unheeded, and the leaders had come to the conclusion that further fighting was futile. As part of the terms of the surrender, Warsaw was to be evacuated.

As soon as news of the capitulation spread, the atmosphere changed and a spirit of enterprise energised the city.

'You wouldn't believe it but some fellows have already set up a street market on Krucza Street,' one of the nurses announced breathlessly. 'They're selling electric lamps and exchanging dollars. You can even buy filtertip Junaki if you've got twenty or thirty zloty to spare!'

'What does capulation mean?' Gittel asked Elżunia. They had both come outside for a breath of fresh air.

An elderly woman who had emerged from a nearby shelter said tartly, 'Capitulation is the humiliation we get in return for the torment we've put up with over the past two months.'

Gittel tugged Elżunia's arm. 'But what does capulation mean?' she repeated.

'It means the fighting's going to end, silly,' Zbyszek cut in. 'Everyone knows that.'

'It means that the Uprising's over,' Elżunia said. She stroked Gittel's brown curls. The child had already lived through two uprisings, and the war still wasn't over.

She felt flat. The news of the ceasefire and imminent capitulation that heralded the end of this two-month-long struggle seemed an anti-climax. It was good to be alive but how could they rejoice when most of the city lay in ruins after an insurrection that had achieved nothing? It had been a display of courage, patriotism and defiance that had cost about two hundred thousand Polish lives, and the Germans were still masters of Warsaw. She thought of Andrzej and a tonne of sadness crushed her chest. If there was anything to celebrate, she had missed it.

No longer listless and resigned, the people who emerged from the shelters had become animated, as though touched by a wizard's wand. Elżunia listened to their conversations, but was in too much turmoil to take part.

As she stood there, staring into space later that afternoon, Stefan rushed over, full of news.

'I've just been to Polytechnic Square to watch the formal ceasefire,' he said, and described the ceremony. A group of German officers with a white flag had entered from one side of the square and were met by AK officers coming from the opposite direction, holding a white cloth on a stick.

'Anyway it's all agreed now,' he said. 'The AK fighters are going to be treated as prisoners of war. Our captain has already divided up the food and cash that was left. Not that there was much left to share.'

Hardly pausing for breath, he launched into a discussion about firearms. 'We have to surrender our weapons but some of the guys said they'd rather bury their Stens than hand them in. One of the fighters in our unit shot himself through the head. He said he'd joined up to win or die, not to become a German prisoner.'

He trailed off and looked more closely at his sister, realising that she hadn't taken in a word he'd said.

'What will you do?' he asked. 'The Germans said everyone has to get out of Warsaw but the women who helped the AK can choose to be prisoners of war with the insurgents or be evacuated, together with the civilians.' He looked down at Gittel, who was clinging to Elżunia's skirt. 'You'd be better off to go with the civilians.'

'I suppose so,' she said in a dull voice. 'But that means taking off the AK armband. After all we've been through, it feels like betrayal.'

'You have to think of the children,' he admonished her in his older-brother tone. 'Anyway, why not make things easier for yourself?'

She shrugged. 'How easy will it be wandering around the countryside with two children? Where will I go? How will I support the three of us?'

She was close to tears and he put his arm awkwardly around her. 'If you've survived here with all this going on, you'll survive anywhere.' To distract her, he listed what he was taking on the march into captivity: a blanket, a coat and a spoon. Plunging his hand into the pocket of his trousers, he pulled out a small wad of notes and pressed it into her hand.

She didn't want to take it but he insisted. He kissed Gittel's cheek, patted Zbyszek on the head, gave Elżunia a tentative hug and sprinted away.

Out in the street, an anxious mood had replaced the earlier euphoria, as everyone discussed their options. Should they leave with the insurgents and be treated as prisoners of war, or leave with the civilians and hope to survive in the countryside without any means of support or a place to sleep? Women with old parents or small children wondered how they'd manage on the road. As long as the AK units remained in the city, people were reluctant to leave, but the alternative was to be left without any protection after they'd gone.

Witek hobbled outside on his crutches and stood quietly beside Elżunia. 'You know what I'm dreading the most? Worse than going into captivity even? It's how the civilians are going to react when they see us leaving. They're so mad at us for bringing all this on their heads — what if they throw things and curse us?'

Back at the hospital, the patients had begun preparing for the evacuation. One of the patients, an architect recovering from pneumonia, was sitting on his camp bed, sketching.

'I'm drawing up plans to reconstruct Warsaw when the war's over,' he explained when he saw Elżunia looking at his notepad with its neat sketch of apartment blocks and parks in a part of the city she'd come to know only too well.

'But that's where the Ghetto used to be,' she said.

He nodded. 'It was pretty run-down before the war, and now it's just a heap of ruins, but we'll transform it into a brand-new suburb with modern shops and buildings that will be the envy of all Poland.'

In a voice hoarse with suppressed emotion she said, 'Do you realise you'll be building over the ashes and remains of half-a-million people? That's like desecrating a cemetery by tearing out tombstones to make room for apartment blocks. You should be designing a memorial instead of obliterating all trace of them.'

'This whole city is a pile of ruins and ashes,' he said. 'We can't let the past stand in the way of the future.'

'But it's all about the past,' she retorted. 'Everything we do is governed by the past. We carry it inside us. Covering it up with bricks doesn't turn it into the future. It just cements in the anger and the pain.'

She was still shaking with anger when she reached her room, where Gittel and Zbyszek were playing with their paper cutouts. She pulled out her haversack and tried to figure out what to pack. They'd be on foot and she might have to carry the children from time to time. If only Andrzej could be waiting at the end of the journey. She blinked away the tears and straightened her back. She had to be strong.

The following morning, she watched as the insurgents marched through the city towards the surrender point. While the Germans watched with impassive faces, thousands of fighters walked four abreast, heads held high, their red-and-white armbands on their sleeves and the white eagle emblems pinned to their shirts.

The commanding officer at the head of the long procession turned and issued an order, and the insurgents stood smartly to attention. Clearing his throat several times, he thanked them for their courage and sacrifice. In response, the fighters started singing the Polish national anthem, and bystanders took up the chant with so much emotion that chills ran down Elżunia's spine. *'Poland hasn't perished yet and it won't perish as long as we live,'* they sang as they were about to pass into German captivity.

As the column proceeded slowly along the road, Elżunia was moved by the extreme youth of the fighters. The street was lined with civilians watching the exodus, and glancing around at the emaciated bodies and gaunt faces in the crowd, she remembered Witek's anxiety. Suddenly, a woman pushed forward towards the column and Elżunia held her

461

breath waiting for the stream of abuse, but the woman pressed an enamel cup into a young fighter's surprised hands. Her action was a signal to others who started bringing out little gifts that the fighters might need during their internment: handkerchiefs, spoons, bowls, socks and combs. Someone pressed a dog-eared exercise book into a girl's hand and called out, 'Make sure you write to your mama!'

A woman with a big peasant headscarf tied under her chin climbed onto some broken masonry and, making the sign of the cross in the air above their heads, shouted in a voice trembling with emotion, 'They're taking our children away!'

Those around her repeated her words and stretched out their arms to bless the long column of young people passing before them. The lump in Elżunia's throat was so huge she couldn't swallow. As the fighters acknowledged the bystanders with waves and brave smiles, they looked like proud soldiers, not a defeated army.

As the long column slowed and came to a halt, Elżunia felt someone staring at her. She turned and caught her breath. It was her father. Her first instinct was to run, melt into the crowd and disappear, but she froze, and a moment later he was standing beside her.

'Elżunia!' he cried in a strangled voice. 'Elżunia! I can't believe it! You're alive after all! This is incredible! It's you, isn't it?'

He broke into harsh sobs and held her so tightly she couldn't breathe. He was less solid than she remembered and no longer smelled of the expensive pomade he'd once rubbed through his hair. His hair had thinned, his jacket hung loosely on him, his moustache looked bigger than ever on his thin face, and the lines on his forehead had deepened. His embrace, though, was as enveloping as ever and in its warmth she felt her anger and resentment dissolving. She had her father back.

But a moment later the pain returned. 'You deserted us,' she said bitterly, pulling away. 'You just left us to rot inside the Ghetto while you ran around with your girlfriend.'

He gripped her shoulders with both hands. 'What are you talking about? I was told you and your mother and Stefan were dead.'

'That must have been convenient.'

'Elżunia, listen to me. They kept me in Szuch Avenue for five months because of my Underground work. The minute I escaped, I went home but the three of you had gone. I nearly went out of my mind trying to find you. I asked everyone I knew. No one had any idea where you were but I never stopped trying to find you.'

Elżunia felt dizzy. She longed to believe him but there were too many questions buzzing around in her head.

He saw the doubt in her eyes and intensified his grip. 'You have to believe me. By the time I was told you were all in the Ghetto, it was closed.' His voice was unsteady. 'Then one of the AK operatives who had a contact inside the Gestapo told me he'd got hold of a list of people who had been killed in there and you three were on it.' His voice was dull with pain. 'How could you possibly think I'd abandoned you?'

Elżunia blinked back tears, and, seeing her distress, Gittel tugged her arm.

'Can we go now? I want to go back,' she whimpered.

'Can't we stay and watch the soldiers?' Zbyszek chimed in.

But Elżunia didn't hear either of them. 'What else could we think when we didn't hear from you?' she retorted. 'And then that business with Marta. I never told Mama you had a girlfriend. I didn't think she'd be able to cope with it. It was better to let her think you were still in prison. Or dead.'

His face was drawn and white. 'Marta was my liaison girl.' He looked around. 'Where is your mother? Let me explain to her.'

But he didn't need a reply. He could tell what had happened by the tears streaming down Elżunia's face.

'Where's Stefan?'

'He escaped from the Ghetto and joined one of the AK units. He's probably somewhere in this column.'

Her father was holding her against him and she didn't have the strength to pull away.

'My little Elżunia. I can't believe I've found you. It's like the Resurrection. Thank God you and Stefan survived. What you must have been through.' He looked down at her lovingly. 'You were a little girl when I was taken away, and now you're a woman.'

Elżunia sighed. It wasn't just her appearance that had changed. So much had happened since they'd seen each other and so many doubts filled her head that she feared the gap between them could never be bridged.

The column started moving again.

'We don't have much time,' he said. 'Listen. My sister Amalia has moved to Saska Kępa in Praga, across the river. Go to her. We'll get together after the war is over. It can't last much longer. God bless you my darling,' he said. Giving her one last hug, he marched off with the insurgents, and kept looking back until she disappeared from view.

'Who was that man?' Gittel asked.

'My father.'

'I didn't know you had a father.'

'Neither did I,' Elżunia said. She could feel her heart skipping with joy.

Gittel looked at her quizzically. 'Was he lost?'

'That's silly. Grown-ups don't get lost,' Zbyszek said.
'Sometimes they do,' Elżunia replied.

That evening she listened as the announcer at the AK
station, Radio Błyskawica, recited his elegy for Warsaw.

We are relaying a message from Warsaw.
An extraordinary message from Warsaw.
The AK station would like to report that the fight is over.
There's nothing left but honour.
So we're bringing the news to every nation.
To colleagues, friends and brothers:
The people of the capital have paid for freedom
With their lives.
A hundred thousand insurgents lie dead in the rubble of Warsaw.
Free. Free from shackles and from life.

We end our transmission.
The AK station has broadcast its final program.
Błyskawica. Warsaw. Victory.
Trumpets. Fanfares.
Curses.

The following afternoon, in the fading rays of the setting sun,
Elżunia joined the river of people trudging into the unknown.
Laden with knapsacks, bundles and parcels, and carrying babies
and small children, they stumbled over piles of rubble and
tripped over craters in the road. The more fortunate among
them pushed barrows laden with bundles tied together, or
prams overflowing with small children.

Many people supported old parents who hobbled on the
broken pavements, or held children in their tired arms.
They moved in silence, preoccupied with their own thoughts
and focused on getting across the next stretch of potholed

road or mound of rubble, afraid of losing one another. The procession, slow and sad, took up the entire width of the road and wound as far as Elżunia could see. Warsaw was disgorging the last of its inhabitants. She took Gittel and Zbyszek by the hand, took one last look at the ruined city, and wondered where this journey would end.

Part III

Fifty-Four

Elżunia sat on the hard wooden bunk, her arms around the shivering children. The chill rose in an icy mist from the cement floor and settled on their clothes. Through the grimy window, the grey sky hung low, and the air had the sharp smell of snow about to fall.

'My tummy hurts. I'm hungry,' Zbyszek wailed.

'Me too,' Gittel whimpered.

Elżunia looked at them and her heart ached. In the month since they'd been deported to Germany, they'd become skin and bone and there were dark circles around their eyes. She tried to rub some warmth into their arms but every movement of her blistered, raw hands made her wince.

Every day, as she scraped the rust off bits of broken machinery and breathed in the pungent smell of the synthetic oil that the factory produced, she was forced to listen to the insulting comments of the German foreman who gloated over the fate of his Polish workers and reminded them several times a day how lucky they were to be living in a civilised country among cultured people.

'Your friends, the British, bombed our factories, so now you have to repair the damage,' he had said, delighted at the divine retribution that had presented him with this workforce of slaves.

Weak from hunger, Elżunia tried to ignore the pain in her hands, the exhaustion, and the misery of her existence, while Gittel and Zbyszek sat on the floor at her feet all day, careful not to draw attention to themselves.

When the local *Arbeitsamt* office had assigned her to this factory, they ordered her to place the children in a crèche, but the idea of leaving them in a Nazi institution for foreign children was unthinkable. Elżunia had begged them to let the children to stay with her, insisting that they wouldn't create any disturbance or interfere with her work.

But although they had reluctantly agreed to let the children stay with her on probation, they refused to give them any food. The children didn't contribute to the German war effort so they didn't warrant being fed, the foreman explained, his piggy eyes sinking deeper into the folds of his plump face.

Every morning, Elżunia cut her slice of black bread into three pieces, and every evening, as she shared her cabbage and turnip soup, she wondered how long the three of them could survive on this diet. But no matter what happened, she was determined they'd stay together. As she scrubbed machine parts with blackened fingers, she reproached herself for the thousandth time. If only she hadn't been so impatient, they would now be in a camp for evacuees instead of being worked to death in a German factory.

The long column of refugees leaving Warsaw that sad October day had proceeded at such a slow pace as it made its way over rubble and bomb craters that it scarcely moved. The journey ahead had seemed endless. Even before they'd left the city centre, the children had complained they were tired, and Elżunia could only carry them a few steps at a time.

Looking around for another route to bypass the throng, she had turned into a side street that seemed deserted. She was congratulating herself for being so enterprising when her path was blocked by two SS men, who forced her at gunpoint on to a cattle truck bound for Germany with a group of other frightened Polish women.

Elżunia could still hear the hollow clang of the carriage being bolted from the outside, and could still feel the jolt as the train moved off. A plump girl called Agnieszka was sobbing. 'We'll end up in one of those death camps and I'll never see my mother again.'

Gittel pulled Elżunia's sleeve. 'Why's that lady crying?'

Elżunia felt like crying herself but gritted her teeth.

The train had lurched on for several hours but there was no way of knowing where they were because the tiny window covered by a metal grille was too high up. Banging on the sides and shouting for water, food and toilet stops had been futile. No bucket had been provided in the carriage, so they'd been forced to use one corner as a toilet. Elżunia had shared the last of her bread and water, but the children were thirsty again. 'We'll be getting off soon and then you can have a drink,' she kept telling them.

'It's all because of the Jews,' one of the women was saying. 'They've always caused Poland's problems.' Some of the others chimed in with stories to illustrate Jewish vices. Elżunia was on the point of making a cutting remark but stopped herself in time. Revealing that she was Jewish would endanger not only herself but the children as well. She had known she'd have to conceal her identity from the Germans, but knowing that she couldn't trust her companions made her feel bitter and alone.

Finally the train lurched to a halt. As the guards unhasped the doors, Elżunia could see a group of officials and SS men standing on the platform, surveying them with distaste.

'*Mein Gott*, what animals!' a stout, uniformed woman exclaimed, screwing up her face as she peered into the carriage. She pulled her jacket more tightly around her as though to shrink into it. 'Look how filthy they are! It's disgusting.'

The man beside her shrugged. 'What can one expect from Slav *Untermenschen?*'

Agnieszka nudged Elżunia. 'I'd like to see how clean they'd be if they were locked up for days with nowhere to shit,' she whispered.

A wind as sharp as a butcher's knife blew across the platform, and, while they shivered, the *Arbeitsamt* official, wrapped in his greatcoat, began to pontificate about their good fortune.

'You are fortunate to have been brought here to work for the Vaterland,' he announced. 'If you work hard, you will be well treated. But if you steal, sabotage or try to escape, you will be severely punished.'

The lorries that sped them towards their destination passed neat fields and farmhouses as immaculate as illustrations in picture books. Not a speck of paint was missing, not a paling hung crookedly from a fence, not a leaf littered a front path. Despite her anxiety, Elżunia was intrigued by this relentless perfection.

She was still lost in thought about her arrival in Germany, while her fingers kept moving to avoid the foreman's threats to report her to the *Arbeitsamt*, when Gittel's high voice piped up from under the workbench.

'I need to do wee-wee.'

Elżunia bit her lip. She always made sure the children went to the toilet before she started work.

'I need to go — badly.' Gittel squeezed her legs together to emphasise the point.

Agnieszka gave Elżunia a sympathetic glance but the others kept their eyes on their work. No one wanted to antagonise the foreman.

'I'm sorry but I have to take her to the toilet,' Elżunia told the foreman.

He placed his beefy hands on his hips. 'I told you this is not a kindergarten!' he thundered. 'You are not permitted to leave the factory and take time off work — '

'It will only take a minute,' she pleaded.

'This is essential work. We can't have disruptions.' He waved a threatening finger at her. 'Tomorrow they will go to the kindergarten to learn German discipline.'

In desperation, Elżunia grabbed his arm. 'I'll stay back this evening and work longer to make up the time. Just don't send them away.'

He studied her for a moment. 'When you finish here this evening, go and clean the kitchen,' he snapped. 'But if this happens again, they go.'

The chef was a gruff German whose bulging stomach nudged his apron. From his lumpy red nose and face veined with broken capillaries, Elżunia guessed that he was fond of the drink and probably had a volatile temperament. Pointing to a wobbling pile of dishes stacked so high that she could hardly see over the top of them, he told her to wash and dry them, then scour the saucepans, wipe down the tables and scrub the floor.

Exhausted after working in the factory for twelve hours, she didn't think she'd have the strength to get it all done, but driven by the threat of Gittel and Zbyszek being sent away, she didn't stop until she'd finished everything. Then she sank into a chair and fell asleep.

Someone was shaking her arm and she opened her eyes to see the chef holding out a mug of strong coffee. She breathed it in and felt light-headed. It was real coffee, not the chicory substitute the workers received.

'For a Pole, you're not a bad worker,' the chef was saying. 'The kitchen maid was taken to hospital today. You can take her place. Be here at five-thirty sharp to make breakfast.'

Elżunia's tiredness evaporated and she felt like pirouetting around the kitchen. No matter how hard she'd have to work for the chef, it would be better than slaving in the factory, and there was always the possibility of obtaining scraps of food for the children.

The chef was a hard taskmaster. He insisted on everything being done to immaculate, gleaming perfection. Whenever he wasn't satisfied, he roared so loudly that she jumped, and he often abused her for being a dirty, lazy Pole who didn't know what work was. By the end of the first day, her hands and feet were so numb that she wished she was back in the factory and she suspected that the previous kitchen maid had collapsed from nervous exhaustion.

But she discovered that when she did exactly what he wanted, he left her alone. And as long as the children sat quietly in the corner and kept out of his way, he didn't object to them. After spending the day on her feet in the kitchen, she'd stagger back to the dormitory and fall onto her bunk, exhausted. One night, at the end of the first week in the kitchen, she sensed a strained atmosphere in the hut. Some of the women stopped talking when she came in, while others continued whispering as they glanced in her direction.

'Here's our privileged princess,' said the woman with the sharp face.

'Meaning what?' Elżunia asked, but with a sarcastic laugh the woman turned away.

Long after the whispers ceased, Elżunia tossed on her hard bunk, unable to sleep. A figure moved quietly towards her in the dark and she sat up, careful not to disturb the sleeping children.

It was Agnieszka. 'She said she's going to tell the chef you're Jewish,' she whispered. 'I told her it was a load of crap, and some of the others said we were all in the same boat so we shouldn't rat on each other, but she's had it in for you ever since you got that job in the kitchen. She said the kids looked Jewish and it would be easy to tell if the boy was.'

Elżunia couldn't close her eyes. She lay awake listening to the night. It was quiet, but this wasn't the quietness of repose. It was the stillness of the antelope twitching in the undergrowth under the lion's gaze. By the time the grudging winter light appeared in the sky, she knew what she had to do.

Fifty-Five

It was the kind of winter's day that Adam regarded as typically English: grey and non-committal. Heavy and dull without rain, cold and damp without snow. Just a relentless chill that seeped into your body and made your bones ache. But inside the officers' mess, the atmosphere was lively. Everyone knew that the war was almost over, and the right side had won. Only the details remained to be ironed out.

Although after his conversations with Feliks, Adam was less sanguine about the outcome for Poland than his colleagues, he was relieved at the prospect of ending his flying career. Life for bomb crews resembled a deadly form of Russian roulette in which five out of six chambers were loaded.

Each time he climbed into the Lanc, he knew he might not return, and, each time he returned, his joy at having survived was marred by reading the names of those who hadn't, whose kits and belongings would stealthily be removed from their lockers as though they'd never existed. Only a few more missions to go and it would all be over and normal life would resume. What that life would consist of, he wasn't certain. Until recently, only one thought was uppermost in his mind: Poland. But for the past few months he'd found his thoughts increasingly returning to Judith, and he wondered whether she would agree to go to his homeland with him.

The other airmen were sprawled out in the deep leather armchairs or standing around the small bar, telling jokes and discussing what they'd do when the war ended. Tomasz couldn't wait to return to Lwów, whose beauty he extolled at every opportunity.

'You can keep your Guild Hall in Kraków and your Royal Palace in Warsaw. You haven't seen anything if you haven't seen the buildings and parks in Lwów. Our opera house is the most beautiful in Europe,' he said, then added hastily because they were shouting him down, 'next to Paris.'

Stewart was coming towards Adam with two tankards of dark liquid. 'You can't leave England without trying this stuff,' he said.

Adam took a sip, shuddered and pushed it away. 'It's like mead that's gone bad.'

Stewart laughed. 'They call it Guinness. Not my brew either, but I thought I'd give it a go.' He glanced at his watch. 'I'm going to London this afternoon to see Nancy. I'm trying to talk her into coming back with me to Australia. Best bloody country in the world, mate.'

Adam couldn't understand these Australians who regarded England as home but compared it unfavourably with their own country, a distant backwater that didn't count in the conference rooms where major world decisions were made. Whenever he asked Judith what it was she loved so much about Australia, she would look at him helplessly and launch into a list that included skylarking on the beach, greeting strangers in the street, giving people a fair go, and not being snobbish. According to her, the garbage man in Australia thought he was as good a bloke as the prime minister. 'You just feel good there,' she would conclude with a shrug, frustrated by his bemused expression.

In the background, the voice of the BBC announcer, who always sounded to Adam as though he were juggling marbles in his throat, was droning on. Suddenly, the word 'Poland' leapt out of the bulky wooden wireless and they stopped talking and turned up the volume.

At a conference in Yalta, a place none of them had ever heard of, the fate of their nation had been decided by the leaders of Great Britain, the United States and the Soviet Union. The eastern part of Poland, including Lwów, had been ceded to Russia, while the rest of the country was to be governed by a provisional government installed by the Soviet Union until elections could be held.

The silence was broken by a harsh sob. It was Tomasz. 'Looks like I won't be going home after all,' he said in an unsteady voice.

Adam clenched his fists so tightly that it looked as though his knuckles would burst through the skin. Unable to sit still, he paced around the mess. From what Feliks had said, he had known that the Allies would cave in to Stalin to some extent, but he hadn't expected such a devastating betrayal. The fifth partition of Poland had just been completed but this time the country had been dismembered not by her enemies but by her allies.

He gave a bitter laugh. No satirist could have invented such a scenario. To appease Stalin, Churchill and Roosevelt had made him an offering of the nation on behalf of which they had declared war in 1939. They had conquered one dictator only to strengthen another.

'Those Judases have sold us out,' Romek fumed, throwing his head back to toss down a whiskey. 'Instead of three pieces of silver, they got a pat on the back from Comrade Stalin. Fucking hypocrites.'

'What fools we were,' Olek said. 'We joined the RAF thinking that if we helped Britain win the war, we'd be helping Poland get its independence. Now our country's fucked and so are we.'

Some of the other men were shouting while others sat in glum silence, trying to absorb the news and the likely effect it would have on their lives.

Stewart was shaking his head in disbelief. 'To think of the three of them — sitting there like bloody emperors, deciding the fate of Poland!'

Adam looked grim. 'Not just Poland. They've sealed the fate of Europe for decades to come.'

In the midst of the furore, the intercom crackled and they listed to the announcement. All leave had been cancelled and they were summoned to an operational briefing.

'Damned if I'm going to fly any more missions and risk my neck for the bastards who betrayed us,' Romek shouted.

'Me neither,' Tomasz said. 'They can go to hell, where they belong. Churchill and Eden were telling us how they'd never abandon us, but in the end they sucked up to Stalin and sold us out.'

Adam rose heavily to his feet. There was a tortured look on his face but his voice was expressionless. 'No matter how we feel, we have to see this through to the end. If we don't behave with honour, they'll say Poles are cowards and deserters.'

In a mutinous mood, cursing under their breath, they filed slowly into the operations room for the briefing. The operations officer tapped on the map of Germany with his pointer.

'Your target tonight will be Dresden.'

There was a sharp intake of breath. This city was often described as the Florence of the north, but they were told that those baroque churches and palaces concealed state-of-the-art factories producing radar and listening devices, which had to be obliterated.

'Dresden is a major centre of communications for Germany's defence,' the officer explained. 'The German army is still capable of reinforcing its eastern front with up to forty-two divisions from other fronts. We have to destroy their communications to hinder the movement of half-a-million German troops from the west, so that we can help the advance of the Red Army.'

Ignoring the muttering, the officer continued. 'It's not generally known that Dresden is an industrial centre of military importance. There are over a hundred factories and industrial plants on its outskirts that build radar and electronic parts, fuses for anti-aircraft shells, gas masks, engines for their Junkers, and cockpit parts for the Messerschmitts. Our aim is to hit the Jerries where it hurts and, by Jove, we'll show the Russians what Bomber Command is capable of!'

As his plane lifted off three hours after the first wave of Lancasters had flown away, Adam thought about the other major cities they had bombed. Cologne, Berlin and Hamburg had also had their cultural and ecclesiastical showpieces and civilian populations. As always, he felt calmer as soon as he was airborne. The comforting drone of the engines had stilled the jangling of his nerves, which on this occasion had been more insistent than usual.

During these bombing raids, he always kept his mind focused on the impersonal concept of 'the target', but this time his mind kept straying to the statistics.

They'd been told that, within two minutes, 529 Lancs would drop 1800 tonnes of incendiary bombs onto a city crowded with refugees fleeing from the east, a city with few anti-aircraft defences.

He knew what these incendiary bombs would do. The roaring rush of overheated air would create a tornado of flames that sucked people in and reduced them to cinders. In London, Judith spent her days healing maimed and burnt patients, while he was on a mission that would maim and burn others. The more he tried to stifle that thought, the more powerfully it gripped his mind. In their desperate struggle to win the war, were they losing the moral values for which they'd been fighting?

He knew that each member of the crew had his own demons and none of them were as nonchalant as they appeared. Negative feelings were best kept to oneself. But one question kept running through his mind.

'Do you ever think about what we're actually doing?' he asked Stewart.

His navigator looked surprised. 'Too right I do,' he said. 'We're giving them a dose of their own medicine. We're repaying them for starting all this, for the Blitz, for Coventry, for Warsaw, and for their death camps. If we let up now, they could still win this fucking war. Just think what sort of world we'd be living in then.'

Adam fell silent.

It was a textbook flight. The cloud that had obscured the city the day before had lifted, and there was less flak than on previous raids. The Pathfinders had flown ahead, marking the target with flares to guide the flotilla of bombers.

Suddenly Adam called out, 'Look at that!' Twenty thousand feet below, they could see Dresden lit up by the red glow of fires. The rear gunner whistled through his teeth. 'What a target!'

The bomb-run began and they felt that familiar rush of adrenalin as the navigator called 'Steady, steady, left, left' while they ran the gauntlet of the flak and searchlights. The bomb doors opened and the Lanc lurched each time a bomb was released and hurtled through the waiting air.

No one spoke as the plane turned and headed for home above a solid sheet of fire that resembled Vulcan's workshop. As the plane rose, it flew through banks of clouds whose unearthly colour startled them. Even a hundred miles from Dresden, the clouds were tinted red.

Adam glanced at his fingers that protruded from the ends of his cut-off gloves, as though he expected to see blood on them. They were all staring, struggling with conflicting thoughts and emotions. Tomasz's voice was hoarse. 'Those poor buggers down there.'

At the wireless controls, Romek pushed his hair back from his forehead. 'Don't ask me to shed tears for Germans, for Christ's sake. Do you think they're crying for the millions of Poles they've murdered?'

Adam didn't speak. No one emerged from war with clean hands.

All around them, the returning Lancs looked like black darts flying through the air. There were flak shells slicing through the sky now, and below them black smoke trailed from one of their planes. The starboard wing was on fire.

A moment later, Stewart said, 'He's gone.' Adam looked down and was startled by the horrifying beauty of the plummeting plane, which resembled a huge flower bursting into flames.

Suddenly he heard a loud crumping sound. The plane was being buffeted about. Adam tried to keep it steady but his right shoulder hurt so much he couldn't move his arm. When he touched his shoulder, there was blood on his left glove. He'd been hit. He gritted his teeth to avoid making a sound and alarming the others.

A moment later they started losing height. He smelled smoke. The plane was engulfed in flames and spinning out of control.

'Hit the silk and bail out!' he shouted.

With trembling fingers, they fastened their parachutes and, one by one, jumped out. But when Adam tried to pull on his parachute, he froze. It had disintegrated in the fire. There was no time to panic, no time to think. Either he stayed in the burning plane and became incinerated, or he jumped out without a parachute. He felt for the cigarette case in his breast pocket, closed his eyes and launched himself into space, hoping for a swift death as he hurtled towards earth like a broken missile.

Fifty-Six

Light was starting to break through the charcoal sky when Elżunia hurried to the kitchen, rehearsing what she was about to say. Her stomach was grinding as she wondered how the chef would react. His moods could change so rapidly from bonhomie to hostility, and there had been times when he'd brandished one of his sharp knives and threatened to kill her, yelling that the filthy Slavs were the scum of the earth and should be exterminated. She could always tell what the day would be like by looking at his hands. If they shook, it meant he'd already started on the schnapps and would soon be stumbling around the kitchen, bellowing. But somehow he always managed to finish cooking before collapsing in an alcoholic stupor. The following morning, he had no recollection of his drunken outbursts and reverted to his gruff manner, which, as Elżunia had discovered, concealed a good heart. While grumbling about useless Polish kitchen maids, he often slipped her and the children some of the leftovers. For the first time since they arrived, they weren't starving, and the dark hollows disappeared from their faces.

As soon as she saw him, she glanced nervously at his hands and was relieved to see that they were steady as he bustled at the stove preparing eggs, *Weisswurst* and *Späetzle* potatoes for the staff. After breakfast, she scrubbed the kitchen more meticulously than ever and made sure that the frying pans sparkled and the floor shone before saying, 'Herr Schnabel, can I speak to you for a moment?'

He waved an impatient hand. 'Go on, get on with it; we have to start preparing lunch.'

She swallowed. 'I thought you should know that one of the women in my hut intends to come and see you to tell you something about me,' she began.

His neck seemed to swell and his face turned a forbidding shade of red. 'What the hell are you gabbling about? What woman? What business has she got with me?'

'She's going to tell you that I'm Jewish.' Hearing herself say the word, her legs almost gave way. She watched him anxiously. Would he denounce her? Her decision to forestall the Polish woman's accusation was a dangerous gamble and could go either way.

He stared hard at her. 'Why are you bothering me with this rubbish?'

'Well, because if she tells you, then you'll wonder ... you might think that ... and then ...' she stammered.

'I'm not interested in women's idiotic gossip. And, as for you,' he poked a warning finger at her, 'stop wasting my time and get on with your work. Peel those potatoes and don't stop till they're done. Rumours indeed,' he muttered as he waddled off to the pantry.

As she reached for the potatoes, it struck her that he hadn't even asked whether it was true.

A few days later, when she arrived in the kitchen at five-thirty as usual, ready to light the stove, she was dismayed to see him lurching around and hiccuping.

'Herr Schnabel,' she said, 'the people from the *Arbeitsamt* office are coming for lunch today. What would you like me to prepare?' She wanted to jog his memory without arousing his fury.

He reached for the bottle, took a long swig and swore loudly. '*Scheisse!* A bunch of nobodies throwing their weight around, that's all they are.'

She looked around to make sure no one heard him. With her help, he managed to get breakfast ready for the staff but as soon as it was over he staggered to a chair, flung himself into it and drained the rest of the bottle.

She was alarmed. He was making dangerous comments and in this state he wouldn't even be capable of preparing the soup, let alone the three-course meal the officials would expect. The factory manager would be furious and the chef would get the sack. And if he was fired, what would happen to her?

The chef was already snoring, his mouth wide open, his legs sprawled out. She couldn't risk the manager or one of the foremen coming into the kitchen and finding him in this condition.

With Gittel and Zbyszek's help, she dragged the chair with him in it into the storeroom adjoining the kitchen and closed the door. If someone came in, she could say he'd stepped into the storeroom. On the back of the door he'd pinned the menu for that day's lunch: pea-and-ham soup, wiener schnitzel, fried potatoes, sauerkraut and *Apfelstrudl*. She knew how to make schnitzel and fried potatoes, and the sauerkraut came from a huge barrel in the cellar, but *Apfelstrudl* was another matter.

The richness and profusion of the food in the larder made her dizzy with longing, the hams glistening with fat, the pork neck tinged delicately pink, the smooth, brown-shelled eggs lined up in rows. The pantry smelled of vanilla, apples and lemon rind but she forced herself to focus on her task. If she failed, the chef wouldn't be the only one in trouble.

Boiling potatoes and crumbing the veal was no problem but when she tried to roll out and stretch the *strudl* dough, just as she'd seen the chef doing, it kept tearing and breaking, and in frustration she tossed it into the rubbish bin. Time was marching on and her hands shook so much that she could hardly hold a spoon. Lunch was always served on the dot of one. What if she wasn't ready on time? Searching desperately in the pantry, she found some *Eierküchen* in a metal tin. If she crumbled these sponge cakes, beat up some eggs and stirred plum jam through the mixture, perhaps she could pass it off as *Kaiserschmarren*.

Delighted at having the freedom to move around the kitchen, Gittel and Zbyszek ran around, eager to help. The preparations were progressing well when Elżunia suddenly stopped and swore aloud. She'd forgotten about the soup. While the children ran to and from the pantry, bringing peas and carrots, she threw the vegetables into the huge vat with the ham hocks and surveyed the bubbling broth with satisfaction. She'd made enough for the factory workers as well. For once they would eat a nourishing soup.

Just before one, she peered into the storeroom. The chef was still asleep but he was stirring. If he woke up and found the door closed, he might start shouting.

Leaving the door ajar, she put on her white cap and apron, poured the soup into the porcelain tureen and carried it into the staff dining-room as usual, praying that her culinary efforts wouldn't arouse suspicion.

She was arranging the schnitzels on the Rosenthal platter while Gittel was decorating the edges with sprigs of dill when a booming voice almost made her drop the plate.

'What the bloody hell is going on?' he roared.

Her heart was banging against her ribs. 'You weren't well, so I thought I'd better let you rest,' she said, motioning for the children to return to their usual place in the recess beside the stove.

He stared at the schnitzels and examined the fried potatoes.

'Where's the soup?' he shouted.

'They're having it now.'

'And what's this supposed to be?'

'*Kaiserschmarren*.'

He snorted with derision. With a sheepish look in her direction, he threw the empty schnapps bottle into the rubbish bin. 'Go on, don't hang around,' he said gruffly. 'Clear the soup plates and serve the main course.'

'Your chef has excelled himself today,' she heard one of the officials telling the manager as she cleared the table after the dessert. 'If you ever get tired of his cooking, send him to me.'

While she was cleaning the kitchen and putting away the dishes, she caught the chef watching her speculatively.

'When the war is over, I suppose you'll go home and tell everyone how terrible we Germans were.'

Elżunia didn't answer. She waited for him to say it was the fault of the Versailles Treaty, or the Allies, or war in general, but he took several slow puffs of his cigarette and shrugged. 'We all believed the ravings of a lunatic.'

Elżunia was silent. People were willing to believe any lie, as long as it confirmed their prejudices and blamed others for their troubles.

From snippets of conversations she overheard at the table, it seemed the Germans realised that the end wasn't far off, and they knew they had lost. If only she could cling to this safe little corner until the end came.

'You're a clever little thing for a Pole,' the chef grunted. 'I'm going to promote you to assistant chef, and we'll get another girl in to do the washing up. But your *Kaiserschmarren* stinks.'

Fifty-Seven

Adam's eyelids fluttered open and quickly closed, speared by the light. A few moments later he opened his eyes again, more carefully this time. He heard himself groan. As a schoolboy, he had been fascinated by an illustration in his physics textbook in which two horses strained in opposite directions in a futile effort to pull apart massive metal domes that had formed a vacuum. As he floated in and out of consciousness, it seemed to him that in some incomprehensible way he had become a vacuum and his body was being pulled apart.

Something was restraining him, preventing him from turning his head, but by swivelling his eyes sideways he could see a window criss-crossed by leadlights, its diamond-shaped panes glistening with a tracery of ice.

So he was still alive. He must have been captured by the Germans, yet this room didn't look like a prisoner-of-war camp. Perhaps it was a fortress like Colditz, where they'd imprisoned the AK leaders after the Uprising, although he couldn't imagine they had been accommodated in individual rooms. He tried to raise his head but his neck was restricted by a brace, while his right leg was attached to a pulley.

He closed his eyes. When he opened them again, someone was standing by the bed, holding a glass of water.

'Ah, you are awake at last. Take this.'

The woman holding out two large white tablets had wiry grey hair cut very short, and a brisk manner to match. Her apron had a bib over her chest, and her laced-up black shoes made no sound as she walked towards the window.

'Where am I?' he asked.

'Schaffenburg Castle.' She walked over to the window and ran a cloth over the misted panes.

'I'd like to see the person in charge,' he said.

'You're seeing her now.' The woman's mouth twitched in amusement. 'I'm Baroness Maria von Schaffenburg. The castle has been in my family for generations. But you will rest now, *ja*?' She walked out of the room, leaving him tormented by a hundred unanswered questions.

His mind became a whirlpool that threatened to suck him in as he tried to remember what had happened. There was the crumping sound of the flak and the sudden searing pain in his shoulder. But where were the others? Had there really been flames inside the fuselage or had he dreamed it? He'd ordered them to bail out. He must have bailed out too. But he didn't have a parachute. Then he remembered his stomach crashing into his throat, suffocating him, as he'd catapulted from the plane, turning helpless somersaults and screaming as the earth rushed towards him. How come he'd survived? It wasn't possible. He closed his eyes and slept. In his dream, Judith was standing beside him, holding his hand.

Bathed in perspiration despite the cold, he woke, mumbling and confused. Which was reality and which was fantasy? His tongue stuck to his mouth. He was at the mercy of a stranger who could have a sinister motive for keeping him there.

What a fool he had been to swallow the tablets. When he looked down, he saw he was wearing pyjamas instead of his air-force uniform. Had they taken away his clothes so he couldn't escape? And where was his cigarette case?

He didn't hear the baroness enter.

'You are looking a little better now,' she said, holding a glass of water to his lips. 'You didn't look so good after you fell out of the sky.'

She had seen the enemy plane turn into a ball of fire, plummet down, and crash somewhere to the east of the castle. Several days later, while walking around her estate with her dogs, she heard them barking and whining under a giant spruce.

'You were stuck upside down in that tree, wedged in the top branches, almost frozen stiff. The caretaker had to use a ladder to get you down.'

'Why did you bring me here?' he asked incredulously.

'You were injured,' she said. 'You needed a doctor.'

He rephrased the question. 'How come you didn't send for the Gestapo?'

'Ah. That's another story.' She rose. 'Rest now. The doctor will come soon.' And she disappeared once more.

Dr Hermann checked Adam's pulse, listened to his heartbeat, and told him to cough while he tapped his back.

Then he looked up. 'The human body is as resilient as the mind is weak,' he said.

His pink scalp showed through the thin strands of greying hair, and the bony face was covered in brown splotches but the bright eyes behind the shiny glasses showed no sign of age.

'With your fractures and internal injuries, I wouldn't have given you much of a chance,' the doctor said. 'Someone has been watching over you.'

Adam thought about the missing cigarette case and wondered whether his luck would now run out.

'So when —' he began and stopped. There was no point hurrying to get away. He was probably safer there than outside. British airmen wouldn't be very popular in Germany.

The doctor answered his unspoken question. 'Be patient. In two weeks we'll remove the dressings, then we'll see about your collarbone and leg, and work out a regime of exercise to strengthen your muscles.'

As they were leaving the room, Adam heard the baroness urging the doctor to slip out through the back door, and realised the risk they were taking, looking after an enemy airman.

The light was fading when Maria von Schaffenburg returned with some clear broth in a Dresden porcelain bowl. She pulled up a straight-backed wooden chair beside the bed, and, while he ate, she answered his questions in a quiet, unemotional voice.

She was a widow when the war broke out, and was proud that her sons were fighting for the Fatherland. Ernst had joined the Luftwaffe while Friedrich had become an officer in the Wehrmacht. While they were away, the local authorities started rounding up the local Jews and taking them away. One night, Dr Hermann came to see her, white-faced. His wife was Jewish. Would the baroness hide her and their daughter? The following night, the Jewish estate manager brought his wife and two small children. By the end of the week, she was hiding eight Jews in the cellar.

'I love my country and believed that the Führer was building a better Germany,' she said, fingering the gold cross around her neck. 'I thought Dachau was a place for criminals, but when Jewish people I knew were rounded up, beaten and deported, I knew something was wrong.

So when they came to me for help, I couldn't turn them away. I prayed for guidance and God gave me the strength to do it.'

Whether it was the surly housemaid who was envious of her employer's wealth, or the self-righteous cook trying to ingratiate herself with the local Gestapo chief, she never found out. But late one night she was woken by someone banging on the heavy oak door. Two Gestapo officers pushed past her with the flat unseeing stare of dead fish, and started searching the house. Soon she heard screams and scuffles as they dragged the fugitives outside at gunpoint. When she pleaded with them to leave the children at least, they warned her to watch out or she'd be arrested for harbouring Jews.

'I didn't know we were waging war on our own women and children,' she retorted.

They grabbed her, drove her to the station and kept her in a damp cell for a week, threatening to send her to Dachau to teach her a lesson. They only released her because of her position in the village, and the fact that her sons were fighting for the Reich. But every few days Gestapo agents turned up — ostensibly to search the castle but really to threaten her.

When Friedrich came home on leave from the Eastern front, he was shocked to hear that his mother had been terrorised. From his strained white face, she sensed he was brooding over something, until one evening he told her what he had witnessed in some Ukrainian villages.

'I enlisted to be a soldier to defend the Fatherland, not to supervise death squads that shot women and children,' he told her. She still shuddered at the recollection of the massacres in the forests he had described.

The following morning he had visited the Gestapo chief to complain about the way his mother had been treated, and filed a report to the authorities about the carnage he'd witnessed on the Eastern front.

She paused and stared past Adam as she fiddled with her cross. A few days after Friedrich's return, there was a military parade in town, which he had attended. Late that afternoon, there was a knock on her door.

'*Gnädige Frau*,' the uniformed policeman said, clicking his heels. 'There has been an accident. Unfortunately your son was run over. We took him to the hospital but it was too late.'

Something seemed to be stuck in her throat. She stopped speaking and stared at her hands.

'But you don't think it was an accident,' Adam said.

She shook her head. 'The Gestapo killed him. He was making a nuisance of himself, with his complaints and stories of what was going on in the east.'

After a long silence, Adam asked, 'What about your other son?'

'Ernst's plane crashed over Britain early in the war. I pray for him every night.'

'You're risking your life having me here.'

'A risk is better than a sin,' she said. 'I talk to God every night and listen to what he tells me. I also listen to Dr Hermann. He says there's a camp not far from here, like Dachau, where they do terrible things. I'm too old to close my eyes and pretend it has nothing to do with me. I can't allow others to mould my thoughts any more.'

She looked at him with a steadfast gaze. 'When I found you hanging upside down in that tree, I made a pact with God. If I looked after you like my own son, He would bring my son home to me.'

The light had gone, night fell, and they sat in the dark, unwilling to break the silence.

'From what I've seen, God doesn't always keep his part of the bargain,' Adam said.

She sighed. 'That's a risk I'm prepared to take. It looks as though the war will end soon, so I'll find out.'

She was about to go out of the room but turned back and took something from the pocket of her apron. 'I had to burn your uniform, but I found this inside your shirt.'

It was the cigarette case.

Fifty-Eight

As the jeep lurched and jolted over potholes and craters, past abandoned trucks, overturned tanks and burnt-out cannon, along a road jammed with lorries, carts and barrows that May morning, Judith felt as if every bone in her body was being dislocated. After a time, she gave up trying to brush off the grit or smooth down her hair. She had wanted to make a good impression but resigned herself to arriving bedraggled, dusty and windswept.

The driver turned off the main road into a region of sturdy farmhouses and neat fields. Occasionally the clouds parted to allow shafts of sunlight to slant over the countryside of Lower Saxony with its picture-book villages and baroque churches.

The light shining on the mullioned windows of an imposing mansion above the road caught Judith's eye and she pointed to the stone turrets.

'That's Schaffenburg Castle,' the driver said. 'They say the owner's a bit of a recluse.'

Birds twittered and whistled from the branches of beech, spruce and birch trees and the air had the bracing scent of pine trees. The war in this part of Germany was over and, as they drove on, Judith's thoughts turned to

Adam. It was four months since they'd seen each other. Determined not to consider the possibility that something had happened to him, she assumed he had dropped her, to use Nancy's blunt phrase. She wasn't surprised. Often when they had been out together, she had seen him eye attractive women, and marvelled that he'd been interested in her at all. But it made her angry to think that he had used her when it suited him and now he'd probably found someone else. Nancy had been right all along. What she had been naïve enough to interpret as deep affection had probably been no more than lust.

Shortly after their last meeting, she had received a brief letter from Stewart, with a German postmark. She was relieved to know that although he was in a POW camp, he was being well treated. But where was Adam? She reread the letter, searching for some clue, something hinted at or concealed, but found nothing. She supposed their plane had crashed but why hadn't Adam written? She made desperate calls to the RAF but courteous voices told her that they had no information.

Uncertainty and dread gnawed at her. The only man she had ever wanted, the only one who had ever cared about her, had disappeared without a trace. She often dreamed about him and woke in despair when she realised that the warm caress she had felt on her skin had been created by her hungry mind.

She was too restless to stay in London, and, when she read a notice that the United Nations Relief and Rehabilitation Administration (UNRRA) was looking for nurses to work in the hospital that had been set up in a death camp recently liberated by the British army, she applied at once.

She spent hours at the UNRRA office in Portman Square attending interviews and undergoing a barrage of tests, but when she hadn't heard back from them for weeks, she had come to the conclusion that her qualifications and personality must be deficient. Then, out of the blue, she received a call from the director. She had been appointed matron of the hospital.

That night she had dreamed about Adam again. She was walking through a wintry landscape, past trees pillowed with snow, when she looked up and to her astonishment saw him sitting on a branch high in a tree. When she asked what he was doing there, he gave her that crooked smile and said, 'Waiting for you.' Judith had no time for psychics, clairvoyants, theosophists or Madame Blavatsky's pseudo-mystics, but, for the first time since his disappearance, she woke feeling comforted.

The jeep passed forests that were solid and impenetrable, so different from the pale, airy Australian bushland she knew, and, as they drove along, she imagined shadowy shapes slipping among the dark trees. These were the menacing forests of the Brothers Grimm where wolves preyed on small girls and witches lay in wait for innocent children.

Don't let your imagination run away with you, she chided herself. It's just a forest.

But knowing what had taken place nearby made it difficult to shake off a sense of evil.

Past the forest, they bumped over the cobblestones of a little Saxon town whose houses had half-timbered façades and flower boxes filled with bright geraniums. These villagers must have watered their geraniums, tended their fields and prayed in their baroque churches while only three kilometres away, trainloads of men, women and children were being starved, tortured and killed.

As they approached the camp, a strange odour, sweet and putrid, hung in the air. She pulled a face. 'What on earth is that?'

The driver took a few moments to reply. He had been part of the British anti-tank regiment that had liberated the camp four weeks before, and knew that what he had seen would haunt him for the rest of his life. He looked at the woman beside him. She had no idea what she was letting herself in for.

That was also Judith's reaction when they reached the camp and she saw the burnt-out huts, the mountains of boots and shoes, and the pyramid of ashes beside the tall chimney. The visions they conjured up were all the more powerful for being imagined. She felt she should offer a prayer for those who had died here in such filth and inhumanity, but the words stuck in her throat. It made no sense to pray to a God who had looked down on these atrocities and been powerless or unwilling to prevent them. She straightened her shoulders. God was derelict in his duty but she wouldn't be. Her job was to look after the living and there were thousands of walking skeletons too weak to move or feed themselves. The sooner she got going, the better.

Fifty-Nine

Judith pushed the typewriter carriage back so vehemently that the machine almost toppled off her desk. Unrolling the sheet of paper, she reread her letter. It was more fiery than the previous ones but she'd given up being diplomatic. In the month since she had taken over as matron, she had sent dozens of tactful, pleading letters that had resulted in promises and prevarications but no action. Now she was demanding that UNRRA send the British nurses that they had promised, not 'as soon as possible' but immediately. Thankfully she no longer had to beg for soap, but she desperately needed more drugs, sterilisers, splints and bed-pans.

She threaded the paper back into the machine and added a biting postscript. She appreciated their faith in her ability to establish a hospital for three thousand desperately ill patients, but her healing powers would be vastly improved with medication, disinfectant and thermometers.

Until the British nurses arrived, she'd have to manage with the German ones. They were clean and efficient but lacked empathy with the patients, who complained that one lot of Nazis had been replaced with another.

She set aside the letter. The truck would soon arrive to collect the bodies and she had to record the names and details of patients who had died that day.

With its Poles, Czechs, Hungarians, Russians, Romanians and Slovaks, the hospital resembled the Tower of Babel. Her best interpreter was Anna Silbermann, a diminutive Polish doctor who spoke five languages. It was Anna's skills that Judith needed now to check the details she'd recorded about the dead patients. The nurse who had informed her that one of the pulmonary tuberculosis cases had died spoke very little English, and Judith's German was too basic to be reliable. She closed the ledger, switched off the lamp, locked the door behind her and went in search of her interpreter.

Dr Silbermann was leaning over an elderly man, listening to his heartbeat. When she saw Judith approaching, she shook her head. 'His wife died yesterday,' she said. 'He doesn't want to go on living.'

Judith looked at her with interest. 'Do you believe people can die of a broken heart?'

'Hearts don't break,' Anna said. 'They harden.'

Something in her tone warned Judith to drop the subject.

Back in her office, she pulled out the report and Anna pointed out some spelling errors.

'I'll never get all those sz's and cz's right,' Judith said. 'Polish must be the most consonant-heavy language in the world.'

Anna lapsed into a preoccupied silence.

'You try to keep everyone alive, Matron, but deep inside we're already dead.' Her voice sounded dull and remote. 'I died in Auschwitz two years ago. What you see is a machine that keeps pumping from habit.'

After Anna had gone, Judith sat for a long time without moving. Probably most of the people in her care had gone through experiences that could add volumes to the annals of human cruelty and suffering. She might succeed in patching up their bodies, but doubted whether their psychological scars would ever heal.

She had to get some air. On her way out, she passed one of the female wards and looked inside. Three of the patients were sitting on a bed, chatting as they bent over their sewing. Curious to see what they were doing, she walked towards them and saw that they were stitching lengths of blue material. They were Slovakian and spoke no English, so the conversation took place in mime. She pointed to the material and spread her hands in an inquiring gesture, and they laughed and indicated that they were making skirts. They didn't seem to understand that she was trying to find out where the material had come from. It wasn't until she walked away that it struck her. They were cutting up the mattress covers. Her initial reaction was anger. With all the thieving that went on in this place, what they needed was a detective, not a matron. The previous week she had been horrified to discover that thousands of sheets donated by American corporations were missing, probably stolen by the staff. As though she hadn't enough to do, she now issued requisition slips for the linen so the girls had to come to her every morning and sign for the sheets before changing the beds.

And now the patients were pilfering what was left of their dwindling store of bed linen to make clothes. Standing in the hospital forecourt, breathing in the cool night air, Judith felt her anger evaporating as she smiled to herself. These women, who only three weeks earlier had been more dead than alive, still cared enough about their appearance to raid cupboards and sew new clothes. Their entrepreneurial spirit was probably more therapeutic than any medication.

*

Light rain fell the following morning, and, seated at her desk, Judith watched the raindrops threading down the window. She was waiting for Frau Wohlberg, the housekeeper, to tell her that she needed to keep a closer watch on the German and Hungarian cleaners. They made an exaggerated show of scrubbing and polishing whenever she appeared, but lounged around smoking and gossiping the minute her back was turned.

There was a knock on the door. She looked up, expecting to see the housekeeper, but it was one of the nurses.

'There is a woman here. She wants work,' she said.

'Can't the housekeeper deal with it? I can't interview every kitchen maid myself,' Judith said.

'*Ja*, but Frau Wohlberg is talking to the cook, and the woman wants to see you only.'

Judith sighed. 'All right, send her in.'

The door opened and a young woman entered, holding two children by the hand.

Sixty

As soon as the news of Germany's surrender was announced, the foreman had opened the factory gates and told the Polish slave labourers that they were free to leave. Within a few hours, the guards and officials had slunk away like rats, terrified of capture and execution by the Russians. Elżunia was dazed. The end of the war was such a huge, long-awaited moment, but she seemed incapable of grasping its significance. The war was over, she kept repeating to herself as though repetition might create the exhilaration she wanted to feel. She was free. But free to do what?

While the other women danced around the factory floor, hugging and kissing each other, she had sat in the kitchen trying to collect her thoughts. Herr Schnabel, who was packing up his implements in preparation for departure, watched her from across the room.

'What will you do now?' he asked. 'Where will you go?'

She shook her head. The moment she had dreamed of for so long had caught her unawares.

He thrust his meaty hand into his pocket and pulled out a wad of banknotes. 'Here, take this,' he said gruffly. 'You've earned it.'

He was still looking at her. 'You could come and keep house for me. You'll be safe there, you and the children. The roads aren't safe for women any more, with those Russian bastards prowling around.'

She almost laughed. After all the atrocities the Germans had committed over the past six years, he was warning her to beware of the Russians. She thanked him for the offer but shook her head.

He sighed. 'I will prepare food for your journey,' he said, and before she had time to reply he was already slicing smoked ham and cutting wedges of cheese and packing them into a basket.

Although the war was over in this part of Germany, the situation in Poland was still unclear. She'd heard that in some areas the fighting was still continuing, while in others there were skirmishes, ambushes and sniper attacks. There were rumours that the communists were now in control, and anyone who had taken part in the Uprising was regarded with suspicion. She didn't know what to do.

'You are nurse, *ja?*' the chef was asking.

He told her that his niece Ulli was working in a hospital that the British had set up in the grounds of some camp or other in Saxony. Ulli hadn't finished her training but they were short of nurses, so they'd taken her on. 'Maybe you could get a job there,' he suggested, then added, 'At least you'll be safe from the Russians. But it won't be easy work like here, mind you. Ulli says that the matron is like a prison commandant.'

It had taken Elżunia several days to get on to a train because the carriages were jammed with desperate evacuees, displaced people and former Nazis who had hurriedly stripped off all signs of their service to the Third Reich in an attempt to pass for innocent civilians. She had trudged the last few kilometres on foot, her knapsack on her back, with the children lagging behind, complaining and squabbling.

'Where are we going? When will we get there?' Zbyszek kept asking.

'Make him wait for me,' Gittel said in a querulous tone as Zbyszek ran past her. She flopped down on the ground. 'I can't walk any more. I'm tired.'

Elżunia knelt beside them and took out the thermos from her rucksack. 'Have a drink and then we'll keep going. We're nearly there. See that building ahead of us? That's the hospital.'

Her knees shook when she was ushered into Matron's office, and she sank gratefully into a chair and looked around. On the bookshelf above Matron's desk lay a worn volume. Its title, *Notes on a Hospital*, didn't mean anything to her, but the author's name leapt out at her. It was Florence Nightingale, whose story had inspired her to become a nurse, and whose portrait hung on the wall of the nursing school in the Ghetto. She felt the matron's eyes resting gently on her and knew she had come to the right place.

'That lady has orange hair,' Gittel said.

Embarrassed, Elżunia hushed her, relieved that the matron couldn't speak Polish, although from the amused gleam in her eyes it looked as if she had sensed that the child had made a comment about her.

'You need nurse, yes?' Elżunia said. She hoped she remembered enough of her English lessons at school to make herself understood.

Judith looked at her with interest. 'You're a nurse, are you?'

'I good nurse. Long time. Polish.'

'And these children,' Judith asked, 'are they yours?'

Elżunia shook her head and held the children closer. 'Not mine but stay with me always.'

There was something about the girl's resolute manner and devotion to the children that touched Judith. And she needed nurses with experience.

After showing Elżunia to the room that she would share with five other nurses, Judith looked at the children.

'We can put two beds in here for them. During the day they can go to the kindergarten in the grounds,' she said.

Elżunia's response was sharp and swift. 'Children with me, always,' she said. 'If kindergarten, I go.'

Taken aback by the girl's ferocity, Judith decided to drop the subject for the time being. 'You must be very tired,' she said. 'Have something to eat, unpack, and then I'll show you around and explain your duties.'

'I don't know what's going to become of these people when they're well enough to leave,' Judith said with a sigh an hour later as they walked around a ward where over a hundred beds were jammed, one next to the other. 'The Jews don't want to go back to the countries where they were persecuted and the British won't let them into Palestine. The Poles refuse to live under a communist government, the Estonians, Latvians and Lithuanians are afraid of reprisals if they go back, and there's a civil war raging in Greece. The world's in a bloody mess.'

Elżunia didn't say anything. Although she understood the gist of what Matron had said, her spoken English was poor, and, in any case, she preferred to keep her thoughts to herself. Hospitals evoked bad memories. Hard work didn't frighten her but she needed all her energy to suppress the ghosts of the past. As she followed the matron around the hospital, she was impressed by what this woman had achieved in such a short time.

Without saying any more about the kindergarten, Judith took Elżunia around the hospital grounds. They ended the tour at the kindergarten that she had equipped with toys and books sent by her friends in Australia.

Gittel and Zbyszek looked around. Gittel's eyes were shining as she picked up some bright wooden blocks and held them out to Zbyszek, who was examining a red truck. 'Look at all these toys!' she shouted.

A few minutes later, they crept forward and sat on the floor beside the other children, who were gazing at a picture book the young teacher held up.

As Elżunia watched them, she realised that probably for the first time in their lives, Gittel and Zbyszek were able to play like normal children.

'Kindergarten good,' she said. 'Children stay.'

Judith was impressed with the efficiency and dedication of her new nurse but she was puzzled by her selective understanding of English. Elżunia carried out all her instructions but whenever she asked where she had studied or which hospitals she had worked in, the girl looked blank and clammed up.

Judith knew that it was essential to tread delicately. Dealing with the bruised personalities of these people was like treading across a minefield where even the lightest step could cause an explosion.

Elżunia knew that she should answer Matron's questions but although this was the first hospital she had ever worked in that wasn't under fire, she couldn't bring herself to talk about her other nursing experiences. She kept reminding herself that no bombs or rockets would fall on them here, and no SS officers would burst into her ward, but she still caught herself listening out for the thumping of boots and the bellowing of mortars.

She was on her way to see Matron early one morning when the sound of dishes crashing in the kitchen made her jump. She was still trembling when she entered the office, but saw that Matron was also in a nervous state, pacing up and down, not like her usual cheerful self.

'There's no power today,' Judith said. 'I was thinking of using wood to fire the bath heaters, but without electricity we can't pump the water. The buggers have cut the power off without any warning, so we didn't even get time to fill the tanks or tubs. I don't know how we're going to manage to wash the patients and cook the food. To say nothing of the dance this evening.'

She spoke more rapidly than usual, and Elżunia could only make out one word in ten, but she understood that it was about the blackout and the dance. She knew from Dr Silbermann that Matron had organised a dance that evening to boost the patients' spirits, but it looked as if she had picked the wrong night.

Judith was still talking. 'One of these days I'll have to write a manual about how to run a three-thousand-bed hospital without water, power or disinfectant. It's bound to be a bestseller!'

Although the power was not restored in time, Judith resolved that nothing would stand in her way. If there was no electricity, the dance would take place by candlelight.

The flickering candles cast long shadows on the walls and transformed the bare hall into a romantic ballroom. One of the patients, an old man whose hunched back and pointy ears reminded Elżunia of a gnome, rushed to the piano with surprising alacrity, and proceeded to play a Strauss waltz. As soon as he pressed one key, four others sounded simultaneously, but neither the jangling music nor the bizarre surroundings dampened the enthusiasm of the patients who had decked themselves out in whatever clothes they could lay their hands on.

The more sprightly among them grabbed a partner and shuffled around with euphoric expressions while the rest looked on, humming the tunes, tapping their feet or clapping to the music. Judith noticed that Anna Silbermann was standing on the edge of the dance floor with her back to the dancers. One of the men hobbled up to her, bowed, and said something. She shook her head and turned away but he persisted and with obvious reluctance she followed him on to the dance floor. Her movements, unenthusiastic at first, gradually loosened up, and soon she was twirling to the infectious rhythm of a Hungarian *czardas*. Watching them, Judith felt her throat close up. It wasn't just the hall that had been transformed. The music had released a flow of energy and emotion that had been bottled up for so long. From the flirtatious smiles of some of the women, and the gallant gestures of the men, it was clear that the juices of life were flowing again.

But she felt that her own juices had dried up. The relentless effort of establishing and running this hospital had taken up all her waking thoughts, and when she fell into bed each night she sank into a dreamless sleep. But as she watched the patients bouncing around the wooden floor or swaying in time to the music, she felt such a surge of longing for Adam and the warmth of his embrace that she had to close her eyes to conceal her emotion.

She saw the new Polish nurse standing quietly beside her, thin and pale as a wafer. 'What about you?' she said. 'Why don't you take a partner and kick up your heels? It would do you the world of good.'

Elżunia started. Her eyes were pools of sadness and Judith wondered whether she, too, was thinking of someone she loved.

510

Sixty-One

A murky twilight had descended over the hospital as Judith quickened her step on the way to her office. At last she'd be able to sit down and read the letter from London.

Nancy's exuberance leapt off the page. Stewart had been released from the POW camp and they were making plans for the future. 'Your brother keeps on about Australia and how much better life would be there for our children. He's jumping the gun as usual but you know how impetuous he is,' she wrote. 'Anyway he's managed to talk me round, so as soon as I finish up here we'll be off. Who knows, maybe one day we'll be neighbours as well as sisters-in-law. Wouldn't that be a hoot?'

Judith put the letter down and sighed. Apart from her work, she had nothing. She felt a pang of guilt that, instead of being happy for Nancy and her brother, she was envious and upset. She forced herself to keep reading. On the reverse side, the handwriting changed.

'Hi Sis,' Stewart had written. 'Nancy's given you all the gen so I'll just add a few words. I couldn't let you know from the POW camp that our Lanc was shot down, so we all had to bail out. Whew! Wouldn't want to do that again in a hurry. The Jerries were waiting for us of course, and we ended up in the camp, except for Adam. I don't know where he ended up but keep your chin up — the moody Pole is bound to turn up.'

He ended with a postscript. 'You should have been in Trafalgar Square the day Churchill announced the war was over. Lights were blazing, firecrackers were exploding like on New Year's Eve. Everyone was jammed into the square waving flags, singing *Rule Britannia* and *God Save the King*, and kissing and hugging — even total strangers. The only people who weren't falling over themselves with joy were the Polish airmen. They reckon Poland has lost more territory than Germany. The way they put it, they won the war but lost the peace. You know what an intense lot they are.'

Judith sighed again. She could imagine how bitter Adam would be to know that people were dancing in London and Paris while Warsaw was dark and silent.

What had become of him? The war was over, so how come he hadn't written to her or contacted Stewart? There was one alternative that her brother hadn't mentioned, one that she had resolutely ignored, but the letter made her jittery.

The walls of her small office were crowding in on her. She picked up a lantern from her desk and headed for the kitchen. A cup of tea would settle her nerves.

The power was switched off at night, and the kitchen was in darkness. As she held up the lantern, she saw that someone was already in there. A small figure was sitting at the table, her head in her hands.

Judith slipped into the chair beside Elżunia.

'Are you ill?' she asked. 'Do you need anything?'

Elżunia shook her head.

Judith boiled water on the primus stove, filled the teapot, poured two cups and slid one in front of the young nurse.

'We Aussies have great faith in the restorative power of tea,' she said. 'Try it. You'll feel better.'

Elżunia gave a wan smile. It would take more than tea to boost her spirits and she didn't like milk in her tea anyway, but Matron was being kind and she didn't want to offend her.

The steam rose from the tea cups and wisped towards the ceiling as they sipped the tea by the weak light of the lantern, filling the silence with their own thoughts.

Matron was studying her with a kind expression and Elżunia suddenly felt an urge to talk. It would be a relief to talk about the grief that was suffocating her.

'I'm speak bad English,' she said.

Judith leaned over. 'Don't let that stop you. I've become quite good at figuring out what people are trying to say. Fire away.'

She tried to speak but the softness of Matron's gaze brought tears to her eyes. She finished the milky tea and wondered where to begin.

'I can tell you've had a terrible time,' Matron murmured. 'But you've still got Gittel and Zbyszek.'

At the mention of the children, Elżunia looked up. Perhaps she'd tell her how she found them. But that would mean talking about the Ghetto. That story was too complicated and too painful. Maybe she could tell her about her nursing experience instead. But if she did, she'd have to talk about the hospitals in the Ghetto and the ones during the Uprising and that would bring her to Andrzej and that was the one subject she couldn't bear to talk about. The memory of their last night together was still so vivid in her mind that every night before she went to sleep she replayed every detail in her mind, and heard his voice murmuring endearments as he gazed at her. Whenever she closed her eyes, she could still feel his lips and his hands, and could hear him saying, 'Life is a brief gift.'

Happiness was even briefer, she thought bitterly. Every night before falling asleep, she cried for him, and every morning she kept her eyes closed as long as possible to keep his image in her mind and wished that the dream were real, and the reality was the nightmare.

But that she would never share with Matron, even if she had the words for it. While she wondered where to start, the ticking of the large wall clock punctuated the silence in the dark kitchen. It reminded her of the grandfather clock in Andrzej's empty apartment that night, and tears were running down her cheeks faster than she could wipe them away.

Judith waited, still and silent. Perhaps the comforting darkness of the kitchen would help the girl elicit memories she found so painful to confront. Focused on the Polish nurse in front of her, she had forgotten about her own grief that had propelled her into the kitchen.

Elżunia brushed a strand of hair from her forehead, blew her nose, and started to speak, haltingly at first, conscious of her inadequate English, but gathering momentum until the words flowed rapidly, regardless of grammar and limited vocabulary.

Judith was transfixed. Although she couldn't understand everything the girl said, she didn't ask her to repeat anything. She sensed that it was more important for Elżunia to tell her story without interruptions than for her to understand every single word. At times the sheer force of Elżunia's intensity communicated the meaning of her words. It was like watching a tragedy enacted in mime. As she listened, Elżunia's life seemed to embody the chaos of war. Adam had once said that the history of Warsaw had been written in the blood of past generations, and as she listened

514

to Elżunia she saw the story of the world encapsulated in the fate of a single city.

Elżunia cried as she described the doomed Ghetto Uprising and the death of her mother and her friends. She talked about the heroic airman who had saved her life just after the war began, and who reappeared miraculously when she was interned inside the Ghetto. Touched by her tragic experiences, Judith felt tears spring to her eyes.

'I never forget this man,' Elżunia concluded. 'I think about him every day.'

Judith sighed. She knew only too well how unexpectedly war threw people together and how brutally it tore them apart. She looked at Elżunia's sad face and took her hand.

'Don't give up hope,' she said. 'Life is full of surprising twists and turns. Perhaps fate will throw you both together again.'

As she walked back to her office, she wished she could believe that fate would produce a miracle for her as well.

Sixty-Two

Judith sat in her office, blowing on her hands. She could cope with the other shortages in the hospital but the lack of coal made her miserable. She was drawing up a nurses' training program for dealing with displaced people, but, as she reread the program, she wondered whether UNRRA would supply the psychologists she had recommended. Probably not. She would have to include a psychological component in her program to give nurses an insight into the problems of survivors and suggest strategies for preparing them for life outside the hospital.

Now that a small contingent of nurses had finally arrived from England, the hospital was filled with the cheery descant of English voices. It was a relief to know that she could entrust the care of the patients to well-trained women, some of whom she had taught herself. The number of acute cases had decreased and although there were still far too many cases of gastroenteritis and pulmonary tuberculosis, she had more time now to talk to the patients.

During her ward rounds, Judith sensed their restlessness as attempts to find a country that would accept them ended in one rejection after another. Affluent Western countries didn't want to admit displaced and dispossessed people who had lost everyone and everything. It was a bloody disgrace. Where was the humanity? The governments were willing to go to war but not to pick up the pieces afterwards.

As she hurried out of the hospital for her daily stroll, she passed Elżunia spooning soup into the mouth of an old woman whose hands shook so violently that she couldn't feed herself. Ever since the girl had talked about her life, Judith's admiration for her had grown. If anyone deserved to find happiness, it was Elżunia.

This was her favourite time of day, just before sunset, when she set off for her daily stroll to the woods. Twigs snapped and leaves rustled under her feet as she walked along the rough track. The day was coming to an end and only the twittering and whistling of birds as they flitted back to their nests broke the silence. The trees almost obscured the sky and the forest seemed to be alive and watching her.

As soon as Judith came to the small clearing, she felt her mind unwinding like a skein of wool loosened from a tight spindle. The bluebells had withered but new plants had sprung up. Under their leaves she found small blue-black berries that stained her fingers like ink, but tasted gritty, sharp and sweet.

She was sitting on a grassy hummock, picking berries and listening to the birds when a ray of sunlight shone so brightly into her eyes that she had to look away. She turned her head in the direction of a stand of birches some distance away. Depending on the angle of her vision, their knobbly trunks leaned towards each other or pulled away, fusing design and disorder into an artistic whole. The wonderful anarchy of life, she chuckled to herself as she headed back to the hospital.

❋

Judith was finishing her paperwork for the day when the sister in charge of Intensive Care knocked on her door. Kathleen was one of the nurses she had trained in London, a cheerful Irish girl who spoke so fast that she sometimes had trouble following her.

'One of the locals just brought a fellow in. He found him unconscious in the forest. Someone didn't like him, judging by the state he's in. He's got some broken ribs and the bruises on his body look like they were made by a boot. And his face! I've never seen such a mess in all me born days. He's still unconscious.'

Judith put down her pen. 'What did the doctor say?'

'Doctor thinks he'll pull through but it looks like some of his broken ribs have perforated the lungs, so he'll need a lot of nursing. I once had a case like that in London —'

'Do we know who he is? Any papers on him?'

Kathleen shook her head. 'No papers at all. I got the girls to go through all his pockets, the ones in his jacket and his trousers and that —'

Judith nodded impatiently. Kathleen always gave the impression of having all the time in the world to chat and drink endless cups of tea. 'So we'll have to wait until he's conscious to find out who he is,' Judith said.

Kathleen nodded. 'That's right, so it is. Because the way he looks now, not even his own ma would recognise him.'

There was no stopping the girl. Judith drummed her fingers on the desk until she rose to leave. She was at the door when, to Judith's annoyance, she turned around.

'I almost forgot,' she said. 'We did find something on him when they brought him in.'

She put her hand into her apron pocket and held out a slim silver cigarette case.

Sixty-Three

When Adam opened his eyes and saw the blurred shape near his bed, he thought he was back in Schaffenburg Castle. He wanted to thank the person leaning over him, but the words came out in a mumble and ended in a groan. His face was bandaged, and, from the difficulty he had breathing, he knew his nose was broken. There was a grinding ache in his right eye, and, when he tried to move, there was hardly a centimetre of his body that didn't hurt. His head was pounding, his vision was blurred and he could hardly open his jaw.

'There now, love, don't you try and move, I'll bring you whatever you need,' a woman was saying. She spoke English in a soft lilting accent that soothed him. As he began to focus, he saw that she wore a white apron and a little starched cap. This time he really was in a hospital. But where were the Germans?

Then it came back to him. The war was over. He'd heard the announcement on the baroness's wireless. Germany had surrendered. Six years of senseless carnage and destruction had finally come to an end.

As soon as he'd heard the news, he had sprung towards the baroness to hug her but held back in time. Exuberance was not her style.

'Thank God Dr Hermann and I have lived to see the end of this madness,' was all she said, and continued polishing the furniture.

That afternoon, Adam heard her discussing the situation with Dr Hermann in tones that sounded like weary relief rather than boundless joy. Over dinner that evening, the baroness looked pensive.

'I'm sure you'll want to leave as soon as possible but we both think you should stay here until you're stronger and the situation becomes more stable,' she'd said. 'Dr Hermann said there are a lot of angry people in town looking for vengeance. Not a good time for you to be wandering around.'

'What about you? Suppose they find out you've been sheltering an enemy airman?'

She shrugged. '*Ach*, for me I don't care so much any more. I've lived my life. But war has stolen the best years of yours. Find a woman and start living.'

Her words startled him. Totally consumed by war, he hadn't made any plans for peace. Although he had come to care more and more for Judith, their trysts had been interludes between missions rather than preludes to the future.

In the next few weeks, the doctor's warning was validated by a succession of beatings and murders in the area, but Adam was too restless to remain in this cocoon any longer. He walked with a limp and his shoulder still ached, but the war had ended and he was impatient to find a place for himself in the changing world.

On the evening before his departure, he sat with the baroness in the chamber where a stag's head with massive antlers hung above the ornately carved mahogany sideboard, and a balding brown bearskin rug lay on the flagstone floor. On other walls, generations of self-satisfied von Schaffenburgs looked down from elaborate gilt frames, their canvas crisscrossed by cracking paint. There were generals encased in armour and hunters mounted on horseback. The women, stern matriarchs with small eyes and wide hips, were surrounded by children dressed like miniature adults. The lives of this family, like his own, had been interwoven with the history of their nation through the centuries.

Like him, the baroness was the last of the clan. On the walls of a Warsaw apartment, portraits of his ancestors had once hung just like these, but the walls had probably crumpled and collapsed and the portraits had been buried beneath the rubble.

Although it was summer, a chill rose from the stone floors. Adam threw more logs into the fireplace and drew their high-backed chairs closer to the crackling fire. The Lenzkirch clock on the marble mantelpiece struck the hour and Maria von Schaffenburg wiped a bottle and placed it on the small oak table between them. 'I was saving this for the end of the war,' she said. 'I had hoped to share it with my sons, but I would like to open it now.'

Adam looked at the label. It was a vintage riesling *Deutschersekt* from a local vineyard. The cork popped and catapulted into the fireplace, and, as he poured the foaming wine, he chuckled at the vagaries of life. He had never envisaged toasting the end of the war with sparkling wine in a German castle. Taking a cigarette from his case, he tapped it on the lid, lit it and inhaled, releasing a column of smoke that curled towards the ceiling.

They clinked glasses without speaking. The significance of the occasion and the depth of their emotion made words unnecessary.

The fire was dying and he stirred it with the poker until the embers glowed again and sparks flew up. 'I hope God keeps his side of the bargain you made when you saved me,' he said.

She touched her cross. 'It was God who spared you. I was only his instrument,' she said.

'But you took the risk. Why?'

She stared into the fireplace. 'After Stalingrad, I became completely disillusioned with the Führer. I could see he was willing to sacrifice his people for his own grandiose ambitions. But after Friedrich was murdered, I saw things in a different light. Hitler wasn't the only one to blame. Our catastrophe was caused by people who followed Satan instead of their conscience.'

She drained her flute and he leaned forward to refill it.

'You see, our national strength is also our weakness,' she continued. 'We're obedient, industrious and meticulous, but we lack imagination and individuality. With you Poles, it's the opposite. Your way leads to recklessness and anarchy but leaves room for moral judgment.'

The following morning, she accompanied him to the gate at the entrance of the estate.

'I want you to know that no matter what happens, I will always be glad I helped you,' she said.

He kissed her hand and walked quickly from the castle, into the unknown.

As Adam strode towards the village, he breathed in the summer scent of ripe corn and sun-warmed flowers. But his cheerful mood faded when he considered the future. As a former courier for the AK, returning to Poland would be risky now that the Russian-sponsored communists were in power. Feliks had told him that Stalin referred to members of the exiled Polish government as 'white Poles,' and regarded the insurgents as a band of criminals who collaborated with the Nazis. No political satire could match this bitter reality, that those who had fought to free their country from a common enemy were reviled and persecuted by their allies as collaborators.

But if he didn't return to Poland, where could he go? He spoke English but was disgusted by the duplicity of the British and American governments. Stewart and Judith enthused about Australia but the prospect of living in a colonial backwater far from the heartbeat of the world was unthinkable. Canada was a possibility. Perhaps he could persuade Judith to go there. Nurses were always in demand, and with his diplomatic background and knowledge of English, he should be able to find work.

He realised with a shock that about six months had passed since they'd last been in touch. Perhaps she had given him up for dead and found someone else. She might even have gone back to Australia.

Preoccupied with his thoughts, he didn't notice two men walking stealthily behind him along the road. One looked like a boxer gone to seed, while the other had the tense watchfulness of an underworld bodyguard.

The baroness had warned Adam not to take the main road, and he had just turned on to the path that led to the woods when the two men grabbed his arms and pushed him along until they came to a forest clearing. He started explaining in German that he'd come looking for work and had no money, but they laughed and laid into him with staves until he lay moaning on the forest floor. Between blows, one of them panted, 'This is for Cologne, Hamburg and Dresden.' He gave Adam's head one final punch and kicked his ribs. The last thing he heard before he lost consciousness was a voice snarling, 'Well, we've fixed him. Now let's pay *her* a visit.'

Sunlight was streaming through the open window and Adam was watching motes of light quivering in the air when he heard firm footsteps coming towards him. He turned his head and knew he must be dreaming because Judith was standing there.

'Adam?' she said in a tremulous voice he hardly recognised. 'It is you, isn't it?'

His voice seemed caught so deep inside his throat that he couldn't get it out. All he could do was nod and grip her hand, as though clinging to the edge of a precipice.

Judith brushed her hand across her eyes and smeared moisture across her cheek. She cleared her throat several times but it kept clogging up. Her gaze slid from his bandaged face to his splinted arm. 'You went to an incredible amount of trouble to find me,' she said. 'Next time just write.'

'Writing is too easy,' he rasped. Under his bandages, he was smiling so broadly that his face felt as though it would split in two. He clasped her hand tightly and felt the sun shining down on his head.

They were sitting like that, not speaking or moving, when Elżunia put her head around the door and drew back. There was the new patient, half-dead and swathed in bandages, holding the hand of Matron, who looked as though she was in a trance.

Elżunia had been sent by the sister to check on the bandages and the temperature of the patient they all referred to as the Mystery Man, but now she hovered around the door, not wanting to break the spell that bound them. She walked on, intrigued. Improbable as it was, it looked like a love scene.

When she returned half an hour later, Matron had gone and the patient was lying with his back to her. As she approached the bed, the sunlight streaming through the window lit up the cigarette case on his bedside table.

Shaking with indignation, Elżunia rushed to find Matron to warn her. She obviously had no idea what kind of man he was.

'I think new patient is thief,' Elżunia blurted out.

Judith looked at her in surprise. 'Why on earth do you think that?'

Elżunia was tapping herself on the chest to make her meaning clearer. 'I give that cigarette case to man in 1942. This man is thief.'

Judith's fingers tightened around her pen and she took a deep breath. Steady on, she told herself. Take it slowly. Don't go jumping to conclusions.

'Are you saying that this was your cigarette case and you gave it to someone?'

Elżunia was nodding. 'I give father's cigarette case to Polish man in Ghetto.' She dropped her voice. 'Special man for me.'

'Leave it with me,' Judith said in a voice she struggled to keep even. 'I'll look into it.'

As Elżunia left the office, she wondered why Matron was staring at her so strangely.

Sixty-Four

Judith rose from her chair, picked up a file and opened it, only to close it a moment later. She sat down again, fiddled with her pen and stared out of the window. Three English nurses were walking from their dormitory across the courtyard, and their bright young voices bounced off the walls. Judith stood up and paced up and down her office. How could it happen that just as she'd received the gift she hadn't even dared to wish for, it was snatched away?

She slumped in her chair. The night they had met in the kitchen, Elżunia had talked about the man she had been in love with for the past six years whom she knew only by his code name, Eagle. Like a maths student who tries desperately to find a way of making an equation produce the desired answer, Judith considered every possibility in the hope of arriving at a different solution, but each time the basic premise defeated her. If Elżunia had given him the cigarette case, then Eagle was Adam. She knew that he had never parted with the case, that he'd kept it with him even during his aerial missions. The first night they had spent together, he described the girl who had given him the case as extraordinary. She had been fooling herself all along. It was Elżunia he loved.

The laughing voices of the young nurses in the yard irritated her and she slammed the window shut so hard that the glass rattled. What a fool she'd been, imagining that he cared for her when all the time it was this girl he longed for.

For the rest of the day, nurses knocked on Judith's door to ask for instructions, housekeepers requested keys, the chef threatened to resign, and doctors discussed treatment regimes for problem patients, and she dealt with them one by one, hardly aware of what she was doing. Inside she felt as stiff and frozen as an iceberg.

The only person who noticed the change in her was Kathleen, who came to discuss Adam's progress, a subject Judith would have preferred to avoid.

'You look worn out, love. Shall I bring you a cup of tea?' she said in her Irish brogue as she looked searchingly into Matron's face.

Judith shook her head. Tea couldn't solve her problems. But a few minutes later, Kathleen reappeared with a tray.

'Come on, now, it'll do you the world of good,' she coaxed as she poured the steaming tea.

As she settled back and sipped the tea, Judith felt her spirits reviving. Why had she been so quick to give up on the man she wanted so much? Almost three years had passed since he and Elżunia had last met, and in that time everything had changed. He was no longer an Underground courier, Poland was no longer independent, the world had moved on, and Elżunia now had two children to care for. For all she knew, their feelings for each other might have changed as well.

Judith thought about the night she had spent with Adam in the London hotel and her blood quickened. Why had she assumed he didn't care for her? Her mind began to concoct a wild scheme. Elżunia didn't know yet who the patient was. Perhaps she could find some pretext to transfer her before she found out. The British Red Cross was desperate for experienced nurses. With Elżunia out of the picture, nothing would stand in her way. She would give her an excellent reference of course, and recommend her for a senior position. After all, didn't they say all was fair in love and war?

Pleased with her solution, Judith sat back and glanced out the window. But as she watched Elżunia walking across the yard with her arms around the children, skipping and singing with them, she felt sick. She couldn't base her happiness on deceit. A wave of compassion for Elżunia swept over her. After all she had suffered and all she had lost, she deserved some happiness in her life. And if Adam represented that happiness, she had no right to stand in their way.

Sitting in Judith's office, Elżunia's eyes widened with disbelief. It must be her bad English. She must have misunderstood what Matron was saying. But Matron kept repeating the same words over and over, a little louder each time, as though increased volume might ensure her comprehension.

'The new patient is the man from the Polish Underground.'

'Is not possible,' Elżunia insisted. 'He steal cigarette case.'

Judith stood up. 'Come with me.'

As soon as Adam saw Elżunia, he struggled to sit up. She was taller and thinner than he remembered, and her eyes were even larger and more luminous than before, but she had the same defiant tilt of the head and air of unshakeable determination that had impressed him in the Ghetto. What was her name? Ela? Eulalia? Then he remembered.

'Elżunia!' he cried out. 'I can't believe it's you! What on earth are you doing here? Look, I still have the cigarette case you gave me.'

She tried to speak but could only stammer. She stared at his bandaged face that bore no resemblance to the man she had dreamed about for so long. How could it possibly be him? And yet he had recognised her.

'I've often thought about you,' he was saying. 'Especially during the Ghetto Uprising.'

Although he spoke in Polish, Judith could hear the affection in his tone. It felt as though someone had picked up her heart and hurled it to the ground.

'I've thought about you too,' Elżunia whispered.

There was so much she wanted to tell him and so many questions she wanted to ask but she couldn't get her thoughts together.

'Does it hurt?' she asked.

'Only if I move or cough. Sister said the bandages can come off my face tomorrow.'

She was trying not to stare at him. 'I can't believe it's you either,' she said and blushed. Words were so inadequate.

She returned later that afternoon, lugging a gramophone and some records in brown paper sleeves. Placing one on the turntable, she cranked the handle, raised the arm from its cradle, and gently lowered the needle onto the edge of the disc. A moment later the sound of Paderewski playing Chopin nocturnes filled the ward. They listened in reverent silence and Elżunia felt that the tenderness of the music expressed her feelings more profoundly than words ever could. Beneath the delicate ecstasy of the poignant Nocturne in C, she heard a lament and a palpitating sense of loss. She looked down to blink away her tears. That was the nocturne she had heard in Andrzej's apartment the last night they spent together. As she touched his hand, she felt sadness spreading through her veins. Our dreams betray and deceive us, especially when they are answered, she thought. When she had met Andrzej, it was Adam's embrace she longed for. Now, with an intensity that made her dizzy, she wished it was Andrzej lying there.

It was at this moment that Judith walked past the Intensive Care ward and knew that her world had changed forever. Jealousy scorched her as she took in the sight of their faces so close together, and she regretted not having sent Elżunia away. The girl stood between her and the only man she had ever wanted, the only man who had ever cared about her, and perhaps still would, if Elżunia hadn't reappeared in his life.

The bandages had come off but when Adam looked in the mirror, he hardly recognised himself. He was looking at a puffy face with hardly any contours, a nose that had splayed across his face, purple bruises under his eyes and a swollen jaw that looked like a severe case of mumps.

'You're no oil painting, love, that's for sure,' Kathleen said as she surveyed him. Then she chuckled. 'Picasso, maybe.'

He couldn't wait to tell Judith about his reunion with Elżunia and was disappointed that she hadn't come to see him all day. As the day wore on, he grew increasingly impatient to see her, and show her that the bandages had been removed. Restless, he tried to find reasons for her absence and concluded that she must be dealing with emergencies and would come as soon as she had time. Elżunia, on the other hand, had put her head around the door many times, and each time he saw her, he marvelled at the serendipity that had brought him to the hospital where she and Judith were both working. War usually separated people but it had brought the three of them together in a way that was miraculous.

In her office, Judith was tearing herself apart as she struggled with the longing to see him and the determination to avoid visiting his ward. She couldn't bear the thought that he might feel sorry for her, or try to make excuses. To save her pride, she decided to keep away but it took all her strength to keep that resolve.

Kathleen knocked on the door to report that the Mystery Man — she still referred to him that way because she couldn't get her tongue around his unpronounceable surname — had had his bandages and dressings removed.

'He's been askin' for you, Matron,' she said. 'Every time I go in.'

Judith made a dismissive gesture. 'I haven't got time,' she said, and continued writing her report, her knuckles white as she gripped the pen.

From his bed, Adam occasionally caught sight of Judith walking past on her rounds. He was baffled by her continued absence and the fact that she seemed to avert her face and hasten her step whenever she passed the Intensive Care ward. Women were fickle and unfathomable and often played hard to get, but he had believed that Judith was different. She'd been overcome with joy at seeing him at first, but now, for some inexplicable reason, she was ignoring him.

After a few days, he managed to hobble along the corridor, leaning on crutches. Panting, he had to stop every few steps because the searing pain in his ribs brought tears to his eyes, but he gritted his teeth and kept going until he reached her office and tapped on the door with a crutch.

She caught her breath when she saw his scarred, bruised face, and restraining an impulse to stroke it, hurriedly looked away.

'Sit down a minute, but I can't talk long,' she said crisply.

'Judith, tell me what's going on,' he said.

'What do you mean?'

'You know what I mean.'

'Perhaps you don't realise that I'm running a hospital here, not a social club. I'm run off my feet from morning till night. I'm not just the head of nursing here. I'm the administrator, negotiator, welfare worker, counsellor and peacemaker. And I still don't have enough thermometers or bed pans.'

He was staring at her. 'I have never seen such a change in anyone.'

She toyed with a glass paperweight, not trusting herself to reply.

He hauled himself to his feet. At the door, he turned and gave her an icy look. 'Don't worry. I won't waste any more of your time.'

The door closed behind him. She turned to the window and buried her face in her hands.

Sixty-Five

Elżunia went about her duties as usual, taking temperatures, sponging fevered bodies and giving injections, but beneath her calm exterior she was churning with anxiety. The patients were making plans for the future and soon she too would have to move on and make a new life for herself and the children, but the world seemed a huge and frightening place.

There was no one waiting for her and she didn't belong anywhere. For the first few weeks after the unexpected meeting with her father, she'd basked in the afterglow of his presence, and had wanted to believe his explanations and assurances, but now that the elation had faded, too many doubts lingered and too many issues remained unresolved. Had he really been told they were dead? What was his true relationship with Marta, and when did it begin? She strained her memory to recall what she had observed or overheard in the room next door to Granny's in case she had overlooked some significant clue, but nothing came to mind.

Frustrating thoughts swirled through her mind as she replaced the drenched pillowcase of the young Czech patient who was watching her with his intense gaze. She plumped his pillow, shook a thermometer and placed it under his tongue.

'Temperature's come down,' she said, assuming her cheerful professional tone. 'You'll probably be able to leave soon.'

'What about you, Miss Elżunia?' he asked. 'Will you go too?'

'I don't know,' she said. Adam's sudden reappearance in her life had left her more confused than ever. For the past six years, from the moment they met, she had thought about him every day, and the fact that he'd kept her cigarette case in his breast pocket all this time must mean he cared about her too. And now, for the third time, their paths had crossed. It had to be destiny.

But something had changed. It wasn't just because his face was swollen and bruised and had lost its gaunt look. Or because the bitter curve of his mouth that had given him the haunted, moody expression she'd found so alluring had gone. Something gnawed at her and she lay in bed night after night trying to work it out.

Almost every night for the past six years she had fallen asleep with his face and voice imprinted on her mind, but now that he was here in the flesh he seemed less real and more distant than before. Perhaps the idea of Adam was more powerful than the reality. It was like looking at a relative with a family resemblance rather than at Adam himself. She tried to dismiss these disturbing thoughts that continued to swirl around in her head. Although it was painful to let go of the dream that had sustained her for so long, she had to admit that he didn't arouse the unsettling excitement that had made her body quiver and grow hot whenever she had thought about him. These days it was Andrzej who haunted her dreams, Andrzej who held her close and stroked her and made her dizzy with longing as she melted into his arms. Whenever she woke up, she tried to sink back into the dream and felt guilty, as though she was disloyal to them both.

From the scene she had witnessed the previous week between Adam and Matron, it seemed they had a strong connection, even though Matron never came into his ward any more. This was puzzling but Adam never mentioned it and Elżunia didn't feel she had the right to ask. She was also baffled by Matron's changed attitude towards her. These days she never smiled or made friendly comments, and whenever she spoke she sounded abrupt.

Adam was sitting in a chair, looking out the window when Elżunia put her head around the door.

'You look sad today,' he said.

She picked at her thumbnail. 'For six years I lived one hour at a time, and when night came I couldn't believe I was still alive. But now it's over, I don't know what to do.' It was a relief to drop the cheerful mask and say what was on her mind.

He was nodding. 'We both have to learn how to live a normal life.'

'For me, war became normal,' she said. She looked up at him. 'You look sad too. Can I help?'

He shook his head. Ever since Judith had started avoiding him, he had been depressed. It was such a brutal way of showing that she had lost interest. He studied the girl beside him and was touched that she had noticed his distress.

Propping her chin on her clasped hands, Elżunia glanced outside. The sky had darkened and gusts of wind lashed the rain against the window panes. She turned back to Adam.

'During the war I made life-and-death decisions all the time,' she mused, 'but now I feel worn out at the thought of having to decide anything.'

'Thinking complicates matters,' he said. 'When your life is at stake, instinct takes over. Like leaping from a Lanc without a parachute.'

She fiddled with the watch pinned to her starched apron. 'Will you go back to Poland?' she asked.

He stared moodily out of the window. The wind had suddenly dropped and the rain had eased, but the clouds still hung low and dark. He sat forward and Elżunia was struck by the intensity and hunger in his face and turned to follow his gaze. Judith was crossing the courtyard towards the general ward. She looked up at his window and, for a moment, their eyes met. Then she looked away and kept walking until she disappeared from view. His mouth tightened and Elżunia saw the pain in his eyes. With what seemed like effort, he turned his attention back to the room and asked her to repeat the question.

'I was wondering whether you'd planned to go back to Poland.'

He shook his head. 'For six years I risked my life in the AK and bombed German cities so the war would end and Poland would be free.' He spoke with such bitterness that she felt a chill sliding down her back. 'It never occurred to me that, when it was over, the Poland I'd fought for would no longer exist and, instead of the Nazis, the communists would be in power. I've heard that the jails are full of AK activists and RAF pilots who were naïve enough to go back. The communists don't want freedom fighters stirring up trouble. I won't go back until they've been overthrown.'

Footsteps sounded in the corridor again and he swivelled around, but it was Sister who had come into the ward. He turned back towards Elżunia and there was an angry glint in his eyes.

'The sooner I get out of here the better,' he said. 'I was thinking of going to Canada.'

'Do you know anyone there?' she asked.

He shook his head and for a few minutes they sat in silence. Then he looked into her face and was overcome by a rush of affection. He had admired this spirited girl ever since she had been his guide in the Ghetto and now, for the third time, fate had thrown her in his path. He had saved her from a bomb, and she had saved him from a bullet. There was a saying that if you saved someone's life, you became responsible for it. He looked at her again. They were both alone in a foreign country, without any plans for the future. On impulse, he said, 'How would you feel about going to Canada with me?'

The world stopped turning. The whole universe hung in the balance, suspended in the miracle of that moment.

'I've never thought about it,' she stammered.

'Well, think about it now,' he said.

The wind had picked up, driving the stinging rain against Elżunia's skin. She pulled her navy-blue cape close around her as she ran across the uncovered passageway to the dormitory and crept into bed, careful not to disturb Zbyszek and Gittel who were asleep. She was trembling. What had Adam's sudden invitation meant? Was it a proposal, a proposition, or merely a friendly suggestion? Although he always looked pleased to see her, he'd never given any indication of anything other than friendship. So why did he want her to go to Canada?

Only a few weeks before, she would have given anything just to see him again. Even in her most fevered flights of fantasy, she had never envisaged that one day he would want her to go away with him. Perhaps it didn't really matter why he had asked her. All she had to do was to accept, and her dreams would come true and she wouldn't be alone any more. Even if he felt no more than friendship, there was always a chance that in time his feelings might deepen. She fell asleep but woke an hour later and tossed from side to side. Her thoughts see-sawed back and forth.

I might as well pull petals off a daisy and chant *I'll go, I won't go*, she thought. Then she recalled the hungry look in his eyes when he'd watched Matron crossing the courtyard, so different from the way he looked at her, and then the disappointment on his face when Matron walked past. She saw it now with startling clarity. It was Matron he really wanted.

The door opened and closed again. Kathleen was rummaging through her valise, throwing her belongings on the floor in a growing pile. She looked up and caught sight of Elżunia lying on her bed, staring at the ceiling.

'What's up, love? she asked. 'You look that forlorn. Man trouble?'

Elżunia propped herself up on her elbow. 'I don't know what to do.'

Kathleen sat on the edge of her bed and gave her a shrewd look. 'You probably do know, but you're scared of followin' your heart.'

Elżunia dropped off to sleep again. She was standing under an oak tree in a dark forest, looking for a path that would lead her home. Suddenly the sky darkened and thunder rumbled. A bolt of lightning flashed across her eyelids, so close that she felt the electrical charge. She flung herself to the ground and covered her head with her hands, just as the tree trunk split and crashed to the ground, missing her by centimetres. As she lay there, trembling, she heard something whizzing through the air and raised her head. An arrow lay quivering at her feet.

She sprang up but more arrows flew past, thousands of them, fired by invisible archers, and all aimed at her. She was running now, her heart hammering in her ears. Any moment now those arrows would pierce her, but she was too exhausted to keep running. She stopped, resigned to her fate, but everything around her was silent and still.

Without realising it, she had outrun the arrows. She sank to her knees in gratitude but a second later she sprang up. The children! Where were the children? She had left them near the oak tree. How could she have forgotten about them? She was already running back, faster than before, not stopping to think about the arrows. Nothing mattered but finding the children. She bolted through the forest, weaving crazily among the oaks and birches while arrows flew through the air. Let them still be there, she sobbed over and over, and her breath came in violent gasps. In front of her, the track split off in various directions. She was panic-stricken. Which one led to the children? If she took the wrong path and lost her way in the forest, she would never find them.

The white trunks of birch trees gleamed in the darkness and she ran towards them, calling, shouting their names, panting, until, exhausted, she threw herself onto the soft forest floor and wept.

As she lay there, she felt a soft tap on her shoulder and looked up. It was Andrzej, and he was looking down at her with that lopsided smile of his, the tram-driver's cap on the back of his head, and she thought she'd explode with joy. 'You almost took the wrong path, didn't you?' he was saying. Behind him, Zbyszek and Gittel were sitting on a grassy hummock, picking blueberries.

Elżunia woke up with a start, drenched in perspiration. Tears were streaming down her cheeks. She glanced at the sleeping children to make sure they were still there and covered them up. She sat on her bed in the dark until the first rays of the sun speared through the space where the curtains didn't meet. She pulled them aside, threw open the window and leaned out. The air was fresh and clear, as though the preceding day's rain had cleansed the dust and grime and brought everything into sharp relief.

Sixty-Six

Judith was in her office reading through the nurses' training program she had drawn up. In the corridor outside, nurses were hurrying to the wards, chatting about their boyfriends in Britain. For the third time, she turned back to the report but couldn't take any of it in. Knowing that Adam was under the same roof, breathing the same air, but as inaccessible as if he were on Jupiter, made her feel she was being skinned alive, one strip at a time.

When she had glanced up at his window that afternoon, she'd felt an impulse to go to him. There was still time to explain why she had become so distant, and admit that she still cared for him but didn't want to stand in the way of his love for Elżunia. But when she came to the door of his ward, she saw him and Elżunia engrossed in what appeared an intimate conversation, and she had kept walking. By speaking out, she would only make a fool of herself. The pain and turmoil were bad enough without adding humiliation. Better to let him go on thinking she'd lost interest.

For the first time since her arrival in Germany, her thoughts strayed to the future. The hospital was running well now and she ticked off in her mind what she had accomplished. Under her regime, the health and morale of the patients had improved beyond anything she'd thought possible when she had arrived in this tragic place. But she had no illusions about being indispensable. Any competent matron could take over from her now. Perhaps it was time to move on.

With a sigh, she returned to her report when she heard a tap on the door. Elżunia was standing there with a resolute expression on her face.

'Matron, I'm want to talk to you, please.'

Judith lay down the file. 'Yes, what is it?'

'I'm want to go,' Elżunia said.

'Go?' Judith repeated. 'Go where?'

'Go from hospital.'

Judith gripped the fountain pen. Kathleen had already told her that Adam would be discharged in a day or two. So that was it. 'I suppose you'll be leaving together?' she said through dry lips.

Elżunia nodded, surprised that Matron needed to ask whether she was taking the children.

Well, that takes care of my dilemma, Judith thought as she stared into space. She glanced at her watch and with an effort heaved herself to her feet. It was time for her ward round. 'I'll give you a reference,' she said stiffly, and left the room.

She glanced perfunctorily at the patients' charts and continued on her way without stopping to chat to anyone. When she came to the men's ward, instead of hovering at the door to speak to the sister and then hurrying on, as she had been doing for the past two weeks, her eyes sought out the figure sitting by the window. Adam held a newspaper in his hands but was staring straight ahead. He turned and she was impaled on his stare. It was too late to retreat.

She walked slowly towards him. 'I hear you're leaving soon.'

He nodded.

There were razors in her throat. 'Where will you go?'

'Canada.'

'They have very cold winters there,' she said.

He gave a bitter laugh. 'It will be less cold than in here.'

She looked down at her hands. 'I suppose the children will enjoy the snow.'

He frowned. 'What children?'

'Zbyszek and Gittel. Elżunia's taking them, isn't she?'

'What the hell are you talking about?'

'I thought you ... I thought Elżunia and you ...' She didn't know how to finish.

He flung his newspaper aside. 'Thought what?'

'I thought Elżunia would be going with you,' she said in a small voice.

'Judith, what are you playing at?' he shouted. 'You told me in London that you were no good at games but I think you underestimated your deviousness and overestimated your honesty.'

'You think *I've* been devious? What about you, pretending to care about me when all the time Elżunia was the one you wanted?'

His face was taut and white. '*Cholera psia krew,*' he swore. 'Bloody hell! You're crazy, you know that? Absolutely crazy!' He stared at her for a moment. 'So this is what it's been about! You decided I was in love with Elżunia. And you didn't even think of asking me. You just assumed you knew it all.'

He was digging his fingers into her shoulder and she moved away from his grasp. She wanted to explain that it wasn't like that, but he was too angry to listen. Whatever she said, she'd sound like a fool and, anyway, it was too late.

Her face was flaming and she couldn't meet his eyes. 'You're right,' she said. 'I should have asked you. I'm sorry.'

'Sorry?' he repeated. 'You ruin everything and say sorry as if you're late for lunch?'

She rose. There was no point prolonging this torture. She was already walking towards the door when he said, almost under his breath, 'Judith, why didn't you trust me?'

There was nothing she could say. His words resounded in her head as she strode to her office with a grim expression that defied anyone to stop her on the way. She closed the door but didn't know what to do with herself. It reminded her of the time she had visited a friend's sheep property near Bathurst and had sat on an ants' nest. Thousands of furious insects had swarmed all over her but jumping up and down, stamping and flailing her arms had failed to dislodge them. She had wished she could run away from herself, and that's how she felt now.

She had to get away to some secluded spot where no one would hear her shouting in frustration. After giving Kathleen instructions to take over, she hurried from the hospital. The morning air felt cool on her skin and as soon as she turned towards the woods, she breathed in the scent of pine needles and began to relax. Sunlight dappled the ground between the trees and larks were twittering in the branches. When she reached the clearing, she sat down at the base of a massive oak, leaned against its hard, ridged trunk, and closed her eyes. Somewhere a cuckoo was calling to its mate. Coming to the woods was usually as calming as a meditation, but this time her agitated mind would not be stilled.

What hurt most was knowing that it was all her fault. Arrogance and false pride. The cuckoo's mate called back and the birds flew off. Judith scrambled to her feet and walked slowly back, shoulders hunched, head down. There was no escape from the pain and no solace in nature. As she returned through the hospital gate, she wondered whether she had thrown away her chance of happiness because she didn't think she deserved to be loved.

Back at her desk, she tried to focus on the report again when there was a knock at the door. Probably morning tea.

'No, thank you,' she called out.

But the door opened and her heart stopped beating because Adam was standing there. She took a deep breath. From the look on his face, she supposed he'd come to tear strips off her again.

He was already inside the office and had closed the door behind him. 'I want to know one thing,' he said between clenched teeth. 'If you didn't want me, why didn't you just say so? Or did you invent this absurd story because you didn't have the courage to tell me the truth?'

'If you think that, you don't know the first thing about me,' she said quietly.

'How can I know you? You are completely irrational.'

Judith opened her mouth to justify herself and stopped. Words could never explain or convey the regret that threatened to choke her.

He was looking into her face with a searching expression. Then he gripped her arms and pressed her against him. Judith closed her eyes. When this moment ends, it will all be over, she thought.

'Judith,' he said hoarsely.

She held her breath.

'When I woke up in here that day and saw you standing there, I knew there was a God,' he whispered.

She tried to speak but no words came out, and all she could do was tighten her arms around him and press her face against his cheek. Then she looked up. For the first time since they had met, Adam was smiling.

Sixty-Seven

Dreams and premonitions were all very well, Elżunia thought as the train rushed through the Polish countryside, but what if she'd made a terrible mistake? Now that she had said goodbye to Adam, she felt like an empty husk. For six years she had fantasised about him, longed for him and idolised him, and now she had tossed the dream away. The train emitted a piercing shriek, hurtled around a bend, then gathered speed. Zbyszek sat with his nose pressed against the dust-streaked window, but Gittel was already dozing, her head against Elżunia's shoulder.

One cluster of small wooden houses with chicken coops and straggly tomato plants followed another until it seemed as if the whole country were a single village intersected by fields. Flocks of jays winged across the ripening wheat, corn and barley, which swayed in the light breeze. On the banks of slow-flowing streams, willows dipped their drooping boughs into the water. In contrast to the summery brightness of the countryside, she sensed a tired greyness about the people who bent over the fields or leaned against their fences.

The other occupants of the compartment looked preoccupied and spoke little, except for a garrulous fellow who scratched his blotchy hands while eyeing his neighbours with an inquisitive gaze as he tried to engage them in conversation.

'Just look at this country,' he said in a querulous voice. 'Small fields, smaller fields, and peasants ploughing with horses. How's this country ever going to pick itself up, can you tell me that?' he said to no one in particular. 'Did we win the war or did we lose the war, that's what I want to know.' He scanned the faces around him for a response.

The man who'd boarded the train at the last station unbuttoned his trenchcoat, placed his felt hat on the rack, and leaned forward. 'What did you expect?' he said with a shrug. 'Our so-called allies sold us down the river and no one gives a shit.' He lit a cigarette with fingers stained with nicotine and inhaled, releasing a column of smoke towards the ceiling. 'Twenty years of independence and three hundred years of oppression — that's been our lot.'

They continued complaining, but, from the way they skirted around the current political situation, Elżunia figured they were sounding each other out. After all, you never knew who you were talking to these days. Your fellow passenger could be working for the secret police.

After a desultory conversation about postwar shortages and the problems of relocation, their glance rested on a young man with semitic features sleeping in the opposite corner. The man with the skin condition lowered his voice as he scratched his hands. 'They reckon the Nazis killed them all off in those camps, but how come there's so many of them left? People are shaking in their boots because they're coming back in droves and demanding their houses back.'

The smoker nodded as he blew another column of smoke towards the ceiling.

'Why shouldn't the Jews reclaim what's theirs?' Elżunia blurted out. 'Wouldn't you?'

The two men exchanged glances. 'What's it to you?' the smoker said.

'I can't stand prejudice,' she said and turned away.

Gittel mumbled something and wriggled around until her head lay in Elżunia's lap. The train clattered around a sweeping curve so that they could see the engine through the window.

'Look at our train!' Zbyszek shouted, pressing his nose harder against the glass for a better view. Elżunia nodded absently. This was her country, but, for people like these men, she and the children weren't part of it and never would be. They were doomed to sit between two worlds, belonging neither to one nor the other, always listening out for what was said and what was left unsaid.

As the train approached Warsaw, her heart beat wildly. In her haste to leave Germany and begin a new life, she hadn't anticipated how emotional her return would be. Memories she had managed to suppress for the past year overwhelmed her. She fixed her eyes on the view and set her jaw. Perhaps one day she would let go and grieve, but for now she had to keep herself together.

The train jerked to a halt at Gdańsk Station, where sombre-faced people waited on the windswept platform. Downstairs, in the bare forecourt, she gripped the children's hands and felt hers become damp with sweat. Hawkers hovered around the entrance selling books, touts offered accommodation, while black marketeers, their hats pulled low over their foreheads, looked over their shoulders as they accosted passersby with offers to exchange currency.

It seemed to Elżunia that her whole life consisted of arrivals and departures, and once again she was alone in a strange place. She asked for a telephone book at the ticket office and scanned the pages for Aunt Amalia's new address, wondering what kind of welcome she would receive. She hardly knew her father's sister, who had moved from Warsaw many years ago after her husband died. If her father hadn't mentioned it, she wouldn't have known that her aunt had returned to her husband's family home. Let her be home, please let her be home, she thought as she dialled her aunt's number.

Half an hour later, as the tram rattled towards her aunt's place, she looked out of the window at the damaged tenements and bullet-scarred apartment buildings and her heart sank. This was Praga, the part of Warsaw on the right bank of the Vistula. Now that the bridges linking it with the Old Town had been destroyed, it seemed cut adrift from the rest of the city. Past the industrial section, with its vodka distillery, conserve factory and desolate streets lined with shabby buildings, they came to the leafy suburb of Saska Kępa. Before the war, international diplomats and affluent residents like her aunt had lived in handsome villas on streets that were named after their countries. Elżunia checked the scrap of paper on which she'd jotted down Aunt Amalia's address. Her house was on Francuzka Street, where the French embassy had once stood.

Before Elżunia had time to ring the doorbell, her father's sister was already at the door, arms outstretched to enfold her. Several times Aunt Amalia tried to say something but each time the words died inside her throat. She drew Elżunia and the children inside and, without speaking, gazed at her niece with such compassion in her eyes that Elżunia choked up. Stroking her head, Aunt Amalia kept saying, 'Thank God. Thank God you're alive.'

Tears flowed down Elżunia's cheeks. She had found her own flesh and blood, someone who cared about her. At last there was a warm corner of the world where she belonged, someone's affection she could count on.

Aunt Amalia's glance fell on the children, who were watching her, wide-eyed and silent. 'Poor little mites!' she cried. 'Look at them; they're as quiet as mice. They must be hungry and exhausted.'

She disappeared into the kitchen. A moment later she emerged, and Gittel and Zbyszek's eyes lit up when they saw her carrying glasses of milk and big slices of yeast cake. She watched with an indulgent smile as the children tucked in.

After the children were in bed, Elżunia and her aunt sat up talking late into the night. All the pent-up sadness, grief and disillusionment of the past six years finally poured out and Elżunia cried as she hadn't cried since she was a child.

She cried for her mother and for all the parts of her own life that had died with her, for the world that had vanished never to return, and for the innocence buried beneath the ashes. She cried for the betrayal of humanity and the betrayal of nations. She cried for those who had enriched the world by their courage and those who had besmirched it by their cruelty. She cried for her friends whose future had been swept away, but most of all she cried for the love that had been snatched from her.

And then she cried because Aunt Amalia was holding her and crying with her. When her sobs finally subsided, she felt lighter, as though the tears had washed away her loneliness.

When she woke the following morning, Aunt Amalia was fussing over Gittel and Zbyszek, who were already at the table, stuffing themselves with bread and cottage cheese. She beamed when she saw Elżunia, and, sitting down beside her, took her hand.

'I couldn't sleep last night, thinking about your poor mother, and what you both went through,' she said softly.

She poured Elżunia some black coffee from the enamel jug and sighed. 'There's so much cruelty in the world. The priests say it's because of original sin, but I don't believe that.'

She buttered another slice of bread for Zbyszek. 'You know, my science teacher used to say that the stars in the sky outnumber all the people that have ever lived on earth. Whenever I'm upset with the human race, I look up at the stars.' She shook her grey head. 'I can't begin to comprehend how you managed to survive in the Old Town during the Uprising, let alone look after these two.'

At the mention of the Old Town, Elżunia winced. Now that she was back in Warsaw, memories of Andrzej hovered in the air around her like wasps waiting to sting. She swallowed and forced herself to turn her attention to Aunt Amalia. Absorbed in her own experiences, she hadn't asked how she had managed during the war.

'There were times I thought I'd go deaf from all the bombing and shelling, but we didn't have it nearly as bad on this side of the river as you did,' she said. 'We thought it was all over when the Red Army stopped practically on our doorstep just before the Uprising broke out. But, as you know, instead of advancing to help the insurgents, they stayed put.' She sighed. 'Life is so strange. One of my most vivid memories of the war was the day they bombed the zoo in 1939. The power of the blast made the metal grilles fly off the cages like iron filings. The poor animals were either wounded or covered in flames. The keepers shot some of them to put them out of their misery, but most of the animals died in agony. I'll never forget the sight of the elephants' hides all blistered from the white phosphorus,' she said. 'I can still hear them trumpeting and screaming, as though they were crying over their dead.'

She blew her nose. 'It seems to me that during the war, the animals behaved like humans, but so many humans behaved like wild beasts.'

After a pause, she sat forward. 'I'll tell you something interesting. After the zoo was destroyed, the director found another use for it. He used the empty cages to hide the Jews whom he and his wife rescued from the Ghetto. Isn't it strange how life takes so much away but gives something back when you least expect it?'

While Aunt Amalia was talking, Elżunia looked for some resemblance to her father. Her hair, twisted into a bun, was completely grey but the well-shaped head was the same, and they both had a long upper lip, which her father concealed with his moustache. Although their features were different, there was something similar about their smile.

At first, whenever Aunt Amalia asked about her brother, Elżunia's curt, detached replies discouraged her from pursuing the subject. But after several days had passed, she broached the subject again.

'I sense you're reluctant to talk about him, and I'm sure you have your reasons,' she said gently, 'but I need to know what's happened to my brother.'

Unable to suppress her confusion and anger any longer, Elżunia launched into a lengthy, disjointed account about her father. 'He said someone told him we were dead,' she said at the end. 'But how come he never checked if it was true? And then there was that business about the girl next door ...' She trailed off, tearing at her thumbnail.

Aunt Amalia placed her wrinkled hands on Elżunia's shoulders and looked into her eyes. 'That must be very upsetting for you,' she said quietly. 'I don't know how easy it was to find out what was going in the Ghetto after it was closed. And I have no idea whether my brother told you the truth about that girl or not. All I know is that he has always been a man of his word, but war sometimes changes people.'

She looked around and lowered her voice. 'Do you know where he is?'

Elżunia shook her head and started to say something but her aunt placed a finger over her lips to indicate that she should whisper.

'There's no one here, Aunty.' Elżunia couldn't help smiling. 'You should relax. The war is over.'

Her aunt didn't smile back. 'That's what you don't understand,' she said. 'One war is over but another has just begun.'

In a voice that was barely audible, she proceeded to describe the poisonous atmosphere of mistrust and suspicion that had spread over Poland. 'This communist government that's been foisted on us is paranoid,' she whispered. 'They've arrested and tried leaders of the AK, as well as airmen who flew for the RAF. They're treating the people who fought for our freedom as traitors and fascists. Even the priests are being arrested and tortured.'

Elżunia stared at her aunt. If anyone else had told her these things, she would have been sceptical but there was no doubting her sincerity.

Her aunt gave a heavy sigh. 'Like you, I thought we'd won the war, but we've just exchanged one lot of oppressors for another.'

She looked at Elżunia's worried face and put her arm around her shoulders. 'I'm sure your father knows the situation and that's why he hasn't returned. It isn't even safe for him to write, because censors open all the letters from non-communist countries. But I'm sure one day it will be safe for him to come back, and, when he does, you'll be able to sort everything out.'

Elżunia sat for a long time in dejected silence, mulling over her aunt's words. Returning to Warsaw, she had expected blackouts, food rationing and shortages, but not a new kind of tyranny. Perhaps Aunt Amalia was right. You had to keep looking up at the stars to remind yourself of the beauty of the world.

Sixty-Eight

On a bright April morning, Elżunia was strolling along the quiet paths of the Praski Park on her way to the hospital. As usual, thoughts of the past threatened to overwhelm her, and to dispel them she kept her eyes fixed on the beds of irises and hyacinths, and her thoughts on Gittel and Zbyszek. Whenever her eyes strayed across the river to the Old Town, she averted her gaze. Too many memories. Like a tightrope walker feeling her way across the wire, she knew how easy it would be to slip, lose her balance, and plunge into the blackness.

Elżunia glanced at her watch. She still had half an hour before her shift. Sitting down on a wooden bench she closed her eyes and felt the warmth of the spring sun on her eyelids. She touched the amber brooch she always wore pinned to her blouse and felt that her mother was close by, watching over her.

The park, peaceful and shady, was conducive to contemplation, and its serenity calmed her mind. In the six months since she had arrived at her aunt's place, most things had fallen into place. The children had settled in at school, and Aunt Amalia took care of them while Elżunia worked at the hospital.

Even Stefan seemed to be getting his life in order, judging from the letter he sent from Kraków. He enthused about the city and a girl he had met there. He was working as a clerk but assured Elżunia that as soon as he'd saved enough money he would study law at the Jagellonian University.

Elżunia looked across at the ruins on the other side of the river, and reflected on Stefan's letter. He was wise to move to a city that hadn't been bombed. She thought about Granny's building, damaged beyond repair, and sighed. As Toughie had predicted, the old woman had been forced to move, and Elżunia's efforts to find her had so far been fruitless, but, as she sat in the park and recalled Granny's kindness, she strengthened her resolve to keep searching for her.

Her reverie was interrupted by a pair of young lovers walking past. They stopped by the huge beech tree on the other side of the path and, leaning against its trunk, began kissing passionately. Elżunia looked away so that the envy in her eyes wouldn't stab them. Her tranquillity shattered, she rose and walked slowly to the hospital.

Some of the other nurses had already arrived for the afternoon shift and the common room was filled with light-hearted chatter about boyfriends, scandals, clothes and movies. Elżunia rarely joined in their conversations. She was changing into her uniform and pulling on her black stockings when she overheard two nurses chatting.

'My sister is in charge of the surgical ward over at St John's Hospital and she says their new medical superintendent is really strange,' one of them said. 'He wears a funny cap and tells everyone to call him by his first name ...'

Elżunia shot up so suddenly that her chair fell backwards and clattered to the floor. Without waiting to change her clothes, she bolted outside. She longed to rush straight to St John's, but fear and apprehension held her back. She needed time to collect her thoughts and find the strength to cope with possible disappointment.

Surely there couldn't be any doubt. It had to be him. But what if it wasn't? And suppose it was, and he'd found someone else?

Calm down, she kept telling herself. Calm down. But the more she tried to compose herself, the more jittery her mind became as it jumped from one disturbing thought to another. Without realising it, she had returned to the park and was walking along a path where the interlaced branches of the chestnut trees formed a canopy overhead. A breeze sprang up and the fallen leaves scattered around until they came to rest in soft drifts along the edge of the path. A young mother was wheeling a high-sided pram. The baby gurgled and its mother cooed back. Despite her tension, Elżunia smiled. Wars had been lost and won, maps of the world had been redrawn, old nations had vanished and new ones had emerged, and, in the process, millions had been senselessly slaughtered, but the chain of life was infinite, like the stars.

Babies were a symbol of hope for the future but what kind of world would that baby grow up in? Would it find out how easily evil men can convince their followers to commit atrocities? Would it learn anything from all the courage and all the cruelty that the war had exposed? And would that baby ever comprehend the excruciating complexity of being human? Or would the war soon recede into the shadows of a distant and irrelevant past so that its lessons would one day have to be learnt all over again?

Turning into a dappled alley of beech trees, Elżunia sat down on a bench and breathed in the musty smell of the leaves. The light that slanted through the trees shone with a brilliance that made her catch her breath. It was the kind of intense golden light that artists painted to depict a sacred moment or to suggest an impending miracle. She looked around, almost expecting a revelation that would imbue the scene with some monumental significance. But there was only the rustling of the leaves, and, when she turned her face up to the sky, she saw that each bough of the massive beech was swaying to its own rhythm.

A young man walked past, whistling a tune she recognised. It was a lovesong from a Lehar operetta that her father used to whistle while shaving. An exquisite pain gripped her chest. The beauty of the melody became enmeshed with recollections of her parents and the world that now lived only in her memory. She closed her eyes and her mind became a kaleidoscope of faces, trees, birds and music. She could hear Andrzej saying, 'Life is a brief gift.' Time stopped and she felt her soul floating past the treetops towards the sky.

Being alive was extraordinary. Life was an impenetrable mystery, a network of beauty and ugliness, wonders and horrors that were intertwined and interconnected, where happiness trembled on the brink of disaster, and the good could not be untangled from the bad.

As though awakening from a trance, Elżunia looked around in wonder. Something mystical had brushed her soul and she sat very still so as not to smudge its delicate fingerprints. The moment passed. The conflict and hesitation were gone, and, in their place, she felt a calm sense of purpose.

As she rose, she looked back to capture the moment and imprint it on her memory but the light had lost its incandescence and that corner of the park no longer glowed with an ethereal light.

Elżunia started walking towards St John's Hospital until she could no longer contain herself and broke into a run. For the first time, she felt that the war was over.

Acknowledgments

Nocturne is a work of fiction based on historical events that took place during and immediately after World War II. Although most of the characters are fictional, I have taken the liberty of interpolating several historical figures into my story. They are Adam Czerniakow, the controversial president of the Jewish Council inside the Warsaw Ghetto, the famous pianist Władysław Szpilman, and the heroic educationalist Dr Janusz Korczak, who could have survived but chose to die together with the children in his charge.

Some of the characters in *Nocturne* have been partly inspired by remarkable people I have met over the years. One of them is H., whose courage and fearlessness during the darkest days of the war have made an indelible impression on me. Among others who have generously shared their stories with me are Cesia Glazer, Lena Goldstein, Yola Schneider, Dora Grynberg, Leo Zettel and the late David Landau.

Emeritus Professor Jerzy Zubricki, who played an important part in some of the events I have described, was kind enough to read sections of this manuscript and provide me with valuable details.

Joanna Kalowski took time to help me translate some phrases into German.

I'd like to acknowledge the following authors whose books I have found invaluable sources of information. Lynne Olson and Stanley Gould for their enthralling account of the plight of Polish airmen who served in the RAF during World War II, *A Question of Honor*; Jan Karski for his illuminating memoir, *Story of a Secret State*; and

Barbara Engelking and Jacek Leociak for their meticulously researched *The Warsaw Ghetto: a Guide to the Perished City*.

Other books and memoirs that have given me unique insights into life during this tragic period are *Justyna's Diary* by Gusta Draenger, *The Ghetto Fighters* by Marek Edelman, *Caged* by David Landau, *A Chronicle of the Years of War and Occupation* by Ludwik Landau, *Participants and Witnesses of the Warsaw Uprising*, edited by Janusz Zawodny, *Letters from Belsen 1945* by Muriel Knox Doherty, *Rising '44* by Norman Davies, *A Chronicle of the Fighting Capital* by Władysław Bartoszewski, *Janek: A Gentile in the Warsaw Ghetto* by Janek Kostanski, *The Cigarette Sellers* by Joseph Ziemian, and *Off the Record: the Life and Times of Muriel Knox Doherty*, edited by R. Lynette Russell.

Living with an author whose mind is fixed on uprisings, invasions, bombing raids and battles for three whole years can test a spouse's understanding and forbearance, but my dear Michael has dealt with this as he deals with everything else — with grace, good humour and generosity. As always, he was my first reader, and I'm very grateful for his understanding, literary taste and helpful suggestions.

It's a pleasure to work with the supportive team at HarperCollins. I'm especially grateful to my publisher, Linda Funnell, for her enthusiasm and sensitivity. Jo Butler has been a meticulous and thoughtful editor, whose probing questions have enhanced this manuscript.

I'm extremely fortunate in having Selwa Anthony as my agent. I appreciate her empathy and wisdom, and the fact that, no matter how busy she is, she always has time to listen and advise.

P.S.

Ideas,
interviews
& features
included
in a new
section…

Meet the author

DIANE WAS born in Poland and arrived in Australia in 1948.

At the age of seven she decided to become a writer. Her first article, about teaching at a Blackboard Jungle school in London, was published in *The Australian Women's Weekly* in 1965. Diane subsequently became a freelance journalist, and over three thousand of her investigative articles, personal experience stories, profiles and travel stories have been published in newspapers and magazines such as *Reader's Digest*, *Vogue*, *The Bulletin*, *Harper's Bazaar*, *The Australian*, the *Sydney Morning Herald*, *Good Weekend* and *The Age*. Her articles have also appeared in major publications in the UK, Canada, Poland, Hong Kong, Hungary, Holland and South Africa.

Over the years she has received numerous awards for journalism, including the Pluma de Plata awarded by the Government of Mexico for the best article written about that country, and the Gold Award given by the Pacific Asia Tourist Association. In 1993 she received an award for an investigative article about Creutzfeldt-Jakob disease. In 1998, she received the George Munster Award for Independent Journalism.

In 1998 her first book, *Mosaic, a Chronicle of Five Generations* was published by Random House with the help of a grant from the Australia Council. This memoir was nominated for the Victorian Premier's Literary Award for Non-Fiction as well as for the National Biography Award. In 2001 it was published in the United States and

Canada by St Martin's Press, and was selected as one of the year's best memoirs by Amazon.com. In May 2009, *Mosaic* will be re-issued by HarperCollins.

In 2000 Diane received her second grant from the Australia Council. *The Voyage of their Life, the Story of the SS Derna and its Passengers* was published by HarperCollins, and was shortlisted in the New South Wales Premier's Literary Awards.

Her first novel, *Winter Journey*, was published by HarperCollins in 2004 and was shortlisted for the Commonwealth Writers' Literary Award. It has been published in Poland. In 2010 it will be published in Israel.

Diane is married to Sydney medico and photographer Michael Armstrong, has two children, Justine and Jonathan, and three grand-daughters, Sarah, Maya and Allie. She is a member of the Australian Society of Authors, the Society of Women Writers, the NSW Writers' Centre and Sydney PEN International. ■

Diane Armstrong's
favourite ten books:

1. *Great Expectations* by Charles Dickens.
I love the vitality of Dickens's characters and his brilliant plots. The irony at the heart of this novel about arrogance and self-deception is very powerful.

2. *The First Circle* by Alexander Solzhenitsyn.
This is a devastating description of life under the Soviet system, and has a masterly plot that leads to its inevitable conclusion.

3. *If This is a Man* by Primo Levi.
This is a stark memoir of the author's experiences at Auschwitz and is told in spare, objective and compelling language.

4. *The Long Voyage* by Jorge Semprun.
I have been profoundly moved by this Spanish writer's insights about the choices that we can make, even in extreme situations.

5. *An Evil Cradling* by Brian Keenan.
This is an inspiring memoir written by a man who was kidnapped and held captive by extremists in Lebanon, but who never lost his courage or humanity.

6. *The Diaries of Anaïs Nin* by Anaïs Nin.
I am beguiled by her lyrical writing and willingness to reveal herself.

7. *The Roots of Heaven* by Romain Gary.
This beautifully written novel about an idealist who tries to save the elephants of Africa from extinction resonated with me when I read it many years ago.

8. *In My Father's Court* by Isaac Bashevis Singer.
These vignettes of life in the home of his father are written with Singer's usual acerbic wit and probing insight into human nature.

9. *Catch-22* by Joseph Heller.
A black satire about the American armed forces during World War II, this is a hilarious, original and also shocking look at war and those who find ways to profit from it. Joseph Heller has been one of my favourite writers ever since I read *Catch-22*, so when he offered to write a comment for the jacket of my first book, *Mosaic*, I couldn't believe my good fortune.

10. *A Severed Head* by Iris Murdoch.
I think Iris Murdoch was one of the twentieth century's best novelists and I was delighted by the unexpected twists and turns of this particular incisive novel of hers. ■

The critical eye

Reviewers have responded enthusiastically to Diane Armstrong's novel Nocturne.

Alan Gold from *Good Reading* declared that '*Nocturne* ... is an extraordinary, complex and compelling book ... Diane Armstrong is one of the most important writers in Australia today.'

The Age admired the way the author made a little-known part of World War II history accessible to readers in a page-turning, fast-paced style: 'Easy reading, racy ... Diane Armstrong's *Nocturne* is in the category of blockbuster with extra heart. The stories of the role played by young women in the Warsaw revolt are extraordinary. Through her central character, Elżunia, she explicitly points the story with resonances from *Gone with the Wind*. Armstrong keeps us turning the pages and may well introduce a new readership to a story that must keep on being told.'

Australian Jewish News also recognised the blockbuster and filmic quality of *Nocturne*: 'I found myself replaying the scenes in the book like a film reel in my mind ... Nocturne is one of those novels that will leave you reading into the night and will stay with you, like the notes of an unforgettable melody, long after you've read the last line.'

Sharon Ellison, writing for *MEAP Careers*, gave the book a wholehearted endorsement: 'If you're looking for a book that really leaves you thinking about life and its transience, then *Nocturne* is a have-to read ... I found this book very hard to put down ... The Warsaw Ghetto Uprising, and later the Warsaw uprising of 1944 have not received a great deal of publicity, yet they were integral parts of Poland's history. *Nocturne* offers a great read for fans of history, or of dramatic or romantic novels. Although it is quite long, every word is worthwhile.'

Australian Bookseller + Publisher acknowledged the depth of Diane Armstrong's research in writing about the Ghetto and Warsaw Uprisings: 'Like Geraldine Brooks, Diane Armstrong's historical research is expertly woven into the fabric of a fictional tale, providing an engrossing "faction" of heroism and resilience which will appeal to both fans of fictional dramatic/romantic sagas, as well as lovers of insightful history' while *Australian Book Review* admired her ability to re-create the despair, terror and hope of those involved in the uprisings in her writing: 'A gallant and gut-wrenching story. The accounts of the two uprisings ... are dramatic and heart-breaking ... superb reading.'

Reviewers have also responded well to one of the most important themes Diane Armstrong brings to the fore in all of her writing: the way people are able to rise to the challenges that confront them in difficult times. *Vibewire* commented: '*Nocturne* had me captured from its opening chapters ... it is an inspirational account of how ordinary people are forced to find strength and courage within themselves when the world around them falls apart.'

Peter Pierce of the *Sydney Morning Herald* recognised the way the author portrays the human cost of war through her characters: 'Armstrong writes vividly of the shocks of displacement, the loss of stable identity, both en masse and for individuals ... lavishing time on characters who reward her efforts.' ■

Q&A about *Nocturne*

Elżunia is an interesting and unusual heroine. What made you decide to tell much of the story from her point of view?

Most stories about the Warsaw Ghetto are told through Jewish eyes, so I thought it would be more interesting to have a heroine who at the start of the novel not only has no connection with Jews or Judaism, but doesn't even know that she is Jewish. Ambivalence about religious and ethnic identity has been a recurring theme in my work, as a result of my own experiences, so I felt that to create a heroine who also has this ambivalence towards her own identity would set up an inner conflict within the exterior tension of the story.

Do you remember anything about the Holocaust yourself when you were a child in Poland?

Not consciously. Don't forget that I was a very small child at the time and my parents shielded me from the trauma they themselves experienced. My parents fled with me to a small village in eastern Poland where we had to pose as Catholics to survive. From what they told me, I know that we went to church on Sundays, and I took part in the church processions, scattering petals with the other little girls. But although I didn't know the truth, I must have sensed their tension and anxiety, must have noticed them exchanging glances and heard them whispering late at night, because I sensed that there was something different about us, and that secrets were being kept from me. So that when, after the war, my father told me that we were Jewish, I felt as though I had always

6 Ambivalence about religious and ethnic identity has been a recurring theme in my work 9

8

known. Finally the secret was out. By this stage I was seven, and we were living back in Krakow.

So did your own experiences influence your choice of subject matter in *Nocturne*?
To some extent they did. Being a child Holocaust survivor, it's not surprising that I find this period of history so compelling. But what fascinates me as a writer is the behaviour of ordinary people when they are trapped in extraordinary situations. In all my books, I explore the choices people make when their lives are on the line and they have to try to maintain their humanity at a time when violence rules.

In *Nocturne* many of your characters are children and teenagers. Why did you choose to tell your story through such young characters?
Not many novels set in wartime focus on the heroism of children, and the more I read about the war, and listened to survivors and witnesses, the more impressed I became at the maturity and resourcefulness of even very young children, some of whom knowingly risked their lives to smuggle food for their starving families. One of the most astonishing stories I heard was about youngsters who had escaped from the Ghetto and lived in the streets of Warsaw, selling cigarettes not only under the noses of the Germans soldiers but to the Germans themselves. I was moved when I read that in spite of their risky business and their own tenuous hold on life, the older kids looked after the younger ones. Their story said so

❝ I explore the choices people make when their lives are on the line ❞

9

much about the power of love and endurance, and the triumph of courage over brutality. When I started writing *Nocturne*, some of these incidents, and these street children, found their way into one of the threads of the plot.

The most dramatic incidents in *Nocturne* take place during two insurrections that broke out in Warsaw. Although many people have heard of the Ghetto Uprising, not so many have heard of the Warsaw Uprising that took place one year later. Is this why you decided to write about the Warsaw Uprising as well?

When the Jews rose up inside the Warsaw Ghetto in 1943, they staged the first armed insurrection against the Germans in World War II. Armed with only a few pistols and home-made Molotov cocktails, the young Ghetto fighters managed to resist German tanks and artillery for five weeks, until the entire Ghetto was finally razed to the ground, set on fire, and most of its inhabitants killed. The Warsaw Uprising broke out in the entire city sixteen months later, in 1944, as the war was coming to an end. The leaders of the Polish Underground decided to rise up against the Germans before the Russians arrived, so that Poles would be in control of their capital city. Like the uprising by the Jews inside the Ghetto the previous year, this revolt ended with defeat, destruction and death. Warsaw was razed to the ground, and 250,000 people were killed. But although it was a military failure, it was a triumph of moral courage over oppression and brutality. The political machinations behind the scenes, as well as the personal dramas, enthralled me and as I researched I came

6 the Warsaw Uprising was a triumph of moral courage over oppression and brutality 9

across such dramatic and powerful events that I felt compelled to write about it, especially as so few people seemed to know anything about the Warsaw Uprising.

Some of your main characters were inspired by real people. Tell us about that.
The Australian nurse in *Nocturne* is based on Muriel Knox Doherty, the remarkable Australian nurse who was placed in charge of the hospital set up in the grounds of the Belsen–Bergen concentration camp. Having read about Muriel and seen an exhibition about her at the Sydney Jewish Museum, I was so inspired by her skill and compassion that she found her way into my novel in the person of Judith McAllister.

Many years ago I watched a Polish resistance activist being interviewed in a documentary called *Shoah* by Claude Lanzmann. Jan Karski, a courier in the Polish Underground, was smuggled into the Warsaw Ghetto, and later from Poland to the West. His task was to let Allied leaders know about the genocide taking place in Poland and to enlist their aid. I couldn't get his haunted expression out of my mind as he described what he witnessed inside the Warsaw Ghetto, and my hero Adam was inspired by this man. The way that real people become transformed into fictional characters is quite mystifying.

Music plays an important role in the book. Why is that?
I think music expresses emotions that are too deep and too complex for words. While writing *Nocturne*, I often listened to the nocturnes of Chopin, and the anguished symphonies of Shostakovich. I have woven

❝ While writing *Nocturne*, I often listened to the nocturnes of Chopin ❞

music into key scenes of *Nocturne* to reinforce its themes and increase emotional impact. For instance, Elżunia hears the strains of a Chopin nocturne while she and Andrzej make love for the last time in his family's ruined apartment. And when the starving, destitute musicians inside the Ghetto stage a concert, they are defying the Germans and showing the strength of the human spirit.

Why did you call your novel *Nocturne*?
The word 'nocturne' refers to night-time, and my novel is set during the darkest days of the twentieth century. Nocturnes are poignant, haunting pieces of music that are particularly associated with Chopin, who is Poland's national composer, so it seemed to me that this title was very evocative for a novel set in Poland during the war.

For me, Chopin's nocturnes express sadness and joy, and evoke the heights that the human spirit can reach.

History always seems to be tightly woven into what you write. Why is this?
I'm fascinated by the way that we never learn from history, and by the parallels I see between past and present. I wanted to write about Warsaw because in some ways its fate seemed to encapsulate the history of the world. *Nocturne* deals with uncertainty, anxiety and terror, and in many ways we're dealing with all these things today, especially with regard to the threat of terrorism. So I was interested to look back and see how people reacted when that terror did fall on them, and how they behaved. It seems as though we never learn the lessons that history teaches.

‘ I'm fascinated by the way that we never learn from history ’

What other themes have you explored through your characters?

I'm fascinated with how ordinary people behave in extraordinary situations, when they have to struggle to survive, when their values are put to the test, and when they face the challenge of maintaining their humanity at a time when violence rules. Some people descend into cruelty while others find strength they never suspected they possessed. Those who never lose their humanity are the true heroes. We all have the potential for good and evil in our natures, and my characters are not perfect: they have flaws and weaknesses. The traumatic events of war give a writer the opportunity to explore many aspects of human nature. Although *Nocturne* covers some of the most dramatic events of World War II, war is the backdrop against which relationships develop, love affairs blossom, and people discover their inner strength as well as their weaknesses.

How did you research *Nocturne*?

Long before I ever thought of writing a novel set in Poland and England during World War II, I'd started collecting memoirs, biographies, autobiographies and history books written about this period, so when I decided to write *Nocturne* I already had a whole library of relevant books at home. Fortunately, there are still many Holocaust survivors and World War II participants and witnesses and talking to them gave me a wealth of details and personal experiences. I also found the Internet a treasure trove of photographs, maps, memoirs and biographies. Listening to survivors and reading memoirs not only increased my

⟨ Those who never lose their humanity are the true heroes ⟩

knowledge and enriched my understanding but gave me ideas for the plot. I'm lucky in that I can read Polish because some of the most valuable material I obtained was written in Polish. My father brought with him to Australia some eyewitness accounts of events during the Holocaust. One of them was a short but powerful account of the Warsaw Ghetto Uprising that was written immediately after the war by Marek Edelman, one of the few fighters who survived. My most invaluable resource about the Warsaw Ghetto was the detailed and exhaustive tome *The Ghetto: a Guide to the Perished City* by Barbara Engelking and Jacek Leonciak, which was published recently in Poland and is publishing in English in 2009. Books by Władysław Bartoszewski and other Polish historians and journalists about the Warsaw Uprising gave me startling insights about the military and political leaders of the Uprising, the conflicts that raged behind the scenes, as well as the dramatic personal experiences of those who participated in this revolt. ■

Discussion questions

1. Can love survive great trauma? How do you imagine the relationship of Elżunia and Andrzej after the end of the novel? What about Adam and Judith? Do you think each couple has a future?

2. If you were Elżunia, would you be able to reconcile with your father at a later date? Do you find it plausible that Elżunia's father believed that his family was dead or do you think that he deserted his wife and children?

3. The novel explores the heroism of children and young people forced to fend for themselves and having to assume responsibility way beyond their years. Which particular scenes most struck a chord with you? Do you believe children who have faced the trauma of war can ever truly regain their childhood?

4. What do you think about the way Elżunia responded to the news that she was Jewish?

5. How does Elżunia's relationship with her brother, Stefan, change throughout the story? What do you think of him?

6. Do you understand Adam's decision to seek a post-war life far from Poland when he had been so patriotic throughout the course of the novel?

7. Throughout the story, there are many examples of heroism by ordinary people. Which particular instances moved you the most?

8. Many of the characters in *Nocturne* risk their lives to defend themselves, their people and their city against their oppressors. Can you imagine being in that situation? How do you think you'd react?

9. Do the events that take place in *Nocturne* during World War II have any relevance for us today? Can you think of any instances of history repeating itself today?

10. Some of the characters in *Nocturne* behave in despicable ways but as the story develops, they gradually become transformed. Is the author showing us that circumstances can affect people's behaviour? Do you think people can redeem themselves?

11. Why do you think that Chopin's nocturnes are heard at particular points in the story? What effect does this have? What role do you think music plays in the novel? ■

Read on

Have you read?

Mosaic: A Chronicle of Five Generations
(2009, HarperCollins Australia,
ISBN 978 07322 8431 2)
Starting in Krakow, Poland, in 1890, and
spanning more than 100 years, five
generations and four continents, *Mosaic* is
Diane Armstrong's moving account of her
remarkable, resilient family. An
extraordinary story of a family and one
woman's journey to reclaim her heritage.

'Diane Armstrong's book is a source of
delight to the reader. Written with fervour
and talent, it will capture your attention and
retain it to the last page' — Nobel Prize
winner Elie Wiesel

'*Mosaic* flows like a novel, which once
started, is hard to put down. It is a compelling
family history of extraordinary people played
out against some of the most frightening
events of our century. The depth of emotions
evoked is stunning. I was thrilled and deeply
moved' — Joseph Heller, author of *Catch-22*

'It is no small achievement and it bristles
with life ... *Mosaic* is a work of many levels.
But ultimately it succeeds because most of its
characters demonstrate how the human
spirit can soar way, way above adversity' —
Sydney Morning Herald

'A most remarkable book about one
family's experience ... a rich and compelling
history ... Just as A.B. Facey's *A Fortunate Life*
and Sally Morgan's *My Place* have become
part of the national literary heritage, so too
has *Mosaic* earned its place in our social
dialogue as part of our cultural tapestry' —
Daily Telegraph

The Voyage of Their Life: The Story of the
SS Derna and its Passengers
(2001, HarperCollins Australia,
ISBN 978 0 7322 8150 2)
In August 1948, 545 passengers — from
displaced persons camps in Germany, death
camps in Poland, labour camps in Hungary,
gulags in Siberia and stony Aegean islands —
boarded an overcrowded, clapped-out vessel in
Marseilles to face an uncertain future in
Australia and New Zealand. The epic voyage on
this hellship lasted almost three months and
was marked by conflict and controversy. As the
conditions on board deteriorated, tension and
violence simmered above and below decks. But
romances and seductions also flourished, and
lifelong bonds were formed.

Diane Armstrong set sail on the *Derna*
with her parents when she was nine years old,
and as an adult she located over a hundred of
the passengers to retell their stories.

'She is a natural sleuth ... her writing is
clear, incisive, yet imaginative' — *Sydney
Morning Herald*

'Armstrong's triumph in this history is
to avoid judgment or argument ... she
allows readers to enter into the mindset of
the refugees, to empathise with them'
— *Weekend Australian*

'Armstrong weaves in these individual
tales with great skill. They flow in and out of
the narrative in rhythm with the ship's slow
movement from the old world to the new'
— *The Age*

'The characters become familiar and
absorbing ... almost unbearably moving'
— *Australian Book Review*

'Diane Armstrong's study of the *Derna* is an important contribution to postwar Australian history' — Dr Suzanne Rutland, *Australian Historical Society Journal*

Winter Journey: a novel

(2006, HarperCollins Australia, ISBN 978 0 7322 7695 9)

When forensic dentist Halina Shore arrives in Nowa Kalwaria to take part in a war crimes investigation, she finds herself at the centre of a bitter struggle in a community that has been divided by a grim legacy. What she does not realise is that she has also embarked on a confronting personal journey.

Inspired by a true incident that took place in Poland in 1941, Diane Armstrong's powerful novel is part mystery, part forensic investigation, and a moving and confronting story of love, loss and sacrifice.

'A bold adventure of a novel ... Here is a consummate writer at the top of her form. A fine fictional debut from a writer who's already made her mark' — *Canberra Times*

'Profoundly moving, compelling and superbly written' — *Australian Women's Weekly*

'A deeply moving and inspiring novel' — *Good Reading*

'Diane Armstrong has done it again with an absorbing page-turner from the opening sentence' — *Australian Jewish News* ∎

Find out more

WARSAW GHETTO UPRISING OF 1943

WEBSITES:
Holocaust Research Project. See:
http://www.holocaustresearchproject.net/
ghettos/warsawghetto.html

Jewish Virtual Library: the Warsaw Ghetto.
See: http://www.jewishvirtuallibrary.org/
jsource/Holocaust/warsawtoc.html

Photographs of the Warsaw Ghetto. See:
http://www.zwoje-scrolls.com/shoah/
wghetto.html

BOOKS:
Draenger, Gusta. *Justyna's Diary* (available as
Justyna's Narrative, University of
Massachusetts Press, 1996).

Edelman, Marek. *The Ghetto Fights: Warsaw,
1941–43*. London: Bookmarks Publications,
1990.

Engelking, Barbara, and Leociak, Jacek. *The
Warsaw Ghetto: a Guide to the Perished City*.
New Haven, Yale University Press, 2009.

Goldstein, Bernard. *Five Years in the Warsaw
Ghetto*. Oakland: AK Press, 2005.

Kostanski, Janek. *Janek: a Gentile in the
Warsaw Ghetto*. Janek Kostanski,
Melbourne, 1998.

Landau, David. *Caged: a Story of Jewish
Resistance*. Macmillan, 2000.

Landau, Ludwik. *A Chronicle of the Years of
War and Occupation*. Warsaw, 1962.

Paulsson, Gunnar S. *Secret City: The Hidden Jews of Warsaw, 1940–1945*. New Haven: Yale University Press, 2002.

Ziemian, Joseph. *The Cigarette Sellers of Three Crosses Square*. Lerner Publishing Group, 1975.

DOCUMENTARIES AND FILMS:

Border Street (*Ulica Graniczna*), Aleksander Ford, Polart, DVD/VHS, 1950.

A Generation, Andrzej Wajda, 1955.

Uprising, Jon Avnet (director), Warner Home Video, VHS, 2001.

The Pianist, Roman Polanski (producer and director), Universal Studios, DVD/VHS, 2002.

Three War Films: A Generation, Kanal, and Ashes & Diamonds, Andrzej Wajda, Criterion, DVD/VHS, 1961 edition.

MUSEUMS:

Museum of the History of Polish Jews, Warsaw (as of May 2009 under construction on the site of the Warsaw Ghetto). See: http://www.jewishmuseum.org.pl/

Jewish Holocaust Centre, Melbourne. See: http://www.jhc.org.au/
13-15 Selwyn Street, Elsternwick, VIC 3185

Sydney Jewish Museum. See: http://www.sydneyjewishmuseum.com.au/

148 Darlinghurst Road, Darlinghurst, NSW 2010 (corner of Burton St and Darlinghurst Rd)

WEBSITES:

Website dedicated to the Warsaw Uprising.
See: http://www.warsawuprising.com/
State University of New York at Buffalo:
Warsaw Uprising 1944. Portal.

See: http://info-poland.buffalo.edu/web/
history/WWII/powstanie/link.shtml

BOOKS:

Borodziej, Włodzimierz. *The Warsaw Uprising of 1944.* Translated by Barbara Harshav. University of Wisconsin Press, 2006.

Borowiec, Andrew. *Destroy Warsaw! Hitler's punishment, Stalin's revenge.* Westport, Connecticut: Praeger, 2001.

Ciechanowski, Jan M. *The Warsaw Rising of 1944.* Cambridge University Press, 2002.

Davies, Norman. *Rising '44. The Battle for Warsaw* (1st U.S. ed.) New York: Viking, 2004.

Karski, Jan. *Story of a Secret State.* Safety Harbor, FL: Simon Publications, 2001.

Walker, Jonathan. *Poland Alone: Britain, SOE and the Collapse of Polish Resistance, 1944.* The History Press, 2008.

Woody, Thomas E. & Jankowski, Stanislaw (1994). *Karski: How One Man Tried to Stop the Holocaust.* John Wiley & Sons, 1994.

DOCUMENTARIES AND FILMS:

*Battle for Warsaw. The Nazi Annihilation of Poland's Historic Capital.*Peter Batty documentary. Beckmann Visual Publishing, 2004, DVD.

Battle for Warsaw. Wanda Koscia (director and producer). BBC and The Discovery Channel, 2005, DVD.

Betrayal: The Battle for Warsaw. Andrew Rothstein (producer). The History Channel documentary, 2005, DVD.

MUSEUMS:
Warsaw Uprising Museum, Warsaw, Poland.
See: http://www.1944.pl/
79 Grzybowska St, 00-844 Warsaw
(enter from Przyokopowa St)

OTHER READING:

Olson, Lynne, and Gould, Stanley. *A Question of Honor: The Kosciuszko Squadron: forgotten heroes of World War II.* Alfred A. Knopf, 2003.

Russell, R. Lynette. *Off the Record: the Life and Times of Muriel Knox Doherty 1896–1988: An autobiography.* New South Wales College of Nursing, Glebe, 1996.